BARBARA TAYLOR BRADFORD

Emma's Secret

WHEELER PUBLISHING

Published in 2004 by arrangement with St. Martin's Press, LLC.

Wheeler Large Print Hardcover.

The text of this Large Print edition is unabridged.
Other aspects of the book may vary from the original edition.

Set in 16 pt. Plantin by Elena Picard.

Printed in the United States on permanent paper.

Library of Congress Cataloging-in-Publication Data

Bradford, Barbara Taylor.

    Emma's secret / Barbara Taylor Bradford.
      p. cm.
    ISBN 1-58724-660-0 (lg. print : hc : alk. paper)
    1. Family-owned business enterprises — Fiction.
2. Grandparent and adult child — Fiction. 3. Inheritance and succession — Fiction. 4. London (England) — Fiction.
5. Terminally ill — Fiction. 6. Businesswomen — Fiction.
7. Large Print Edition. I. Title.
PS3552.R2147E46 2004b
813'.54—dc22   2004044047

For Bob, as always, with my love

As the Founder/CEO of NAVH, the only national health agency solely devoted to those who, although not totally blind, have an eye disease which could lead to serious visual impairment, I am pleased to recognize Thorndike Press★ as one of the leading publishers in the large print field.

Founded in 1954 in San Francisco to prepare large print textbooks for partially seeing children, NAVH became the pioneer and standard setting agency in the preparation of large type.

Today, those publishers who meet our standards carry the prestigious "Seal of Approval" indicating high quality large print. We are delighted that Thorndike Press is one of the publishers whose titles meet these standards. We are also pleased to recognize the significant contribution Thorndike Press is making in this important and growing field.

Lorraine H. Marchi, L.H.D.
Founder/CEO
NAVH

★ Thorndike Press encompasses the following imprints: Thorndike, Wheeler, Walker and Large Print Press.

Contents

The Three Clans

The Hartes
(Shown in line of descent)

EMMA HARTE. Matriarch. Founder of the dynasty and business empire.

EMMA'S CHILDREN

EDWINA HARTE LOWTHER, Dowager Countess of Dunvale. Emma's daughter by Edwin Fairley. (Illegitimate.) First born.

CHRISTOPHER "KIT" LOWTHER. Emma's son by her first husband, Joe Lowther. Second born.

ROBIN AINSLEY. Emma's son by her second husband, Arthur Ainsley. Twin of Elizabeth. Third born.

ELIZABETH AINSLEY DEBOYNE. Emma's daughter by her second husband, Arthur Ainsley. Twin of Robin. Third born.

DAISY AINSLEY. Emma's daughter by Paul McGill. (Illegitimate.) Fourth born.

EMMA'S GRANDCHILDREN

ANTHONY STANDISH, Earl of Dunvale. Son of Edwina and Jeremy Standish, Earl and Countess of Dunvale.

SARAH LOWTHER PASCAL. Daughter of Kit and June Lowther.

JONATHAN AINSLEY. Son of Robin and Valerie Ainsley.

PAULA MCGILL HARTE AMORY FAIRLEY O'NEILL. Daughter of Daisy and David Amory. Sister of Philip.

PHILIP MCGILL HARTE AMORY. Son of Daisy and David Amory. Brother of Paula.

EMILY BARKSTONE HARTE. Daughter of Elizabeth Ainsley and Tony Barkstone. Half sister of Amanda.

AMANDA LINDE. Daughter of Elizabeth Ainsley and her second husband, Derek Linde. Half sister of Emily.

EMMA'S GREAT-GRANDCHILDREN

TESSA FAIRLEY LONGDEN. Daughter of Paula and Jim Fairley (her first husband). Twin of Lorne.

LORNE FAIRLEY. Son of Paula and Jim Fairley. Twin of Tessa.

LADY INDIA STANDISH. Daughter of Anthony Standish and Sally Harte, Earl and Countess of Dunvale.

LINNET O'NEILL. Daughter of Paula and

Shane O'Neill (her second husband). Sister of Emsie and Desmond.

CHLOE PASCAL. Daughter of Sarah Lowther and Yves Pascal.

FIONA MCGILL AMORY. Daughter of Philip McGill Amory and Madelana O'Shea Amory (deceased).

EMSIE O'NEILL. Daughter of Paula and Shane O'Neill. Sister of Linnet and Desmond.

DESMOND O'NEILL. Son of Paula and Shane O'Neill. Brother of Linnet and Emsie.

The Hartes
(continued)

WINSTON HARTE. Emma's older brother and business partner.

RANDOLPH HARTE. Son of Winston and Charlotte Harte.

WINSTON HARTE II. Son of Randolph and Georgina Harte.

TOBY HARTE. Son of Winston Harte II and Emily Harte. Brother of Gideon.

GIDEON HARTE. Son of Winston Harte II and Emily Harte. Brother of Toby.

FRANK HARTE. Emma's younger brother.

ROSAMUND HARTE. Daughter of Frank and Natalie Harte. Sister of Simon.

SIMON HARTE. Son of Frank and Natalie Harte. Brother of Rosamund.

The O'Neills

SHANE PATRICK DESMOND "BLACKIE" O'NEILL. Founding father of the dynasty and business empire.

BRYAN O'NEILL. Son of Blackie and Laura Spencer O'Neill.

SHANE O'NEILL. Son of Bryan and Geraldine O'Neill.

LINNET O'NEILL. Daughter of Shane and Paula O'Neill.

EMMA "EMSIE" O'NEILL. Daughter of Shane and Paula O'Neill.

DESMOND O'NEILL. Son of Shane and Paula O'Neill.

The Kallinskis

DAVID KALLINSKI. Founding father of the dynasty and business empire.

SIR RONALD KALLINSKI. Son of David and Rebecca Kallinski.

MICHAEL KALLINSKI. Son of Ronald and Helen "Posy" Kallinski.

JULIAN KALLINSKI. Son of Michael and Valentine Kallinski.

PROLOGUE

2000

In my end is my beginning.
— MARY STUART,
MARY QUEEN OF SCOTS

Prologue

She sat very still in the chair next to the bed, holding her grandmother's hand. It was so quiet in the hospital room she could hear her breathing, the breath coming in soft little intakes and exhalations.

The old woman's face was relaxed, the tension gone from it as she dozed, and she appeared to be younger than her years, younger than she had looked in a very long time.

Perhaps she *will* get better, Evan thought, her eyes riveted on her grandmother, the person whom she loved most in the whole world except for her father. She wished he would get here. He was driving into Manhattan from Connecticut, and he had left several hours ago; she couldn't imagine what was making him this late. Evan glanced at her watch, and when she saw the time she realized he was probably snarled up in the late-afternoon traffic of Manhattan . . . rush hour was imminent and Thanksgiving was next week. A small sigh escaped her; she couldn't imagine her life without her beloved gran in it. But her grandmother had been suffering with a kidney infection and had gone into kidney failure. It was only a question of time.

Glynnis Jenkins Hughes. The Welsh girl from the Rhondda Valley, who had arrived in America fifty-four years ago as a GI bride. Come to these shores to join her GI husband, Richard Hughes, and bringing with her their small son, Owen, conceived and born in England when Richard had been stationed there in the Second World War.

And she's been as much a mother to me as she has to Dad, Evan decided, leaning back in the chair, closing her eyes, allowing a fund of childhood memories to come flooding back. Gran always there for them . . . always laughing, full of fun and gaiety, her warmth and love so abundant.

Evan's own mother had been ill for as long as Evan could remember, and still was, a manic-depressive living in a world of her own, out of reality, out of their lives in a certain sense.

One day, many years ago, Gran had come up to Connecticut from New York City and taken over, muttering that they were all too little to fend for themselves. And adding, in a quieter voice, but not so quiet Evan didn't hear, that a man needed a hot meal to come home to at night, as well as loving arms to hold him, a good woman to give him comfort and warmth and understanding. To boost

16

him, when he needed it, to underscore his confidence.

Gran had spent several years taking care of Evan and her two sisters, Elayne and Angharad, running their young lives. She had been full of robust energy and goodwill, comfortable in her own skin, wanting only to share her joy in living with them and their father, her only child. Which she did so profoundly, Evan thought, and she is the best part of me. She made me what I am.

Finally opening her eyes, Evan glanced toward her grandmother, and a smile broke across her troubled face when she saw that Glynnis was awake.

"You were dozing, Evan," Glynnis said, her voice whispery.

"Not really. Just resting my eyes and thinking, Grandma."

"About?"

"You, and how you took care of us so well when we were little girls. And Dad, too."

A smile touched Glynnis's lips, and quite unexpectedly her rheumy old eyes cleared, became alive, the blueness remarkable in its shining intensity.

Squeezing her grandmother's hand, Evan exclaimed, "You'll be out of here soon! You'll see."

"Where's Owen?" Glynnis murmured, her voice barely audible.

"Dad's on his way. He'll be arriving any

minute . . . he's probably caught in traffic."

"Leave here," Glynnis instructed hoarsely.

"I can't leave you alone, Gran!" Evan protested, shaking her head. Wondering what this was all about, she frowned and added, "I *want* to be here to take care of you, and so does Dad."

"Leave New York . . . that's what I meant . . . you're twenty-six . . . should be out . . . in the world . . ." Glynnis's voice trailed off wearily. And she sighed, seemed to sink further into the pillows.

Evan leaned closer to her grandmother, her eyes fixed on her unwaveringly. "I'm happy here, I love my job at Saks, and anyway, I want to be near you."

"I'm dying." Glynnis's lids fluttered, and she stared back at Evan, held her granddaughter with her steady gaze.

"Don't say that, Gran! You're going to get better. I know you are." Evan's eyes filled, and she tightened her grip on Glynnis's fragile fingers.

"Old," Glynnis whispered, "too old now."

"No, you're not! You're only seventy-nine, that's not old these days," Evan protested, her voice rising.

Glynnis sighed, and her heart clenched. It was unbearable for her to see her granddaughter's pain. My one true love, she thought; well, there was the other, but that was so long ago it doesn't matter anymore.

18

Evan was always mine. Like my own daughter, the daughter I never had with Richard. Dearest, dearest Richard. The truest husband a woman could ever want. Such a good man. The best man I ever knew, the right man to spend a lifetime with after all. So much to say to Evan. So little time left. I must get my thoughts unscrambled . . . get them straight. I should have told her before . . . but I was afraid . . .

"Gran! Gran!" Evan cried. "Please, Gran, open your eyes!"

Slowly Glynnis's lids lifted, and as she gazed at her granddaughter again, a sudden radiance flooded her wrinkled face. "I was thinking of your grandfather, Evan. Such a good man, Richard Hughes."

"We loved him, too, Grandma."

"Do you think he's waiting for me? Do you believe in an afterlife, Evan? Is there a heaven, do you think?"

"I don't know, Gran." Evan brushed her eyes with her fingertips, flicked away the tears. "I hope so, I really do."

"I think perhaps there is . . . don't weep for me, Evan, I've had a good life . . . sad at times . . . painful, too. . . . But I've enjoyed it all . . . there's always the bad along with the good . . ." Glynnis drifted off once more, lost in her thoughts, endeavoring to summon the last vestiges of her strength.

Evan bent closer, touching Glynnis's cheek

19

very gently. "I'm here, Grandma."

"I know, dear." Glynnis sighed, and a faint smile flickered on her wide and generous mouth.

Evan said, "Dad'll be here any minute now," and she hoped that he would. She pushed her spiraling anxiety away.

"I loved him too much," Glynnis muttered suddenly.

"You can never love a child too much, you said that yourself, Gran."

"Did I?"

"Yes, long ago, to me, when I was a little girl."

"I don't remember. *Evan?*"

"Yes, Gran?"

"Go to Emma."

"Emma? Who's *Emma?*"

"Emma Harte. In London. She has . . . the key. To your future. Oh, Evan —" Glynnis stopped speaking abruptly, stared at her granddaughter with enormous intensity, as though committing her face to memory, and then she closed her eyes. A long, fluttering sigh rippled through her before she lay absolutely still.

"Gran," Evan said in a low, insistent tone. *"Gran."*

There was no response, not even the flicker of an eyelash. Evan glanced down at their hands clasped together on top of the sheet, and she saw that her grandmother's hand had gone slack in hers. She felt her throat closing. Her eyes welled.

Gran's gone, Evan thought. Gone to another place. She's out of her pain and suffering, at peace. Evan hoped that there was a heaven, and that her grandfather was waiting there for her beloved gran.

Bending forward, Evan kissed Glynnis's still-warm cheek; the tears spilled out of her eyes and slid down her face as grief engulfed her. So distraught was she that Evan did not hear her father come into the room. It was only when she felt his hand resting lightly on her shoulder that she became aware of his presence.

"She's gone?" Owen asked, a catch in his voice.

"Yes, Dad, but only a second ago." As she spoke, Evan smoothed her hand over Glynnis's silver hair, and then she got up, turned to her father. When she saw the tears in his blue eyes, the anguish on his face, she stepped into his arms, wanting to comfort him and needing his comfort in return.

They clung together for a few seconds. Finally, Owen said, "I tried to get here before she died."

"I know, Dad, and Gran knew that, too."

"Did she have any last word for me?"

"She said she loved you too much."

Her father was silent, a reflective look crossing his face. A moment later he released

Evan and went to sit beside his mother, his dark head bent over her, his sorrow apparent.

Evan, watching him, concerned for him, did not think of her grandmother's last words to *her*. When she did, she was baffled.

And some time later she went to London. To find Emma Harte. To find her future.

PART ONE

Dynasty

2001

Hold your friends close,
Your enemies closer.

ANONYMOUS

Be not forgetful to entertain strangers:
For thereby some have entertained
angels unaware.

THE BIBLE: HEBREWS

One

It was a blustery morning.

The penetrating wind blowing in from the North Sea was laden with moisture, and the dampness was heavy on the air, and icy. Linnet O'Neill felt as though it were seeping into her bones.

She huddled further into her thick, loden green wool coat and tied her scarf tighter around her head. Then, thrusting her gloved hands into her pockets, she trudged on, doggedly following the winding path which would bring her to the crest of the moors.

After a moment she lifted her head and glanced up.

Above her, the arc of the sky appeared hollowed out, resembled the inside of a vast, polished bowl. It was the color of steel, its metallic grayness relieved by a few scudding clouds, pale and wispy in the clear, crystalline light so peculiar to these northern climes. It was an eerie light that seemed to emanate from some hidden source below the horizon.

When she'd set out to walk up into the

high country which soared above Pennistone Royal, Linnet had anticipated rain, but the massed black clouds of earlier had been scuttled by the gusting wind.

Since she had lived here all her life, she knew about the weather and its unpredictability, knew that the skies of Yorkshire were ever-changing. By lunchtime the sun could easily be creeping out from behind the grayness to fill the heavens with radiance, or rain might be slashing down in a relentless stream.

You took your chances when you went walking on the Yorkshire moors. But she didn't care. Ever since she had been a small child, these moors had been irresistible to her; she had loved to come here with her mother when she was little, to wander amongst the heather and the bracken, content to play alone with her stuffed animals in the vast emptiness surrounding her. It was her world; she had even believed it belonged to her, and in a way, she still did.

It was quiet on the moors this morning.

In the spring and summer, even in the autumn, there was always the splash and tinkle of water as it tumbled down over rock formations into pebble-strewn becks, and the whistling of little birds, the rapid whirring of their wings, was ever-present.

All were absent on this cold January Saturday. The birds had long ago flown off to warmer places, the becks had a layer of ice, and it was curiously silent as she climbed higher and higher, the land rising steeply.

Linnet missed the sounds of nature so prevalent in the summer months. To her there was nothing sweeter than the twittering and trilling of the songbirds as they wheeled and turned in the lucent air. On those lovely, balmy days it was a treat to come up here just to hear the choruses of the larks and linnets, often delivered with gusto from an exposed branch of a bramble bush. They loved those bushes, these little birds, as well as the gorse that grew on the moors, where they often made their nests or searched for seeds.

And on those days, in the sunlight and under cerulean skies, were the scurry of rabbits, the calls of larger birds, the scent of warm grass, wildflowers, bracken, and bilberry mingling, all so sweet and redolent on the air. Then the moors were at their most beautiful, except for late August and September, when the heather bloomed and transformed the dun-colored hills into a rolling sea of royal purple and soft, muted greens.

Suddenly the wind became fiercer, buffeting her forward, and taken by surprise, she almost stumbled on the path but quickly regained her balance. No wonder the wildlife has gone to ground, or gone away, she thought, and she couldn't help asking herself if she had been foolish to come out in this bitter cold weather.

But whenever she returned to Pennistone Royal, even after only a short absence, she headed for the moors at the first opportunity. When she was walking across them, she felt at peace and at ease with herself. Up here she could collect her thoughts and sort things out. Most especially if she was troubled. These days her troubles centered on her sister, Tessa, who had become her rival in various ways, especially at Harte's, the store where they both worked.

It pleased her to know that she was home again, in the place where she truly belonged.

Her mother also loved the moors, but only in the spring and summer months; Paula did not entirely share her daughter's feelings about this wild and desolate landscape in the winter, considered by some to be the bleakest country in England at this time of year.

It was her father, Shane O'Neill, who had a deep affinity for the high country all year round and a rare, almost tender love of nature. She always thought of her father as a true Celt, a throwback to a much earlier century, and it was he who had nurtured her own love of the outdoors, of wild things, and of the flora and fauna which abounded in Yorkshire.

She knew from her mother that her great-grandmother had been just as passionate about the moors as she was, and had spent a considerable amount of time on them. "Whenever she was troubled, Grandy headed for her beloved moors," her mother had told Linnet years ago. Linnet fully understood why they had given Grandy such solace; after all, she had been born in one of the moor villages, had grown up in the Pennine hills.

Her great-grandmother was the renowned Emma Harte, a legend in her own time; people who had known Emma said *she* was like her. Linnet laughed somewhat dismissively, but secretly she was thrilled. Who wouldn't want to be favorably compared with that most extraordinary woman, who single-handedly had created a family dynasty and a business empire circling the globe?

Her mother said Linnet was a chip off the old block because she had considerable business acumen and a talent for merchandising and retailing. "Just like Grandy," Paula would point out constantly, and with a proud smile.

Linnet felt warm inside when she thought about her mother, Paula McGill Harte Amory Fairley O'Neill. She was a very special person, and fair and just in her dealings with everyone, whatever others might believe. As for Linnet's father, he was awesome.

Linnet had always enjoyed a most harmonious relationship with Shane, and they had drawn even closer after Patrick's death ten years ago. Her elder brother had died of a rare blood disease when he was seventeen, and they had all mourned the sweet-natured Patrick, retarded from birth but so loving and caring. He had been everybody's favorite; each of them, especially Linnet, had protected and nurtured him in her or his own way. She still missed him, missed mothering him.

As she tramped on, moving ever upward, Linnet noticed tiny icicles dripping from the bramble bushes; the ground was hard as iron. It was becoming colder now that she was almost at the summit, and the wind was raw. She was glad she was wearing warm clothes and boots, and a woolen scarf around her head.

Just as she knew it would, the path suddenly rose sharply, and she felt her calves tightening as she climbed higher. Within minutes she was puffing hard, so she paused to rest. Peering ahead, she realized she was only a few feet from the crest; there, a formation of jagged black rocks jutted up into the sky like some giant monolith erected as a monument to an ancient Celtic god.

Once she had suggested to Gideon Harte, her cousin and best friend, that the monolith was man-made, perhaps even by the Celts themselves. Or the Druids. But Gideon, who was well informed about a lot of things, had immediately dismissed that idea. He had explained that the black boulders piled so precariously on their pedestal had been carried there by a vast glacier during the Ice Age, long before man had existed in Britain. Then he had pointed out that the rocks had been sitting there for aeons and aeons, and therefore were not actually precariously balanced. They merely looked as if they were.

Anxious to reach the top, Linnet set off again, and suddenly there she was, stepping onto the plateau to stand in the shadow of the monolith floating immediately above her. Its pedestal of limestone, formed by nature millennia ago, was an odd shape, with two pieces protruding on either side of a tall, flat slab, which was set back. Thus was created a narrow niche, a niche protected from the winds that blew at gale force up here on the high fells.

Years ago Emma had placed a boulder in the niche, and this served as a makeshift bench. Linnet sat down on it, as she always did, and gazed out at the vista in front of her. Her breath caught in her throat; she never ceased to be awed by this panoramic spread. Her eyes roamed across bare, untenanted fells, windswept under the lowering sky, stark, implacable, and lonely, yet she never felt lonely or afraid up here. The wild beauty of the moors filled her with wonder, and she relished the solitude, found it soothing.

Far below her Linnet could see the pastures of the Dales, their verdant lushness temporarily obliterated in this harsh weather. The fields were gleaming whitely, covered as they were with winter frost, and the river flowing through the bucolic valley was a winding, silver rope that glittered in the cold northern light.

And there, in the center, sitting amidst the peaceful meadows punctuated by drystone walls, was Pennistone Royal, that ancient and stately house acquired by Emma Harte in 1932, almost seventy years ago. In the years she had lived there, Emma had turned it into the most magical of places. The grounds were extensive and picturesque. Lawns rolled down to the river, and in the spring and summer months the flower beds and shrubs were ablaze with riotous color.

But there were no roses anywhere in those lovely rambling gardens. It was a family legend that Emma Harte had detested roses because she had been spurned by Edwin Fairley in the rose garden at Fairley Hall. On that day, when she was just a young girl, she had told Edwin she was carrying his child. In his panic, and fearing his powerful father, Adam Fairley, he had repudiated her. He had offered her a few shillings; she had asked to borrow a suitcase.

Emma had run away. From her family and Fairley village, nestling in the shadow of the Pennine Chain of hills. She had traveled to Leeds to find her dear friend Blackie O'Neill, whom she knew would help her.

And of course he had. He had taken her to live with his friend Laura Spencer, later his wife, who had looked after her until Edwina was born. It was then that Emma Harte made a vow: She would become a rich and powerful woman to protect herself and her child. She had worked like a drudge to accomplish this, and as it happened, everything she touched had turned to gold.

Linnet's grandfather Bryan O'Neill had told her that her great-grandmother had never once looked back. As a young woman she had gone from success to success, reaching even higher, always attaining the seemingly impossible, becoming a true woman of substance in every way.

According to Linnet's grandfather, Emma had apparently never forgotten that horrible day in the rose garden at Fairley Hall. Her senses had been swimming, and she had vomited violently when she was alone. Emma had blamed her attack of nausea on the roses, and for the rest of her life she had felt overcome when she smelled them.

Out of deference to her beloved grandy, Paula had never permitted roses to be grown at Pennistone Royal, nor were they used in floral arrangements in the house. Emma's ruling still held.

Linnet had been born in her great-grandmother's house twenty-five years ago, in the middle of May. Her grandmother Daisy had inherited Pennistone Royal from Emma. But she had immediately gifted it to *her* daughter, Paula, because Daisy preferred to live in London, and also to save death duties later. Paula had lived there since Emma's death. The house meant more to Linnet than any other place on earth; even though she worked in London during the week, she came up to Yorkshire every weekend.

This past November, Paula had taken Linnet into her confidence about a matter close to Paula's heart. "Grandy made a rule years ago," she explained. "And it was this . . . Pennistone Royal must go to the one who loves it the most, as long as that person has the intelligence and the knowledge to look after the estate properly. I know that Tessa, as the eldest, believes I'm going to leave it to her, but I just can't, Linnet. She doesn't even like the house and grounds, they're meaningless to her. She's only concerned with what they represent in terms of power and prestige in the family. That's certainly not what Grandy wanted or intended." Paula had shaken her head and gone on: "Lorne has no interest in the house, and Emsie cares only about her stables."

A loving smile had crossed her mother's face as she continued. "I doubt she'll ever change, bless her heart. And as for Desmond, he'll have his grandfather's house in

Harrogate one day, when Grandfather Bryan is gone."

Her mother had reached out and taken her hand, saying, "And so I am planning to leave Pennistone Royal to you, Linnet, because I know how much it means to you, how much you really care. But not a word to anyone about this. Understand, darling?"

Linnet had thanked her mother profusely, and promised not to betray her confidence. She fully understood the ramifications. But Paula's words had startled her; her mother's intention was the last thing she had expected. Deep down she was thrilled, but she did not like to dwell on anything she might one day inherit, especially if it involved her mother and father. She wanted them to have long lives.

Leaning back against the limestone slab in the niche, Linnet sighed, still dwelling on Paula's words. There would be trouble with Tessa if she ever found out about their mother's intentions.

It was true that Tessa did not have any genuine feelings for the house and the estate, but she did covet them, greed being one of her least attractive traits. And Paula was correct, Lorne wouldn't care at all. London was his bailiwick; he rarely came north anymore, except for special family occasions and holidays. He was caught up in the world of the West End theater, where he was a successful and popular young actor. He was truly dedicated to his career, and unlike his twin sister, Lorne was not avaricious or combative. He had a loving, gentle heart and had often been Linnet's fierce and loyal champion against Tessa. This did not mean he did not love Tessa, because he really did. Like most twins, he and Tessa were very close and saw a lot of each other. Put simply, Lorne was not particularly interested in his mother's business, nor did he have a desire to inherit any part of it. Tessa was welcome to it.

As for the two youngest of the O'Neill brood, they didn't figure in the scheme of things as far as Tessa was concerned. Emsie was a dreamy-eyed girl, rather whimsical, with an artistic nature. Linnet thought of her as a true Celt, like their father. Possessions were of no consequence to Emsie; she loved her horses and her dogs more than new dresses and pretty things. Nonsenses, she called the latter, and rather disdainfully, preferring to muck out the stables in a pair of jeans and an old sweater.

Linnet smiled inwardly, reflecting on her sister, of whom she was extremely protective and whom she loved dearly. Emsie, at seventeen, was vulnerable and sensitive, but also riotously funny when she wanted to amuse the family. Named for Emma Harte, she had become Emsie a few days after her birth, her parents suddenly realizing that there was no room for another *Emma* in the family. The Emma who was dead still dominated them all.

The last-born child of the O'Neills was the son Linnet's father had yearned for, especially after Patrick's death. Desmond, who was now fifteen, was the spitting image of Shane: six feet tall, dark haired, and ruggedly handsome, he was looking very grown-up already.

Linnet had always thought Desmond was the most gorgeous child, and he was turning into a stunning young man. There was no doubt in her mind that women were going to fall at his feet like ninepins, as they apparently had at her father's before he was married to their mother. Desmond was the apple of Shane's eye and the much-desired heir to the O'Neill hotel empire founded by Blackie and built up into a worldwide company by Bryan O'Neill and his only son, Shane, who ran it today.

Funnily enough, Tessa had always been rather taken with Desmond, favoring her youngest half brother over her O'Neill half sisters. "Mostly, that's because he doesn't represent a threat to her," Linnet had said to Gideon recently, and her cousin had nodded. "But he *is* irresistible," Gideon had thought to add.

For a few seconds Linnet focused on Tessa, and her face took on a grim aspect. Her half sister had been born to her mother and Jim Fairley, Paula's first husband. But when the twins were small Jim had died in a massive avalanche in Chamonix.

Because Tessa had been born a few minutes before Lorne, she was the eldest, and never allowed him, or anyone else for that matter, to forget this fact. She forever reminded them she was Paula's heir apparent as the first of her six children, only five of whom were now living.

Contemplating Tessa's competitiveness, Linnet cringed inside. She hated confrontation and infighting, and was usually the peacemaker in the family. Perhaps this was no longer a viable role.

Linnet and Gideon had discussed Tessa's attitude just the other day, and he had reminded her that Tessa was jealous of her, and envious. Although she loathed the thought, Linnet had found herself in agreement with her cousin. He had pointed out how mean-spirited Tessa had been when they were children. "A leopard doesn't change its spots that easily," he had muttered, throwing Linnet one of his knowing looks.

A feeling of dismay now lodged in her stomach. Nothing had changed really, even though she and her half sister were now grown up. Tessa had bullied her when she was little, and in some ways she was still attempting to do so, however indirectly.

Quite unexpectedly, Linnet remembered how she had once stood up to Tessa when she was a child, surprising everyone, herself included, and Tessa most of all. Certainly she had shown that she was feisty and had the spirit of Emma Harte in her. Her twelve-year-old sister had finally backed off.

Linnet laughed out loud, her laughter floating out across the empty fells, reverberating back to her in a series of echoes. She had just recalled an incident with Tessa's bright yellow sun hat, of which Tessa had been so proud. It had been ruined in the swimming pool at the Villa Faviola in France, and Linnet could see it in her mind's eye, floating so serenely in the pool. Where *she* had deliberately tossed it . . . how pleased with herself she had been.

How angry Tessa had been with her that day, screaming that she had willfully destroyed her brand-new hat, purchased with a whole week's pocket money at the open-air market in Nice.

On that particular morning, Gideon had roared with laughter, and so had his brother, Toby, much to Tessa's annoyance, since Toby was one of her sycophants, fawning all over her. As he still did to this day.

As for Tessa, it had been obvious that she was flabbergasted by Linnet's audacity. Their mother had had a hard time smothering her laughter.

Tessa was nearly thirty-two and a married woman. Her husband, Mark Longden, was an architect who had made something of a name for himself with his ultramodern buildings. They had a three-year-old daughter, Adele, named in honor of Tessa's great-great-grandmother, Adele Fairley. Tessa was very proud of her connection to that aristocratic family, and this was another point she liked to ram home to people, at least those who would listen.

In spite of her age and position in the world, Tessa could be mean, often for no apparent reason. The family was conscious of this tendency and appalled at her behavior, which they deemed immature and frequently rather ugly.

Linnet and Tessa worked for their mother at Harte's in Knightsbridge, the chain's flagship store. But Tessa had a much more important job than Linnet did; Tessa managed a number of departments, while Linnet ran only the fashion floors, and assisted her mother with merchandising and marketing. There was no question that Tessa had the most power, yet in the last few months her sister had grown increasingly hostile toward her.

Only the other day Linnet had experienced a peculiar premonition that trouble was brewing. The mere idea was alarming, especially since the cause of Tessa's recent animosity eluded her.

The distant rumble of thunder brought Linnet out of her reverie and, startled, she sat up straighter on the boulder, lifted her eyes to the sky. It looked curdled, suddenly darker, and there was no denying that a storm threatened.

Not wanting to be caught here in the rain, or even a blizzard since it was so cold, she jumped up. Turning away from the extraordinary view, she headed down the steep path. It had been a long, steady pull on the way up, but it was much easier going down, and she moved at a fairly rapid pace. Thoughts of her elder sister continued to preoccupy her. Linnet was baffled by Tessa's increased coldness in these last few weeks. There seemed to be no reason for the change in her demeanor . . . unless she knew, somehow, about their mother's intentions regarding Pennistone Royal.

But how could she know?

The question hovered there. Linnet pondered on it, casting her mind back to the meeting she had had with their mother in November. The conversation had been held in private, in her mother's inner sanctum at the Leeds store. They had been entirely alone, and in any case Tessa was in London at the time. No, she couldn't possibly have any inkling of it, Linnet now decided.

And yet . . . she thought of the way Tessa

had directed some of her hostility toward their mother in December, at least that was how Linnet had read it, and she had been surprised at the time. Tessa had announced that she would not be coming to Pennistone Royal for Christmas. This was tantamount to sacrilege in the family, and everyone was taken aback.

The Hartes, the O'Neills, and the Kallinskis celebrated all the important holidays together at Pennistone Royal. It was a tradition that had begun in 1933, just after Emma Harte had purchased the grand house and its vast estate outside Ripon. "The gathering of the three clans," her grandfather called it, and that was exactly what it was. Emma Harte, Blackie O'Neill, and David Kallinski had become friends very early in the twentieth century, and had remained friends throughout their lives, as had their growing families. And the Hartes and the O'Neills were now joined in marriage and by blood.

"Ninety-five, ninety-six years, Linnet," her grandfather had explained to her this past Christmas. "That's how far our relationships go back. Spending Christmas together is mandatory. As David Kallinski used to say, we're *mishpocheh* . . . family."

Naturally their mother had been very upset when she learned of Tessa's intention to remain in London over the holidays. Paula had finally laid down the law as only she could, in her inimitable Emma Harte style.

Of course Tessa, in the end, had had no alternative but to acquiesce, no doubt encouraged by her husband, who knew a good thing when he saw it. Like any smart gambler, he always had his eye on the main chance.

Ever since Mark had slithered so skillfully, and in such a reptilian way, into their lives five years ago, Linnet had been scrutinizing him surreptitiously. And she saw how obsequiously attentive he was to their mother. It was quite apparent to her that he regarded Paula not only as the matriarch to be kowtowed to but as Mrs. Moneybags to be endlessly flattered.

Linnet had been suspicious of Mark from the beginning, had considered him an opportunist and a gold digger. And she had often wondered what the beautiful Tessa had ever seen in him. For beautiful her sister was, and she had enormous charm and grace when she wanted, along with considerable intelligence. There were many other qualities in Tessa which balanced her less attractive traits. Linnet cared about Tessa; her half sister was nobody's fool, she knew that. Yet she had chosen Mark. It troubled Linnet that Tessa had married someone not quite up to par.

Somewhat grudgingly, Tessa had agreed to spend Christmas at Pennistone Royal, but it had been a clever compromise. She had explained that they would arrive on the afternoon of Christmas Eve, in time for tea and the lighting of the tree, and depart after lunch on Christmas Day. Her excuse for such a short visit was the necessity of spending Boxing Day with Mark's parents in Cirencester.

But in essence Tessa had given her family only twenty-four hours of her time, and Grandfather Bryan, in particular, had been put out, mainly on her mother's behalf. He had made a few adverse comments to Linnet after Tessa left with Mark and Adele. He frequently confided his thoughts to her, and in this instance he had said that Tessa was as manipulative now as she had been as a child.

Despite the Christmas activities, and the presence of the other clans, Tessa had acted rather strangely, in Linnet's opinion. In her childhood Tessa had been prone to throwing tantrums, and her temperamental nature seemed to get the better of her at Christmas. She had not even bothered to disguise her moodiness or ill temper. Furthermore, she seemed hell-bent on doing battle. There appeared to be no valid reason for this combativeness, and Linnet thought Tessa was being reckless in the way she constantly annoyed their mother.

Paula had not said anything to Linnet at Christmas, or since, regarding Tessa's behavior. But understanding her mother the

44

way she did, Linnet knew she had not missed a trick. It was unlikely that Paula would put up with Tessa's moods for long. She was a practical woman, with her feet firmly on the ground, and emotional outbursts for no apparent reason left her totally unmoved.

What will be, will be, Linnet muttered to herself. In the meantime, I'm not going to worry. But despite this promise, Linnet *did* worry as she continued her trek down. She was far too astute to underestimate her sister, and she knew that Tessa could fight a mean fight.

She hoped it wouldn't come to that. But if it did she would have to defend herself. She had no other choice.

Two

Bryan O'Neill had arrived at Pennistone Royal over an hour ago, and once he had looked in on his grandson, Desmond, who was recovering from the flu, he had made his way to the upstairs parlor. He had stood at a window ever since, looking out at the moors, waiting for Linnet to return, worried about her.

Now, as he saw her sprinting along the path, he relaxed. With her in his line of vision, his spirits lifted considerably. A small sigh escaped. He tried so hard not to have favorites among his grandchildren, and he loved them all, but there was no denying he loved this one the best, even though Desmond, the long-awaited male heir apparent, happened to be the apple of his eye.

Linnet was a wonderful young woman in so many ways, but then so were his other granddaughters. However, there was a special reason she was precious to him, and it was bound up with his memories and his childhood.

Bryan strode across the room and into the

corridor. In December he had celebrated his eighty-fourth birthday, but he looked nowhere near it. In robust health, he was a fine figure of a man, tall and broad-shouldered with a shock of silver hair and the merry black eyes his father, Blackie, had had, which his son, Shane, had inherited from them both.

As he headed toward the grand staircase, Bryan heard the front door slam, and by the time he reached the top of the stairs Linnet was standing in the Stone Hall, struggling out of her coat and scarf. Unobserved, he watched her as she put them away in an antique armoire near the front door.

It was her coloring, of course, that so captivated, drew the eye to her: the glorious red hair shot through with golden lights, the translucent skin, the oval-shaped face with its fine, chiseled features, the wide-set eyes of a green so deep their color appeared almost unnatural. She had been endowed with the famous Harte coloring, the famous Harte looks, and he thought she was the embodiment of true beauty.

Unexpectedly, in the inner recesses of his mind, he heard Edwina's voice reverberating, and he instantly fell into the past as he recalled her comments, uttered over thirty years ago. "All the Hartes have is pots and pots of money. Oh, and their looks, of course. There's no denying they are a good-looking family. Each and every one of them."

Bryan had never forgotten what she said that day, and with such disdain it was chilling to the bone. It had been at the party after the christening of Lorne and Tessa at Fairley Church, in the little village at the foot of the moors. He had been shocked by her tone, and truly angered by her attitude.

Edwina was a Harte herself, Emma's first-born child, now over ninety years old, yet all she had ever wanted was to be a Fairley. Blackie had frequently said her attitude was an insult to Emma, and Bryan had fully agreed with his father.

Yet what Edwina had said all those years ago did have a certain ring of truth to it. The Hartes *were* good-looking, and they had been for four generations. Even the men were beautiful, and there were others in the family with Linnet's coloring. But it was she who resembled Emma Harte *exactly*, right down to the widow's peak so dramatic above her broad, smooth brow.

"Grandpops! What are you doing here so early? You weren't expected until teatime!" Linnet cried, having suddenly spotted Bryan on the landing. As she spoke she ran to the bottom of the staircase, stood looking up at him, her face ringed in smiles. These two had been confidants since her childhood, and they were still close.

"I was bored and lonely rattling around in

that big old house in Harrogate all by myself, don't you know," Bryan answered and started down the stairs toward her.

"There's nobody here but us chickens! Well, except for Desmond, who's still sick in bed," she informed him, laughing, draping herself around the banister. "Paula and Shane are out."

It still startled him when she called her parents by their first names, even though she'd been doing it for years, and he asked, "And where are your *mother* and *father*?"

"Dad's gone to Harrogate to meet Uncle Winston for lunch —"

"At the Drum and Monkey, I've no doubt," he interrupted.

She grinned. "That's right, and Mummy's at the Harrogate store."

"I looked in on Desmond," Bryan said. "Your father told me he was under the weather, but where's Emsie on a nasty day like this? Margaret said *she* was out, too."

"Emsie went down to the village to see her friend Anne's new horse, and she mumbled something about staying there for lunch. But you've got *me*, Gramps, and we can have a nice cozy lunch together. Margaret will be able to rustle up something special for you."

Smiling, his black eyes sparkling, Bryan stepped into the hall and pulled his granddaughter to him in a big bear hug, holding her close, loving this girl. Releasing her, he

49

held her away from him for 'a moment and said, "You're looking especially bonny today, mavourneen."

Linnet smiled up at him, linked her arm through his, and led him across the Stone Hall to the grand fireplace, where a pile of huge logs were blazing up the chimney back. "Now, Gramps, how about a drop of your favorite Irish whiskey before lunch?" she asked, patting his arm, giving him a wide, warm smile.

"I wouldn't say no, Linnet, thanks, me darlin'."

"It'll warm the cockles of your heart . . . just what you need on a day like this," she remarked, gliding across to a chest in one corner, where an array of bottles, glasses, and an ice bucket had been lined up on a tray.

Bryan remained standing with his back to the fire, enjoying the warmth. His eyes followed Linnet, and he couldn't help smiling to himself at the way she mothered him. She had been doing it since she was a child, just as she had been a little mother to her brother Patrick. It was instinctive with her, he supposed. One day, when she married, she would make a wonderful parent.

Instantly his thoughts veered to Julian Kallinski. Good-looking young man. Clever, too. Heir to the Kallinski empire. Now if he and Linnet did tie the knot, Emma's greatest wish would be fulfilled. The *three* clans would finally be united in marriage. He wanted that, so did Ronald Kallinski and the rest of the Kallinskis, Hartes, and O'Neills.

He was just about to ask Linnet about Julian when he remembered Shane's warning of only last week. Apparently there had been too much pressure put upon the young couple to get married, and so they were no longer seeing each other; they were "cooling it," to use Shane's expression. No, better not mention Julian today, he decided. No point in fanning the fire.

Instead, he shifted his stance and glanced around the Stone Hall. It was large, with a high-flung ceiling crisscrossed with dark wood beams, and it took its name from the local gray stone, which was used every-where — on the walls, the ceiling, the floor, and the fireplace facade.

He had been sixteen years old when he had first stepped into the Stone Hall with Emma and his father. She had wanted to show them the house she had just bought, and they had been impressed with its gran-deur. "Wasted space," she had muttered to Blackie that day, glancing around the great hall. And in the end she had turned it into one of the most splendid living rooms he had ever seen. Despite its grand size, it had warmth and intimacy because Emma had used large pieces of handsome Jacobean and Tudor furniture made of dark mellow woods, and comfortable oversized sofas and chairs.

To Bryan it looked exactly the way it had the day Emma finished it, although he knew Paula had done a lot of refurbishing over the years. But she had kept Emma's basic style, as she usually did in these things. And like Emma she had filled the room with flowering plants, in blue-and-white pots and copper buckets. Today the tops of the polished wood tables and consoles were alive with pink, amber, and yellow chrysanthemums, orange-red amaryllis, and many of the white orchids Paula loved and nurtured in the greenhouse.

A moment later Linnet was back with his whiskey and a small glass of sherry for herself. After handing him the whiskey, she clinked her glass to his. "Cheers," they said in unison.

Bryan took a sip, then murmured in a reflective tone, "I suppose you were up on those godforsaken moors because something is troubling you."

Linnet nodded but did not volunteer anything.

He wondered if she was worrying about her relationship with Julian, and he asked, as casually as possible, "Want to talk about it?"

Linnet hesitated fractionally, then answered in a slightly hesitant voice, "It's Tessa. I'm worried about her. What I mean is I'm concerned about her attitude toward me, Gramps. She's so hostile these days."

"Nothing new about that, is there?" he asked, a snowy brow lifting quizzically.

"Not really . . . I suppose. She's often been odd with me at different times. Somewhat bullying when I was little, as you well remember. And bossy since we've been working at Harte's."

"Competitive with you, Linnet, wouldn't you say?"

"I guess so," she agreed finally.

Bryan was silent for a moment, and then he remarked softly, "Ants in her pants, I'm afraid."

Linnet threw her grandfather a puzzled look. "What do you mean?"

"Mentally she has ants in her pants, can't be still in her mind. And I'm quite sure that's because she's full of anxiety about her position at Harte's. She desperately wants to be reassured that she will one day succeed your mother."

Linnet nodded vigorously. "*Absolutely.* She thinks she will. She expects to, actually."

"And what do you think, mavourneen?" Bryan probed, his dark eyes resting on her with great interest.

"I don't know what my mother plans to do. But Tessa *is* the eldest of Paula's children, and I suppose she's entitled to inherit my mother's job when she retires."

Bryan shook his head vehemently, then taking hold of her arm, he led her toward the sofa placed nearest to the fire. "Let's sit down," he murmured, and after settling himself in a corner against the tapestry cushions, he continued: "Your mother doesn't operate that way, she's not into those kinds of rules, or the law or primogeniture. I'm certain Paula will choose someone *she* wants to be her successor in the family business. After all, she is the largest single stockholder, not to mention CEO."

When Linnet made no comment, Bryan added, "Let's not forget she was trained by Emma Harte for many, many years, and that was *her* policy. *She* gave the key jobs to those who deserved them and could handle them. Paula will do the same."

"I guess you're right, Gramps, but Tessa does very well at Harte's, you know. She's a pretty good executive."

"Could she run the store in Knightsbridge? And the whole chain as well?" Bryan asked, looking at her keenly.

Linnet bit her lip and glanced away, acutely aware of her grandfather's penetrating gaze, thinking of the discussions she'd had with Gideon about this very subject. And with her cousin India, who worked at Harte's. They believed that Tessa would never be able to cut it, but she fully acknowledged they were prejudiced, having suffered at Tessa's hands, especially when they were children.

Clearing her throat, Linnet said, "As an executive Tessa's very good, well organized, practical, and she handles the daily problems with skill . . ." Her voice trailed off as she thought of the rows her mother had with Tessa about planning ahead. She stared at Bryan, then sighed. "Oh gosh, Gramps, Tessa's my sister and I love her . . ."

"There's a big *but* I suspect when it comes to certain things to do with her work."

"I think so. She's great on a day-to-day basis, as I said. But Tessa never considers the future."

"No real vision perhaps," Bryan pronounced. "There's got to be vision in any business, but especially in retailing, otherwise the stores will go nowhere. Except down the drain eventually. That's always been one of your mother's strong suits, Linnet. Paula has had tremendous vision over the years, still does, and Emma often commented on it to me. It made your great-grandmother very proud, and she felt secure about leaving Harte's to your mother."

"Mummy's a genius in so many ways. You know, she's really been annoyed about Tessa's attitude regarding my project. Tessa thinks my idea for a fashion retrospective is ridiculous, that it won't succeed. But I know it will, and Mummy's given me her blessing."

Bryan frowned and shook his head. After a moment's thought he murmured, "But your retrospective is a natural, it's bound to bring in hundreds of women, and when they're in the store they'll spend money on the fashion floors."

"Exactly, Gramps! That's the whole idea, but Tessa doesn't get it."

Or doesn't want to, Bryan thought, but he said, "The main thing is that it's going to be a big success. You mustn't worry about what Tessa says or thinks . . . only your immediate boss, and that's your mother."

Linnet nodded. "Mummy's thrilled I'm using such a lot of Grandy's haute couture clothes. Vintage clothes are very *in* these days, and the retrospective does cover eighty years. It'll pull in a lot of young women. India agrees."

"And tell me, how is little India working out?"

"Very well, Grandfather, and she's not so little either. She's quite the dashing young woman."

"So I noticed on New Year's Eve." He chuckled. "I always think of India as being little. You know, in the sense of petite, dainty, very delicate and feminine."

"That she is. But getting back to Tessa, Gideon says she doesn't know how to handle people, that she has no empathy or compassion." Linnet sat back and made a small grimace. "Mummy's always said it's important to feel compassion for people if you're an employer, and Gideon thinks Tessa lacks that quality."

"Do you?"

When Linnet was silent, Bryan knew the answer. But he knew how much she disliked criticizing others. Deciding not to press for an answer, he leaned back against the cushions once more and studied her for a moment. Quite unexpectedly his throat tightened with emotion. For he saw not Linnet O'Neill, his twenty-five-year-old granddaughter, but Emma Harte when she was twenty-seven and his surrogate mother. He had been born in December 1916, and his biological mother, Laura O'Neill, had died almost immediately after his birth. With his father, Blackie, fighting in the First World War, there was only Emma Harte, his parents' best friend, to look after him. And so she had taken him home from the hospital and brought him up as her own. And it was *her* face he had gazed up at from his crib, *her* face he had learned to love at such a tender age.

Now, eighty-four years later, he was staring into that same face. Of course it was not Emma he was looking at, it was Linnet, but to him she was Emma Harte reincarnated; the resemblance was uncanny.

"Gramps, are you all right? You've got such a funny look on your face," Linnet said.

Sitting up straighter, Bryan blinked several times, then smiled at her. He coughed behind his hand and after a moment replied, "I have some photographs at home of your great-grandmother when she was about your age, maybe a couple of years older. And you *are* her, Linnet. Why, it's as if Emma has been reborn in you. It's not only that you're the spitting image of her physically, as everyone tells you these days, but you have so many of her facial expressions and her gestures, and you think like her. Certainly you have her drive, energy, and talent for retailing, and you're a good businesswoman. You'll get even better, too, with a bit of age on you." He smiled at her. "You're the best, in my opinion."

"You're prejudiced, Gramps."

"Perhaps. But you're going to be fine . . . another Emma Harte."

"I'll try to live up to all the things she was, and stood for. I know she had great integrity, that she was a most honorable woman, one who had ethics, knew right from wrong, and was just and fair in all her dealings."

"That she was indeed, and you'll do her justice, I've no qualms about you, mavourneen." He took her hand in his. "My money's on you, Linnet. In my opinion it's *you* who should take over from your mother when she retires. Harte's should be yours."

"I'd like that very much, but it really is up to my mother."

She's probably chosen you already, Bryan

58

thought, but he did not confide in his granddaughter. Instead he said, "I want you to have those photographs of Emma. I'll bring them with me the next time I come over."

"Oh, thanks, Gramps, I'd love to have them. I'll treasure them."

A moment later Margaret came hurrying in, and in her usual quiet and efficient way, she said, "Lunch is ready, Mr. O'Neill . . . Linnet. If you'd like to come into the morning room, I'll serve it in there, it's much cozier than the dining room, with the fire an' all."

"Thanks, we'll come right away, Margaret," Bryan said, pushing himself to his feet. "Linnet did tell me that you'd be rustling up something special for me. Well, that's the way she put it. So what's for lunch?"

Margaret laughed and explained, "Oh, some of your *real* favorites, Mr. O'Neill. I had a crock of Morecambe Bay potted shrimps put away for lunch tomorrow, but I thought you'd like to have them today with some of that nice thin brown bread and butter of mine, and I've made a cottage pie with fresh ground beef and a crust of mashed potatoes, pureed parsnips, and peas. And for pudding you can have either freshly baked apple crumble with warm custard, just the way you like it, or trifle."

"Goodness, Margaret, you've done me proud! Everything sounds delicious," Bryan answered, smiling at the housekeeper; then turning to Linnet, he added, "I'm seriously thinking of moving in here."

"I wish you would, Gramps!" Linnet exclaimed, tucking her arm through his, meaning every word she said.

"The idea is tempting, mavourneen, but I think it's best I remain in Harrogate. After all, Blackie built that house, and I've lived in it forever it seems, and I'm keeping it warm for Desmond, so to speak. It'll be his one day, when I'm gone."

"Let's not talk about you going anywhere!" Linnet cried, bustling him toward the morning room. "You've got lots of years ahead of you."

"I hope so, Linny, but as Blackie used to say, when you get to be over eighty, you're living on borrowed time."

The two of them sat down for lunch at the round walnut table which stood in the bay window of the morning room. Until very recently this had been a rarely used office, which Paula had considered wasted space. A few months before Christmas she had turned it into a spot for casual meals, such as breakfast and light lunches, or tea in the afternoon. Now everyone used it.

The morning room had a springlike feeling because of Paula's decorative scheme, based on pale apple green and white: green walls, green-and-white-striped balloon shades at the windows, green-and-white-checked fabric on the chairs around the table. Accentuating this look were a collection of thirty-six botanical prints hanging on one wall and jugs of yellow and white chrysanthemums, which stood on a long, carved wooden sideboard and a Queen Anne chest placed in a corner. Adding a welcoming touch on this snowy day was the blazing fire in the hearth; a small love seat and armchairs covered in rose-colored linen were arranged around a coffee table in front of the fire, and it was here that tea was often served.

As always, Bryan admired Paula's decorating. Like his late wife, Geraldine, his daughter-in-law had a way of making a room look elegant. But it was never intimidating because she had the happy knack of creating a sense of comfort in the midst of the elegance.

Linnet said, "A penny for your thoughts, Gramps."

He smiled at her. "Wasn't thinking of anything much. But . . ." He paused, leaned across the table, and asked in a conspiratorial voice, "Any more information about Paula's plans for Shane's birthday?"

Linnet nodded. "Mummy spoke to me about it the other day. Uncle Winston's also going to be sixty in June, and she said she was considering making it a joint birthday party. Actually, she told me she was going to speak to you about it." Linnet gave him a hard stare, and her brows pinched together in a frown. "I guess she didn't."

"That's correct —" Bryan broke off as Margaret came hurrying in with a tray; a moment later she was placing a plate of potted shrimps in front of him, then brought one over for Linnet. "The brown bread and butter is already on the table, Mr. O'Neill," she said, then glancing from one to the other, she asked, "Do you need anything else?"

"We're fine, Margaret," Linnet replied. "Thanks very much."

The housekeeper nodded, flashed a smile, and disappeared.

Bryan picked up a fork and plunged it into the tiny pale pink shrimps encased in the round of hardened butter. "Mmmm. They're delicious," he said after a moment. "A *joint* party, eh? And where does your mother plan to have it?"

"Here at Pennistone Royal . . ." Her voice faltered as she noticed that his expression seemed to change. "Don't you like the idea of a party for the two of them?"

"Sure an' I do, I think it makes great sense, Linny, me darlin'. Your father and Winston have been best friends since they were boys, and then as young men they shared Beck House in West Tanfield. What rascals they were when they were little," he said, chuckling, "*and* when they were young spalpeens chasing after the girls. Handsome they were, too."

"They still are," she shot back, laughter echoing in her voice.

"True, only too true. But they got their wings clipped all right, that and they did! And by Emma's favorites . . . your mother and Emily." Bryan grinned at her. "Fell like ninepins, the two of them, when those beautiful Harte girls batted their eyelashes." He shook his head, still smiling, and continued to spear the blush pink shrimps with his fork.

When they'd finished eating, Bryan sat back and stared across the table at Linnet. In the cool light coming in through the bay window, her coloring was so vivid it startled. Yet there was a translucent quality to her skin today, and she looked quite fragile. Still, Bryan knew how strong she was, both mentally and physically. She had enormous willpower, as well as stamina and energy, even though she was a slender girl of medium height.

She is going to need all the strength she has, he thought, just as she'll need her wits about her. Tessa wants it all, has convinced herself she's entitled to it all, and she'll fight for what she believes are her rights. Intuitively, he knew that Paula would give everything to Linnet. This was her child by Shane, the great love of her life, the hero of her childhood, her true soul mate, and Linnet had been much desired, and conceived in great passion. Furthermore, Linnet was cast in the image of the woman who had founded the Harte dynasty and a great business empire. There was no question about it, Linnet was irresistible to Paula. Also, she was best suited to take Paula's place. She was steady as a rock, with a cool nerve and insight quite remarkable for her age.

Tessa did not have Linnet's business acumen, her vision, or her stamina, all necessary for running the Harte stores. Paula, with a mind like a steel trap when it came to business, knew this. She might not discuss it with anyone, but Bryan *knew* she knew what Tessa's shortcomings were.

Even when Tessa was little, long before Shane and Paula were married, he had been resistant to her charms. He had been wary of Jim Fairley's child, detecting in her vanity, duplicity, and a tendency to lie. And later it had irritated him that she had been so envious of Linnet. Now that they were grown up, not only was Tessa envious but she resented Linnet, most especially her looks. Those were simply an accident of birth; there was nothing anybody could do about them.

Tessa's other resentments were bound up with the Fairleys, with Shane, who had been a loving father to her but was nonetheless perceived as the stepfather, and with Emma Harte. The last was easy enough to fathom; at least he had fathomed it all out finally.

There'll be tears before midnight one day very soon, he thought, taking a sip of his water. His instincts told him that Tessa had Linnet in her line of fire. It was going to be nasty. He wished it could be different, but he knew that was not possible.

The die was cast. It had been cast long ago.

Three

"It's only the flu, Dad, I'm not dying," Evan said, balancing the phone between her ear and her shoulder, reaching for the box of tissues on the bedside table. "I'll be better in a couple of days," she added, then blew her nose several times. "Give my love to everyone."

"I will. 'Bye, sweetheart."

"Bye, Daddy."

When she hung up, Evan slid down in the bed, pulling the covers up to her chin. The flu had started the night she arrived from New York. That was Wednesday. Now it was Saturday, and she still didn't feel all that much better, even though the doctor had prescribed various medicines, which she had been taking religiously.

But better to be sick *here* than in some awful commercial hotel, Evan thought glumly. Once she had made the decision to come to London, her father had insisted she stay at the small family hotel in Belgravia owned and run by his old friend George Thomas. Her father had met George when he had gone to live in London as a young man, and they had been friends ever since. She was glad now that she had agreed. George, whom she barely remembered from her toddler years, was a lovely Welshman, and his wife, Arlette, was one of those take-charge French-women who seemed to know everything about everything. They had been warm and welcoming when she arrived and given her a room that was both inviting and full of charm.

It was on the top floor, one level down from the attics under the eaves of this grand Victorian town house, which they had turned into a small but attractive hotel some years before. The room was decorated with lovely, colorful floral chintz fabrics and handsome Victorian furniture, including this four-poster bed where she now lay cocooned in two feather-light duvets. She felt coddled and cared for.

Despite Arlette's tender loving care, Evan would have given anything not to be sick. Her plan had been to go to Harte's depart-ment store in Knightsbridge without wasting any time. Once there she had intended to seek an appointment with Emma Harte, using her grandmother's name as an intro-duction. Next week, she thought, I'll go next week to see Emma Harte.

Ever since Glynnis Hughes had died last November, Evan had felt lost. Her gran had forever been cheering her on, telling her she could do anything she wanted, as long as she put her mind to it and worked hard.

An image of her mother suddenly insinuated itself into her mind, and Evan focused on her for a split second. Marietta Hughes had been a talented artist once, but something awful had gone wrong, and she had given up, given up on life in so many ways.

When Evan had told her father she was considering going to London for a year, he had been instantly enthusiastic. But almost immediately she had noticed the look of sorrow enter his eyes, seen a dulling of their brightness, and she had realized at once that he, above all others, would miss her. Her mother wouldn't miss her. Marietta hadn't even noticed her absence when she moved to New York, and that had been seven years ago.

On that day in the middle of December, she had quickly backtracked, told her father that perhaps she wouldn't go after all. But he had insisted she take this sabbatical, as he called it, reminding her that he had done the same thing himself over thirty years ago, had gone back to visit London, where he had been born during the Second World War. It was at this time that he had met her mother, then an art student at the Royal College of Art. Marietta Glenn. A beautiful blond girl from California with whom he had fallen madly in love. He had married her in London. "And don't forget, *you* were born there," he had reminded Evan.

After they had talked about London Evan had confided her grandmother's last words to her father. He had been just as startled, and baffled, as she had been. "But Emma Harte must be very old now. I vaguely remember my mother once saying that she had met her during the war, just before she married her wonderful GI Joe, as she called my dad, and came to America. As you well know by now . . . it's family history. I doubt my mother's name will mean anything to her, so don't be disappointed, honey, if you don't get a reaction."

She had promised him that she would not let anything disappoint her on this trip, and she had meant it. Her father had hugged her and told her how important she was to him. Then he had explained that she would have no problem working in London because she had dual nationality, as he did. Having been born in England to a British-born American father and an American mother meant that she was a legal citizen on both sides of the Atlantic.

Finally a date had been set for her departure, and her father had made all the arrangements with his old pal George, saying that she should think of George and Arlette as family. "Have fun, and most of all be happy, Evan," he had said with a big smile, hugging her to him again. "Life's too short for misery."

That day she had thought what a wonderfully courageous man her father was. He was cheerful, and had an even temper most of the time, despite the burden of her mother. What had gone wrong in her mother's psyche? How often she had asked herself that, but she had no answers. There were women, she knew, who enjoyed being ill, but surely no woman could enjoy being a manic-depressive.

Her mother had doctors, and they prescribed medications all the time, and her mother took them. Yet she was still wrapped in a cloak of depression. Or was she? Evan had often asked herself if her mother faked it at times, in order to retreat from her husband, from them all, from responsibility. What an awful thing, if that were true.

I want to live my life to the fullest, Evan thought. I want to follow my dreams, fulfill my ambitions. I want the career in fashion I always dreamed of having. I want to meet a wonderful man, get married, have children. I want a life. *My own life.*

Curled up under the duvets, Evan half-dozed, half-drifted with her thoughts.

She wasn't sure she would be happy in London, but it was worth a try. That was why she had come, to meet a challenge, seek her destiny. This was the city of her birth, and she had lived here until she was almost four. It was then that her parents had returned to New York; soon after, they had settled in Connecticut. There Elayne and Angharad had been adopted, just a year apart. Evan's mother had had a hysterectomy but wanted more children.

Owen Hughes had raised his family in a rambling old house in Kent, sometimes with the help of his mother, while launching his antiques business. He was following in the footsteps of his father; Richard Hughes had taught his son everything he knew, and Owen had studied on his own, enhancing his knowledge to the fullest.

It was her grandparents who had brought Evan back to London when she was twelve. Richard had been coming to London on a buying trip, and he had invited Glynnis and Evan to accompany him.

Part of the time she and her grandmother had gone with him in search of beautiful antiques, making trips to the country towns just outside London or driving down to Gloucestershire and Sussex. It had been an adventure for her, and she had loved every moment.

The two of them, she and her gran, were sometimes alone when Grandfather was off making transactions with other dealers, and it was then that Glynnis had taken her out to see Windsor Castle, Hampton Court, and

Kew Gardens. And she had learned about British history, and Welsh history, from her grandmother, who knew a lot and was articulate in the telling of it all.

It had been lovely weather that summer, and the three of them had enjoyed the time they spent together. Her grandfather loved the theater, so they had gone to see plays in the West End, and one night they even had supper at the Savoy Hotel, in the elegant dining room overlooking the river Thames; another evening after a play Grandfather had taken them to Rules, an old and very famous restaurant which her grandparents had favored for years. She had never forgotten these treats.

After almost two weeks in London, they had crossed the English Channel to France. Her grandfather had been an expert in English Georgian furniture and also specialized in English and European china. That was the real reason for their trip to France . . . the quest for rare porcelains in perfect condition.

It was from his father that her father had learned all about English and European porcelains, as well as furniture. "I studied at the knee of the master," Owen often said, and he was now a leading expert in the field. Over the years he had made something of a name for himself, and people came from all over to hear him speak. Evan knew how much her father loved antiques, and she was well aware that his work had been his great savior over the years.

Angharad, the youngest, had shown a talent for spotting "the good stuff," as her grandmother had called it. Knowing that she had what he called "a good eye," Owen had taken his daughter into the business when she was old enough, and she worked with him at the New Milford shop for part of the week and on Sundays.

Elayne, the middle child, was an artist, and she had a small studio near the family home in Kent. Her paintings were shown in a gallery their father had created within his New Milford shop, and they sold very well. People liked her evocative landscapes and sun-filled beach scenes, and especially her mother-and-child studies.

In a certain way Evan had thought Glynnis was her best friend as she was growing up, especially when she was in her late teens. She had gone to live with her grandparents in Manhattan at the age of seventeen, and after six months, when she became eighteen, she had enrolled in the Fashion Institute of Technology on West Twenty-seventh Street, where she had studied fashion design, her true vocation.

Now, suddenly, her thoughts focused on her grandmother's will. She and her father had been taken aback by it. Glynnis had left almost four hundred thousand dollars; the amount had taken their breath away. "Where did it all come from?" Evan had asked her father, once they left the lawyer's office.

Owen had shrugged, looking nonplussed. "Damned if I know, honey, but my mother was always frugal, and also a good business-woman. She kept my father's books at the shop for years, and she had a good head for figures, he told me. I know she liked to dabble in the stock market a bit. Over the years she did quite well, but your gran was cautious, and she also tended to scrimp and scrape. I guess that's where her money came from . . . her own thrift and prudence."

Owen had received the bulk of the money and his mother's apartment, which Glynnis had inherited from Richard after his death several years earlier. There had been nice be-quests to Elayne and Angharad, and Evan herself had received thirty thousand dollars, much more than the other two girls. But she was the eldest grandchild, and they had un-derstood. Their grandmother's few pieces of jewelry and small trinkets had been left to her sisters and herself. Glynnis had passed on several of the really good pieces to their mother, obviously not wanting to slight her daughter-in-law.

Follow your dreams, her dad had said to Evan. She would try. Certainly her grand-mother had made that possible. Evan had been able to come to London without asking her father for money, and for this she was grateful.

Her grandmother's dying words again reverberated in her head, and she couldn't help wondering why Emma Harte was her future. What had Glynnis meant? Evan wouldn't know until next week, when she was well enough to go out.

Rousing herself, she went over to the chest of drawers near the fireplace. On top of it she had arranged a selection of family photographs. She picked up the one of her grandparents and herself when she was twelve, taken here in London.

She stared at the photograph for a few moments. In the background were the gates of Buckingham Palace. It had been a sunny day, and she was squinting into the light, looking sedate in khaki pants, a white blouse, and white sneakers. She half-smiled at the youthful image of herself, thinking she looked so awkward with her long legs and skinny shoulders. Her hair had been cut in bangs, a straight, dark line across her forehead, and this style did not suit her. She recognized that now, but she hadn't known it then.

Her grandfather, tall, almost military in his bearing, was wearing a dark blazer and gray trousers, and looked very smart with his pale blue shirt and navy tie. His hair was pepper-and-salt, and his light gray eyes twinkled in his lean, craggy face. Still a handsome man, just as he had been in his younger days.

Her grandmother was quite amazing looking in the photograph. She had been sixty-five at the time, and she had stopped tinting her hair long before. It was a cloud of silver around her still-youthful face, and the blueness of her eyes appeared very sharp in the picture. That wide smile Evan had known and loved all of her life was in place on Glynnis's face, which as usual reflected her loving nature.

Grandparents were important, Evan was fully aware of that. It was only through them that you really knew who you were, where you came from, what you were all about. In a sense, great-grandparents were of even more importance, for what you gleaned about *them* gave you considerably more insight into your grandparents, your parents, and yourself. You carried their genes, and also their hopes and dreams and aspirations. All of these elements were there in you, flowing down through the bloodlines. Knowing about your family background gave you a sense of direction, she thought, and told you so much about who and what you could become. It gave you and your life meaning.

It was because of her grandmother that she was here. And next week, if her grandmother was to be believed, she would come face-to-face with her future on the day she went to Harte's in Knightsbridge. She had faith in Glynnis, she had always had faith in her.

Four

In the late afternoon, Linnet made her way to the attics in the East Wing of Pennistone Royal. She had been working up there on weekends for several months, and had almost finished cataloging Emma's couture clothes.

After opening the door with her key, she stepped inside and switched on the light, then stood for a moment, glancing around, a smile of pleasure flitting across her face. These attics were special to her, more than ever since she had arranged everything the way she wanted. What made them unique was their size; they were not at all like the small, low-ceilinged rooms found under the eaves of most houses.

Spacious, with fairly high ceilings, they had been remodeled by her great-grandmother many, many years before. Emma had had the walls lined with cedar, the floors covered with carpeting, and she had installed excellent lighting. Cupboards with deep shelves had been designed to hold boxes of varying sizes, where all manner of things could be safely kept free from dust. In essence, Emma had created a series of splendid storage rooms for all her clothes and accessories, such as shoes, hats and handbags, and costume jewelry.

As she moved forward, Linnet couldn't help congratulating herself on the reorganization she and her cousin India Standish had done in the last few months. When her mother had asked her to sort out the muddle in the attics, it had not taken her very long to realize there was no *real* muddle. The basic problem was that many racks had been pushed close together and filled with innumerable outfits and ensembles.

She and India had decided there was only one way to organize the clothes, once the racks had been properly arranged. They did it by designer rather than by category of clothing, as her mother and Aunt Emily had done some years before. Each designer now had a rack, or racks, with his or her name posted in bold letters.

It had always been something of a wonder to Linnet that so much had been kept. Even as a child she had liked to roam amongst the racks of clothes, admiring the beading and the embroidery, touching the beautiful chiffons, satins, silks, and velvets.

Her great-grandmother had had excellent taste, and everything had been kept in near-perfect condition by her, and later by Paula and Emily. Some years earlier her mother had installed air-conditioning, which was kept on low the whole year round to preserve the clothing.

Normally the ensembles were kept in dust-proof, zip-up garment bags made of cotton, but she and India had taken many of the outfits out of the bags in order to make decisions about them. She glanced at them now as she walked between the racks; it struck her that she could use almost all of her great-grandmother's clothes in her retrospective, especially since she was covering eighty years.

Emma's ensembles dated back to the 1920s and featured many great designers. In particular she had favored three French designers in their heyday — Pierre Balmain, Cristóbal Balenciaga, and Christian Dior. But she had bought from Vionnet and Chanel in Paris; Hardy Amies in London; the French American designer Pauline Trigère, based in New York; and the Russian designer Valentina, whose couture house had also been in New York until her retirement in 1957. And there were all those wonderful accessories. It was a treasure trove of elegance and style.

Linnet knew she could easily finish the last of the cataloging tomorrow. Now she had a specific purpose — finding a missing evening gown which her aunt Emily had told her about last week. Emily had discovered it years ago in Emma's Belgrave Square flat and had used it in a display of fashion Paula had put on in the early seventies, which she had called Fashion Fantasia.

"You have to use it," Emily had told Linnet. "It's really not lost, just mislaid. I'll bet you anything it's in the attics at Pennistone Royal, since it's not in London. Look for a very large flat box, a dress box, and I think it has a Harte's label on it, rather faded. I found it in that box, and I put it back there, as far as I remember. As you well know, beaded dresses are heavy, the weight of the beads pulls the fabric down and makes a mess of the shape. So I know it's not hanging in a dress bag."

Emily had gone on to describe the dress: "A sheath of pale blue chiffon covered with thousands of tiny bugle beads of pale blue and emerald green. It's simply gorgeous. Oh, and there's a pair of emerald green silk evening shoes by Pinet of Paris."

When Linnet came to the end of the first aisle of racks, she headed for the long worktable and put her shopping basket of tools down on it. Dragging the stepladder closer to one of the tall built-in cupboards, she opened its doors and climbed the steps. As she leaned forward and pulled out a large box, a number of others tumbled to the floor. Backing down the ladder, she put the box she was carrying on the table, surmising that it did not contain the dress. It was very heavy, and when she lifted the lid she saw it contained shoe boxes neatly lined up next to one another.

At this moment her cell phone began to ring; reaching into her basket, she grabbed it. "Hello?"

"It's me," her cousin Gideon announced.

"Hi! Where are you, Gid?"

"At the stables in Middleham. When I phoned the house, Margaret told me to call you on your cell. Where on earth are you? You sound as if you're on the moon."

She laughed. "Not quite. But I am in the attics."

"Good Lord, it's years since we've been up there . . . playing with all those old toys."

"Not those attics, silly. I'm in the East Wing, where all of Grandy's clothes are stored. I'm actually looking for an evening gown your mother told me about last week."

"Oh gosh, that's right. Your big project is in the works. Eighty Years of Elegance and Style," he said, laughter in his voice.

"Don't make fun of me, Gideon. The retrospective is going to generate a lot of traffic in the fashion department, and that means sales."

He was suddenly chagrined, knowing how seriously she took her work. Swiftly he exclaimed, "Now *you're* being silly. It's a great idea and I wouldn't make fun of it."

"I don't suppose you would, Gid. You are

coming to dinner tonight, aren't you?"

" 'Course I am. That's why I'm phoning actually. . . . Listen, do you think it will be all right for me to bring a guest? Will your mother mind?"

"I'm sure she won't. You know how she likes to play Earth Mother, invites the whole world to partake of her food. Who do you want to bring?"

"Actually, Linnet, it's Julian."

"Kallinski!"

"Is there another Julian in your life?"

"No, and he's not either. Mummy won't mind if you bring him to dinner, but I certainly will."

"Oh come on, Linnet, you know how you feel about him."

"And how's that, Gid?"

"You love him."

"Yes, that's true . . . in the way I love you. Like a cousin, or a big brother."

"Liar!"

"I'm not a liar. Since we grew up together, as you well know, Julian and I have a very fraternal relationship."

Gideon did not respond, and she was wondering if the connection had gone dead when he said, "It's not the way Julian portrays your relationship."

"I think you're fibbing, Gideon Harte."

"No. I'm not. I *know* he loves you, *and* in the most sexual, romantic, man-woman sense."

"Is that what he said to you?"

"Yes, it is. More or less. Scout's honor," Gideon answered, sounding suddenly serious.

"I knew men were worse gossips than women," Linnet muttered. "What else did he say?"

Ignoring her gibe, he answered, "I believe he wants to tell you *that* himself."

"When?"

"Tonight."

"He's not with you now?" she asked, riddled with curiosity.

"No, he went to see his grandfather. Sir Ronald's not been feeling well. But Julian's staying with us in Middleham."

She was silent, her mind racing.

"Well, can he come to dinner or not? Come on, you know you want to see him."

Linnet hesitated, then said, "I guess it'll be all right. My mother's having a bit of a crowd, I think."

"She is?" Gideon sounded alarmed. "Who's coming?"

"Well, Gramps is here for the weekend, so that's another O'Neill, making six of us altogether *if* Desmond and Emsie join us for sups. And then there's Emily and Winston —"

"I know my parents are coming," he cut in.

"India said she might fly up from London to help me with the last of the cataloging and the packing of the clothes, but she hasn't appeared so far. Oh, and Mummy said something about Aunt Amanda coming also."

"She was supposed to be staying with us, but she's not arrived either."

"The blizzard didn't amount to anything much after all. So Amanda's probably just late, not lost in a snowdrift somewhere. Oh, and by the way, Gid, I think Mummy invited Anita Shaw, just to even out the numbers."

"Good God, I hope not!" Gideon exclaimed. "I can't bear that girl. . . . I do wish your mother would stop trying to fix me up with women. I'm quite happy as I am, the proverbial bachelor."

Linnet laughed. "Somebody's going to catch you one day, Gid."

"You will tell your mother about Julian coming, won't you?"

"Yes. And listen, I was teasing you about Anita. She's not invited. I think my mother's given up on trying to get you married. I suppose we're going to have to rely on a total stranger to sweep you off your feet."

"That'll be the day!" he shot back, chuckling. "I'll see you later then, and don't work too hard."

"Bye, Gid," she answered.

Linnet stood leaning against the stepladder for a moment, her mind focused on Julian. She wondered if she had made a mistake, allowing her cousin to bring him to dinner. In the last year she had felt totally confused about their relationship, which was why she had pulled away from him six months ago. Julian had agreed they should have some breathing space, and they had stopped seeing each other by mutual consent.

Despite the closeness of their families, they had run into each other only once, and that was at Christmas here at Pennistone Royal. But like Tessa, Julian had fled as quickly as he could without appearing rude.

She closed her eyes, saw him in her mind's eye. Tall, slender, darkly handsome, with the most penetrating blue eyes she had ever seen. His cold blues, she called them, when he got angry. Linnet felt a sudden and terrible longing for him, and she was momentarily startled. He had been part of her life for as long as she could remember, from the time they were toddlers, and an indispensable part of her existence since she was fifteen. She missed him . . .

"I'm sorry I'm so late."

Linnet snapped her eyes open with a start and straightened against the ladder. Her cousin India was hovering in the doorway, carrying her own shopping basket, her tortoiseshell glasses pushed up on top of her mass of curly, pale blond hair.

India was twenty-seven but looked much younger, and she was pretty in a soft, delicate way. She had large, luminous silvery gray eyes and an expressive, sensitive face reminiscent of the Fairleys. She had their blood running through her veins. Without a doubt India was the most popular person in the family; she was considerate and gentle, and had an understanding heart. Everyone loved her.

She asked, with a small frown, "Is something wrong, Linnet?"

"No, I'm fine. Why?"

"You're rather pale, and you look . . . well, slightly troubled."

"Oh, it's nothing of any importance, India," Linnet answered, and pushing her cell phone into the pocket of her loden green trousers, she continued more briskly, "I pulled out that big box over there on the table, and a lot of others fell down. We'd better pick them up. Maybe the missing dress is in one of them."

"Don't worry, darling, we'll find it," India murmured in her soothing voice, which held a lovely lilt, a hint of her upbringing on the estate at Clonloughlin, which belonged to her father, Anthony Standish, the Earl of Dunvale.

Placing her shopping basket of tools on the table, India added, "I'm quite sure we can finish everything by tomorrow night, so don't worry."

"I hope we can. We have to go back to London on Monday morning. Early. We've a lot to do at the store, India." As she spoke, Linnet carried one of the larger boxes to the table; India did likewise.

Together, two great-granddaughters of Emma Harte sorted through the flat boxes. But after an hour the beaded dress had not turned up. "It can't have walked away. It must be somewhere," Linnet remarked to India. "Let's look in that big built-in next door in the smaller attic," she said, disappearing from view.

India hurried after her. "I think that particular built-in is full of old leather suitcases that belonged to Grandy."

"I don't remember seeing any there," Linnet answered, sounding puzzled. "I wonder who could have put them there."

"Who knows? But Aunt Emily might easily have packed the evening gown in one of them," India suggested.

"She was positive she'd put it back in the box she found it in, one with a faded Harte's label on the lid. But she could be mistaken," Linnet said over her shoulder. "After all, it was years ago."

"To be sure it was," India murmured.

A moment later the cousins stood in the smaller attic, staring at the shelves in the tall cupboard. It was stacked with boxes. But there were also a number of leather cases on the lower shelves.

The young women lost no time in taking

out all the boxes, and as soon as Linnet saw one with an old Harte's label attached to the lid, she shrieked. "*Voilà!* I bet it's in here!" At once she pulled the lid off and was staring down at a glittering mass of pale blue and emerald green bugle beads. "We've found it!" she exclaimed triumphantly, then lifted the gown out of the box, gazing at it in the light.

"Isn't it beautiful, India?" She pressed the beaded sheath against her body, stood looking down at the dress.

"Grandy must have been a sensation when she wore it," India said. "What with her red hair and green eyes. And you don't look half bad yourself, the way you're holding it against your body. The colors are wonderful for you. You know, Linnet, it has a sealike effect, all those blues and greens mingling." India gave Linnet a big smile. "The gown seems to undulate when you move. Maybe you should keep it. You love vintage clothes more than anyone I know."

"It's too valuable," Linnet responded, laughing. "And the beading has been very cleverly worked, that's why it undulates," she explained, then carefully laid the dress on top of a long table. She began to examine the embroidery and the overall workmanship, marveling at both. She was amazed at the gown's condition; it looked almost new.

In the meantime, India had made a discovery of her own. She exclaimed, "Linnet, come here and look at this."

"What is it?" Linnet asked, her attention still focused on the lining of the evening gown.

"It's a suitcase that belonged to Grandy. I just opened it up, and there's a smaller case inside marked 'Private and Confidential.' Her name is on the same luggage label. Oh, and here's a little key attached with a bit of string to the handle."

"What's inside the smaller case?"

"I don't know, I haven't looked. After all, it is marked 'private and confidential' . . ." India's sentence trailed off as she untied the small key and opened the case, murmuring, "Since our great-grandmother has been dead for years, I suppose I can lift the lid at least."

"Of course you can," Linnet said confidently.

"Linnet, please do leave that dress and come and look at what I've found. *Please.*"

Struck by the urgency in her cousin's voice, Linnet went to join India on the floor in front of the built-in cupboard.

She crouched down on her haunches and followed India's gaze. "Oh my God!" Linnet's hand flew to her mouth. Her eyes widened, and she reached out, touched the leather-bound books lying side by side in the smaller suitcase. What she was seeing made her heart miss a beat. At last she said in an awed voice, "Emma Harte's wartime diaries. Oh, India, what a find!" She lifted one out and read the date embossed in gold on the black cover. "Nineteen thirty-eight. Long before we were born, and even before our parents were born. Gosh . . ."

"This is a treasure trove, you know," India volunteered. "They run right through to 1947. Did you notice that?"

Linnet nodded, then tried the lock on the 1938 diary, which was still in her hands. It opened easily. She was about to look inside the diary but hesitated, then very resolutely, she closed it again.

India, sounding nervous, said, "I'm glad you didn't read anything. I know Grandy's been dead longer than we've been alive, but I think it is rather an invasion of privacy, reading her diaries, don't you, Linny?"

"I do, and I think it's my mother's decision. After all, she was Emma's chief heir. Paula should see them first. I'll take them down to her when we've finished up here."

"Yes, yes, that's the wisest thing, to be sure."

Linnet put the diary back in its place, then slowly smoothed her hand over the ten books, her expression reflective, her eyes suddenly far away. After a moment or two, she focused her attention back on the diaries. All of them were bound in black, the year embossed in gold, and she was sure none of them were locked. She could not help wondering what secrets they contained; she longed to read them. But her integrity, bred in the bone, would not permit her to violate her mother's trust in her. The golden rule in the family was that anything pertaining to Emma Harte first passed through Paula, head of the Harte dynasty.

Linnet was honor bound to abide by that rule.

Five

Although she was fifty-seven, Paula McGill Harte O'Neill looked younger. Her head of luxuriant dark hair, coming to a widow's peak above her smooth brow, was still the color of jet, although she was the first to admit that it got a little help from her hairdresser these days. Her eyes, her most spectacular feature, were still that amazing deep violet color and thickly fringed with dark lashes. They had always reflected her deep intelligence, but wisdom and compassion dwelt there now as well.

She sat in the upstairs parlor at Pennistone Royal with her cousin Emily Harte, but her thoughts were focused on her daughter Linnet, and Julian Kallinski, whom at one time she had thought Linnet would marry. She wished her daughter had confided in her more, wished that Linnet had not made such sweeping and drastic moves without at least one discussion. But when she herself had been in her twenties she had been headstrong, too, had believed she knew everything.

Oh, what it was to be young and impulsive, and so convinced of the rightness of what one did. She had married Jim Fairley when she was very young, and lived to regret it, as she had come to understand that it was Shane O'Neill who held her heart. But at least things had eventually worked out for her and Shane. They had been married now for almost thirty years, their love growing deeper and deeper with the passing of time.

Eventually Emily said, as if reading her thoughts, "I think Linnet and Julian were made for each other, as you and Shane were —"

"And you and Winston, too," Paula interrupted as she roused herself from her thoughts of her daughter.

"*True.* Anyway, I was going to say I hope those two begin to realize this, and very soon. Wouldn't it be nice to have a family wedding in the summer with the three clans present?"

"You see, there you go, Emily!" Paula exclaimed, shaking her head. "Bringing the clans into it. But yes, you're right, it would be nice. In the meantime, there's Gideon for us to worry about, he's still a bachelor."

"He doesn't settle down with any of the women he dates. Brief encounters I call them," Emily muttered.

"He just hasn't met the right woman yet, that's all," Paula asserted. She pushed herself up from the chair, walked across the floor.

Emily's eyes followed her. She thought her cousin looked beautiful tonight with her new short hairdo, sleek, stylish, and youthful. She was wearing a long, straight amethyst wool skirt and a matching turtleneck sweater that brought out the color of her eyes and was a foil for her hair. The outfit was simple, even a little severe, but it suited Paula, who was tall and slender.

Emily wished she had a figure like Paula's, but try though she did, she always looked slightly plump in comparison. No wonder Paula had affectionately dubbed her Apple Dumpling when she was little. She was still fighting the childhood preponderance to put on weight.

In all the years of their growing up together, they had never exchanged a cross word or had a quarrel, although sometimes the eight-year-old Paula had reprimanded Emily when she was five and they were staying at Heron's Nest, Emma's summer home in Scarborough, and she had been what Paula called "a pest." Cousins, best friends, and confidantes, they had been each other's rocks in times of trouble and adversity.

For the most part, these two had been brought up by Emma, they were trained by her, and today they ran a large part of her empire between them. They were devoted to their grandmother's memory, and in a sense they were the keepers of the flame.

Pausing at the door of the bedroom which adjoined the upstairs parlor, Paula said, "There's something I want to show you before the others arrive."

"What?"

"Linnet and India found it in the storage attics and —"

"The famous beaded dress!" Emily declared triumphantly.

"Oh, they found that all right, but they came across something else, something much more important."

"Hurry up then, I'm intrigued." Emily sat back, an expectant look on her face.

A moment later Paula came back carrying the small brown leather suitcase which contained the diaries. She placed it on the coffee table in front of Emily, and then, leaning forward, she lifted the lid.

"This is it," she said, glancing over her shoulder to look at her cousin.

"What's in it, actually?" Emily asked, full of curiosity.

"Grandy's diaries. From 1938 through 1947. Ten of them, and they're all in the most beautiful condition. I suspect she stored them in this case for years, and that's why they're so well preserved."

"Oh my God, what a find!" Emily cried, leaning forward, staring at the set of black-leather, gold-embossed diaries within the case. "But where on earth have they been all these years? And how is it the girls just found them? I mean, why didn't *we?*" She glanced at Paula, frowning. "How could we have missed them?"

"You're going to have a good laugh when I tell you where they were stored for years, Emily."

"*Where?*"

"In that walk-in closet in the ground-floor office."

"Not the one that's now called the morning room?" Emily asked, her eyes wide with surprise.

"Exactly. They'd been there for years. This one and five others, all part of a matched set of luggage from Asprey. Grandy used that office every day when she was at Pennistone Royal, for years and years. So it was definitely she who put them there. This case was actually inside a larger one, otherwise I would have noticed the label marked confidential. Anyway, I moved them when I revamped that room a few months ago."

"And you never looked inside any of the cases?" Emily asked, incredulity in her voice.

"No. Why would I? They weren't heavy. I just assumed Grandy had kept them there because there was no space left in the luggage room. Which there isn't. And it was a convenient place. Actually, I never gave them a second thought, not even when I used that office myself. I had Margaret put them down in the basement when I redecorated."

"So how did they find their way to the attics?"

"Margaret took them up there. We had a dreadful flood in the basement two weeks ago, and she remembered the cases when she was taking other things out to safety. She knew they were good, hardly used, and she put them in the smaller attic, in the first cupboard where there was space."

"Thank God she did. If she hadn't, the cases and the diaries would have been destroyed."

"You're right, we're lucky she acted so promptly."

Emily glanced at the open suitcase again, then swung her eyes to her cousin. "Have you read any of them?"

"I haven't. Linnet only gave them to me a couple of hours ago."

"Are you going to?"

"Eventually, I suppose."

"Shall we look inside one now?" Emily asked. "I'm very curious."

Paula hesitated, then nodded. "All right, if you want to, Emily."

Reaching into the case, Emily pulled out the diary dated 1938, opened it, and glanced at the first page. Then she handed it to Paula silently.

After scanning the page in the same cursory way Emily had done, Paula put the diary back in the small suitcase. "I don't think we should be reading these . . ."

"I know what you mean, they're very private. On the other hand, Paula, I have the feeling Gran wouldn't mind *us* looking at them. I think she'd want us to read them, actually."

"Perhaps you're right. But for now I'm going to lock the case and put it away somewhere safe. Maybe in a few weeks we can read them together."

"Oh yes, that's a good idea. Grandy was articulate, you know, and so was her brother Winston. She expressed herself most eloquently at times." Emily paused, then, leaning toward Paula, she said quietly, "I'm sure there are a few secrets in there, don't you agree?"

"I don't really know. . . . Did she have any during the war years? Paul was dead, and she was grieving, coping with our uncles being in the services, running a big business under wartime conditions. What kinds of secrets could she possibly have had?"

"Well, I didn't mean sexual, or anything like that! I bet she never wrote that kind of thing down. Really, Paula, Gran was very proper."

"She also had a number of husbands, let's not forget that."

"Only two. And two lovers."

"And that was that. So I'm sure there are no secrets buried in those diaries."

"You never know. Anyway, everyone has secrets," Emily pronounced.

"They do?" Shane said from the doorway, making them both jump.

"Are you quite positive of that?" He was smiling broadly as he came to join them by the fireside.

Paula said, "I didn't get a chance to tell you earlier, Shane, but India found a case full of Grandy's diaries in the attic. I was just showing them to Emily."

"How wonderful," he said, glancing at the case on the coffee table. "I see they're her private diaries."

"Yes, it's a great find, but we've decided not to read any of them. At least not now."

Shane looked down at her, his eyes loving as he said, "You've made a good decision. . . . Wait for the right moment. After all, these are sacrosanct . . . a woman's private thoughts and feelings. Those should be treated with great respect."

Later, as she sat near the fireplace in the great Stone Hall, Paula glanced around at her family, as always happy to have them gathered around her at Pennistone Royal.

Everyone had finally arrived. Shane had mixed drinks for those who wanted whiskey or vodka, and Linnet and India had poured champagne into tall Venetian flutes and passed them around.

As Paula sat back in her chair, sipping her champagne, she let her gaze finally rest on the son of one of her dearest friends . . . *Julian*. He had, in the last few minutes, edged closer to Linnet, and now they were speaking quietly, standing a little apart from the others. Oh to be a fly on the wall, Paula thought, and hoped they were ending their silly separation, which had been Linnet's idea.

Julian was already a member of the family by virtue of his birth, and a full-blown member of the third clan; everyone liked and admired him. He was a truly nice young man, perhaps too nice in some ways. He adored Linnet and always had; because of this he was a little too submissive to her will, Paula thought. He's so right for her, though, and he understands that she will have so much responsibility one day. Just as he will. And they have a shared history, and their childhood that binds them together. He *is* admirable, thoughtful, kind, intelligent, even a bit of an intellectual, and fun loving. The last is so important for Linnet, who tends to be a workaholic.

Suddenly there he was, moving across the floor in rapid strides, looking hell-bent and determined about . . . something. And something important at that, she decided, if the look on his face was anything to go by.

Then he was hovering over her, tall, dark haired, just like his father, Michael, his eyes clear, bright blue, and unblinking. Filled with the sincerity she had first seen there when he was only a little boy. Julian was a pleasant-looking young man, lean and slender . . . perhaps a little too thin right now, Paula thought. He was, as usual, well dressed, in a dark blazer worn with dark gray trousers and a black turtleneck sweater.

"I need to talk to you for a moment," he said, smiling down at her. "In private," he added softly.

Paula nodded, stood up instantly, her hopes soaring unexpectedly. Perhaps he was going to speak about Linnet, about their becoming engaged, and was testing the waters with her before jumping in the deep end with Shane. But surely he knew they were all for this match. . . .

He placed his hand under her elbow and led her to a quiet corner. "Let's sit here for a moment." He indicated two straight-backed chairs covered in tapestry, placed near a circular table.

Always straightforward, Julian got right to the point. "My grandfather wondered if you could pop over to see him tomorrow. If you're not too busy."

"Why of course I'm not. But is something

the matter? I know he's not been feeling well." Her face clouded over with concern.

"Oh he's all right, suffering from a bit of rheumatism, and he's had a bad cold. But Grandfather's a tough old bird, don't you know, and as sharp as he ever was. He actually wants to talk to you about —" Julian broke off, leaned closer, lowered his voice, and murmured, "Jonathan Ainsley."

Paula stared at him, her body instantly stiffening. *"Jonathan,"* she repeated. "What on earth could Uncle Ronnie have to say about him?"

"Apparently your cousin Jonathan has returned to England. Permanently. Grandfather heard through his bankers in the City that he plans to open a business in London."

For a moment she could not respond. She felt a trickle of apprehension run through her, and although she did not know it, she had turned considerably paler.

"But is Uncle Ronnie sure of this?" she asked at last. As the words left her mouth she knew the question was a foolish one. Ronald Kallinski, her wise rabbi ever since Emma's death, always knew exactly what he was talking about.

Julian nodded. "Oh yes, he's *quite* sure. He feels you and he need to talk. He's obviously not very joyful about this turn of events."

"Jonathan Ainsley can't hurt me, or create problems with the company. I own fifty-four percent of the stock, and that's what matters in regard to the Harte stores. Even if he bought some of the stock that's being traded on the London Stock Exchange, it would be meaningless because I own the majority of the shares and control many more. And as far as the other companies are concerned, they're all controlled by me, Winston, Emily, and Amanda. Privately held by the family, and as tight as a drum. Emma saw to that before she died. We are invulnerable. But you know all this, Julian," she pointed out, sounding sure of herself. "We've never had any secrets within the three clans."

"I know, and I agree with you. On the other hand, Grandfather did sound rather concerned about the advent of the dreaded Mr. Ainsley."

Paula laughed, then responded, "I'll go and see him tomorrow, if only to reassure myself that he's all right."

Julian gave her the benefit of a wide smile. "You've worried about everyone for as long as I can remember. Linnet's right when she says you're a genuine earth mother. And look, I can come and get you tomorrow, drive you over to Harrogate to see Grandfather."

"Well, if you're sure it's no trouble." It suddenly occurred to her that she might use the opportunity to speak to him about Linnet.

"It's no problem at all. And anyway, it will give us a chance to chat about Linnet." He threw her a coolly calculated look and added, with a small smile, "I bet you were thinking exactly the same thing, weren't you?"

He's astute, just like his grandfather, she thought, then nodded. "Well, yes, I was," she admitted.

Leaning even closer to her, Julian said in a low, confiding voice, "It's all going to be fine, so don't worry. I know Linnet better than I know myself. She wanted to step away from our situation to take stock. She thought we were being pressured into marriage. We weren't, not really, but . . ." He paused, shook his head, finished, "Please don't worry."

"I can't help it," Paula answered, and then hesitated.

"You know, life does have a way of taking care of itself," he announced in a firm voice, before she had a chance to say anything else. "Tell me later what time you want me to come and fetch you tomorrow, and I'll be here."

Paula watched him return to Linnet's side, then at once her thoughts went to Jonathan Ainsley. He had betrayed the family and tried to steal the stores from her, but she had out-witted him, and in a certain sense she had destroyed him. He had called her his nem-esis, and she was. He had vowed to wreak his revenge. And she knew he would. A cold chill settled around her heart.

Six

Harte's was the most imposing edifice in Knightsbridge, an important landmark ever since the day it was finished, and its glamour and prestige were renowned the world over. Almost everyone who visited London felt compelled to make a stop at Harte's, always to browse and marvel, and usually to buy . . . *something*, however small.

On this cold Tuesday morning in the middle of January, Evan Hughes was finally hurrying toward the magnificent store, filled with excitement. It was acting like a magnet, pulling her forward, and she couldn't wait to enter its stately portals.

Evan paused, but only for a moment, to peer into the beautifully dressed windows that fronted onto Knightsbridge. She felt a little frisson of anticipation as she pushed open the doors and went inside the vast and impressive establishment.

She stood for a moment blinking in the bright lights and glancing around. How spectacular it all was. She was in the cosmetics department, and there was a glitter and shine to everything, from the product to the decorative elements, which added their own unique touches. Slowly Evan walked through the department, admiring the flair that was evident in the displays of creams and lotions, lipsticks, powders and perfumes, breathing in the scented air.

Suddenly she caught sight of her own reflection in one of the counter mirrors, and she paused to check her appearance before moving on, satisfied that she looked well put together. Her makeup was perfectly applied, her hair fresh and glossy, and she felt better than she had in days.

After her bout with the flu, which had lasted ten days in the end, she had been drained. But last night she had decided she did not want to put off visiting Harte's any longer. Earlier that morning she had dressed with care. Her choice was a stylish black pantsuit which emphasized her slenderness and height, and black leather boots. Over the pantsuit she wore a black wool coat that came down to her ankles; not only was it well tailored and elegant but it had a certain dash to it. Adding a flash of color to the ensemble was a long red wool scarf, which she had thrown around her neck. Otherwise her only adornments were gold earrings and a watch.

A number of people turned to look and admire as she strolled on through the cosmetics department. But Evan was oblivious to the attention she drew, endeavoring to feel more at ease, and lost in her thoughts as she headed toward the information booth.

The young woman in the booth looked up, smiled, and asked pleasantly, "Can I help you, madame?"

"Well. Er. Yes. What floor are the management offices on?"

"The ninth," the young woman answered.

"I'm assuming Mrs. Harte's office is on the same floor," Evan ventured, staring at her questioningly.

"*Mrs. Harte,*" the young woman repeated and frowned, shook her head. Then she exclaimed, "Oh, you must mean Mrs. O'Neill . . . Mrs. Paula O'Neill. A lot of people get her confused with her grandmother."

"And her grandmother is Emma Harte?"

"Was her grandmother. Mrs. Harte's dead. Has been for quite a while."

Taken aback though she was, Evan said quickly, "Yes. Yes, I was getting them confused, that's true. And Mrs. O'Neill's office is on the ninth floor?"

"It is."

"Thanks very much," Evan murmured and with a nod she hurried away. She wasn't quite sure where she was heading, but she certainly wasn't moving toward the bank of elevators which would whiz her up to the management offices.

At this moment what she really wanted was to have a cup of coffee and think about her grandmother's last words to her. Because the girl at the information desk had just negated her grandmother's instructions to "go to Emma . . . She has the key. To your future."

Emma Harte was dead. Had been for quite a while, the young woman had said. That could mean anything. A few months, a few years, maybe even decades. It struck Evan now that her grandmother and Emma Harte must have been about the same age, since they seemed to have known each other in the Second World War. Mrs. Harte had probably passed away recently, just as her gran had. Well, so much for that, she muttered and glanced around.

Evan now realized she was in the jewelry department. Approaching a salesperson, she said, "Excuse me. . . . Is there a restaurant on this floor?"

"There's the Coffee Café on the other side of the Food Halls. Just keep walking straight ahead, you'll come to it," the young man told her with a smile.

"Thanks," Evan said. Within a couple of minutes she had traversed the huge, well-stocked Food Halls and was standing in front of the Coffee Café. Pushing open the opaque-glass doors, she went inside. The café was small and attractive, and redolent with the smell of coffee. It was almost empty; she made for a booth, where she sat down and took off her scarf.

A split second later she was ordering a pot of coffee, and as she waited for the waitress to bring it, Evan pondered on her predicament. She had come to the store hoping to see Emma Harte and hoping to get a job; without this important contact, there was no possibility of a job now.

Sighing, she leaned back against the banquette and closed her eyes. Her thoughts were on Glynnis. Had her grandmother been delirious? Or living in the past? Didn't that sometimes happen to people when they were dying? Didn't parts of their lives flash before them like a reel of film unraveling? Evan had believed her grandmother that day, because she had no reason not to. Yet just before she left for London, her father had pointed out that she might not get a reaction from Mrs. Harte, since Glynnis had known her in the Second World War. That had been sixty years ago, after all.

How foolish she had been to take everything at face value. Why hadn't she checked things out? Because she had trusted Gran. She experienced a rush of frustration. Here she was in London with no prospects. The trip had been a waste of time, and more important, money.

No, that's not really true, she thought, sitting up straighter. The pot of coffee had materialized while she had been lost in her thoughts, and she poured herself a cup, added milk. As she sipped it she decided she deserved a vacation, and she reminded herself she had no real reason to worry, at least not for the moment, thanks to the money her grandmother had left her.

Immediately she zeroed in on the legacy she, her siblings, and her father had received from his mother. The overall amount Gran had left was enormous, at least to them, and it was something of a mystery. Her father had attempted to explain it away, yet it did seem incredible to Evan that Gran had accumulated such a sum.

Her grandparents had lived comfortably, but there had never been any great wealth. In fact, it struck Evan that they had always lived rather modestly. *Why?* They could have indulged themselves a bit with the kind of bank balance Glynnis obviously had. But perhaps Gran had been hoarding the money for her son and granddaughters.

Suddenly her father's puzzled expression flashed before Evan's eyes, how surprised he had been in the lawyer's office that day. Startled really, now that she thought about it, and confused. Just as she had been.

Her father deserved this windfall, deserved to inherit his parents' apartment. Evan was glad he had finally decided to keep it. The apartment was on East Seventy-second Street at Madison Avenue, a great location; and real estate was bringing excellent prices at the moment, so the idea of selling it had been tempting to him. But it pleased Evan that her father now had somewhere to stay overnight when he went into Manhattan; also, it was his own private space, a safe haven away from her mother. She wondered again, why had Marietta turned into a recluse?

Evan bit her lip, shook her head sadly. So many mysteries in her life . . . so many questions . . . and no answers. She pushed these thoughts away. Mysteries were for another day.

The cup of coffee had given her a boost. Slowly she began to formulate a plan.

She had given up her job in New York, so why go back? Why not stay in London for a few months? The weather would get better soon, and she'd always wanted to come back here . . . after all, this *was* the city where she was born.

But what to *do*, how to occupy herself? Her kind of sightseeing would be finished in a couple of weeks, then what? Get a job, of course. And why not a job here at Harte's? She liked the look of this grand store. No, it was more like an emporium, she decided, and somehow it had a connection, however tenuous, to her gran.

So why not go up to the management offices and apply for a position here? A voice whispered in her head, Go for it, girl. Evan smiled to herself. Glynnis would have said exactly that, and she would have added, "You've nothing to lose and everything to gain." Another smile flitted across her face as she thought of her grandmother.

When she was absolutely truthful with herself, Evan knew she had seized on her grandmother's dying words in order to leave New York and her family. She loved them all, especially her father, but she needed to be on her own, she needed to be free. London had beckoned her. And here she would stay, at least for a while. You never knew what was going to happen. As her gran had always said, "Life is full of surprises, Evan, make the most of the good ones." Perhaps her future *was* here after all, she thought, her face brightening.

Evan stepped out of the elevator on the ninth floor and found herself in a small lobby. To her left was a blank wall, to her right a pair of wooden swinging doors with glass windows set in the upper panels. Only way to go, she thought, as she turned right and pushed through the doors into the vast corridor. Slowly she walked along, reading the names on the various doors.

Halfway down the corridor, arched alcoves on each side broke up the flow of doors, and Evan paused, staring at a large oil painting hanging above a narrow side table in one of the alcoves. She stepped closer, marveling at the beauty of the woman in the portrait, who had red hair shot through with gold and coming to a widow's peak on her forehead. She had expressive eyes, very green, and small hands clasped in her lap.

The woman wore a pale blue silk dress, with an emerald bow pinned on one shoulder and large, square-cut emerald earrings on her ears. The ring on her left hand was another large emerald. There was a lovely warm smile on her face, and her eyes were alive and sparkling with intelligence. She looked to be about fifty years old.

Evan knew exactly who it was before she leaned forward and read the small engraved plaque attached to the elaborate gilded wood frame: "Emma Harte: 1889–1970."

Momentarily dumbfounded, she read the plaque again. Finally it sank in . . . *Emma Harte had been dead for thirty-one years.* Surely her grandmother had known this if they had once been friends. So what had made Gran utter those words on her deathbed? Evan shook her head, baffled more than ever about what her gran had been trying to accomplish.

After several seconds staring at the painting, Evan turned away, and it was then she noticed the painting in the alcove on the opposite wall. As she stepped up to it, she thought the woman in the portrait seemed vaguely familiar, but she couldn't quite place her. The plaque on this simply gave the name of the subject: "Paula McGill Harte O'Neill." Emma's granddaughter, Evan murmured under her breath, looking at it more closely.

She studied the portrait for a few minutes, struck by the dominant widow's peak obviously inherited from Emma. But here the resemblance stopped. Paula O'Neill's hair was jet black, worn in a pageboy style that ended at her strong jawline. Her complexion was pale as ivory, and she had a broad brow, high cheekbones, dimples, and large, expressive eyes the color of pansies. Truly beautiful eyes, Evan thought, unusual, and she decided Paula looked about forty-five in the portrait. She was striking in a dark, exotic way. In the painting she was wearing a silver-gray silk dress, and Emma Harte's emeralds were very much in evidence.

Evan was completely mesmerized by this painting, it was extraordinary, an accomplished portrait of —

"Can I help you?"

She almost jumped out of her skin, startled by a male voice, which had broken the silence in the corridor. She swung around and came face-to-face with a tall, good-looking young man.

A surprised look was flashing across his face as he stared at her, and then he said

115

again, "Do you need some assistance?"

"Yes. Yes, I do. I'm looking for the management offices."

He nodded. "They're at the end of the corridor. I'm heading in that direction, I'll show you where they are." Stepping closer to her, he held out his hand.

Evan took it, smiled up at him.

"Gideon Harte," he announced, shaking her hand.

"Oh!" she exclaimed, and automatically her eyes swung to Emma's portrait. "And that's your grandmother!"

"No, it isn't, actually," he answered. "That's my *great*-grandmother."

"I see."

"And you are?"

"Oh, excuse me, I'm forgetting my manners. I'm Evan Hughes."

"A Welsh name. A *boy's* Welsh name, to be precise," he responded.

"My grandmother was Welsh, and she told her son, my father, that she expected him to name his first child Evan. She was sure I was going to be a boy. I turned out to be a girl."

"So I can see," he said, giving her a swift, appraising look.

"But now I think the name Evan is used for a boy or a girl," she went on, ignoring his gaze, and then gently extricated her hand from his.

He said, "Let's go along to the offices,"

and began to walk slowly down the corridor.

Evan fell in step with him.

After a moment's silence, Gideon said, "You're an American, aren't you?"

"Yes, I am. From New York."

"Great city." He glanced at her. "And are you here on business?"

"Well, no, not exactly. I decided to come to London for a year or so," she quickly invented. "And that's why I'm here at Harte's today. I'm looking for a job."

"Are you now. In what area?"

"Fashion. I studied design in New York, and worked in the fashion departments of several stores. I also did a year's apprenticeship with Arnold Scaasi, the American couturier."

He nodded, seemed about to say something, then merely cleared his throat. "Here's where you want to be . . . Human Resources," he explained, indicating the door. "But Miss Hughes . . ." He stopped, cleared his throat again, and then said, "Do you have a work permit?"

"No, I don't, but I don't need one. I was born in London. I have an English passport and dual nationality."

"Well then, that's fine," he answered, giving her a broad smile.

Opening the door, he ushered her into a large office. A young woman seated at a desk looked up as they entered.

"Oh, hello, Mr. Harte," she said.

"Hello, Jennifer. This is Miss Evan Hughes. She's come to apply for a job at Harte's. In fashion." Looking at Evan, he added, "I wish you lots of luck, Miss Hughes."

"Thank you, Mr. Harte," she answered, smiling up at him again. "Thanks for everything."

Seven

Gideon walked down the corridor, thinking of the young woman he had just ushered inside. Evan Hughes. Unusual name. Unusual woman.

From the moment he set eyes on her, he had been struck by her fine looks, and not the least by her likeness to Paula O'Neill. For a second he had thought this quite uncanny. Their facial characteristics were very similar, as was their coloring, and he had recoiled in surprise when she had swung around to face him.

But then, in a flash, he had realized the likeness meant nothing. A lot of people resembled each other without being in any way related. In any case, how could this young American woman be related to Paula, of all people?

Gideon walked on, heading for Linnet's office, where he had been going when he had come across Evan Hughes looking lost in the middle of the corridor. But, in fact, she had been studying the portrait of Paula, he realized that now. Maybe she herself had noticed her likeness to the lady boss of the store.

Opening the door to the executive offices, he crossed the small central foyer and turned right.

Linnet's outer office was usually occupied by Cassie Littleton, her secretary, but this morning Cassie was nowhere in sight. His cousin's office door was wide open, and he strode toward it but paused in the doorway when he saw she was on the phone.

Linnet was staring out of the window as she talked, and he hovered on the threshold, not wanting to intrude on her privacy. Suddenly she swung around, saw him and beamed, then beckoned. Immediately she hung up the phone, exclaimed, "Gid, come in and sit down!"

He hesitated.

"What's the matter?" she asked, frowning, seating herself behind her desk.

"I'm not sure where I *could* sit, or how I could possibly navigate myself through this —"

"Don't you dare say *mess*," she cut in peremptorily.

"I wasn't going to," Gideon answered, strolling into the room, being careful not to knock over any of the precariously balanced boxes. "I was going to call it a minefield, because I know if I did accidentally tangle with something you'd explode."

"Ha! Ha! Very funny, Gid. But seriously,

just maneuver your way through and come and sit here." As she spoke Linnet leapt to her feet, ran around the desk, and lifted a pile of manila folders off the chair on the other side. "You'll be comfortable here," she remarked as she stacked the folders on the floor near the window.

"Thanks," Gideon said as he stepped warily around the many boxes, sat down, crossed his legs, and continued, "What did you think about the pictures I had them dig up in the photo morgue at the *Gazette*?"

"They're great. Grandy Emma gave some party in the fifties, by the look of the pictures anyway, and they'll be helpful to us. So, we're in charge it seems." She threw him a quizzical look.

"We are indeed, but I don't mind, do you? Stupid question!" he exclaimed, answering himself. "I can see very well what's going on here, and your fashion retrospective has become somewhat demanding, according to Julian."

Linnet nodded. "Too true. I just haven't had a chance to see him, and before you start chastising me, I will have dinner with him, as I promised I would. But I've got to get some of this work under my belt first."

"I know that. By the way, where's Cassie? She's usually keeping guard out there." He half-glanced toward the door as he spoke.

"She has the flu. And so does India.

121

Actually, poor old India sounds awful. Very chesty, and she has a nasty cough. I hope she doesn't get bronchitis again. She's prone to that, as you know. It's a Fairley characteristic, at least that's what Mummy says. Tessa's got a weak chest, too. Anyway, not to digress . . . I'm trying to cope on my own while they're both off nursing their ailments."

"So I can see."

"It's going to be a super show, I can promise you that, and I know my mother's going to be pleased. It'll be a great boost for the store."

"I know it will, I've always said that to you. But listen, Linnet, getting back to the birthday party for our respective fathers for a moment, have you come up with any ideas yet? Ideas about a theme, that kind of thing?"

"No, not really. But I haven't had much time to focus on it. Are you going to Yorkshire this weekend?"

"Yes, I am. Why?"

"I'm staying in London for once, to work through this lot, and I was thinking we might have supper on Saturday or Sunday, and brainstorm the party. But if you're going to Middleham . . ." Her voice trailed off and she gave a small, dismissive shrug.

"I'm sorry, but I promised Dad. We have to work on some business papers. I really do have to go, especially since I wasn't up there last weekend." He gave her a small, rueful smile. "But I promise I'll put my thinking cap on and brainstorm by myself. We can get together next week, if you can manage it."

"That'll be okay. Is Julian going with you?"

"No, as a matter of fact he isn't. But if he were, and he knew you were staying in town, I can assure you he would cancel *me* out immediately."

She laughed, then said swiftly, "Well, I'm going to have to dig into this pile, no matter what, and however long it takes. What *I* need, actually, is two assistants, and right *now*."

Gideon sat up straighter in the chair, a knowing look crossing his face, and exclaimed, "How about one assistant right *now*? Would that help?"

"Are you joking, of course it would!"

"Then I think I might have just the right person for you."

"Who?"

"Evan Hughes."

"A man. Oh, I'm not sure —"

"No, a woman," he cut in. "And yes, before you say it, I am fully aware that Evan is a Welsh boy's name. But apparently in America it's used as a girl's name as well."

"Oh, she's an American?"

"Yes. And well trained, I think. Studied fashion, worked for a well-known American couturier. She comes from New York, she's about twenty-six. And she's very personable."

"And she's a friend of yours, Gid?"

"Not exactly." He cleared his throat, gave Linnet a faint smile. "Actually I just met her in the corridor on her way to the personnel office."

"You mean you picked her up in the corridor, you Don Juan, you!"

"Don't be so ridiculous, Linnet. She was looking rather lost, and I asked her if I could help her," he shot back in a slightly injured tone, wondering how he had managed to acquire the reputation as a womanizer. He wasn't that at all.

"I bet you did." Linnet leered at him and added, "Well, one thing's for sure, if she grabbed *your* attention —"

"What's that?" he interrupted.

"She must be good-looking."

Gideon began to laugh. "Well, yes, she is. I must admit that."

"And where is she now?"

"I think she must still be in Human Resources." He glanced at his watch, nodded. "Definitely. She has to be still there."

Linnet, always decisive, picked up the phone and dialed. "Jennifer, it's Linnet," she said. "Do you still have a Miss Evan Hughes with you?"

"We do, Linnet. She's in with Maggie right now. Her application read very well, and so did her résumé."

"Very good. Transfer me to Maggie, would you, please, Jennifer."

"Right away."

A second later Maggie Hemmings answered her phone with a crisp, "Human Resources here."

"It's Linnet, Maggie. I understand Evan Hughes is with you."

"Correct."

"Jennifer says her papers are good."

"That's right."

"I'm looking for an assistant. Would she fit the bill?"

"I don't know."

"Oh. Well, once you've finished your interview, I'd appreciate it if you would bring her along to my office. I'd like to talk to her myself."

Maggie said, "See you shortly."

"I'll be waiting," Linnet replied and hung up. Looking across at Gideon, she remarked, "Apparently your Miss Hughes has made a reasonable impression."

"She's not *my* Miss Hughes. She's not even an acquaintance."

Linnet nodded. "Don't be so snarly, Gid. You know we've always enjoyed teasing each other."

"I'm not being snarly. Merely factual." He smiled at her; his expression was loving.

She stared back at him, also smiling, thinking how well he looked today in his impeccably tailored Savile Row suit, dark gray with a white pinstripe, pale blue shirt, and a silk tie of a similar hue. There were moments, like the present when he was looking serious and intent, that he reminded her of his father, Winston. The Harte looks were predominant in them both, except that Uncle Winston's vivid coloring had begun to fade. Gideon's hair was a rich russet color, his eyes light green, and he had clean, sharply defined features.

She and Gideon looked a lot like each other, and strangers often thought they were brother and sister. Certainly their relationship was close, and had been since they were small. But then their parents were cousins and best friends, in each other's company constantly, and as a consequence as children they had been thrown together a lot, along with his sister, Natalie, and brother, Toby, and Tessa and Lorne. Her other siblings were not yet born at that time.

At the thought of Toby, Linnet winced inside. He was not one of her favorites in the family, and she had always believed he was her enemy. He had been forever allied with Tessa, paying court and drooling all over her, which Tessa blatantly encouraged. Perhaps now that he was a married man things had changed somewhat, although she doubted it.

"Penny for your thoughts," Gideon said.

"I was thinking how smart you looked

today, very dashing, actually."

"Thanks for those kind words, my pet."

"And then Toby jumped into my head. . . . What's *he* up to at the moment? He's been awfully quiet of late, wouldn't you say?"

"Yes, he has. But he's very busy with work; he's got a hugely demanding job, as a matter of fact. I know he's not your favorite, Linny, and sometimes I have problems with him myself, always did, as you know only too well. Still, I've got to say he's good at what he does. Brilliant. He loves working in television, and Dad's pleased with the way he's been managing the television company. None of us can possibly fault him there, you know." Gideon shifted in the chair slightly and continued, "And of course, he's a newlywed. . . . I suppose he's rather preoccupied with his bride."

"You're right —" Linnet paused, threw him a direct look, her head on one side. "Do you like Adrianna Massingham, Gid?"

"She's all right. Not *my* type, but that doesn't mean anything really. Even though her appearance is very contrived, it's all that makeup I guess, she's still a beautiful young woman, and pleasant enough, I suppose —" He cut his sentence off abruptly and sat back in the chair, his face growing more serious than usual.

"But what? There's definitely a *but* here," Linnet asserted.

127

"True. Look, to be honest, I'm not sure that the marriage will weather the storms that are bound to erupt. Toby's not easy, we know that, and he wants kids, wants to start a family, while Adrianna is very intent on pursuing her acting career. Everyone's aware of that at home, especially my mother. No children for Adrianna, at least not right now. Maybe her attitude will change in time. What does Tessa think? Whoops, that's a stupid question!" he exclaimed. "Of course *you* don't know what *she* thinks, because she never confides in you."

"No, she doesn't, she never did. However, I suspect her nose is out of joint because he got married."

"But she's married herself!"

"Tessa's a bit odd, Gid. She's always thought of Toby as her property. Have you forgotten that?"

"Not really, but I was certain she'd out-grown her possessiveness."

A sudden thought occurred to Linnet, and leaning forward, she exclaimed, "Gideon, you said your Miss Hughes was an American. So how could I employ her immediately? She'll need a work permit. Oh God, all that red tape to go through!" She groaned.

"Not necessary, my pet. I should have mentioned that she was born in London, has a British passport and dual nationality. No work permit required."

"That's good to know, and I must say, you certainly found out a lot about her in only a few minutes."

He grinned. "You are now in possession of the sum total of every blessed thing I know about Miss Evan Hughes."

Eight

Two things were instantly apparent to Linnet after Maggie Hemmings had introduced Evan Hughes and then left her office.

First, the young woman was the same type as her mother — slender, willowy, dark haired, pale of skin, and exotic-looking. And, Linnet thought, there was a curious likeness between the two of them.

Second, Gideon and Evan were transfixed in the middle of the room, completely oblivious to her presence. They were taken with each other. But hadn't she known that because of the way Gid had spoken about Evan earlier?

Certainly she had never seen this particular expression on Gid's face before; it was a dazed look, and she felt a sudden twinge of jealousy. He was her favorite cousin, her best friend since childhood, closer even than India. And he belonged to her.

No, stop thinking like that, she told herself. She wasn't like Tessa. Silently, she chastised herself. She loved Gideon, wanted only the best for him, and of course, he *would* meet someone special one day, and he would get married. But it hadn't happened thus far, so he was available. And she had come to rely on him more and more since she had put her relationship with Julian on hold.

Linnet reminded herself that Gideon had never been jealous of Julian, but then the three of them had grown up together, and Julian was Gideon's greatest male friend. Her father had called them the Three Musketeers when they were kids because they were inseparable and devoted to one another.

Julian. He had been part of her life, part of her, for as long as she could remember, and he was always there, hovering at the back of her mind, however much she tried to block him out. Was he her one true love? Had she made a terrible mistake in turning away from him for, well, for so many reasons actually? Perhaps those reasons were not quite as valid as she thought. She couldn't help wondering about this from time to time. But not now, an inner voice suddenly cautioned. Now it's time to concentrate on this young woman, to concentrate on work, on the retrospective.

Linnet dropped her eyes to the folder on the desk which Maggie had just given her, opened it, and looked at the application forms and the detailed résumé.

But riddled with curiosity as she was, she glanced up after only a second, focusing her eyes on Gideon and Evan Hughes. Now he was solicitously shepherding the young American to the chair near her desk, his glazed expression having been replaced by a most beatific smile. Evan was looking slightly flushed, a little shy, perhaps even flustered, but her eyes held a distinct sparkle.

Clearing her throat somewhat noisily, Linnet looked directly at Evan and said pleasantly, "I'll finish reading your résumé and application forms later."

Evan nodded, looking pleased. She was thrilled to be sitting here; she could scarcely believe her luck.

Returning Evan's steady gaze, Linnet noticed that the young woman's resemblance to her mother was stronger than she had realized a moment ago. Evan's face was the same shape as Paula's, finely sculpted, and the dark brows sweeping along the broad forehead were identical. But her eyes were a light bluish gray, large and translucent. At this moment those eyes were full of eagerness, and there was a sense of earnestness about her that Linnet couldn't help liking. In fact, there was something truly appealing about Evan Hughes, and Linnet smiled at her warmly.

Evan smiled back and was just about to say something when she was cut off by Gideon.

Hovering behind Evan's chair, his hand resting on the back, he exclaimed, "Well, I'd better skedaddle, leave you both to get down to the nitty-gritty." Striding purposefully toward the door, he swung around before exiting. Blowing a kiss to Linnet, he said, "I'll give you a ring later, so that we can discuss the big bash in June. And Miss Hughes, I wish *you* lots of luck at Harte's."

Before either woman could make any kind of response, the door closed softly behind him.

"I've been looking to hire another assistant," Linnet explained to Evan once they were alone. "I already have one, actually. Her name's India Standish, and she's my cousin. We work well together, we've run the fashion floors for several years. Unfortunately, India's out sick right now; she has the flu. So does my secretary, Cassie Littleton." Linnet stopped, shook her head, and then, making a face, she glanced around the room. "Hence this *mess*. It's not usually like this, I'm a fairly tidy person. Anyway, I don't think either of them will be in this week. I just hope *I* don't come down with it. I can't afford to be sick right now."

"I think there's a bit of an epidemic," Evan warned in a worried voice. "I've just recovered from a bout of the flu myself."

"I'm glad you're better," Linnet murmured. "Anyway, not to digress. I understand from Gideon and Maggie that you studied design and had a career in fashion in New York."

"That's correct. I was a student at the Fashion Institute of Technology, and later I was an apprentice with the couturier Arnold Scaasi for a year. I even worked in the fashion department at Bergdorf Goodman for a while."

Evan shifted slightly in her chair and continued, "I also helped Pauline Trigère with a retrospective of her couture. That was about six years ago, when I was still at FIT. She's a friend of my father's, and he asked if I could help her with the exhibit, just to gain experience. I learned a lot simply from being around her. She has great personal style, and her clothes are marvelous."

"That I know. My great-grandmother was a fan of hers, according to my mother, and the clothes I found in storage are proof of that. There are a number of Trigère gowns, suits, and coats in Emma's vast collection."

Evan's face lit up as she exclaimed, "That's wonderful. They will be in the fashion retrospective, won't they?"

"Yes, they will. Obviously Maggie Hemmings told you about the exhibition which India and I are planning."

"She did touch on it, yes. How comprehensive is it going to be?"

Leaning across the desk, Linnet explained in an enthusiastic voice, "Very comprehensive. We're going to be showing eighty years of fashion, going all the way back to 1920. We're basing part of the exhibition on the clothes which belonged to my great-grandmother. She was Emma Harte, the founder of the Harte stores."

"Yes, I know," Evan said, and then before she could stop herself, she blurted out, "I saw her portrait in the corridor. You certainly look like a younger version of her."

Laughing, Linnet opened the center drawer of her desk and murmured, "Oh yes, I know . . . everybody tells me that. I just hope I'm a little bit like her in other ways, particularly in character. She was pretty special, and a very brilliant woman."

Bringing out a sheet of paper, Linnet handed it to Evan. "These are some of the designers we're planning to feature. The clothes that belonged to Emma are also listed, and they're from her haute couture collection." She laughed. "Actually, I think I've taken *all* of the collection."

Quickly scanning the list, Evan read out some of the names in an awed voice. "Pierre Balmain, Coco Chanel, Cristóbal Balenciaga, Christian Dior, Trigère, Lanvin, Vionnet, Hubert de Givenchy, Yves Saint Laurent, Scaasi, Cardin. Heavens, what fantastic names. Your great-grandmother must have had wonderful taste."

"*I* think she did."

"I notice you're also listing separately Valentino, Oscar de la Renta, Karl Lagerfeld,

Zandra Rhodes, Lacroix, Versace, and many other designers. Do you have their clothes already?"

"Only some. We have Emma's collection, of course. That's recently been brought down here from Pennistone Royal, my mother's house in Yorkshire, where they are stored. And we do have a certain number of items by other designers which you read off. However, I think we need to find more vintage pieces, and I was hoping you could handle that. Naturally I'm assuming that you would like to work on the retrospective, if you come onboard at Harte's."

Leaning forward urgently, her face full of that engaging eagerness Linnet had noted before, Evan exclaimed, "I'd love to work at Harte's, and I'd be thrilled to be involved with the retrospective. A project like this is always challenging, Miss O'Neill."

"And very hard work," Linnet pointed out, giving her a direct look. "I hope you don't mind long hours."

"Not me. I've been told I'm a workaholic by most people I've worked with."

Linnet burst out laughing. "That's good to know, and join the club! India and I suffer from that same ailment, I'm afraid. But I think I happen to be worse than she is sometimes. Anyway, do you have any thoughts about where and how to acquire vintage clothes for the exhibition?"

"Yes, I do. There are several good vintage clothing shops in New York. The best I think is Keni Valenti. He's a private dealer of vintage couture, and he has about ten thousand pieces, as well as accessories such as shoes, bags, scarves, and jewelry. He has quite a lot of Yves Saint Laurent, I know that. Anyway, he has an Internet site, and we can pull it up on the computer so you can see some of the clothes. Then there's Didier Ludot in Paris. He has three shops, but the best is the one in the gardens of the Palais Royal, which is dedicated to vintage haute couture from the 1920s up to the 1980s. Almost the time span for your exhibit."

"That's good to know! We do have to investigate, look at Web sites. There are auction houses, of course, such as Christie's and Sotheby's here in London. In fact, we've already bought quite a lot at auction in the past year, which is how long we've been working on the retrospective."

"The William Doyle Galleries in New York also specialize in vintage haute couture. There's probably an auction coming up sometime soon."

"You mentioned accessories a moment ago," Linnet remarked. "And I forgot to tell you that we have shoes and bags from Emma Harte's collection, which we'll be putting on display."

"That's always a great idea, to give the

whole picture," Evan answered. "Also, some fashion designers are willing to loan clothes from their archives for a retrospective like the one you're planning. Have you contacted any of them?"

"Yes we have, and the clothes have already been lent to us. All those wonderful original models the designers have kept for posterity, which is great. And we have a number of current haute couture pieces in the fashion department which we're planning to include. But we still need more items to make the exhibition really impressive . . ." Her voice trailed off, and she shook her head. "It's quite a task, you know."

After a moment's thought, Evan said quietly, "I have an idea. . . . Why not pick out six or eight, or better still, *ten* really chic women in London, and honor them at the retrospective as Fashion Icons? They'd be a wonderful vehicle for publicity, especially if they're well known. And they'd probably agree to lend us some of their own couture clothes to put on display. If we had *ten* icons and each loaned the store five or six pieces, that would mean we'd have fifty or so garments in one fell swoop."

"Brilliant!" Linnet exclaimed, her eyes lighting up. "Let's take it a step further. Why don't we have a best-dressed list? Create one of our own. That would engender some publicity for the retrospective —" Linnet cut herself off, suddenly looking concerned. "I can see from your expression that you don't like *that* idea one bit," she muttered.

Evan responded swiftly. "It's a good idea, but I must admit I am worried about the use of the phrase 'best-dressed list.' I'm not sure whether that's a registered trademark. The best-dressed list was started by Eleanor Lambert in New York, as far as I know, and many years ago. It just might —"

"Belong to her," Linnet interrupted. "I understand your concern. Point well taken. So let's skip it then. I don't want complications, and certainly I don't want to work on something that might prove to be a waste of time. Let's go with the Fashion Icons, though. I love it. India will help with the right names, and so will I. We'll need a long list, more women than ten, because not all of the women we approach will agree to participate. Let's do some research on that."

Evan agreed, and encouraged by Linnet's enthusiastic response to her suggestion, she went on, "I can talk to Arnold Scaasi. I'm sure he would lend us a number of his evening gowns. He has a magnificent collection of his own designs, a great archive."

Linnet nodded. "That'd be fantastic. But we will have to buy some of the vintage couture that's around. Very simply, we just *need* it, to round out certain years in fashion." She sat back, deciding that Evan Hughes was going to be invaluable to her. How lucky it was that Gideon had noticed her in the corridor. But who could fail to miss her? She was an arresting-looking young woman. Linnet felt considerably better about completing all of the work on the exhibition. The young American woman had been in her office for, what? Half an hour at the most. Yet she had a truly good feeling about Evan. And in the most peculiar way she felt as if she had known her for a very long time.

For her part, Evan knew she had made a good impression, and now she said in that lovely, quiet voice of hers, "I guess you're planning to have the retrospective in June, from what Mr. Harte said."

"No, no, it'll be in the middle of May," Linnet responded swiftly, then thought to explain, "My cousin was referring to a birthday party we're helping to plan with my mother. It's for his father and mine. That's what Gideon was talking about when he mentioned the big bash in June."

Evan merely inclined her head, hoping she didn't look foolish for assuming something and then voicing it without knowing the facts.

Linnet went on, "The retrospective will be on view for about four months, perhaps even six. The longer the better, and so I do want it to be really smashing. Sumptuous clothes, elegance all the way."

Evan asked, "Where will it be housed in the store?"

"On the top floor. We have an auditorium up there, which my mother carved out of a number of defunct departments a few years ago. She demolished and remodeled, she's very good at that. It holds about eight hundred people, so it's very spacious. The clothes will be displayed to great advantage there."

"There's a lot of preparation involved in this kind of show," Evan murmured, her mind racing when she thought of all that had to be done by May. It was the middle of January already. Yes, it was a big challenge indeed.

"I agree with you," Linnet was saying. "But the clothes we already have are now in perfect condition. They've been cleaned and repaired, whenever that was necessary, and also steamed or pressed. Touch-ups can be done once the clothes are on the mannequins and in position. But there's still an awful lot to finish. That's why I need extra help. Would you be interested in the job?"

"Oh yes, I would!" Evan's voice echoed her enthusiasm.

"When could you start?"

"Whenever you want me to."

"I'll talk to my mother and get back to you tomorrow morning," Linnet said.

"Thank you, Miss O'Neill."

Once she was alone, Linnet looked at Evan's résumé again, and she liked what she read. She also liked Evan. There was something open and honest about her, and certainly she was enthusiastic about working at Harte's. No shirker here, she thought, as she stood up and walked out of her office.

She headed for Maggie Hemmings's office.

Jennifer looked up as she went in and smiled. "Hello, Miss O'Neill. Can I help you?"

"I was looking for Maggie. Is she in her office? Is she free?"

Jennifer nodded.

Linnet smiled, crossed the room, knocked on the door, and went in. "Do you have a few minutes, Maggie?"

The older woman looked up, gave Linnet a warm smile. "Certainly."

Linnet sat down. "I wanted a word with you about Evan Hughes. I thought you seemed a little reluctant about her, not as enthusiastic as I would expect after reading her résumé."

"The résumé does read well, I can't argue there. But I wasn't sure if she was quite right for Harte's."

"*Oh*. Why not?"

"I can't really put my finger on it . . ." Maggie shrugged. "It's just a feeling. And anyway, I thought it was odd, the way she was introduced by Mr. Gideon, and then she denied knowing him to me. There's another thing." Maggie leaned over the desk and added in a lowered voice, "Don't you think she looks like your mother?"

Linnet laughed. "They're similar types, that's all. And I don't think it's odd, no. As for my cousin, he ran into her in the corridor when she was looking for this office. He simply guided her here. He *doesn't* know her, Maggie."

"I see."

"And even if he did, why would it matter? I think she has excellent credentials, and certainly she would be very helpful to me now."

"Are you going to hire her?" Maggie asked, her voice neutral, her expression cautious.

"I'm certainly going to think about it," Linnet answered, and with a nod and a smile, she rose. "Thanks, Maggie," she murmured as she left the office.

What was *that* about? Linnet asked herself as she went back to her own office, baffled but determined not to be influenced by anyone. Evan could be of great help to her in mounting the retrospective. Perhaps she would hire her on a trial basis.

The following morning Linnet spoke to Evan on the phone. "I'd like you to come in and see me again, Miss Hughes. Around eleven. We can talk some more, and I'll take you to see the collection of clothes we've al-

143

ready assembled."

Evan was thrilled. "I'll be there, Miss O'Neill, and thank you very much."

She arrived at Linnet's office exactly on time. After chatting about the retrospective and her needs, Linnet said, "I'd like to offer you the job on a trial basis, Evan."

Evan beamed. "I accept, Miss O'Neill. Thank you."

Linnet took Evan to a storage room on the seventh floor, behind the haute couture fashion department. Pausing at a large metal-clad door, she took out a set of keys and turned to Evan. "Only India and I have keys to this room. That way we're the only two people responsible, and only we can be blamed if anything goes wrong. Or goes missing."

"I understand."

Linnet unlocked the door, pushed it open, and stepped inside. She paused for a moment on the threshold until she found the light switch. A split second later many overhead lights came blinking on. She beckoned to Evan to follow her into the temperature-controlled storage space.

There were dozens of racks of clothes hanging in cotton bags, and when Linnet saw Evan's face she exclaimed, "Oh, don't worry, I'm not going to show you everything right now. There's far too much to look at. But perhaps you'd be interested to see a few choice pieces that belonged to Emma."

"Yes, I'd like that."

Hurrying to the far end of the room, Linnet moved a rack or two around and explained, "There are a couple of outfits here that are just knockouts." As she spoke she began to untie the drawstring at the top of a cotton bag.

Evan watched her taking out a black suit on a padded hanger, and she remarked, "What a marvelous idea these cotton bags are. Did you have them made?"

Linnet swung around. "Not these, no. They came from Paris. But we have had them copied for the other clothes hanging here. Actually, the bag is called an *oooss*."

"An *oooss*," Evan repeated slowly. "What a strange name."

"That's the way it's pronounced, but it's spelled *h o u s s e*, and of course, the letter *h* is dropped in the French pronunciation. It's the French word for 'cover,' in fact."

"They're certainly effective for storage purposes," Evan replied, thinking they looked like voluminous tents.

"Look at this suit." Linnet held it out. "It's by Cristóbal Balenciaga, and Emma had it made in 1951."

Evan inspected the suit closely and nodded. "There's nothing like a piece of haute couture, is there? The cut, the shoulder line, the overall silhouette. It's simply impeccable, a masterpiece of workmanship."

Linnet pulled a dress out of another cotton bag. "And this is a cocktail dress by Balenciaga. Emma also bought it in 1951. I happen to think it's fantastic. Here, Evan, hold it against yourself." She handed her the cocktail gown on its padded hanger; Evan did as she instructed, looking down at the dress, which was made of black tissue taffeta. "I love the way the skirt is flounced in tiers and the bodice wrapped around. It's unique, and the wonderful thing is that, like the suit, it's not a bit dated."

"I agree with you. There's a picture of Emma in the dress, and it looks as if it was taken only yesterday. Over there" — Linnet swung her head, gestured toward more racks — "are some couture outfits lent by my mother, India's mother, and my aunts Emily and Amanda. Their pieces will also help to flesh out certain years in design."

Evan helped Linnet put the two garments back in their cotton covers, and as they stood at the rack, Linnet remarked, "I think you're going to enjoy working on the retrospective, Evan, and even though we have a tough road ahead, I believe that the three of us will be able to pull it together most effectively."

"I know we will," Evan answered and crossed her fingers, stepping away from the clothes rack and picking up her purse.

"Let's go see Maggie and get you properly hired as my assistant," Linnet said, leading the way out of the storage room.

Nine

Evan felt as if she were walking on air when she left Harte's several hours later. She was not aware of the biting wind, nor did she feel hungry even though it was turning two. I'm on cloud nine, she thought, hurrying toward the cab she had hailed, which had suddenly slithered to a stop close by.

Once inside, she sat back against the leather seat, her thoughts focused on her father. All she wanted now was to get to the hotel so she could put in a call to him.

Since today was Wednesday, she knew he would be at the antiques shop in New Milford; he always did his books when business was slower. She could hardly wait to tell him her news; he would be surprised, she was certain of that. She could scarcely believe it herself . . . that she actually had a job at Harte's.

Once she was in her quarters at the hotel, she shrugged out of her red scarf and long black coat and put them away in the cupboard. And then, after turning on the electric fire in the small sitting room, she sat down next to it in the big easy chair. Picking up the phone, she dialed his Connecticut number and waited for it to ring through. A couple of seconds later, her father answered.

"Good morning. Hughes Antiques."

"Hi, Dad! It's me, Evan."

"Evan, honey, you sound great! You've made a good recovery, I can hear that."

"I'm feeling like my old self, more or less. But listen, Dad, I've got some great news. I've got a job." She paused for maximum effect, and then cried, "At Harte's! I've got a job in the fashion department at Harte's."

There was a moment's silence at his end of the phone, but in her excitement and enthusiasm Evan paid no attention.

"Well," he said at last, rather slowly. "That's good news."

It struck her then that his voice was flat. She exclaimed, "You don't sound a bit excited, and I thought you'd be thrilled for me . . ." Her voice died away, and she clutched the phone a little tighter, frowning.

"Oh I am, Evan, I am. I was simply taken aback, that's all. I hadn't realized you'd already been there and applied for a job."

"I didn't. What I mean is, I hadn't been there before, I just wasn't up to it until yesterday. But I felt so much better I got ready and went to the store. Basically to see Emma Harte, as Grandma told me to do."

"Yes, I know what she told you. And did you see Emma Harte?"

"Dad, she's *dead!* And for thirty-one years. So I don't know what Gran was going on about. If they'd been friends, she must have *known.* Anyway, I was startled. And upset. But you know me, I bounced back after I'd had a cup of coffee and time to think. I liked the look of the store, it's very beautiful, so I decided to go up to management and apply for a position. I mean, what did I have to lose?"

"Nothing. And so they hired you just like that. Is that what you're saying, honey?"

"I was lucky yesterday, *very* lucky. I happened to be in the right place at the right time."

"Were you now," he murmured. "So go ahead, tell me all about it."

"What happened was this . . ." Swiftly but graphically, Evan told her story, finishing, "And before I knew it, Maggie Hemmings, of Human Resources, was taking me to see Linnet O'Neill. She's the head of fashion and the great-granddaughter of Emma Harte."

"It does sound very fortuitous," Owen remarked softly. "And this Linnet O'Neill was impressed enough to hire you on the spot, is that it?"

"Not exactly. I had to go back today for another chat with her, and then she hired me on a trial basis."

"Congratulations, I'm pleased for you. And who was the nice young man you mentioned?"

"His name's Gideon Harte, and I found out later that he works at the family's newspaper company. He runs the *London Evening Post*."

"I see. Well, Elayne and Angharad *are* going to be thrilled when I tell them the news."

"Give them my love. I'll be helping Linnet put on a fashion retrospective for the next few months, and hey, Dad, guess what? Some of Miss Trigère's clothes are going to be in the retrospective. Emma Harte was a fan of hers."

"I'll tell Pauline. She'll be pleased to hear it," Owen replied.

"Dad?"

"Yes, honey?"

"Do you think Grandma *knew* Mrs. Harte was dead?"

There was total silence at his end of the phone.

Evan said insistently, "Dad, are you still there?"

"Yes, I'm here."

"So . . . what do you think? *Did* Gran know? If so, why did she tell me to go there?"

"I've no idea. She never mentioned anything about Emma Harte to me, except that

151

she'd known her during the Second World War. Look, Evan, my mother could've been wandering in her mind, or delirious, in her last moments. I told you that before you left for London."

"I know. At least she pointed me in the right direction . . . as it turns out."

After another short silence, her father said quietly, "That's true, yes."

Evan asked, "How's Mom?"

His voice brightened as he answered, "She's better, she's come out of herself a bit. And she cooked a nice dinner for me last night. I think the new medication's started to kick in."

"Oh I'm so glad! That's great. Give her my love."

"I will. When do you start at Harte's?"

"Tomorrow morning." She began to laugh and quipped, "They really do need me there, Dad."

She expected him to laugh with her, but he did not. "Perhaps," he answered in the same low voice and rapidly changed the subject.

They talked for a few minutes longer about other things, then said their affectionate good-byes.

After she put the receiver down, Evan leaned back in the chair, thinking about her father's reaction to her news. It wasn't what she had expected at all, and she felt oddly disconcerted, even irritated by his response.

The more she thought about it, the more she came to realize that he hadn't sounded pleased. She couldn't help wondering why. Like her grandmother, he had always cheered her on, been her greatest booster. But not today.

Evan had no way of knowing that her father, seated at his desk in his New Milford shop, was staring absently into space. He was wondering what his mother had set in motion on her deathbed, admitting to himself that he should have known Glynnis would be unable to resist pulling a few strings at the end. Owen cursed himself for having so enthusiastically encouraged Evan to go to London, to take a sabbatical there as he himself had done. He should have discouraged the trip. But in December he had not known what he knew now. Anyway, it was too late. Evan was already there . . . and the wheels had begun to turn . . .

Evan liked the public rooms at the little hotel in Belgravia, which George and Arlette had decorated in the manner of an English country house. Not that she had ever been in an English country house, but she had seen photos in magazines, and she was partial to the look: the vivid floral chintzes, the mellow woods, the fine antiques, the porcelain lamps with their cream-colored silk shades, plus the big vases of flowers loosely arranged in the English style.

Of all the rooms on the main floor, her favorite was the sitting room, with its walls painted terra cotta and glazed with light peach, the red-rose-patterned chintz curtains at the three windows, and the overstuffed sofas and chairs upholstered in russet red linen. On the floor, a wonderful old Persian rug had a background color similar to the draperies, with a pattern of deep blues, pinks, and greens. It helped to pull the color scheme together and acted as the perfect anchor for the seating arrangement.

The sitting room was empty when Evan went down for afternoon tea, and as she headed for the fireplace, her spirits lifted. The atmosphere was rich, warm, welcoming, and the huge fire blazing in the hearth added to its coziness.

It was her gran who had introduced Evan to afternoon tea when she was growing up in Connecticut. Glynnis had made quite a ceremony out of it, serving the tea from a silver pot with a silver strainer over the cup and thin slices of lemon, or milk for those who preferred. The tea had always been Twinings brand from London, English breakfast preferred by Glynnis, but sometimes replaced by orange pekoe. Never Earl Grey, because Gran didn't like the flavor. *Smoky,* she called it.

On special occasions her grandmother

would make a light sponge cake, which she sliced through the middle into two flat pieces and filled with whipped cream and raspberry jam. And when Evan had grown older, Glynnis had taught *her* how to make the finger sandwiches, the scones, and the various cakes; in fact, it was her gran who had taught her to cook any number of things, and over the years she had become quite accomplished in the kitchen.

Evan thought of this now as she munched on a smoked salmon sandwich. Should she look for a small apartment in this area? Or should she stay on at the hotel? She had meant to ask her father about this earlier, but she had been so distracted by his lackluster response to her news it had slipped her mind. In many ways the hotel was more convenient; she was so well taken care of here. On the other hand, she had to eat in the hotel dining room, which added to her expenses.

After a few minutes, she made a decision. She would stay on at the hotel for the moment, very simply because she did not have time to look for an apartment. Evan already had a good picture of what working at Harte's was going to be like — long hours and total dedication. Linnet would be a taskmaster, and she would expect everyone to work as hard as she did. Especially a newcomer like Evan, who was bound to be on trial. Evan had discerned that Linnet, for all her sweetness and beauty, was at heart a tough businesswoman. This did not trouble her; rather, she admired that trait.

Yes, it's better to stay here, Evan told herself, where I'm comfortable and have every convenience. Once the retrospective is set up and things are rolling along smoothly, I'll think about finding my own place, one with a decent kitchen, an apartment where I can do a little entertaining even. This thought pleased her, and she reached for a scone, spread it with strawberry jam, and added a large dollop of cream.

As she ate the scone she realized just how hungry she had been, but she also reminded herself how fattening scones and cream cakes were. Not too many of these afternoon teas, she vowed to herself, then smiled inwardly. She would be at the store most of the time anyway, and how she was looking forward to it.

Leaning back against the sofa cushions once again, Evan let her thoughts wander, reviewing the events of the day. Eventually they came to settle on Gideon Harte. He had been pleasant and helpful in the corridor when she was looking for the management offices. But later this pleasantness had turned to genuine masculine charm and much solicitousness. When she had walked into Linnet's office with Maggie Hemmings, he had hurried to greet her. Once she had been introduced by Maggie to his cousin, he had not hidden his interest. In fact, he had been so focused on her she found herself staring back at him.

His light green eyes had been riveted on hers, and she found she could not look away. Now she remembered how her heart had skipped a beat, and that his long, penetrating look had made her go slightly weak at the knees. Nothing had ever happened to her like that before, but then no man had looked at her quite like that. A moment later, when he had taken hold of her arm to lead her over to the chair, his hand had seemed to scorch through the fabric of her jacket. She had been momentarily thrown, so attracted to him was she . . .

"Evan. How are *you?*"

At the sound of Arlette's lilting, lightly accented French voice, she sat up with a start and exclaimed, "I'm fine, Arlette. How nice to see you. And how're you?"

"I am well. Busy, busy. George is away on the business, so I am in command, as he calls it. And one needs the *bon courage* to be in charge of a hotel. Even a small one such as this."

"But you do everything so well, I'm sure you run it exactly the same way George does." As she spoke Evan smiled at Arlette, her face dimpling.

Arlette was captivated by that smile, which she found so infectious, and she smiled in return. There was something unique about this open, outgoing American girl who was full of such charm and grace. Now she asked, "Are you all right? Are you feeling better?"

"I'm back to normal, thank you," Evan reassured her, and then she leaned forward from the waist, looked up at Arlette. "Can you sit for a minute? I've got some news for you."

"Mais oui, chérie." Arlette lowered herself onto the sofa next to Evan.

"I got myself a job today, a wonderful job. At Harte's store in Knightsbridge." Once again Evan enthusiastically launched into the telling of her experience at the store. "And Linnet O'Neill hired me," she finished, settling back, a look of pleasure lighting up her face. "I will be working in fashion with her."

"Très bien, Evan! It is wonderful news. I know you like the fashion. And what made you pick Harte's? Out of all the stores here?"

"I've always wanted to work there. It's the finest store in the world, in my opinion." Evan had no intention of confiding to Arlette her grandmother's dying words; she feared she would appear ridiculous.

Arlette sat studying Evan for a moment, thinking how stunning she looked. The black hair was glossy, the complexion translucent, the blue-gray eyes huge pools in her delicate face. She was a beautiful woman, very feminine. Alluring to men, Arlette had no doubt, and there was an air of refinement about her that the Frenchwoman admired.

"And this young man?" Arlette asked. "The one who helped you yesterday morning . . . will you be meeting him again soon?"

Evan gaped at her. "Oh, but he doesn't work there."

"I didn't mean seeing him at *work*." Arlette gazed at the younger woman indulgently, shaking her head, pursing her lips.

Evan saw the merriment in Arlette's dark eyes, noticed the hidden laughter twitching on her mouth, and for a moment she wondered if this attractive and motherly Frenchwoman was teasing her. After only a moment she realized that she was not. Evan took a deep breath. "He was just trying to be helpful, that's all," she protested.

Arlette sat up a little straighter and crossed her legs, arranging her full red skirt over highly polished brown boots. After a moment's consideration, she explained. "I was thinking of a *rendezvous* . . . the date with him?" Those wise brown eyes lingered on Evan's questioningly, and a brow lifted eloquently.

A deep flush spread from Evan's neck up onto her face, and she said, "I — I don't think I will be meeting him again. Not in the way you mean, Arlette."

"No? You do not think so?" The French-woman shook her head vigorously. "But I do. *Ah oui*. I am sure. You will have a *rendezvous* with him, *mon petite choux à la crème*. And in the not too distant future." Her laughter rippled on the warm air once more. "It is . . . obvious . . . he had a hand in cutting through the red ribbon. At the store. Ah yes. *Absolument*."

"The red ribbon?" Evan frowned at her, looking puzzled.

"*Ah non, non*. I am stupid! Not the red ribbon. The red *tape*."

"You're right about that part, Arlette. But I'm not sure about a date with him. I don't think he's interested in me."

"Trust me, *chérie*. I am *older* than you, *and* I am a *Frenchwoman*. And we know about these things. We know about . . . *amour*."

Unbeknownst to Evan and Arlette, Gideon Harte, at that precise moment, was indeed thinking about a rendezvous with Evan Hughes.

He sat in his office at the Yorkshire Consolidated Newspaper Company, in a building on the other side of London, his mind focused on the young American woman. He had been thinking about her a lot since meeting her in the corridor at Harte's yesterday. There was something about her that was special. She totally held his interest, and there was no doubt that he wanted to see her again. He had discovered that he felt a sense of urgency about her, a need to be in her company, to discover more about her. And at once.

Gideon already knew that Linnet had hired Evan on a trial basis. His cousin had phoned to tell him that a short while ago. Furthermore, Linnet had thanked him profusely, as if he had led Evan by the hand to Harte's, when in fact her arrival at the store had been happenstance, pure luck. And Linnet had been enthusiastic about Evan Hughes, gone into minute detail about their meetings. "She's a real find, Gid, and I know India's going to like her as much as I do. Evan came up with some brilliant ideas. She bodes well for me, Gideon, she really does."

Did she bode well for him? He hoped so. He wished he could call Evan right now, but he had no idea where to find her, and he certainly had no intention of phoning Linnet back to ask for her number. He would deal with that tomorrow by calling Evan herself at the store.

Pushing his chair slightly away from the desk, he put his feet up on it, crossing his long legs at the ankles. He closed his eyes and contemplated the new addition to Linnet's staff.

Since there was a big push on to complete the retrospective, Linnet and Evan would be together a lot, which meant he would have easy access to Evan. In any case, he didn't imagine there would be a problem about dating her. It had struck him that she seemed interested in him, just as he was in her. He had held her with his eyes in Linnet's office, and she had returned his meaningful look. He had seen her blushes, noted her fascination with him, felt the tremor in her arm when he led her over to Linnet's desk. Yes, she was taken with him. Well, he hoped she was.

Although he had never had much trouble with women, Gideon Harte was not a conceited man. In fact, in certain ways it was his lack of male vanity, his gentleness, and a degree of diffidence that women found attractive. Although he was tall, good-looking, and blessed with an easy charm, there was also a little-boy quality in his makeup which appealed to women, made them want to spoil him.

Gideon liked women, respected them, and especially admired those who were accomplished. He didn't have much interest in women who wasted their time, had no job or profession. Yet all types of women flocked to him. The problem was he had never met anyone he had wanted to get serious with. Until now.

Until now! Wow! This thought brought him up with a start.

Snapping open his eyes, he sat straighter in the chair and dropped his feet to the floor. Good God! He was thinking about getting serious with Evan Hughes, and he didn't even *know* her! He must have gone mad.

After a moment's contemplation he had the answer. He had fallen for her, fallen hard, and in the blink of an eye. A *coup de foudre*, the French called it, a flash of lightning. Oh God, he thought, I've gone and fallen for a stranger I know nothing about. Maybe she's involved with another man. And maybe she's not interested in me. Maybe I've imagined that.

Puffing his cheeks, he blew out air, then settled back in the chair, focusing again on Evan Hughes. What was it about her that was so *different?* Not necessarily her looks, even though she was beautiful, because he usually went for tall, slender, dark-haired, exotic-looking women.

Perhaps it was her manner that had captivated him. She had been forthcoming in the corridor, yet he had detected a reticence in her, an air of refinement. And then there was her extraordinary smile, which had made his heart do a flip, and those large, liquid eyes that had seemed to swamp him. Clear, luminous eyes that were full of honesty, and trust.

I'm behaving like a schoolboy, he chastised himself. And I'm twenty-eight years old. I should know better. I mustn't get carried away. That could be fatal for me, especially if she's caught up with someone else.

She might even be engaged. But she hadn't been wearing a ring. Still, that didn't really signify anything these days. People were often engaged without a ring to show for it.

But I'll get her a ring, he thought. A sapphire ring. No, aquamarine, to match the color of her eyes. Hey, slow down, he muttered. You're running ahead of yourself. But he couldn't help it. No two ways about it. He wanted Evan Hughes.

Gideon's eyes shifted to the door at the sound of knocking. "Come in," he called, then jumped to his feet at the sight of his father on the threshold.

"Hi, Dad," he exclaimed, walking toward him.

"Hello, my boy," Winston Harte said, giving him a broad smile.

After they had embraced, and Gideon had led his father to a chair near his desk, he said, "I thought you were in Yorkshire. What're you doing in London?"

"I came up to town for a meeting at the television studios, and I wanted to see you anyway."

Gideon raised a brow. "What about?"

"Christian Palmer."

"Oh God, Dad, I knew you were going to say that. Look, I don't seem to make any inroads with him. You know what he's like, so tough-minded and focused. He won't come back, Dad. He's busy writing his book."

Winston sighed. "I figured you'd say that, although I knew you'd stay on top of it. I've always said you're like a dog with a bone. But look here, there must be some inducement we can offer?"

Sitting down at his desk, Gideon nodded. "I think there is, but it's going to cost us."

"Whatever it is, Christian's worth it. He's the best damned editor we've ever had, and I believe we need him back here. So, what's the price?"

"He loves that house he's renting on the Isle of Man. I'm sure if we offer to buy it for him he'll agree to come back."

"How much?"

"I don't know, Dad. I'll go into it with him, if you're in agreement. It's a nice house, and he's rented it off and on for a number of years. He's become very attached to it."

"Whereabouts is it on the Isle of Man?"

"Just outside Douglas. In an area where he used to go with his parents as a child. He finds the Manx way of life very easy, very compatible, and of course he has peace and quiet there to write his books. Furthermore, it's not difficult to get to, you know, just a plane trip from Lancashire to the middle of the Irish Sea."

"It's not exactly an easy commute," Winston pointed out, shaking his head. "And are you sure the house will be enough of an inducement? He might want something else."

"I doubt it. Christian's not like that, and listen, he might not ever go for the deal. He's hell-bent on doing some serious writing, you know."

"What I know is that he is the best bloody editor Fleet Street has ever seen, except for Arthur Christiansen, and he was king of the heap sixty years ago. He made the *Daily Express*. Palmer's cut from the same cloth. Editors with their talent and brilliance don't often come along. So do your best, my boy. Get him to come back."

"Okay, but it might mean a bigger contract as well."

"That's not a problem, Gideon," Winston said briskly. "I learned years ago from Aunt Emma that when you want someone or something badly enough, the price doesn't really matter. That's how important Christian Palmer is to this company. So do your stuff."

"I think I'll have to go and see him," Gideon said. "I'll talk to him on the phone tomorrow and suggest a visit next week." Gideon chuckled. "I wish it were the middle of the summer, not the dead of winter. The Isle of Man is superb in the warm weather but a bit chilly at this time of year."

"You're right about that. I wish we could tempt Christian to come back to the Land of the White Rose. . . . I always thought he loved Yorkshire, loved his house in Ripon."

"I think there's another inducement on the Isle of Man, Dad. A particular lady he's very attached to, quite aside from his fondness for that cottage."

"Oh, it's a cottage is it?"

Again, Gideon chuckled. "A big one though."

"Make the deal with him, and the sooner the better."

"Listen, Dad, hang on a minute. I think we'll have to wait until he finishes the book. In fact, I'm sure of it. Once he's delivered to the publishers, he'll be lost, bored silly. That's when he'll come back, and only then."

"So be it. I'll agree to whatever he wants. And dangle a new contract. Make it a good offer, an offer he can't refuse. He's worth it at any price. Now, do you have a date tonight, Gideon? Stupid question, I suppose you do."

"No, I don't, as a matter of fact. Why?"

"I'm at a loose end with your mother in Yorkshire. It occurred to me we might have dinner together."

"Great idea, Dad. I'd love it," Gideon said, meaning this. But he couldn't help thinking about Evan Hughes. . . . She insinuated herself into his thoughts again.

Ten

When they arrived at the entrance to the Grill Room in the Dorchester, the maître d' was at the other end of the dining room. They hovered together for a moment, waiting to be shown to a table.

On the way to the hotel, Gideon had decided he wanted to pay for dinner tonight; he realized it would give him immense pleasure to entertain his father, who was so generous with him always, and whom he never got a chance to take out for a meal. He felt around in various pockets, seeking his credit-card wallet.

Preoccupied as he was, Gideon did not notice that his father had moved closer to the screen that created a barrier between the Grill Room and the entrance. Winston was peering into the restaurant through the glass panels of the wooden screen, his eyes widening.

Gideon became aware that something was wrong only when he heard his father curse quietly, felt the sudden hard pressure of Winston's hand on his arm.

"We can't go in there. Come on," Winston muttered and guided Gideon out into the hall.

"Dad, what's wrong?" Gideon was struck by the bony pallor of his father's face, the fierce, dark gleam in his eyes.

When Winston did not at first respond, Gideon asked again, "Dad, whatever is it? You look as if you've just seen a ghost."

"More like the devil. Jonathan Ainsley, to be exact. He's dining in the Grill with Sarah Lowther. They've always plotted against the family, and their presence together in London does not bode well for any of us. Mark my words."

"You and Mother have always alluded to the trouble Jonathan Ainsley and Sarah Lowther caused the family, and I know they were kicked out of Harte Enterprises. But I still don't know exactly *what* it is they did," Gideon said, staring at his father.

The two of them were seated at a table near a window overlooking Green Park in the elegant dining room of the Ritz Hotel on Piccadilly. At Gideon's suggestion they had come here after making a hasty retreat from the Dorchester and his two cousins.

"Well, it's a long story, two stories, really. I'll tell you in a moment, and I'll make it as concise as possible. But first, let's order a drink. What would you like, Gideon?"

169

"White wine, I think."

"And I'll have a glass of champagne."

"Oh that's a good idea, Dad. I'll join you, forget about the white wine."

Winston nodded, beckoned to the waiter, and ordered two glasses of Veuve-Cliquot, then settled back in his chair. Gideon said, "You looked so disturbed at the Dorchester, Dad, I was really alarmed."

"I was *angry*, Gid. Individually, those two are dangerous. But even more dangerous when they're in cahoots together." He sighed and shook his head. "I knew Jonathan Ainsley was in London, but I certainly had no idea Sarah was here from France." He glanced at Gideon, added, "Uncle Ronnie warned Paula that Ainsley had come back to live here. He told her a couple of weeks ago."

"It was the weekend Julian was staying with us, the weekend of all that snow. And we went to Pennistone Royal for dinner on Saturday. I thought Aunt Paula seemed rather perturbed during the latter part of the evening."

"Julian gave her a message from his grandfather. I think it shook her up a bit. Uncle Ronnie was concerned about Ainsley's sudden reappearance after all these years, and when she went to see him the next day he warned her to be on her guard."

"But Julian told me Ainsley can't actually do anything."

"Not as far as the Harte companies are concerned," Winston said. "But he's a trouble-maker. And he always was. It's the nature of the beast, and if he could hurt Paula in any way at all, he would. Actually, it would give him pleasure to upset her applecart. He's vicious, and he always was, even when we were all growing up together."

Their drinks arrived, and after they had clinked glasses and each taken a sip of champagne, Winston continued: "I had a word with Uncle Ronnie, and he told me he'd advised Paula to hire a private investigator to check on Ainsley's activities. Uncle Ronnie explained that his gut instinct tells him Ainsley is out for blood. Paula's blood."

An involuntary shiver ran down Gideon's spine, and he exclaimed, "I hope Aunt Paula *is* going to put a private eye on him, Dad."

"Well . . . she's not all that keen. Let's say she's ambivalent at best."

"What do you think?"

"I'm in favor of it. Uncle Ronnie's a wise old bird. And never forget that the most valuable commodity is *information*. We all learned this from Aunt Emma, and as I reminded Paula the other day, forewarned is forearmed."

Gideon nodded his understanding, turned to the waiter hovering, and took a menu, as did his father. After a few seconds they ordered Colchester oysters to be followed by grilled Dover sole, choosing the same dishes as they had for years. Father and son had similar tastes in many things. So much so that Emily had dubbed them "my two peas in a pod" years before.

After requesting two more glasses of champagne, Gideon turned to his father. "Enlighten me about Jonathan Ainsley, Dad. Tell me what he and Sarah did."

"Ainsley headed up the real estate division of Harte Enterprises in the sixties and seventies, and he ran the company very well. But suddenly business slackened, and he seemed to be missing a lot of big deals. Later we found out that he had been steering these really valuable deals to a company called Stonewall Properties, and —"

"But why?" Gideon cut in.

"Because secretly *he* owned Stonewall Properties with his old friend from his Eton days, Sebastian Cross. Ainsley was actually cheating Harte Enterprises out of thousands of pounds, and he undermined the financial stability of the division."

"And Sarah Lowther was involved in this, too?" Gideon asked, a brow lifting.

"Yes, although somewhat indirectly, I think. She had invested money in Stonewall Properties, but to be honest, Gid, I don't believe Sarah knew of her cousin's treachery to the family. Once Paula and her father had enough evidence against Ainsley, they confronted him, kicked him out of the company and out of the family. And Sarah as well."

"They didn't have any choice," Gideon asserted, giving his father a direct look. "And then *he* went to Hong Kong and made a fortune in real estate."

"That's true. Ainsley was always quite brilliant at business."

"Julian told me Ainsley came back later and tried to get control of Harte stores. How could that happen?"

Winston shook his head, his face suddenly saddened. "It was actually Paula's fault. Ainsley did return to London in the 1980s, just around the time she put ten percent of her shares in Harte's on the market. Naturally he snapped them up. And those shares combined with what he owned gave him an advantage."

"But why did she sell some of her shares?"

"She wanted to buy a chain of stores in the States. Shane and I both understood her desire to create something of her own, but we also knew her judgment was flawed. It's the only mistake she's ever made, to my knowledge. Other than marrying Jim Fairley, of course. *That* was a disaster."

Toward the end of the evening, Winston turned to Gideon and stared at him intently for a moment or two.

Gideon frowned and leaned toward his fa-

173

ther. "What is it, Dad? You're looking perturbed again."

"No, no, I'm fine. I was actually thinking about our great family dynasty that Emma and Winston senior created, and I was hoping you might be the one to continue it . . . continue the line of descent."

"I'm not sure I'm getting what you really mean."

"Toby's not likely to present me with grandchildren as long as he stays married to the actress. Adrianna doesn't want any children, and I don't think Toby will be able to make *her* change her mind, whatever *he* believes."

"But there's Paula, Dad, she's got a large brood —"

"True," Winston interrupted peremptorily. "And she's a Harte. But her name is O'Neill."

Gideon nodded, suddenly understanding what his father was getting at. "We *are* the last of the Hartes to bear the Harte name, that's a fact."

Winston sat back in his chair, pondering for a moment, and finally said, "Far be it from me to prevent you from sowing your wild oats, and admittedly, you're only twenty-eight. But . . . well, I was just wondering if there was anyone on the horizon. A girl you might be *serious* about. A likely prospect, so to speak."

"Not really, Dad." When Gideon saw his father's crestfallen expression, he added swiftly, "Actually, I've just met someone, and I like her a lot. But it's too soon. I don't want to make any wild predictions and then disappoint you."

"But is she the marrying kind?" Winston probed.

Gideon nodded. "I certainly don't think she's the type of woman a man would attempt to sow his wild oats with, no, no, not at all."

Winston beamed at him. "I'm looking forward to meeting her."

Later that night Gideon discovered he was unable to fall asleep. He lay wide awake in the darkness, his mind racing with all the things he and his father had discussed.

He had been startled to discover that Paula, the most brilliant person he knew, had actually made such a mistake that she had almost forfeited her grandmother's beloved stores. In the same vein, he had been shocked that a member of their family had resorted to such treachery for personal gain when he already had so much. "Ego and greed," his father had said. "A fatal combination that has destroyed many other men as well as Jonathan Ainsley."

And finally there had been the conversation about him settling down, getting married and having children. If Winston had been a little obvious, Gideon had not minded. He loved and admired his father, and he fully understood where he was coming from, how much he longed for grandchildren. As did his mother. It was only natural they would feel that way.

Evan Hughes. He had met her only yesterday, yet he had been utterly enchanted. He did not know her, or anything about her, but he felt as if he *did* know her. She was beautiful, and she had been warm, outgoing. He found her sexually attractive, very desirable. And yet he discerned in her a refinement that gave her an added dimension.

Tomorrow he would phone her, invite her out . . . he fell asleep thinking about Evan Hughes and her possibilities.

Eleven

Tessa Fairley Longden picked up her handbag and carryall, glanced at her desk, then hurried across the room, snapping off the light as she left her office.

She was dressed entirely in white, one of her favorite colors; a soft, flowing cashmere cape was thrown over her shoulders on top of a white wool pantsuit and matching silk shirt. Her boots were deep cream color, as were her crocodile handbag and the leather carryall stuffed with files. The all-white ensemble underscored her ethereal appearance, which came from her wonderful head of pale silvery blond hair, her silvery gray eyes, and her perfect ivory complexion. Her delicate face looked as if it had been carved by a master sculptor, and to say she was lovely was an understatement. Tessa was staggeringly beautiful, so striking that heads turned wherever she went. She was tall, willowy, and always wore the most beautiful and costly clothes. They were unique, distinctive, and often by lesser-known designers who catered to her whims. Tessa knew what she wanted and aimed to get it no matter what, when it came to her clothes at least.

She didn't always get what she wanted in other areas of her life, particularly when it came to her husband, Mark Longden. Of late he had been more difficult than usual, bad tempered, irritable, and impatient with her on a variety of levels. It seemed to her that he kept his temper only when their little daughter, Adele, was around, or her family. He wouldn't dare be rude or nasty in the presence of her mother and Shane, but he didn't seem to care how he treated her in front of their friends. Not that they went out much anymore; he was always staying late at the office, or going to see clients on weekends. It occurred to her now that he didn't have much time for her these days unless it was to rant and rave at her about nothing of any great consequence.

A couple of times lately she had smelled liquor on his breath, and he had looked flushed, his eyes glazed. But he had denied he had been drinking too much and had flown into such a violent temper she had quickly retreated behind the safety of the bathroom door.

He was always contrite after his volatile behavior, asking, no begging, her forgiveness. And, of course, fool that she was, she always forgave him. Until the other day, when he had raged at her about some chipped paint in the kitchen. He had been so ridiculous she had abruptly stood away, looking at him objectively and wondering what exactly was wrong with him.

As she turned the corner, walking rapidly toward the bank of elevators, she saw her half sister Linnet, and she immediately called, "*Linnet!* I need to talk to you."

Linnet paused, swung around, a smile lighting up her face. "You look beautiful, absolutely gorgeous, Tess, in all that white!" As she spoke Linnet stepped toward her sister, was about to embrace her. But the smile slipped when she saw Tessa's face.

Tessa moved closer to the elevators and said in a cold tone, "How dare you countermand my orders about the auditorium? You had no right to do that. I am the senior executive here, and what I say goes."

"But I didn't know —"

"I can't stand here wasting time with you. I'm late as it is," Tessa interrupted and stepped into the elevator. "Just don't do things without asking my permission," she snapped as the door closed.

That girl goes too far at times, Tessa thought, as the elevator carried her down to the ground floor. She was suddenly seething about the younger woman, and once again all her resentment and jealousy rose to the surface. There was no question in Tessa's mind that Linnet O'Neill was the favorite child of

179

her mother and Shane. *Shane O'Neill.* In her own way she loved him, he had always been kind, had brought her up as his own. But she was *not* his biological child, and deep down that rankled. How could he love her as much as Linnet when she was not of his blood? In a way, though, she was glad she was not an O'Neill. *She* was a Fairley, came from an aristocratic line that went back centuries. Why, she herself was an aristocrat. Everyone said she looked like the Fairleys, and she knew she resembled Aunt Edwina, who was also part Fairley and a countess. To hell with Linnet, she thought, and pushed her out of her mind.

As she went through the side entrance of the store, nodding to employees who were also leaving for the day, Tessa decided to be especially nice to Mark tonight. She did love him, despite his behavior of late, and she wanted to keep the marriage intact. She had learned that the best way to make sure their time together was absolutely tranquil was to be acquiescent. She had to meet his every demand.

It was cold, and she shivered as she stepped into the street, but within a second her driver had pulled over, was coming around to her side of the car.

"Good evening, Mrs. Longden," Milton said, opening the door.

"Good evening. I'm going straight home,

Milton, thanks," Tessa said, as usual scrupulously polite with the help.

Settling back against the seat, Tessa decided she would make pasta tonight. She had a well-stocked larder because she often worked late herself, and frequently she and Mark did not sit down to supper before nine o'clock. They would eat earlier; she had made a point of leaving at five-thirty so that she could start preparing their meal. Mark liked food and vintage wine, and she aimed to please.

When Milton pulled into the driveway of their Hampstead house, Tessa saw at once that Mark was already home. His car was parked outside the front door.

"Thanks, good night, Milton," she said as she alighted. She gave her driver a faint smile and asked him to come for her at eight the following morning.

Running up the front steps, she let herself into the house, calling as she usually did, "Adele! Cooee! Where's my little girl?"

A split second later Adele came running into the entrance hall, shouting, "Mumma! Mumma! I am here!"

Crouching down, arms outstretched, Tessa caught her child as she hurtled forward into her embrace. Adele kissed her cheek and snuggled closer.

After a moment, Tessa held the little girl away from her. "How's my sweetie pie?"

"I'm fine. Daddy's here."

The words had hardly left the child's mouth when Mark's shadow fell across them. He stood in the archway that led into the large kitchen.

Looking up at him, smiling, Tessa saw that his face was cold, his eyes angry. He seemed somehow menacing. Although her smile congealed, she said evenly, "Hello, darling, you're home early."

"And you're late. As always," he murmured, his tone quiet but icy.

Standing up, taking hold of Adele's hand, Tessa said, "It's only six, Mark. Come on, Adele, let's go and find Elvira." As she spoke she took off her cape and threw it on the bench in the entrance hall.

Elvira, the young nanny, was stacking the dishwasher, and she looked up and smiled at Tessa and Adele as they came into the kitchen together. "Hello, Mrs. Longden, Adele's just had a nice supper. Steamed vegetables and a small piece of grilled sole. And raspberries for dessert."

"It sounds delicious. Thanks, Elvira. You look after her so well."

"Good nutrition, Mrs. Longden." Closing the dishwasher, Elvira added, "I'll take her upstairs in a few minutes to get her ready for bed."

"Oh, I can do that," Tessa replied quickly. Looking down at Adele, she went on, "Shall

I read you a story, darling?"

"Oh yes, Mumma. *Please.*"

"I need to talk to you. Right now, Tessa," Mark said, suddenly looming over her.

"But I want to read a story to Adele. Can't it wait a few minutes?"

"No, it cannot."

There was such a nasty undertone in his voice, Tessa nodded, then bent over Adele and murmured, "Daddy needs me. I'll come up shortly. Elvira can get you ready, and then I'll come and read the story to you before you go to sleep."

Adele smiled up at her mother adoringly.

Taking hold of her arm, Mark led Tessa across the hall into the library, closing the door behind them. This was yet another room in the house that Tessa loathed. She found it cold, dark, and depressing, and she rarely entered it.

"What's so important that it couldn't wait a few minutes?" she asked, smiling, wanting to keep everything tranquil between them.

"I want to talk to you about the hours you keep," he answered. "You stay at that damned store far too late, and you work too hard. And some good it's all going to do you."

"What do you mean?"

"She's not going to leave anything to *you*. Paula O'Neill doesn't care about *you*. Linnet's her *favorite*. She's the love child, born

183

out of Shane's loins. Did you know he was her lover before your father was even *dead?* She was screwing him when she was on her business trips to New York . . . when you were left behind in England with the help. And did you —"

"That's not true!" Tessa exclaimed, automatically defending her mother. "I know Mummy and Shane were friends then, in fact they have been friends all their lives. They grew up together in Yorkshire. You're being ridiculous. I won't have you talk about my parents like that."

"*Oh.* Shane's suddenly a parent, is he?"

"He did bring me up, Mark, and he was kind and loving. I was only a small child when Jim Fairley was killed."

"And wasn't *that* convenient for your mother and her lover."

"Oh stop this! You're being disgusting. And God knows where you got that kind of information. Why it's . . . almost *libelous.*"

"No it's not, because it's true. And I got it from a very good source."

"Who?"

"I never reveal my sources. Rule of the game, you know."

Tessa glared at him. "I demand to know who is making these scurrilous remarks to you about my mother and Shane."

"A little dickey bird. Look, why don't you ask her yourself. Ask her about her weekends in New Milford, Connecticut. The long weekends she spent with Shane in his barn there."

Tessa shifted slightly in the chair, frowning. She stared at Mark and then looked away, puzzled and disturbed.

He broke the silence, saying suddenly, "You won't get to be head of the stores, believe me you won't. And you won't get to inherit Pennistone Royal either. Linnet's going to get it all. Poor little you, you're the one who's going to get a royal screwing." He laughed coldly.

"I don't believe any of this," Tessa said, striving to keep her voice steady. But she was shaking inside, and she wondered if there was any truth in what he was saying. Abruptly, she jumped up, walked toward the door. "I'm going to read to Adele."

"Not so fast," he cried, striding across the room, grabbing her arm before she could reach the door. He pulled her into his arms and kissed her, forcing his tongue into her mouth. With his free hand he locked the door. He walked her over to the sofa and pulled her down with him, throwing a leg over her, pressing his face against hers. In her ear he said, "I'm going to give you a royal screwing right now, Tessa, my love." He fumbled with her white silk shirt, and growing impatient with the buttons, he simply ripped it down the front, put his hand in her bra, and got hold of a breast. He brought his mouth to it, kissed the nipple, then suddenly he bit.

Tessa screamed, struggled, pushed him away, and sat up. Slender though she was, she worked out every day, and she had amazing strength in her arms. She gave him a sudden hard shove, and he rolled off the narrow sofa onto the floor.

"You bloody bitch," he shouted.

"You hurt me, Mark," she said quietly, at once conciliatory, knowing his temper was about to flare up. "Why did you bite me?"

He struggled to his feet without responding.

Standing herself, Tessa edged toward the door. He caught hold of her arm, almost wrenching it out of its socket. "Don't spend too much time with Adele," he murmured, his voice unexpectedly soft. "I have an urgent need for you tonight. You're going to have to meet your wifely obligations."

"I always do, Mark darling," she whispered.

His answer was to grab hold of her hand and press it against his crotch. "See what you do to me? Come on, Tess, let's have a quickie now. Right there on the sofa. The door's locked. No one can get in."

"Later, Mark darling." She leaned into him, kissed him lightly on the mouth. "Let me deal with Adele first." She was desperate to keep him appeased.

He took her face between his hands, squeezing it hard, so hard it hurt, and tears sprang into her eyes. "Don't be too long," he hissed. "Otherwise I might have to —"

"Have to what?" she cut in.

He did not answer. He merely gave her a cold stare, let go of her, walked across to the door, and unlocked it. "Be my guest," he said, his voice menacing again.

Tessa hurried out and ran upstairs, fastening her jacket. She almost stumbled into Adele's room, then took a deep breath to calm herself. With a smile she walked toward the bed, saying, "And what story shall I read to you tonight, darling?"

"Anything you want, Mumma." Adele patted the bed. "Sit here."

Tessa did as her daughter said, picking up one of the books on the bedside table.

Adele leaned closer to her mother and touched her cheeks. "Why are you crying, Mumma?" she whispered. "What's wrong?"

"Nothing, sweetie pie." Tessa smoothed her cheeks with her fingertips and then wrapped her arms around her daughter, holding her close.

Twenty minutes later, when Adele had fallen asleep, Tessa turned out the lamp but left on the night-light and slipped out of the room quietly.

Walking slowly downstairs, she took control

of her emotions and went into the library. Mark was sitting at his desk going through the mail, and he glanced up, instantly smiled at her. "I'm so sorry," he murmured, getting up, coming toward her. "I hope I didn't hurt you."

She shook her head. It was not unusual for him to be suddenly calm after the storm. He had strange mood swings these days, went from being angry to loving.

He said, "I don't know what gets into me sometimes. I suppose it's overwork, stress, pressures. Forgive me?"

"Yes, Mark. But why did you say those things about my mother? Why did you say I'm not going to inherit?"

"It was just some gossip I heard. Forget it, darling. I really shouldn't have repeated it. I was wrong."

"Why won't you tell me who told you?"

"It's not anyone you know, some American chap who was here from New York. He claims he knew Shane in those days when Shane was running the American end of O'Neill Hotels International. Let's forget it, okay?"

"All right. But it wasn't very nice, I mean the things he said about Mummy."

"Oh, I know. And as I said, I was wrong to repeat them. Look, let's go out to dinner, shall we? Why don't we go to Harry's Bar? Go and change, and I'll try and get a table for nine o'clock. Please, Tessa."

"That'll be nice, going out," she murmured. "I'll get ready." But inwardly she was terrified of her own husband.

Twelve

"I have only one question for you," Linnet said, pausing in the middle of Chester Street, staring up at Julian.

"Yes?" he responded, looking down at her, thinking how lovely she looked in the lamplight, curbing the desire to kiss her passionately. "And what's that?"

"How did you manage to get past security at the back door of the store, *and* up to my office without anybody phoning me?"

Amused by the question, he began to laugh. "Joe Pinkerton was on duty at the staff entrance, and he's known me since I was a toddler. So obviously he let me through."

"I see."

Noting her sudden snippy tone, and not wishing to get a senior staff member into trouble, he quickly added, "But Joe did ask me to sign the book."

"I'm glad to hear it."

"Also, I mentioned I was coming to pick you up," Julian thought to add, watching her face carefully.

"And how did Joe react to that?" she asked, her voice a fraction milder.

"He smiled, and winked, and —"

"You *see!* Someone else assuming we're a couple!"

"Well, we are. We always have been, and hopefully we always will be, whatever *you* think. And what's wrong with that anyhow?" he demanded, his voice rising sharply, an irate gleam entering his blue eyes.

Linnet continued to stare up at him, looking slightly put out, and she was about to make another sharp retort when he grabbed hold of her shoulders, pulled her to him, and kissed her fully and deeply on the mouth.

For a moment Linnet endeavored to push him away, then, unexpectedly, and much to her amazement, she crumbled. Clinging to him fiercely, her arms around his neck, she felt her resistance to him dissolve. She began to return his kisses with a passion which equaled his, and she surprised not only herself but Julian.

After a moment, they reluctantly drew apart, stood gaping at each other, both of them startled and for the same reason: Her unbridled response to him after months of forbidding distance was a total turnabout.

Julian touched her cheeks lightly with his fingertips and murmured, "Come on, I've got a surprise for you." As he spoke he tucked her arm through his, and they continued down the street in the direction of his apartment. Once they were inside the entrance hall of the remodeled town house, he kissed her softly on the mouth again, then taking her hand, he hurried her up to the next floor.

"What kind of surprise?" she asked, her curiosity finally getting the better of her.

Julian Kallinski simply smiled enigmatically and led her to his front door. After unlocking it, he ushered her inside, slammed the door behind them with his foot, and took her in his arms once more, his mouth finding hers.

Continuing to kiss her, he began to pull off her heavy topcoat, dropped it to the floor, then shrugged out of his own, let it fall, and they half-walked, half-stumbled toward the living room, still kissing each other.

The room was in darkness except for a pool of light from a small, silk-shaded lamp and the lambent flames from the fire burning in the hearth.

"Our separation is over," Julian announced, impatiently taking off her suit jacket, throwing it on a chair, leading her toward the fire.

"But —"

"No *buts*," he cried, putting two fingers on her lips to silence her; then he took her face between his hands and stared deeply into her eyes. It was a face he loved, had loved since they were children. Heart-shaped, with high cheekbones and a broad brow, it was perfectly sculpted, the lines fine, delicate. She had sweeping auburn brows above those marvelous, deep green eyes, balanced by the widow's peak, which came down onto her forehead in a dramatic V. Her coloring was so vivid, so unique, it was heart-stopping.

He had always loved her bright red-gold hair, and when her siblings and some of her cousins had called her "carrottop" and "red pepper" when they were all growing up, he had angrily shouted rude comments back at them. And he had taken her to one of their secret places, where he had kissed the tears off her cheeks, kissed her small, capable hands, repeatedly told her she was the most beautiful of all girls. It was Gideon who usually came to find them, and he, too, hugged and comforted her, and encouraged her in her defiance of the others. They were her stalwart champions, the two of them, and like him Gideon was a nonparticipant in the teasing.

Now Julian said, very slowly, "I've loved you all of my life, Linnet O'Neill. I'll always love you. Until the day I die I'll love you, and even after that. And I cannot go on like this. Very simply, I *won't*. We have to be together again, and immediately. I can't bear being away from you, I can't live like this, I just can't tolerate the separation you imposed."

She gazed at him, saw the sincerity written on his face, the desperation in his eyes. But she remained silent, afraid to say anything because she knew the wrong word would make him blow up. He was obviously at the end of his patience.

"Tell me you truly want to end our relationship," he said after a moment, "tell me to go away forever, and I will. I promise I'll never bother you again. Tell me you don't love me anymore, Linnet O'Neill, and I'll go."

Looking him straight in the eye, she cried, "Of course I love you, Julian! I always have, but you see, it's —"

"No!" he shouted, more in frustration than annoyance. "This ridiculous nonsense has to stop, do you hear. I am putting a stop to it right now. I'm taking a stand, Linnet. I just won't accept this from you any longer. *This is an ultimatum.* Either we go back to our normal relationship or I'm getting out . . . I'm jumping ship!"

She was taken aback by the authority in his voice, the look of absolute determination on his face. And she knew that if she continued her campaign to keep him at arm's length, to stall the relationship, she would lose him forever.

Julian had just shown her that he was in earnest. And she understood deep within herself that he was far too proud to be treated with the kind of indifference she had been meting out. He was too much in love with her to stand for the separation she had imposed, and too much of a man to be bullied by her. No weakling, he.

She realized with a sudden rush of clarity that she somehow had to make amends to him. At once. Tomorrow would be too late. She had pushed him, to the very limit, and his patience *was* at an end. That was patently obvious from his tone, the stance he had taken, the hard glint reflected in his blue eyes, the tight set of his generous mouth.

Linnet took a step forward and put her arms around him; standing on tiptoe, she kissed him lightly on the mouth. Holding his hand in hers, she gently pulled him toward the fire. "Take this off," she murmured, touching the lapel of his jacket.

He did as she asked, threw it to one side, stepped closer, and took her in his arms, all in one smooth movement. His mouth sought hers hungrily, and they kissed for a long time. Then they sank down onto the rug in front of the blazing fire, wrapped in each other's arms.

Pushing himself up on his elbow, Julian gazed at her for a long moment, trying to read her face.

She saw the question in his eyes and asked, "What is it, Julian?"

"Are you *sure?*"

"What do you mean?"

"Sure about this? Being here with me like this? Are you sure about ending the separation, coming back to me? Sure about *us?*"

"Yes, I'm sure," she whispered, reaching up, touching his face, her eyes spilling her love for him.

He nodded his understanding; a smile flickered on his mouth and was gone. He wanted her so much; he always had. He began to smooth his hand over her breasts. Beneath the thin silk of her shirt her nipples stood erect as they hardened. Just as he himself was erect and rapidly hardening. He bent over her, sucked at her nipple through the silk, staining it, then unbuttoned her shirt, took a breast out of her lacy bra. His mouth came down on her warm flesh, and he kissed her breast tenderly, cupping it, sucking the nipple. And he breathed in the warmth of her.

Linnet's hands went up onto the nape of his neck, into his thick, dark hair, and her fingers felt strong and firm on him.

Julian's desire for her was intensifying, to such an extent he thought he would burst. They had been apart for months now, months that had seemed endless, and he had constantly thought about her, dreamed about her. And of course he had fantasized about being with her like this.

He was terribly excited, his emotions high,

his physical desire flaming through him. He wanted to sink into the deepness of her, into her core. And yet he did not want to rush; he wanted to prolong these moments, savor them, and he wanted to pleasure her, just as he had been doing for years, since they had first understood that they were sexually attracted to each other as teenagers.

He began to kiss her mouth once again, and she opened it slightly for him, and he sought her tongue, gave her his. And they were enraptured with each other, joined in great intimacy, becoming part of each other.

Linnet was on fire, as she always was when they kissed like this, so voluptuously. She wanted him inside her, loving her, making her feel whole once more. She realized now how very much she had missed him, missed their lovemaking, their extraordinary sexual bonding. He had been making love to her since she was sixteen, possessing her constantly and with great feverishness, and how she loved being possessed by him with such fervor. Suddenly she felt the pulse at the core of her beginning to throb, and she was damp and wild with desire. "Julian, Julian . . . please. I want you so much," she moaned softly.

He lifted his head from her breast, looked down at her, and nodded. He began to pull off her blouse, and she unbuttoned his shirt, snatching at it, and finally they shed all of their clothes, which lay scattered around them.

Julian lay down next to her on his side, fitting his body to the curve of hers. He was silent. Observing her. Absorbing her. He enjoyed studying her, devouring her with his eyes.

She thought how marvelously masculine he was. Long and lean, yet muscular with a broad chest, and he was darkly handsome, with high cheekbones, a cleft in his chin, and eyes that were bright blue but dark now with desire. He moved closer to her, and she felt his hardness against her thigh, and it both thrilled and inflamed her; knowing how much he wanted her sexually was an aphrodisiac.

After a moment, Julian raised himself on one elbow, began to stroke her, running his fingers across her breasts, down onto her stomach and then her thigh, until they came to rest on the red-gold hair at the top of her legs. Slowly, tantalizingly, he slid his hand down between her legs, which she parted for him. Linnet sighed, and her body began to relax as his fingers fluttered around her core, probed and then entered her. She stiffened, and a low moan trembled in her throat. He stroked and caressed her until she was crying out, and he bent over her body, brought his mouth down to join his fingers, and he pleasured her until she convulsed, her legs stiffening, and as she came for him she cried out once more.

He could no longer hold back. He was at bursting point, harder than ever, and he knelt between her legs. Gripping her body, he entered her swiftly and hard, thrusting down into the deep darkness of her, loving her. She was part of him, part of his soul, and she had been for as long as he could remember.

Her long, slender legs went around his back, and she locked them at the ankles, locked him into her the way she had learned to do so expertly, the way he had taught her. He pushed his hands under her buttocks, lifting her to him, and she began to thrust her body against his as he thrust into her velvet warmth. And he found himself floating higher and higher, as if he were intoxicated, and he was. With her, with the scent of her red-gold hair, the scent of her womanliness and her sex.

She began to tremble, the core of her suffused with heat and opening up all around him, engulfing him. He crested higher and higher; deep shudders convulsed him as he soared, and dimly, he heard her calling his name as he cried hers, and they were united once more, riding on waves of ecstasy and joy.

The intimacy of their reunion, the power and passion of their coupling after such a long absence left them both shattered, and they lay still for a long time, depleted.

But eventually they began to stir.

Julian watched Linnet as she gathered herself together, smoothed her hand through her auburn curls, settled against the base of the sofa, then reached for her shirt, slipped it on, a trifle shy after their lovemaking. She had always been that way, modest, needing to cover herself, to be proper.

He smiled inwardly, thinking that there were two of her. The Linnet of this moment, covering her bare breasts, saying little, lost in herself; and the Linnet of a short while ago, soaring with him on a sexual high, hot, wild, passionate. Uninhibited. Joyous. She was the joy of his life. He loved both of his Linnets with all his heart.

He pushed himself to his feet, bent over her, kissed the top of her head, walked across the living room and into his bedroom.

She watched him go, then closed her eyes, let herself drift with her thoughts. She was so happy to be with him again, and their lovemaking had been sublime. How had she ever believed that she could give him up? He was part of her. The only man for her. The only man she had ever wanted.

Linnet sensed that he had returned, and she opened her eyes, looked up at him. He leaned down, draped a silk dressing gown around her shoulders, and once more joined her on the rug in front of the fire, pulling his own robe around himself, tying the belt.

"You should always wear that shade of blue," she murmured. "It matches the color of your eyes."

"I know. My favorite woman bought it for me."

She smiled at him, her eyes crinkling with laughter; then she said softly, "I love you, Julian Kallinski." She threw him a long, pointed stare and added, "I love you as much as you love me."

"I know that, Linnet."

There was a small silence; she bent her head, plucked at the dressing gown, then went on, "I'm sorry . . . sorry I did this to you . . . asked for breathing space, and in the process hurt you so much. I did, didn't I?"

"Yes, you did."

"Do you accept my apology?"

"I do, but I have a question."

"Yes?"

"*Why?* Why did you do it, Linnet? I'm still baffled."

She nodded, let out a deep sigh. "I felt I was being manipulated, that *we* were being manipulated into marriage by our grandfathers. I really and truly did feel this. After all, the three clans have always wanted a Kallinski to marry a Harte."

"You're an O'Neill," he teased.

"You know what I mean . . . a descendant of David Kallinski and a descendant of

Emma Harte must marry, because almost a hundred years ago, at the turn of the last century anyway, David loved Emma."

"And Emma walked away from him, just as you walked away from me. History must repeat itself, is that it?" he asked, sounding just a little acerbic.

"No, no, of course not! David Kallinski, your great-grandfather, was a married man, and you know that Emma had immense integrity, and she would never break up a marriage, attempt to build a life on someone else's misery. That's why she walked away, but she remained his friend until he died, and he was her partner in Lady Hamilton Clothes for years. Grandfather Bryan's often told me *that* story. I know it by heart by now."

"And I heard it from Grandfather Ronnie at one point in my life. But feeling manipulated is not a good enough reason, Linnet," Julian murmured.

"I know. And it was only part of the reason. I wanted us both to be sure of the way we felt about each other. I wanted to let you have a few months of . . . well, freedom actually, to find out where you stood with me. You could say I set you free, Julian . . . you know what I mean." She made a small moue with her mouth, shaking her head. "I didn't want you to feel obligated to me. I wanted you to be unattached, in a sense, so you could have a relationship with another woman if you wanted."

He gaped at her, surprise sliding onto his face. Then he burst out laughing. "You mean you set me free so that I could . . . *play around?*" He gasped, still chuckling.

"Yes."

He was so amused he couldn't speak for a moment, and he laughed again.

Linnet frowned. "Did you?" she demanded.

"Did I what?"

"Have an affair in the last few months?"

"No, of course I didn't! I'm not interested in anybody else but you, and surely you know that by now."

"I suppose I do. But I did feel we were being pushed headlong into marriage because of *their* pasts, because the three clans wanted it, and I resented that a whole lot. Also, there was another thing. I thought that once we were well and truly married, you'd get bored. That does happen, you know. A couple are together for years, happy being with each other, and then once that piece of paper's been signed, *it* comes between them. I began to worry that we'd been together for so long . . . I thought the marriage would break up, and then where would we be?"

"Oh, Linnet . . . darling, how could I ever be *bored* with you?"

"Well, we have been sleeping together for ten years . . . that's a long time."

"That's true, and I've loved every minute," he said, staring at her, wondering whether to laugh or cry. She had put him through hell, agonies of mind and body for months, and all because she was full of preconceived ideas about men and their behavior with women. But he was not like other men. Their rules didn't apply to him; he didn't follow anybody's rules.

In a way, she was right about the grandfathers, though. They were to blame, if blame could be attached to anyone. They had not let the matter rest for years, ever since they'd realized, and with delight, that he and Linnet were a twosome. And they had stepped up their campaign this past year, so he knew exactly how troubled she was by their manipulation. He had felt it himself, if the truth be known. He had simply been less affected than she, had been able to shrug it off.

And he supposed, if he were eminently fair, that many women might well think a man could become sexually turned off one day after spending years with the same woman, a woman he had known since her childhood. But he was different. He wished she'd realized that about him; it bothered him, for a moment, that she hadn't understood him better, and then he kicked the thought away, with the force he once used to kick a rugger ball. And dismissed it instantly.

Moving closer, he put his arm around her

and pulled her to him. "Do you remember what we did when you were seven and I was eleven? Up in the attics at Pennistone Royal?"

"What *we* did! You mean what *you* did."

"What did I do that you didn't do?"

"You undressed me, and without my permission."

"I don't remember you objecting, you little beast."

"You didn't think I was a little beast *then*. You were fascinated . . . with every part of me."

"If I remember correctly, you were very willing and able, and an enthusiastic participant in our little games when we were teenagers. In fact, you once undressed me, and quite forcefully, and examined me, and did a lot more, I might add. You even went as far as to —"

"Don't say it, Julian Kallinski, or I'll —"

"You'll what?" he interrupted.

"I'll do it again, right now."

"Yes, please." Smiling at her, he moved even closer, buried his face in her hair that smelled of lemon verbena and a hint of summer flowers and cleanliness. Such a familiar scent . . . her scent. "Oh, I do love you so very much, my Linnet, my darling, my sweetheart. How could you ever think I would want to make love to another woman? I've only ever wanted you . . . only you could give me such joy, such satisfaction."

She smiled to herself. "I *was* your willing pupil, wasn't I?"

He pulled away from her, winked wickedly. "But you did have the best teacher in the world, don't you know."

"Oh I do, I do, only too well!"

He cradled her in his arms, trying to be objective for a second or so. He knew her through and through, better than he knew anyone else, even members of his own family.

She was a complete Harte. She had inherited all of their characteristics . . . their toughness of mind, their loyalty and generosity, their spirit and energy, their many diverse talents, their capacity for backbreaking work. All the Hartes were fierce in their defense of one another, and she was no different. Touch a Harte and the rest of the clan would go for the jugular. He knew full well that she had never really liked Toby, but she would fight until she dropped to defend or avenge him. That was the way they were. They were abiding by Emma's rules, as they did in all things. Emma had set the standards long ago, and they still existed for every one of the Hartes.

Yes, Linnet had inherited *all* of their traits, good and bad, and their marvelous looks. Not to mention their hot-bloodedness. Emma's blood ran in her veins, and Emma's had never been icy. To the contrary. Men had fallen at *her* feet, and there had been a number of men she had loved, had had liaisons with, and several of her children had been born on the wrong side of the blanket. If he was any judge of character, from what he knew about her Emma Harte had more than likely been as uninhibited in bed as her great-granddaughter was with him.

But he loved Linnet because she *was* a Harte, because she was all the things she was. He loved her defiance of the rules, her independence, her pithy bluntness that at times reminded him of her aunt Emily and made him laugh hilariously. And he loved her for her sweetness, her tenderness, her gentleness with children, her kindness to the elderly in the family. He knew how much she cared for Bryan, even though at times her grandfather had driven her crazy with his talk of the final uniting of the three clans.

For her part, Linnet's thoughts were focused on her behavior over the past few months. She was mainly worrying that Julian thought she had been silly. Well, she had been foolish in certain ways; she should have confided her worries in him, instead of insisting on a period of separation. What had been accomplished in the end? Nothing at all. It had only made them both miserable and been a waste of precious time. No, perhaps not such a waste. Certainly she valued him more than ever . . . now she understood that. The very thought of losing him a short while ago had filled her with dread, and she had been determined to make things right between them. Immediately. And she had.

Their attraction for each other was as rampant now as it had been the first time they had made love. She remembered that night very clearly. They had kissed and touched and explored each other for years, and then, not long after her sixteenth birthday, the petting had gone too far. She had enticed him until finally they were carried away by their own feelings, had gone the whole way. Several times that night, in fact. Then they had worried themselves to death until she had her next period. After that Julian had armed himself with contraceptives until she went on birth control pills.

Julian Kallinski. Her *first* love. Her *only* lover. She sometimes wondered if she had been his only conquest; she was not sure. He was four, almost five, years older than she, and had gone away to boarding school, then to Oxford. Once she had heard her father and Uncle Winston talking and laughing about Gideon and Julian, and Uncle Winston had muttered something about them being a couple of "Jack the lads." Which meant only one thing in her mind.

But she did not care. Those days had ended. He was carrying a great deal of responsibility at Kallinski Industries, and he would have to shoulder much more when he took over. They understood each other very well, and she had her own load to carry at Harte's. In a sense, they had been lumbered by their ancestors' great successes; perhaps that was why they were compatible, the shared background and upbringing, the dedication to duty, their acceptance of the circumstances of their lives. No explanations were ever necessary when it came to work and business. Julian was brilliant, hardworking, and dedicated, and they had identical values. For as long as she could remember she had loved him; she also liked, admired, and respected him.

She stirred in his arms and sat up. "You told me you had a surprise for me," she exclaimed, remembering what he had said earlier.

"I do."

"What is it?"

"Close your eyes."

"Okay. They're closed."

Julian reached into the pocket of his robe and fumbled around until his fingers touched the object he was seeking. He took it out, got hold of her hand, and slipped on the ring.

"Open your eyes."

"Oh my God, Julian! It's beautiful," she cried as she stared down at the emerald engagement ring glittering on her finger in the firelight. Swiveling around, she looked up at him. "It's more than beautiful, it's absolutely perfect. Thank you." Reaching up, pulling him down to her, she kissed him on the mouth.

"It matches your eyes," he murmured a moment later, enjoying her pleasure. "Do you accept it?" He drew away, peering at her in the soft light. "You know what it means if you do."

"Of course I accept it, and I *do* know what it means, silly. We're engaged."

"At last." He began to chuckle.

"What is it? Why are you laughing?"

"The grandfathers are going to take credit for our engagement, you know."

"Don't you dare mention *them* to me now," she exclaimed, but she couldn't help laughing with him. "So this is why you came to the store tonight, appeared at my office unexpected and dragged me off, almost by the hair. To get engaged to me."

"I didn't know what was going to happen, how you'd respond," he replied. "But I wanted to be prepared . . . for any situation. I mostly wanted to talk to you, Linnet, to clear the air. You see, I just couldn't stand it any longer. I thought I was going to go insane without you. I wanted to have it out, settle it once and for all."

"And when you kissed me in Chester Street, I knew I couldn't bear to be apart from you any longer. So you see, you were right to come to the store and act so masterfully. And tomorrow I shall thank Joe for sending you up unannounced."

He hugged her to him, and after a moment he said, "I could eat an elephant I'm so hungry. Aren't you?"

"Yes. But you never have any food in your refrigerator."

"I do tonight. This afternoon I did a bit of shopping, and brought dinner home. Mrs. Ludlow prepared it all just before she left at six. She put everything on the tea trolley in the kitchen, left the champagne on ice, lit the fire in here, and departed. We've nothing to do really, just wheel in the trolley. How about a picnic on the rug? Courtesy of Harte's, of course."

"It'll be lovely, but we won't have a fire if you don't put another log on it."

"Right away." He jumped up, removed the fireguard, dropped a log on the smoldering embers.

"I'll come and help you in the kitchen," Linnet said, also rising. "Now that I'm almost, if not quite, your missus."

"You've always been my missus," he shot back, took hold of her hand, and stared at the ring. It was a pool of green fire in the lamplight. "The mister who gave you this must be crazy about you. It's some ring. And then some!"

"The mister who gave me this ring is terrific in every way, but especially in bed. I've always got the hots for him."

He put his arm around her, laughing, and they walked across the living room and into the kitchen.

Thirteen

Lifting her crystal flute, Linnet touched it to Julian's. "Cheers," she said and took a sip. Looking at him over the rim, she added, "When are we going to announce our engagement? Or shall we keep it a secret for a while."

"Cheers, darling." After a long swallow of champagne, Julian shrugged lightly. "It's really up to you. Do you want to have a drinks party? Just for the clans. Maybe on Valentine's Day? Or is that too corny?"

"I don't think it's too corny, but Valentine's Day is next week. There's going to be nobody around. Paula and Shane went to Paris this morning. Uncle Winston left for Toronto yesterday, for a board meeting, and Gideon's on the Isle of Man."

"Oh, that's right. He went to see Christian, I understand. Hoping to lure him back to Fleet Street with all kinds of promises. And goodies."

"If anybody can do it, Gideon can." She laughed and leaned back against the base of the sofa, stretching her legs.

The two of them were sitting on the rug in

front of the fire, the picnic spread out between them. There were plates of cold meats and chicken, slices of cold game pie, potato salad in a crystal dish, a bowl of cornichons, plus a baguette cut up in pieces and a slab of butter on a plate. The bottle of champagne sat in a bucket of ice nearby.

Julian eyed the food, took a slice of the pie, laid it on his plate, and speared a fork into the cornichons. "You used to love these when you were little."

"Still do," she said, and also took a slice of pie and some of the small pickled cucumbers. After munching on one and eating part of the pie, she glanced at Julian. "Why did you agree to take a breather, as I called it?"

"Because you wanted it so much and I decided I must humor you. But very frankly, Linnet, I'd no idea you'd stretch it out for several months. I thought we were talking a few weeks, at the most. It became too unbearable for words."

"I know . . . I'm so sorry." She served herself some potato salad, took a forkful, then murmured, "Gideon's smitten with Evan Hughes."

"*Very.*" Julian gave her a knowing look, drank some more champagne, then stared into the fire, his expression reflective. Finally he turned back to her. "Actually, Linnet, I've never seen him like this before. He's really fallen hard."

"I know. I think it happened the moment he set eyes on her in the corridor at Harte's. He told me the other day that it was a *coup de foudre*."

"He told me the same thing . . . and I believe he's right in that. Has Evan said anything to you, Linnet?"

"Not a lot. She's cautious, but that's only natural, I suppose. After all, he's a Harte, and she's my assistant. Maybe she's a bit awkward because she works for me. But if you want my opinion, I think she feels the same way I feel about you."

Julian sat back.

"She's flipped for him, in other words, and she's got stars in her eyes."

"So that's how you feel, is it?" He leaned forward, looking pleased, and squeezed her arm.

"Yep."

There was a small silence.

It was Julian who broke it when he said quietly, in a thoughtful tone, "What do you know about Evan Hughes, Linnet?"

She met his steady gaze with a puzzled look. "What do you mean? What are you getting at?"

"I was just wondering about her background, where she comes from, that kind of thing. I realize you have her résumé, know all about her previous work in fashion. I was actually thinking about her *personal* background."

"She's only been working for me for about

215

three weeks, but I like her a lot. So does everyone else. And she's good, Julian, really professional. Imaginative, even quite brilliant in certain ways. India's impressed, and so is Cassie. I haven't asked her a lot of questions about her private life, but I think it goes without saying that she was available, not entangled with anyone when Gideon first asked her out. I know she was brought up in Connecticut but lived in New York for about nine years before moving here. Her father's an antiques dealer. I gather her mother is a manic-depressive. She has two sisters. She's never been married. Well educated, nice manners. Great personality. That's about all I can tell you, really."

Julian nodded, took a few sips of champagne, put the glass down. He cut a piece of the game pie still on his plate and ate it, the reflective look intact in his eyes.

Linnet also ate a little of the pie, took a small piece of chicken, reached over for the bottle and poured herself another glass of the champagne. "What a good idea this was, darling. So tell me why you're interested in Evan's background."

"There's something about her that seems . . . well, quite mysterious . . ." He let his sentence trail off because he couldn't quite put into words what he meant. Also, he didn't want to say anything which would be inflammatory to Linnet, or equally important, put her off Evan Hughes. God knew she needed another assistant because of the retrospective, and she had for a long time. Evan Hughes puzzled him, she had done so since he had first met her with Gideon. Not the least of it was her resemblance to Paula, which he found so startling he was actually troubled by it.

Taking a deep breath, Julian plunged in: "Don't you think there's something odd about her? She shows up at Harte's, out of the blue, and gets herself a job with you . . . and everyone's agog because she looks exactly like your mother. Younger version, of course."

"I don't think she looks *exactly* like Paula," Linnet answered swiftly, staring across at him. "They're the same type, that's all — tall, dark, exotic in appearance. Evan has sort of bluish gray eyes, my mother's are violet, and Mummy's got dimples and a much broader forehead. And no, I don't think there's anything odd about Evan, I really don't, Julian. As for her *slight* resemblance to Mummy, it *is* just that . . . *slight*. Very slight. And anyway, lots of people look like each other but it doesn't mean they're related."

"You're right," he agreed, not wishing to upset her or probe further. As far as he was concerned, from her appearance Evan Hughes could easily be Paula's daughter; in fact, she looked more like her than Linnet did. When he had met Evan, he had been truly taken aback by her looks, but he *had* liked her, had found her charming, warm, quite lovely in many respects. And he had understood her appeal for Gideon. For any man, actually. And yet . . . well, he might as well admit it, he was quite suspicious of Miss Evan Hughes and her sudden advent at Harte's. As his grandfather would say, there was something not quite kosher here . . .

"When are your parents coming back?" he asked.

"In a few days. Sometime next week. Dad had some hotel business there, and Mummy just decided to tag along at the last moment. She said they're spending Valentine's Day in Paris. Why?"

"I was thinking about asking your father for your hand in marriage."

"Go on, don't be so daft, lad!" she cried in a broad Yorkshire accent and began to laugh uproariously. "You don't have to ask him, I think he's always known it would happen, that we'd get married one day," she added in her normal voice.

"But I want to ask him, Linnet. I think it's the proper thing to do."

Linnet leaned over, kissed his cheek. "That would be lovely, darling," she said softly, knowing what a close call she had had with him. She had almost lost him because of her own foolishness.

Fourteen

Throwing her long black coat around her shoulders, Evan headed toward the door, but the shrilling of the telephone made her turn back into the little sitting room. She ran to pick it up, exclaiming, "Hello?" and glancing at her watch as she did. She was running late; it was almost seven o'clock.

"It's me, Evan," her father said from far-away Connecticut, sounding as if he was just around the corner.

"Hi, Dad!" she cried brightly, glad to hear his voice. "How are you?"

"I'm okay," he answered in a low mutter. "But you haven't called in over a week, and I started to worry. Are you all right?"

She knew that down-in-the-dumps tone only too well, had always dreaded it, and swiftly she said, "Oh, Dad, I'm so sorry, and yes, everything's fine. I'm great. It's just that we've been so busy with the retrospective I haven't had a minute to spare. But you shouldn't worry, I'm doing great here."

"Well, I'm happy to hear it." He said this in such a grudging voice it was obvious to her that he was not happy at all.

Evan murmured, in a conciliatory way, "I ought to have called you. I mustn't let the pressure of work get in the way again."

"I've got to admit, I *do* worry about you. You seem so far away, Evan."

When there was a small silence at her end of the phone, he said, "Evan . . . Evan . . . are you there?"

"Yes, I am. And don't worry so much. I'm almost twenty-seven, for heaven's sake, Dad."

"I miss you, we all do," he answered, "and I can't help worrying."

"I miss everyone, too, Dad. How's Mom doing? How're the girls?"

"About the same, and your mother is a lot more cheerful at the moment. I even got her out to the movies the other night."

"That's wonderful news!" Evan was startled at this turn of events but pleased. Perhaps her mother was finally coming out of her lethargy and depression.

"So, you like working at Harte's, do you?" her father asked.

"Very much. I'm loving it. The retrospective is going to be something really special, and it's a challenging job. Mounting it properly, giving it cachet and excitement is most important."

"I told Pauline Trigère some of her clothes are going to be in it, and she was thrilled." There was a little pause, and then Owen said, in a careful tone, "And how's your admirer?"

"Admirer?" she repeated, taken aback by the question.

"I hear you have a boyfriend."

"Oh. Well, he's just a friend really, Dad," she responded, knowing at once that he'd been speaking to George Thomas.

"Is it that man you met at the store when you went for the interview?" her father now asked. *"Gideon Harte?"*

"It is Gideon, yes."

"He's the cousin of your immediate boss, isn't he?"

"That's right. But we're just good friends, as I said."

"I hope so, Evan. It wouldn't do for you to get mixed up with your employer, you know."

"He's not my employer!" she exclaimed. "He's in the newspaper business, he has nothing to do with the store." She gripped the phone tighter, endeavoring to remain patient with her father. But he was obviously not pleased with her, and on various levels. This baffled her, and made her feel uneasy.

Owen said, "I don't like the idea of you being mixed up with him, Evan. He's out of your league. It wouldn't work, and you'll get hurt."

"Dad, I told you, he's just a good friend. He's tried to be nice to me, to be helpful. Anyway, who told you about Gideon? George

221

Thomas, I've no doubt."

"No, Arlette. I phoned the other day to speak to George and she answered the phone in his office. In passing, she told me you had an admirer before she put George on."

"What do you mean he's out of my league?"

"All of Emma Harte's offspring are fabulously wealthy, powerful, live a life of privilege. You're not used to their world, Evan —"

"He's not like that," she interrupted. "He's a very nice, hardworking guy, and you wouldn't know he was from great wealth or privilege. He's very down-to-earth, committed to work, as are his cousins Linnet and India. In fact, the whole family has a very strong work ethic, Dad, so I don't know what you're talking about. And in any case, I'm *not* out of his league. That's a very strange thing for *you* to say. You've always said I could have any man I wanted!"

It was Owen's turn to be conciliatory, and he said quickly, "You don't have to get all het up! I'm only being protective of you, honey."

"I am quite capable of looking after myself. I've been doing that since I was seventeen, when I went to live in New York. Remember, Dad?"

"Yes, I do remember, and you weren't on your own, you were living with my parents in Manhattan. And listen to me, Evan, I don't care how nice this guy Gideon is, I know what his type are like, snobby, class conscious, out to get what they can from a woman —"

"Dad! Stop it. And at once! Gideon's not like that, and in any case, I told you we're just good friends. I'm not having an affair with him, if that's what you're getting at. He's taken me out a few times, a number of times actually, but that's it. We have a lovely friendship, he's tried to be kind, to steer me in the right direction, giving me helpful tips about working at Harte's."

"I understand. But remember, he's from a very different world than you're accustomed to, Evan, and I want you to be careful. I don't want anyone ever to take advantage of you."

"They won't," she said in the steadiest voice she could muster. "I'm a big girl, you know, a grown-up now, Dad. And you have always said I'm very levelheaded. So I just don't understand this tack you're taking with me."

"Let's not quarrel, Evan," he said in a less belligerent voice.

"I'm not quarreling," she shot back, thinking *he* was the one trying to pick a fight.

"All right, honey, I trust you, trust your judgment. Anyway, I'd better get off the phone. I have to drive into New York this afternoon."

"Dad, if I'm not here at the hotel and you want to speak to me, you can always call me at the store, you know."

"I don't like to bother you at work."

"You wouldn't be, honest."

"All right then. Take care, honey. I love you."

"I love you, Dad. And give my love to the girls and Mom."

"I will. Bye."

She said good-bye and put the phone down, stood for a moment with her hand on the receiver, thinking about the conversation. Her father just hadn't sounded like himself, and she couldn't help wondering why.

As Evan stepped out of the elevator, she collided with Arlette Thomas, almost knocked her over.

Gripping Evan's arm, steadying herself, the somewhat diminutive Frenchwoman exclaimed, *"Mon Dieu,* Evan, you are in the hurry!"

"I'm sorry, Arlette. Rushing out of the elevator like that was rather stupid of me. You could have fallen and hurt yourself, and it would have been my fault."

"I am perfectly all right, *chérie,"* Arlette answered, looking up at Evan, smiling at her, as usual quite entranced by the young American. "You look *très chic* tonight, but more important, very beautiful. I hope you have the *rendezvous* . . ." She paused, laughing, and her eyes twinkled. "With that nice young man you told me about."

Evan couldn't help smiling back at her, and she realized then that Arlette had not meant to make mischief by mentioning Gideon to her father. She had merely done what came naturally to a romantic Frenchwoman — she had passed on a little bit of harmless information about two young people going out together. Evan had come to know Arlette quite well in the last two months, and she was aware that the charming and motherly woman did not have a bad bone in her body. On the contrary, she was kind, loving, and saw only the best in everyone.

Edging toward the lobby, Evan nonetheless ignored the remark about Gideon and said, "I was just talking to my father. I understand you told him I had an admirer."

"*Mais oui, chérie.* I am so happy for you . . . and I told him *that,* too, and I said it was always nice for a young woman like you to have a lovely male companion."

Evan said nothing, and a tiny silence fell between them.

Arlette, looking at Evan keenly, suddenly wondered if she had done the wrong thing by mentioning Gideon to Owen Hughes, and she frowned. "I hope you did not mind that I spoke in that way. . . . I hope I did not speak out of turn to your father?"

Arlette sounded so troubled, and there was such a worried expression in her dark eyes, Evan exclaimed, "No, no, not at all. He called me because he hadn't heard from me for over a week, I've been so busy with work. I guess he worries. But he shouldn't, Arlette. I'm a grown woman, I'll soon be twenty-seven."

"That's very old, so old it's downright ancient," a masculine voice with a lilting Welsh accent said behind them.

The two women swung around as George Thomas came walking out of the office next to the concierge's small desk. Both of them laughed, and so did George.

The tall, pleasant-looking Welshman drew to a standstill next to Evan and kissed her on the cheek. "You look bonny tonight, my dear."

"Thanks, George," she responded cheerfully, smiling at him. "I was just talking to Dad. I guess he was on the phone to you during the week, worrying about me as usual."

"I told him he should stop doing that, and immediately. You're well grounded, Evan, and he ought to know that. He brought you up. And you're levelheaded. I think I embarrassed him a bit, actually, because I gave him a lecture." George began to laugh. "I told him he was getting to be a fusspot, an old lady."

"He wouldn't like that!" Evan exclaimed. "Anyway, he was fine when we hung up. To be fair, I suppose he misses me a lot."

"Yes, he does." George hesitated, and then he said in a low voice, "I hope you're going to stay on at the hotel, Evan. The other day Arlette told me you had been thinking of finding a flat."

"Oh, but not at the moment though," Evan replied. "I'm far too busy, and I'm so happy and comfortable here at the hotel. Maybe one day I'll look for a flat, but not just yet."

"I'm very happy to hear that," George said.

"And so am I, *chérie*," Arlette agreed. "And now we must let you go. I know you are in a hurry."

"Yes, I am."

"Have a lovely evening," George said.

Arlette merely gave her a knowing glance as she smiled broadly, the look in her eyes soulful and romantic.

Evan smiled back, and she couldn't resist winking at the Frenchwoman.

Evan found a cab immediately and gave the cabbie the address of the newspaper offices. Then she sat back as the taxi swung around and headed toward Belgrave Square. She could not help thinking about the conversation with her father. He had sounded so unlike himself . . . very odd really. There had been a hint of belligerence in his voice, and his tone had been rather critical when it came to the Hartes. But *why?* He didn't even know them. He had told her his mother had only ever mentioned Emma Harte to him once in passing, years ago, when she said she had met her in the war years. It's very peculiar, she said to herself, and then wondered if it had merely been her father's possessiveness coming to the fore. Although she was reluctant to admit it to anyone, she had always known that she came before her adopted sisters, that she was his favorite because she was his biological child. He had favored her in everything, had quietly spoiled her when she was growing up, and even now.

But he had never displayed any kind of possessiveness, much less shown jealousy when she had brought home her various boyfriends over the years. Still, he had known that none of them had been very serious contenders for her hand in marriage. Except for Willard.

With her father's approval, she had become engaged to Willard five years ago, but it hadn't lasted very long. Once she had decided to break it off, Owen had admitted that he had never thought wedding bells would ring for them. "Will wouldn't have been able to handle you, Evan. He's far too weak," her father had said, and they had never mentioned him again. Owen had never even asked her why she had broken her engagement. If he had she would have told him the truth . . . one day it dawned on her that she didn't *like* Will. Certainly she wasn't in love with him.

She had never been in love. But she knew she might easily fall in love with Gideon. Was she simply carried away because of his charm, his savoir faire, his looks, his uniqueness, his very Englishness? She wasn't sure.

Gideon had made it clear he was keen on her, wanted to pursue a relationship. He had been a devoted friend to her since her first working day at Harte's, had made a point of taking her to lunch a couple of times a week, although it was always in the Bird Cage, the restaurant at the store, because of her tough schedule. And they had been out to dinner a number of times. He had held her hand, kissed her good night, but he had never been aggressive; he had handled her with kid gloves, as if he didn't want to scare her off. In fact, he had been the perfect gentleman.

One thing was certain — they got on well, were compatible with each other. They never stopped talking, had many things in common, and similar tastes. She wasn't exactly sure of his true feelings, but she had stars in her eyes about him . . . he was a very desirable man.

As the cab entered the Mall and went down toward Trafalgar Square, it suddenly struck Evan that she hadn't liked the way her father had characterized Gideon, and without even having met him. It was not like the Owen Hughes she had grown up with, and knew so well . . . or thought she knew. Perhaps she didn't, after all.

Looking back over the past few weeks, she realized that her father had been churlish about the Hartes from the moment she had found a job at the store. Did he have something against them? If so, why had he encouraged her to go to see Emma Harte? He hadn't, now that she thought about it. He'd actually made no comment. It was only when she had pressed him that he had said something . . . that Glynnis had known Emma during the Second World War. He had not volunteered anything else. Had her father always known that Emma Harte was dead and buried? If that were so, he had let her go on a wild-goose chase. He had been humoring her perhaps, because of her devotion to her grandmother. That was the only explanation . . .

Her cell phone began to ring, and she fished around for it in her handbag, brought it to her ear. "Hello?"

"Evan, it's me, Gideon."

"Hi."

"Where are you?"

"Just coming down the Mall. I'm almost at Trafalgar Square."

"That's good. I've finished here at the

paper earlier than I expected. Tell the cabbie to take you to the Savoy. I'll meet you in the bar."

"I'll see you in a few minutes," she answered and put the cell back in her bag.

They sat together in a quiet corner of the bar, sipping their glasses of white wine and talking. At least Gideon was talking, about his work mostly, and Evan was listening attentively. Finally he fell silent. As he had been speaking, his eyes had remained on her face, and they were still riveted on her.

She returned his scrutiny steadily. His light green eyes looked as if they were flecked with gold in the dim light of the bar, and it seemed to her that he was trying to convey his innermost feelings to her. She realized they were the same as hers.

After a moment, Gideon said, "I have a confession to make . . ."

"Yes?" she asked quietly, staring into his face, which was now full of yearning.

"I've never felt like this before . . . the way I feel about you."

"Neither have I."

A small smile settled on his mouth.

"I think we share the same feelings for each other," Evan said.

"I hope so." His face filled with sudden happiness. "I'm not playing around with you. I'm very serious about you, so tell me if you don't feel the same. . . . If this is just a *passing thing* for you, then say so now."

She shook her head vehemently. "It's not a passing thing. I'm not in the habit of playing around. But we still have a long way to go. We have to get to know each other better, don't you think? We need to spend more time together."

He nodded his understanding, took hold of her hand again, brought it to his mouth, kissed the back of it. "There's one way I want to get to know you much better. And tonight. Will you come home with me later . . . so that we can be together at last?"

She nodded.

"I booked a table at Rules for dinner."

"Oh, you did."

"You told me you went there with your grandparents when you were twelve. But you don't sound very enthusiastic."

"I'm not hungry."

"I know what you mean. Neither am I." His eyes held hers. "I want to be with you more than anything in the whole world. Would you like to leave now?"

"Yes, I would," she whispered.

Gideon paid the bill and they left the bar. He escorted her through the lobby, his hand under her elbow, and they stepped out into the courtyard of the hotel.

A moment later his driver was pulling up alongside them, and as they got into the car,

Gideon said, "You can drop us off at home, Harry, thanks."

Once they were settled in the backseat and the car edged out of the yard, his arms went around her and she brought her face up to his. He kissed her deeply and continued to kiss her for a few minutes, then he moved his face away from hers. Sitting up a little straighter, he still held her tightly in his arms; against the cloud of her dark hair, he murmured, "I've got to stop this. I can't stand it. I think I'm going to explode."

"I know, I know."

Fifteen

Evan had been to Gideon's flat once before with Linnet and Julian; they had gone there for drinks before the four of them went out to dinner. That night she had been struck by its inherent good taste, but now she saw, at a quick glance, that it also had charm and comfort. The whole was a mingling of grays and soft blues, accented with white, and there were some very good paintings on the walls.

After taking her coat, he led her into the sitting room, where he turned on more lamps. But they did not linger there. In his usual take-charge manner he ushered her in the direction of his bedroom. He said in a low, hoarse voice, "I know you want what I want, so let's not be coy. Let's go in here now, darling. All right?"

"Yes," she answered softly.

Evan knew that she would have been slightly startled if this somewhat cut-and-dried comment had come from anyone else. But not from Gideon; he had meant it in the best possible way. Anyway, she liked his directness. They had come here to make love. Why pretend otherwise?

In the bedroom he snapped on a small lamp in a corner, then turned to her, kissed her lightly on the mouth, and began to unbutton the neckline of her black wool dress. But suddenly he stopped, drew her to him, and held her very close. He said, after a moment, "I can't begin to tell you what this means to me, Evan, having you here with me. And I do want to please you so much . . ." He let the words slide away, held her tighter.

"You do," she whispered.

Later that night she was to remember how tender and loving he was when they undressed, recall how she realized he was being so true to his nature . . . gentle and thoughtful, concerned for her.

Gideon held her in his arms, kissing her, touching her lightly, and she responded to him most ardently. He was as tall as she was, and they fitted well together as they lay alongside each other on the bed. Eventually he began to stroke her, exploring her body, kissing her all over, and then he covered her with his long, lean body, and her arms went around him. Her fingers crept into the hair on the nape of his neck, and then she slid her hands down over his shoulders and onto the small of his back.

He was very still, quiet, hardly speaking except for a few gently murmured endearments. And she was silent, too, enjoying this intense communion without words, enjoying his touching, so experienced and knowing, all over her.

Bracing himself with his hands on either side of her, he looked down into her face. The expression in his eyes was so intense, so penetrating, she felt as if he were seeing into her very soul, and she into his. Unexpectedly his face contorted slightly, and his eyes widened, as if in surprise, as he took her to him finally, sinking deeply into her.

An involuntary moan escaped her as he thrust harder, deeper, and he instantly covered her mouth with his, tasting her, letting his tongue entwine with hers. Almost at once they fell into their own fluid rhythm, moving together as one.

Evan, her arms and legs wrapped around him, felt the heat rushing through her. It was rising from the core of her. She was red-hot with desire, her face flaming under his touch as he stroked it roughly, then brought his hand down onto her breast, cupping it. The heat flowing through her suddenly seemed to intensify; she knew she was on the verge of climaxing, and her body began to tremble under his. She whispered, "*Gideon*. Oh, Gideon. Please don't stop."

He raised himself again, looked down into her face, his eyes piercing, overflowing with desire. "I won't," he said, his voice still hoarse, rasping with his own pent-up emotions. "Come to me, Evan, come to me, darling." Gideon could no longer control himself. Shudders convulsed him, and he gripped her body hard, pulled it tighter to him. They crested together on wave upon wave of pure, unadulterated joy.

They lay together in a mass of tangled sheets, not moving, not speaking. Eventually, Gideon moved closer, half-covered Evan with his body, and pushed strands of hair away from her face. Staring into her luminous gray eyes, he said softly, "Before, you said I pleased you. I hope I please you even *more* now."

She smiled up at him, her eyes crinkling at the corners. "Yes, you do. Very much."

He nodded, still looking at her intently, and then he let his hand wander down from her breasts, over her stomach toward the V of black hair at the top of her legs. He caressed her with tenderness, kissed her passionately, slowly found her core, and began to make love to her with great concentration. Almost immediately her legs started to quiver, her whole body stiffened, and she cried out.

He wrapped his arms around her, held her close to him, and said in a low voice, "I want you to be mine and only mine, Evan."

"I am, Gideon," she whispered and reached up to touch his face.

Evan awakened suddenly, looking about. Disoriented for a moment, she glanced around the dimly lit room; then she realized she was at Gideon's flat in Belgravia.

Turning, she reached for him, only to discover that his side of the bed was empty. She got up, found the terry-cloth robe he had given her last night, and put it on. Padding across the carpet in her bare feet, she found Gideon in the sitting room. Wrapped in a dark blue silk dressing gown, wearing his tortoiseshell glasses, he was seated at his desk, his head down, staring at papers, his briefcase open on the floor.

He must have sensed her presence. He glanced up and instantly smiled at her. "Evan! It's the middle of the night. Go back to bed."

She leaned against the doorjamb for a second, then glided over, stood before him at the desk. "It's three o'clock. Do you always work at this hour?"

"Frequently. But I've already accomplished quite a lot in an hour, so come on, let's get a bit of sleep if we can."

He rose, came around the desk, took hold of her hand, and led her back to the bedroom. They got into bed and he turned out the lamp, took her in his arms, kissed her cheek, and held her close. After a moment he said, "I have to go to the Isle of Man again on business. I want you to come with me. Will you, sweetheart?"

"Yes. If Linnet lets me have the time off."

"She will." He nuzzled the back of her neck, and they settled down. Entwined, comfortable with each other, they soon dozed.

But within the hour Evan woke up again. During sleep they had disentangled themselves; Gideon was laying on his side at the edge of the bed, obviously in a deep slumber, breathing evenly.

She curled against his back and closed her eyes, but sleep eluded her. For a while she thought about every moment of the last few hours; she focused on their rampant desire for each other, their passionate lovemaking. It seemed to her that they were perfect together, perfect in every way, really. They had discovered, right from the beginning of their relationship, that they were completely compatible; that had been patently obvious to them both. In these last few weeks they had come to know each other well, had become friends and, in a way, allies. She was glad of that, happy that they had such a strong foundation for their relationship. There was no question that she was in love with him. She wanted him. It was apparent to her that he felt the same way.

Unexpectedly, her father's words came back

to her. The way he had fitted Gideon into some ridiculous slot in his mind was shocking. How foolish it was to categorize people. And her father wasn't a stupid man. So perhaps it was something else which made him speak in that awful manner. Dislike of the Hartes? But he didn't even *know* them. Or did he? She was becoming very suspicious of her father's reactions as far as Emma Harte's offspring were concerned.

Gideon moved restlessly, made a strange, strangled noise in his throat, as if he were having a bad dream; then almost at once he settled down again. Gently, Evan smoothed her hand across his back, not wanting to wake him but wanting, certainly, to soothe him.

Gideon worked so hard. Sometimes when he met her for dinner it was well after nine o'clock, and he looked exhausted, his face pinched, his eyes dull and weary. It took him a while to relax, to let go of that world he occupied all day. It was a world he loved, she knew that, but it took its toll. He was trying to build the circulation of the *London Evening Post*, and he needed to entice Christian Palmer back to the paper. That was why he had to return to the Isle of Man. Last week he had told her that he was working on the contract for Christian, and that things now looked positive. She hoped Gideon would succeed.

The entire family worked hard; she had realized this from her first day at the store. And she had told her father this earlier tonight, but he hadn't seemed impressed. He just wanted to focus on his own skewed view of them. She had begun to understand that the Hartes were totally dedicated to the great business empire founded by Emma Harte. "A legend in her own time," Linnet had explained the other day. "Imagine that, Evan. Already a legend when she was in her early fifties. It's amazing." But they were all amazing, weren't they?

Eventually Evan fell asleep, curled up against Gideon's back, one arm thrown over his body, one leg entwined with his. Her last thought was that this was where she wanted to be for the rest of her life. With him always.

Sixteen

Paula glanced at the full-sized portrait of Emma hanging over the fireplace in her office and said to Emily, "Grandy would be very proud of you, Dumpling, you've done a wonderful job the way you've run Harte Enterprises."

"She'd be proud of all of us, actually, and I do think you'll have to stop calling me Dumpling. It's a most unsuitable name for a middle-aged woman. Quite embarrassing, actually."

Paula started to laugh. "I agree, but I can't help it. I started calling you Dumpling when you were four or five years old, and it's a habit that's hard to break."

"Try."

"I will."

There was a small pause, and Emily glanced around Paula's office, suddenly exclaiming, "Gosh, it's like spring in here with all your wonderful flowering plants, and the daffodils look beautiful. I wish I had your green fingers. You've been able to make things grow ever since we were little."

"It's just luck really. Well, *Emily,* let's go over the guest lists for Winston and Shane's joint birthday party. I see you have pretty much included everyone I put on my list, so we're in agreement there. I don't think there's anyone to add."

"I think there is. One person is missing, Paula," Emily remarked, settling back in the chair on the other side of Paula's partners' desk, which had once belonged to Emma, as had this office.

With a small frown, Paula asked, "Who did I miss?"

"Evan Hughes."

"But she's not family," Paula began and stopped abruptly. "Of course! Gideon's been taking her out, so Linnet tells me, and obviously you think he'll want to bring her with him. But will it last until June? It's only March now. Or is this serious? I think she's a lovely young woman."

"Yes, and it's the first time he's ever been serious about a woman in his life. You know the story . . . how he found her looking for the management offices in January. Well, he's been seeing her ever since. And I think the initial friendship has blossomed into a love affair."

"Oh! How do you know?"

"Winston told me, and he got it from the horse's mouth, so to speak."

"What did Gideon say to Winston?"

"A few weeks ago, that night Winston spotted Jonathan Ainsley and Sarah Lowther in the Dorchester Grill Room, the two of them had a talk about Gideon's love life. Winston point-blank asked him if there was anyone serious, and Gideon said he'd just met someone he thought *could* be, but it was too soon to really say. Well, a couple of days ago, he told his father he did have serious intentions about Evan."

"And what about Evan? Did he say how she felt?"

"That she was very involved with him, but being sensible and cautious, she thought they should get to know each other properly before making a long-term commitment."

"That sounds like her. Linnet says she's very down-to-earth and practical. And a workaholic, which Linnet loves because she's such a slave driver. But I will add this, Emily, India is crazy about her as well. She can't speak highly enough about her. Evan seems to be rather popular all around."

"So I hear. Amanda thought she had a look of you."

"I didn't know Amanda had met her."

"The other day before she flew to New York she came to the store to see Linnet, to bring a couple of gowns for the retrospective, actually, and Linnet introduced them."

"Do *you* think she looks like me, Em?"

"No, I don't, to be honest. Oh yes, she's

the same type as you, tall, slender, dark haired, exotic-looking, but that's all it is, really. She doesn't have your widow's peak, and her eyes are gray, not violet."

"That's what Linnet says, but oddly enough, Shane did a double take the other day when *he* met her."

Emily shook her head. "I just don't see it. On the other hand, she tends to dress like you, very tailored clothes, which may add to the impression. But who cares, she's obviously not a relative. On the couple of occasions I met her I liked her, Paula." Emily leaned forward slightly and gave her cousin a long, hard stare. "I trust my son, he's a good judge of character, and his happiness is all that matters for me. If he wants to marry Evan, then it's all right by me, and Winston, although he's yet to meet Evan. But you know he's anxious to have grandchildren. He's banking on Gideon to deliver the goods, because he's certain Adrianna will do her best not to get pregnant by Toby."

"I tend to agree with his assessment. Well then, let's add Evan Hughes to the list. I see you didn't," Paula murmured.

"I wouldn't, not until I'd spoken to you. By the way, Mummy's really excited about coming, seeing the family." Emily started to laugh. "She's so excited, in fact, I do believe she's thinking about having another face job before she faces the entire family."

Paula laughed with her. "Poor Aunt Elizabeth, you do malign her, Em, and I'm sure she's not going to have a face job. She looks half her age and perfectly wonderful."

"You're right. But she is hightailing it to Paris. To Balmain on the rue François 1er to be exact. She wants Oscar de la Renta to make her a fabulous evening gown. And she told me she's getting her ill-gotten gains out of the bank."

"Ill-gotten gains?"

"All the diamonds her husbands and lovers have given her over the years."

"Emily, that's a downright lie, and you know it! Your mother bought her own jewelry. Remember what Grandy said — that your mother's husbands all had dubious titles and *empty* wallets."

"Except for my father. Tony Barkstone was a true blue Englishman, and so was Derek Linde, Amanda's father. Mind you, they didn't have a bean between them, but they were nice. Mummy should never have dumped either one of them. But you're right, she did buy her own stuff, except for some rather nice pieces Grandy gave her, with the understanding they came to Amanda, Francesca, and me when she dies."

"You've told me that before. Amanda's doing a great job at Genret, don't you think?"

"I do. She's getting her divorce moving

forward, by the way."

"I'm glad to hear it. I thought that marriage was a mistake right from the beginning," Paula replied and added, "By the way, I spoke to Aunt Edwina in Yorkshire the other day. I couldn't believe how she sounded."

"Well, she *is* very old, you know. Over ninety."

"No, no, what I meant is that she was fantastic. Sounded as if she was about to lead the entire British army into battle."

Emily grinned. "That's Edwina, and I do believe her favorite granddaughter, India, gets that enormous energy from her. It's bred in the bone, I guess."

"I think so. Now, Em, what do we do about Uncle Robin?"

"I think we have to invite him, Paula. He's not responsible for his son's treachery to the family."

"Let's think about it, shall we?" Paula suggested and picked up another sheet of paper. "I like your suggestion about having various food bars during drinks, but we have to settle on the actual dinner menu. How —" Paula stopped, glanced at her private line as it buzzed, and picked up the receiver. "Hello?"

"Mother, it's me. Tessa."

"Yes, Tessa. What can I —"

"I want to see you," Tessa cut in swiftly. "Immediately. I *have* to talk to you. And it can't wait, so I'm going to come up to your office now."

"I'm in a meeting at the moment," Paula responded, her voice cool, contained. "I can't see you for at least half an hour."

"Then I suppose I'm going to have to wait until then." Tessa banged the phone down.

As she replaced the receiver, Paula looked across at her cousin and said in a clipped tone, "The Dauphine is in something of a snit it seems."

"She really *does* think she's the heir apparent, you know," Emily remarked. "She has illusions of grandeur, and she certainly thinks she's going to take over from you, Paula, sooner rather than later."

"Grandy often used a wonderful Yorkshire saying in such instances. 'You know what Thought did, followed a muck cart and thought it was a wedding.' Rather apt, wouldn't you say? I'm afraid Tessa has a few lessons to learn . . . the first one in half an hour."

"What's my problem, you ask? *Really,* Mother! You should know by now it's Linnet and her ridiculous sibling rivalry. It can't possibly have escaped you that she acts as if she owns this store. It boggles the mind the way she walks about, telling everyone what to do, throwing her weight around. She thinks she's in command of everyone, certainly she bosses enough people. Not me, of course, she wouldn't dare, but her underlings, oh yes indeed. And now, on top of everything else, she has another assistant, as well as India. It's preposterous. I don't even have an assistant, merely a secretary. And do you know what she did the other day? She countermanded an order of mine, and I was —"

"*Countermanded!*" Paula exclaimed, cutting her daughter off. "That's a peculiar word to use. This is not the army."

"You know what I mean, Mother. Don't split hairs."

"And you watch your manners, young lady. You're whipping yourself into a fury for no reason at all and dancing around like a whirling dervish gone mad. Calm down, Tessa, and let's get to the bottom of all this nonsense."

"Yes, let's do that!" Tessa exclaimed, glaring at Paula. Nonetheless, she was wise enough to flop into the chair on the other side of her mother's desk.

Paula said, "First of all, Linnet doesn't have one ounce of sibling rivalry in her. *That* exists simply in *your* imagination, yet you are using the idea of it to come in here and make trouble."

"That's not true!" Tessa cried, leaping to her feet.

"Sit down! And shut up!" Paula admonished sharply. "I won't tolerate this kind of behavior. Now you listen to me, and listen very, very carefully, because I'm only going to say this once. Linnet does none of the things you suggest. Nor does she throw her weight around or boss people. She gets on with her work and confines herself to that work. If you have the need for an assistant, or even *two* assistants, do some hiring. I have never, ever prevented you from employing the help you need to do your job efficiently. Do you understand me?"

"Yes, Mother. I'll start looking for an assistant tomorrow," Tessa announced coldly, but at least her voice was lower.

"Let us get to the core of the matter, to the reason you demanded to see me," Paula said, staring at her eldest daughter steadily and very intently.

Tessa squirmed slightly under this unwavering stare but made no comment. She clasped her hands tightly in her lap, endeavoring not to show her nervousness.

Paula continued: "Your agitation springs from your need to know about the succession . . . who will one day have my job."

"No, Mother, it's not —"

"Do not deny it, Tessa, lying doesn't become you. I know that you've been talking about it to members of the family —"

"Toby!" Tessa exclaimed. "I was talking to Toby, my dearest friend in the family, and no doubt his father told you. It was Winston!

Don't pretend otherwise."

"I wasn't going to do that, and you might as well know that under no circumstances will I designate a successor. I have no intention of abdicating! I would be in dereliction of my duty if I did, and I would be breaking a promise I made to Emma Harte over thirty years ago. When Grandy retired on the evening of her eightieth birthday — at her party, in fact — she charged me to hold her dream. I promised I would. And the next day when we had lunch together she asked me to promise her something else, and I did. And it was this . . . that I would not retire from my job as head of the Harte stores unless I was desperately ill and no longer able to execute my duties with due diligence. And so, because I am only fifty-six, in excellent health both mentally and physically, I fully intend to remain as head of Harte Stores. Since I'm a Harte, I will more than likely have Grandy's great health for many years, and I'll probably retire when I am eighty as she did, and not before. So you can shelve any ideas you might harbor about taking over from me."

Tessa was so taken aback she was speechless, and she simply sat staring at her mother, unable to think of a suitable comment. But she was boiling inside.

"I hope you do really understand, Tessa, that I will not name a successor for the future. I will not name you and I will not name Linnet. I will only announce who's taking over from me on the day that I actually retire."

"But why, Mother?"

"Because I don't know who it's going to be."

"But surely you have some idea —"

"I certainly do not," Paula cut in in a stern voice. "You both have a lot to learn, much more experience to gain. Anyway, it might not be either of you. It could well be somebody else in the family."

"*But who?* Surely you're not thinking of silly little Emsie. She's dopey and only interested in horses."

"Emsie is not silly, and she's your loving sister, so please refrain from bad-mouthing her. But for your information, no, I'm not thinking of Emsie. I'm actually not thinking of anyone. I just told you that. Stop trying to pin me down, it's not going to work. I'm a young woman, and I fully intend to keep my promise to Emma Harte for as many years as I can."

"What about Pennistone Royal? Who's going to inherit that?"

Paula gaped at her daughter, flabbergasted. "Good heavens, Tessa, not only do you want my job, you apparently want my home. I'm not dead yet, and I will not discuss my will, or my intentions, with you or anyone else. You've gone too far today. I'm appalled at your behavior. How dare you broach the subject of Pennistone Royal."

Tessa stared at her mother, her lip quivering, and then she burst into tears, sobbing into her hands.

Instantly Paula leapt to her feet, went around her desk, bent over her daughter, and put her arms around her. Tessa flinched slightly, then recoiled.

At once Paula drew away and looked down into Tessa's tearful face. "What's the matter? Why did you flinch like that? Surely I'm not *so* repulsive to you?"

"No, no, I have a bad arm, Mother, that's all."

"And I hurt you as I got hold of you, is that what you're saying?"

Tessa nodded, her large gray eyes brimming.

"What happened to it?"

"I — I — er, well, I fell."

"Here at the store, darling?" Paula asked.

"No. At . . . well, at home."

"Have you seen the doctor?"

"It's not necessary, Mother."

"Come on, take your jacket off, let me see it," Paula murmured, trying to be conciliatory but also concerned.

"It's nothing, really it isn't," Tessa muttered, reluctant to remove her jacket. But Paula insisted, and finally Tessa stood up, slipped off the black cashmere blazer, and allowed her mother to look at her arm.

"Tessa, this is dreadful! You must have fallen very hard to get such huge bruises. They must be awfully painful. No wonder you recoiled the way you did. Are you sure you haven't broken any bones?"

"No, there's nothing broken. I thought at first my shoulder had been damaged, but I had an X ray and it's fine."

Paula frowned, still staring at the purple and black bruises on Tessa's upper arm. "How did you say you fell?"

"I didn't say. But I fell down the stairs at home."

"You must be more careful, darling. So many dangerous accidents happen in the home." Paula shook her head. "Are you sure you don't want Doctor Gill to take a look at it?"

"No, honestly, Mother, I'm okay. But . . . well, thanks for being concerned," she answered, her voice suddenly grown quiet, even meek.

Taking hold of Tessa's other hand, Paula gently pulled her daughter closer, kissed her on the cheek. "I'm *always* concerned about you, Tessa. I love you very much. And we mustn't quarrel like this, it's just not right. I meant what I said, you know, I'm not going to designate a successor for many, many years. So you must relax about it. Enjoy your job here, move up the corporate ladder, and enjoy your husband and your child. Everything's all right at home, isn't it?"

"Oh yes, yes, of course it is."

"I'm glad . . ." Paula sighed as she walked back to her chair, then added softly, "Marriage is relentless . . . no matter how much you love someone."

Seventeen

Tessa paused on the top step and took a deep breath, endeavored to relax her facial muscles. Then she arranged a smile on her face before putting her key in the lock and opening the front door of her house.

It was a smile she had donned for years, her fraudulent smile she called it. When she was a child it had been a useful tool because it disguised so much — hurt, pain, sorrow, anger, discontent. And over the years she had become adept at hiding her real feelings behind that dazzling smile.

"Cooee, cooee," she called as she stepped into the hall, and a moment later she heard Adele's fast-flying feet as her baby daughter came running from the kitchen, calling, "Mumma! Mumma!"

Tessa swept Adele up into her arms and hugged her tightly, then deposited her on the floor carefully. Leaning forward, kissing the child's smiling face, she hunkered down next to her and said, "I've brought you something special, Adele. I know you're going to love it."

The child's face lit up, and she excitedly cried, "A present, Mumma."

"Yes, a present, darling." Reaching for one of the Harte shopping bags she had brought in with her, Tessa pulled out a gift-wrapped package and showed it to her three-year-old. Adele's large, silvery gray eyes became even larger in her delicate face, and she reached out small, plump arms for the package.

"It's too big for you to carry. Come along, let's go to the kitchen and we can unwrap it there." As she spoke Tessa stood up and took hold of Adele's hand, and the two of them walked across the glassy black granite floor.

"Oh, hello, Mrs. Longden," the nanny said, closing the dishwasher door and swinging around as mother and daughter walked in together.

"Good evening, Elvira," Tessa replied, ushering Adele toward the small breakfast area which opened off the spacious, modern kitchen. "I've brought a present for Adele, and now we're going to open it, aren't we, darling?"

Adele nodded, her face full of smiles, her eyes sparkling.

"Aren't you a lucky girl?" Elvira said and then addressed Tessa. "I'm sorry I've got to take the night off, Mrs. Longden, but as I told you on the phone, my mother's fall was a bad one. Fell off a stepladder, she did. A broken arm and a broken leg, both in casts.

Thank goodness her next-door neighbor happened to come in to see her about something. Mrs. Abel found her and was able to get Mum to the hospital. But now she's sort of . . . well, stranded there at home alone."

"I understand, Elvira, and I'm sorry this happened to your mother. Do you know how long you'll be gone?"

"Oh, only tonight, Mrs. Longden. I've been on the phone, and my sister Pearl is driving up from Sussex. She'll be arriving about midnight, and she'll stay with Mum until my other sister, Moira, comes back from her holidays in Spain. Between them, Pearl and Moira can handle everything."

"As I said, I'm sorry your mother hurt herself, Elvira; broken bones are a nuisance and very painful. But I must admit that, rather selfishly, I'm relieved you'll be back tomorrow."

"I know you need me to look after Adele, you work so hard, Mrs. Longden, and I should be here by lunchtime. But you'll have Mrs. Jolles in the morning, and she loves Adele. She can look after her until I arrive."

Tessa nodded and followed her daughter into the breakfast area. After placing the package on the table, Tessa lifted Adele into a chair and said, "Come on, let's untie the ribbon and remove the paper."

Eagerly, the child pulled at the bow of ribbon, tore off the paper, and Tessa helped her to come to the golden cardboard box. Lifting off the lid, Tessa tipped the box up on its end so that Adele could see its contents.

"Oh! Oh!" Adele exclaimed a little breathlessly, her face a picture of delight. "A doll, Mumma! Pretty doll!"

"Yes, it *is* pretty, just like you." Tessa took the exquisitely crafted and beautifully dressed porcelain baby doll out of its box and handed it to Adele, who immediately kissed its cheeks and hugged it to her.

"Do you like her?" Tessa asked, sitting down in a chair opposite her daughter.

"Yes," Adele said, nodding, smiling at her mother, and patting the doll's head.

"What's her name?" Elvira asked, as she came to join them.

Adele looked from Elvira to her mother. "Name, Mumma?"

"She doesn't have a name, not yet. You have to choose one for her, Adele."

"Oh." Adele's eyes opened wider, and she looked at her mother in a puzzled way, then dropped her eyes to the doll she clutched. She stroked its bright blond hair and touched its face, and then she looked up at her mother and said, "Daisy."

"That's a pretty name for a pretty doll," Elvira said, smiling at her young charge, such a beautiful child she was breathtaking.

"Gan-Gan's name," Adele suddenly announced.

"Gran-Gran Daisy *will* be pleased," Tessa murmured, somewhat startled that the child had chosen the name of her great-grandmother. But of course Daisy did have grayish blond hair and a pretty face. Daisy McGill Harte Amory Rickards had worn well over the years. She now lived part of the time in England again, after the death of her second husband, Jason Rickards, in Australia. And she was a frequent visitor to see her granddaughter and her great-granddaughter, especially because she adored little Adele so much.

Glancing at her watch, Tessa rose and, turning to Elvira, remarked, "It's well after six, so you must have given Adele her supper."

"Yes, I have, and I thought I'd start getting her ready for bed in a short while. I was just waiting for you to come home so you could spend a bit of time with her."

"Thanks, Elvira, I do appreciate that. Will you help me to bring the shopping bags into the kitchen, please? Mr. Longden's getting back from his trip later this evening, and I'm going to cook dinner for him."

"That's nice, Mrs. L. What're you going to make?"

"Coq au vin, it's one of his favorite dishes."

It was peaceful in the kitchen.
The only sound was the music playing on

the radio, turned low so that it was merely a background hum. Pleasant but not distracting.

Tessa moved between the stove and the long central island, where she had prepared most of the ingredients for the chicken dish, one of her specialties. After browning the chicken and frying the chopped bacon and chopped onions, she brought all three pans to the island counter and emptied the contents into a large enameled pot. She liked cooking, and she worked easily, as always relaxed when she was preparing food.

Once she had opened a bottle of Beaujolais, she poured herself a glass, then added half of the bottle to the pot. Into this also went a can of tomato paste, a small jug of chicken broth, and two cupfuls of sliced mushrooms. The bouquet garni she had made earlier and tied with a piece of cheesecloth was added, and then she carried the pot to the stove and turned on the gas, setting it at medium.

Tessa stood stirring the contents of the pot with a wooden spoon, and when everything was well mixed she put the lid on and went back to the island. After taking a sip of red wine, she glanced at the ingredients to be added later — a small bowl of pearl onions and another of button mushrooms — then she began to clean up after herself. Within seconds all of the dirty dishes, pans, and utensils were stacked in the dishwasher, and finally Tessa sat down on a stool at the island to enjoy the glass of wine.

Her eyes roamed around the kitchen, taking everything in. She liked this spacious room, with its high-flung cathedral ceiling and the skylights cut into each end, the wide French doors opening onto the patio and the garden beyond. It was light filled and airy, perfect for cooking because it was properly planned and its proportions were excellent.

To Tessa the kitchen was the best room in the house. She thought the rest of the place was cold, a little banal even, and far too modern for her liking. But that was Mark's great claim to fame, ultramodern buildings soaring upward, with great empty spaces inside. Cold spaces, without color or life and with a minimum of furniture. Uncomfortable furniture, she thought, and poured herself a little more wine. She hadn't realized until she moved into this house that she truly detested it. She had watched Mark strip the lovely old Edwardian structure down to its bare bones, then rebuild the interiors the way he wanted. But it was not what she wanted. She had vociferously protested, but he had swept her concern and opinions to one side, telling her that she would love it once it was completed, that she had no vision.

But she had not loved it, and the upsetting thing was that her mother had bought the house for her — it belonged to *her* — and not to have a pleasing place to live affected her badly at times. Furthermore the amount of money he had spent remodeling had been enormous, and that money was hers, too.

She had been brought up at Pennistone Royal and her mother's Belgravia house, which had once been Emma Harte's, and she was used to the warmth and comfort predominant in both places. Pennistone Royal, stately home though it was, with so many huge and soaring spaces, had its smaller rooms, which were intimate, charming, and lovely to be in, to live with.

There were those who thought Mark was a genius. But of late Tessa had come to understand this was not the case at all; she had suddenly realized that much of what he designed was plagiarized from other, more famous architects, most of them dead. These designs he modified until they were bastardizations of the originals. Thus he could claim them as his own, although Tessa often wondered why he would want to do so. She thought that most were monstrosities.

The realization that he was not what she had originally thought him to be had been something of a shock. Yet hadn't she always known deep down inside that he was a bit of a fraud, a blowhard and a boaster? Goodlooking yes, but not as good a catch as she liked to make out to others. And if she were really truthful with herself, she had to admit their marriage was going downhill fast. However, there was Adele to think of; she adored her father. Anyway, Tessa did not want to leave him, even though he was becoming increasingly difficult. The ridiculous thing was that she still loved him.

What was that remark her mother had made this afternoon? "Marriage is relentless."

Yes, that was true. Absolutely true. And *he* was relentless, forever on her back about so many things to do with her mother and the stores, her power, her inheritance, her future in the hierarchy, and her money.

Tessa sighed to herself and got up, carried the remainder of the ingredients over to the stove. Her eye caught the clock on the wall, and she was startled to see it was well past eight. But then she had taken a long time preparing the various ingredients for her dinner. She wondered where Mark was as she added the rest of the items to the pot, stirred them, poured in the additional chicken broth and a bit more of the Beaujolais.

The coq au vin smelled delicious; it was going to come out well and Mark would be pleased. Replacing the lid, she set the table in the breakfast area before returning to the island.

Sitting down on the stool once more, Tessa poured the last of the red wine into her glass and took a sip absently, thinking of her mother and other aspects of their conversation. It suddenly struck her that Paula had looked upset, rattled when they had been discussing the succession, and she reflected on this for a while.

Tessa could not deny that Paula had been a good mother to her; she had been a good mother to all of her children, in fact. But there were times when Tessa resented her attitude. How easy it would be for Paula to make *her* life easy simply by naming her as the heir apparent . . . the Dauphine, as she liked to call herself, borrowing that French royal title. How she loved that word, it sang with power. But her mother was not going to do this. She had made that clear. At least she wasn't going to name Linnet. Or anyone else for that matter.

But wasn't her mother being a bit unfair? After all, she *was* the eldest of Paula's children and also a Fairley. It was family lore that Emma Harte had taken much of what had once belonged to the Fairleys, and so in Tessa's opinion, she was entitled to oversee those family businesses later, just as her mother did now.

The problem was her mother favored Linnet above all others, because she was her child by Shane. Tessa blew out air in a whoosh, suddenly irritated. Her mother blamed *her* for the sibling rivalry that existed between them, but it actually emanated from

Linnet, aided and abetted by India Standish and Gideon Harte. They egged her on, as they always had. But she had Toby on her side, and they had their plans well laid, and one day . . .

The sound of the front door slamming brought Tessa up with a start, and she looked eagerly toward the kitchen door, which stood ajar.

Tessa was determined to save her marriage, make it work . . . because that was what she wanted.

Eighteen

"Hello, darling," Tessa said as Mark walked into the kitchen. Giving him her most brilliant smile, she went on, "I was beginning to worry, you're so late." Sliding off the stool, she went to meet him, gave him a hug, but he was so unresponsive she let her arms fall to her sides. "Where have you been?" she now asked, her voice very quiet.

Pulling away from her, he answered gruffly, "On a bloody train, where the hell do you think I've been?" Making a face, he added, "Public transport is diabolical in this country these days."

"Yes," Tessa murmured, retreating to her stool.

His dark eyes followed her and instantly settled on the bottle of Beaujolais. He was at the island in two or three long strides, and he picked it up, shook it. "This bottle's *empty!* You've been drinking again!" he exclaimed, staring at her, his eyes suddenly full of icy disdain.

"You say that as if I'm an alcoholic, for heaven's sake. All I've had is a glass and a half. Most of that bottle of wine is in the coq au vin." Hoping to avert another outburst of nastiness, she flashed her winning smile again and explained, "I've made a big pot. I know how much you like it, darling."

Ignoring her words, he waved the bottle in front of her face and intoned in a dire voice, "It's a Fairley problem, *drink*. You don't want to end up like your father. Or worse still, your great-grandmother, Adele Fairley. She was so soused one night she fell down the stairs at Fairley Hall and broke her bloody neck." He shook his head, his expression more disdainful than ever. "What a family I've married into."

Tessa was gaping at him, totally taken aback. "Where on earth did that story come from? I've never heard it before, and if it were true I would have. Who told you such a terrible lie?"

Mark ran his hand through his already rumpled brownish blond hair and shrugged carelessly. A look of sudden indifference crossed his disgruntled face, and he muttered, *"I don't know.* But it doesn't matter who told me, it's a well-known fact the Fairleys were huge tipplers, renowned across the county for their drinking. So just watch yourself, do you hear? I won't have my daughter brought up by a drunken mother."

"Mark, stop this! And immediately. I've not even had two glasses of wine, and I rarely drink. *Ever.* You know it. So stop it right now!" Tessa was on her feet, regarding him intently, aware of some kind of implied threat behind his words. She was suddenly on her guard, asking herself if *he* had been drinking. And where had he been? This morning he had told her he was going out of town for the day. But where had he been *exactly?* And who with?

Mark had seated himself on one of the other stools, and he glanced at her and said in a lighter and more normal voice, "I'd like a vodka. Please fix one for me, darling."

Wanting to be conciliatory, Tessa smiled in relief, nodded, and hurried across to the cupboard where the liquor was stored. She returned with a bottle of Russian vodka, put it on the counter, took ice from the refrigerator, then stood at the island mixing a drink for him.

"Cheers," he said as he lifted the glass to his mouth and took a long swallow.

"Cheers." Tessa picked up her glass, which was now empty except for a few drops of wine. "Who was the client you went to see today?" she asked, trying to sound casual, not wishing to start another row.

"A chap up north," he muttered, staring into his drink absently, as if preoccupied.

"*Up north.* Were you in Yorkshire?" she asked, instantly suspicious, especially after his ramblings about Adele Fairley and her father.

"No, I meant the Midlands," he corrected himself, looking across at her. "I'm designing a house for him. Lots of money in it. For the firm." A strange, ironic smile struck his mouth, and he asked, "And what about your day? How did it go? Any quarrels with little sister? Did you talk to your mother? About the bloody succession? I know the answers to those questions. Rows with Linnet, I'm certain, just as I'm certain you haven't spoken to your mother. About when you're taking over as CEO."

Tessa was on the verge of telling him what had transpired but changed her mind. It would cause trouble, she was suddenly very sure of that. He was in a strange mood, and if he had not been drinking then he was definitely on something. She detected a change in him. It was ever so slight, but it was there.

Clearing her throat, she lied, "My mother had important meetings with the board today. I didn't get to see her at all. But I will, darling. Anyway, there's no problem, really, it's obvious I'm going to be the boss. I'm the eldest."

"Let's hope so." He swilled some of the vodka, then put the glass down and looked at her intently. "Is something burning?"

"Oh my God!" Tessa ran to the stove, lifted the lid on the pot, and peered inside. "No, nothing's burnt. It's all right. And the coq au vin looks great. You're going to enjoy it," she said, turning to him.

"I'm not hungry."

"Come on, Mark, you must eat something. You've been gone since dawn, and if I know you, lunch got skipped."

He did not respond. He simply stared at her morosely, his eyes glassy.

It took her a few minutes, but Tessa cajoled him and finally he went into the breakfast area and sat down at the table, nursing his vodka with both hands.

As she served spoonfuls of the coq au vin onto the plates which had been warming on top of the stove, he called out, "Bring a bottle of Beaujolais and I'll open it."

Muttering under her breath, she did as he asked, then continued to serve their dinner. Once she had put the plates on the table, she went into the kitchen again for the bread basket and butter dish. Finally she sat down with him.

He was struggling with the bottle opener but managed, awkwardly, to pull out the cork at last. He poured the wine sloppily, splashing some of it onto the table.

Observing him, Tessa thought of the way he had chastised her about drinking a short time before. He had obviously forgotten that, since he had filled her glass to overflowing. What's wrong with him? she wondered. Her guard went up once more, and she decided to remain silent.

Earlier Tessa had been hungry, but now her appetite had disappeared. Nonetheless, she put a forkful of chicken into her mouth. It was delicious, but her husband was making her feel so nervous she could barely swallow the food.

The slamming down of his fork made her sit up with a jerk. Swiftly she looked across at him. "Mark, what's wrong?"

"This is foul. I don't know what you've cooked, but it's disgusting. *Pig swill!*"

"But it's delicious," she exclaimed, then stopped speaking, not wanting to inflame him further. She felt a surge of panic.

"Don't argue with me, you bitch!" he yelled, his face growing red and contorted. He pushed the plate away so ferociously it slid across the glass table and fell to the floor with a crash.

Tessa did not dare make a move. She simply sat there staring at him, her eyes growing wide with surprise.

"Clean it up!" he shouted angrily. "Or I'll give you a thrashing you won't forget." He half-rose in his chair, raising his hand, and she leapt to her feet before he could touch her. She found the dustpan and brush and ran back to the breakfast area.

Kneeling down, she swept the food and the shattered plate into the dustpan and fled again, shaking inside. A moment later, she returned with a wet dishcloth, knelt, and washed the sticky mess off the polished parquet floor.

Unexpectedly, and so suddenly she went into shock, she felt his hand gripping the back of her neck. He was standing over her, and she sensed, rather than saw, the menace in him. He tightened his grip on her neck.

"Please let go of me, Mark," she said, her voice soft, cajoling.

"What's going on between you and Toby Harte?" he demanded. "You'd better tell me, bitch!"

"Nothing's going on. We're family, we've been best friends since childhood, you know that," she answered as evenly as possible. Staying calm and controlled was important, she realized.

"What I hear is that you're more than friends," he hissed, squeezing her neck even harder. "What I hear is that he's in your knickers and has been since you were kids."

"That's not true, and you know it," she cried. "He's my cousin, for God's sake."

"Ha! Fat lot that means! Par for the course, I'd say, the way your bunch marry each other. Talk about an incestuous lot, your bloody family takes first prize."

"Don't be ridiculous, there's nothing between Toby and me —"

"Daddy! Daddy!" Adele squealed, running into the breakfast area in her nightgown, dragging her rag doll Aggie by its arm.

Instantly Mark let go of Tessa and rushed to his daughter. He gathered her up in his arms, held her close to him. "Hello, sweetheart," he whispered against her softly curling blond hair. "How's Daddy's special little girl? Are you all right, my pet?"

"Yes." She nuzzled her face against his, then said, "Come see my doll, Daddy."

"But I can see her," he responded, taking hold of the rag doll she was dangling in one hand.

"No, new doll," Adele said.

Tessa, who had immediately jumped up and retreated to the safety of the kitchen, explained quickly, "I bought her a doll today. It's upstairs in her bedroom."

Mark glanced at Tessa. "I'll be back in a few minutes," he murmured, and once again his voice sounded much more normal.

That's for the benefit of Adele, Tessa thought, as she watched his retreating figure, wondering how long he would be gone. She was terrified, and she didn't know what to do. Her initial thought was to flee to Toby's flat. But Mark had Adele with him, and she could not leave her child behind. Her eyes flew to her handbag on the far counter. Her cell phone was in it. But who should she call? Toby would come immediately, and if she called Shane he would be here as fast as possible. Yet she did not want either of them to know about Mark's treatment of her.

Wait it out. See what happens, her inner voice told her. But she understood that she must be cautious, and very alert.

After fifteen minutes, when Mark had not returned to the kitchen, Tessa went out to the hall and climbed the stairs, being as quiet as possible. As she crept down the corridor, she saw that the door of Adele's room was open, light shining out, and she held her breath until she got there. All was still inside the room. When she finally tiptoed in, she saw that Adele was fast asleep, clutching the rag doll to her and sucking her thumb.

Bending over her daughter, Tessa smoothed the fair hair from her face and turned off the bedside lamp but left the small night-light burning.

Once she had closed Adele's door behind her, Tessa continued down the corridor to their bedroom. The door was half open, and she pushed it, peered inside. Mark, half undressed, was sprawled across the bed. Snoring, he was in a drunken or drugged sleep.

After closing the bedroom door, Tessa stood in the corridor, debating what to do. Finally she decided to sleep on the single bed which had been put in Adele's room for her or Elvira to use if Adele was ever sick. She knew Mark would never harm their child, so she deemed Adele's room the safest place to be.

★ ★ ★

Tessa lay under the duvet cover, fully dressed except for her cashmere blazer and shoes, and clutching her cell phone in one hand.

Although she had locked Adele and herself in the child's room, she found it impossible to relax. But over the next hour Mark did not emerge from their bedroom. Silence reigned throughout the house.

Eventually she dozed off from sheer exhaustion, and it was only when a glimmering of light began to seep in through the windows that she awakened with a start, for a second feeling out of sorts and disoriented. Then she remembered her husband's strange behavior the night before.

Mark had always had a tendency to be volatile; he was excitable, and even abrasive at times, but it was only in the last six months that he had become verbally and physically abusive, and this had both startled and alarmed her.

She remembered that there had often been unspoken criticism in Mark's attitude toward her, plus a superiority in his manner in the last few years. The superiority had amused her because she was nothing if not self-confident, a trait which she knew she had inherited from her great-grandmother Emma Harte via her grandmother Daisy and her mother. Intimidation rolled off her back like water, and she could be wonderfully articulate if she had to defend herself. The only thing that could make her truly apprehensive was physical violence directed at her daughter. Or her.

Last weekend a quarrel had erupted between her and Mark about who would succeed her mother. In the heat of the moment Mark had lunged at her, as if to punch her in the face. She had adroitly sidestepped him, but then she had tripped and fallen down the six steps that led to the lower-level larder.

He had been at once chagrined, had rushed to pick her up, looking scared and worried. The result of the fall had been her heavily bruised shoulder and upper arm, which her mother had looked at yesterday, appalled and concerned.

This was one of the few times her husband had gone for her in that way during their entire marriage, and she had been shaken to the core. Mark was not the easiest of men, but he had rarely displayed any violence in the past.

Now she contemplated the events of the night before. He might well have become really violent if she had not remained calm and in control of herself, and if little Adele had not walked in precisely when she did. The unexpected appearance of his adored child had evidently brought Mark to his senses.

Tessa was now certain he had been

drinking earlier in the evening, and convinced he was on something else as well, some sort of designer drug rather than hard stuff like cocaine or heroin. Normally he held his drink extremely well. But last night his eyes had been actually glazed over, and he had gone rapidly through several mood swings. She had seen a whole new Mark.

She would have to ask Toby about drugs. As a high-powered executive running a television network, he probably knew quite a lot about them, and if *he* didn't, Gideon surely would. She knew that neither of her cousins would go anywhere near drugs. They had always needed to be in control, of themselves and others, and they were too driven and work-oriented to indulge in substances of oblivion. But in their line of business they would have a certain amount of information at their disposal.

She wondered, suddenly, if she ought to confide in Toby after all. He was the closest to her, except for Lorne. But *they* were tight because they were twins, and Lorne might easily tell their mother about Mark if she took him into her confidence. A still tongue, a wise head, that had been her motto for years. Tell no one . . .

Adele murmured in her sleep and turned over, and Tessa threw off the duvet, swung her feet to the floor, and almost stepped on the cell phone, which must have fallen out of her hand during the night. After looking down at Adele, smoothing her hair gently from her face, smiling with pleasure and love for this gorgeous child of hers, Tessa covered her with the eiderdown, then stepped across the room.

Unlocking the door, she went along the corridor, being careful not to make a noise. It was unusually quiet. Glancing at her watch, she saw that it was just a few minutes past six.

Moving carefully, Tessa paused at their bedroom door, opened it gently, and looked inside. Mark was still passed out, sprawling diagonally across their bed, in almost the same position as last night. Hardly daring to breathe, she closed the door as quietly as possible and continued down the corridor to her own suite.

This was a set of private rooms she had designed herself; she'd had to fight Mark about it but had finally won. It consisted of a fully equipped office, a small gym, a luxurious bathroom, and a huge dressing room, where her clothes hung in well-organized perfection. Also housed there were her shoes, handbags, scarves, shawls, and other accessories. It was her private domain, and it gave her a great deal of pleasure. Perfectionist that she was, she loved to have everything scrupulously arranged.

After a quick shower, Tessa blow-dried her

hair and then sat down at the dressing table to put on makeup. A short while later she went to one of the closets and selected a tailored gray pin-striped pantsuit and a pale blue man-tailored cotton shirt. Within minutes she was hurrying down to the kitchen. After putting on the coffee, she quickly stacked the dishwasher with a few remaining items from last night's cooking, turned it on, threw out the coq au vin, which had congealed overnight, and made herself a slice of toast.

She was halfway through her first cup of coffee when Mark appeared. His hair was still damp from the shower, and he was freshly shaved, dressed in a white shirt, open at the neck, and dark blue trousers. He carried the jacket of his suit and a dark blue tie.

He hesitated fractionally when he saw her, his step seeming to falter; then he recouped and came toward her, a feeble smile playing on his face. After putting the jacket and tie on one of the stools at the island counter, he came around to her side and stood looking down at her, forcing the smile to become a little wider. "Good morning."

When there was no response, he said in a low, contrite voice, "I'm sorry, Tessa darling. I can't remember exactly what happened last night, but when I woke up not long ago I realized I'd probably behaved badly."

Still she remained silent.

He stared, focusing all of his attention on her. "I did, didn't I? Behave badly, I mean. Please tell me what happened. I'm so troubled. . . . We had a row, didn't we?"

"No, we didn't," she said, speaking at last, leveling her steady gaze at him, her face icy cold, her eyes the color of steel.

"*Oh,*" was all he could say. He went and poured himself a cup of coffee, carried the mug back to the island. He stood next to her, drinking it. After a split second, he murmured, "I thought we'd had a quarrel, because I found myself on top of the bed, almost fully dressed, and obviously the bed hadn't been slept in . . . and you were gone."

"Only too true." Tessa let out a sigh. "We didn't have a row, Mark, but you did behave very badly. You came home in an extremely belligerent mood and tried to pick a fight. Your behavior was extraordinary, very strange, in fact, and I thought you were not only drunk but *on* something. You were, weren't you?"

He shook his head vehemently. "No, no, not at all. I'd had a couple of drinks, that's true, but if you're implying I'd taken drugs, or some kind of . . . *substance,* then you're totally mistaken. *Totally.*"

"But there *was* something terribly wrong with you! Your eyes were glazed over and your manner was so erratic." She decided to tell him everything that had happened the night before. And when it came to his physical attack, how he had held her neck in a viselike grip when she was on the floor, she pulled no punches.

Tessa could see that he remembered bits and pieces of what had transpired because he nodded his head several times. Shame and remorse hung heavy on him. "Oh my God! Tessa, I'm so sorry, so terribly sorry. All I can think of is that I took some cold pills on the train. Perhaps they had a bad effect on me, especially since I did have a few drinks afterwards. You see, I thought I was coming down with the flu, and I bought some cold pills at the station . . . swilled them down with Scotch. It was stupid. *I was stupid.*"

Although he was obviously ashamed and wanted to make amends to her, Tessa knew that he was lying. About the cold pills, at least — it was such a phony story. But she remained absolutely cool and unresponsive to his protestations of innocence and his abundance of contrition.

"Who did you meet yesterday?" she asked after a few sips of coffee. She stared at him over the rim of the mug, her silvery gray eyes penetrating, challenging.

"I told you, darling. A client." Mark sat down opposite her and put his coffee mug on the countertop.

"But you didn't say who the client is.

What's his name?" she pressed.

"Oh, I thought I told you before. His name is William Stone, and he's apparently filthy rich. I've designed a house for him . . . he calls it the house of his dreams."

"And where is this dream house?"

"In the Midlands. I thought I'd told you that." He frowned at her.

"Did you drink with him before you left? Maybe that would explain your disastrous condition."

"What do you mean?"

"If you drank with your Mr. Stone and then drank on the train, maybe you were drunker than you realized."

"Possibly." He shook his head and leaned across the counter, taking her hand in his. "Listen, Tessa, I'm truly sorry. This whole thing has been painful, very painful for me to listen to. Please, darling, say you accept my apology. I promise it won't happen again. You know I adore you. Upsetting you is the last thing I want to do. I love you, Tessa."

She stared into his face, remained silent. Despite his bloodshot eyes, he looked surprisingly boyish. Perhaps it was the pink flush on his cheeks or maybe his open shirt; it had always been part of his charm, that collegiate look of his, and his sincerity. Although she was never quite sure if that was genuine.

Finally nodding her head slowly, Tessa said, "I forgive you, Mark." But will I ever forget? she asked herself. Then to him, she added, "But it can't happen again. If you ever again become physically violent with me as you did last night, I'll leave you. Divorce you. I won't stand for that, you know. And neither will Paula and Shane." She had thrown their names into the mix just to remind him of who she was, and who stood behind her. If nothing else, he understood the meaning of money and power, of *clout,* as he usually referred to it.

Mark smiled in relief. He took her hand again, brought it to his mouth, kissed her fingers. "I'm truly, truly sorry. And it will never, *ever* happen again, I promise you, Tessa." His eyes did not leave her face as he added, "I'm so utterly ashamed of myself."

The sound of the key in the back door made them both sit up a little straighter, and Tessa exclaimed, "Oh it's Mrs. Jolles. Elvira asked her to come in early today."

"Why's that?" Mark asked, frowning.

"Because I have to go to work, and so do you, and Elvira had to go home last night to look after her mother."

"Morning all," Mrs. Jolles called. "Don't disturb yourselves, finish your breakfasts. I'll go and see to Adele."

Nineteen

Gideon sat waiting for Evan in the sitting room of the small hotel in Belgravia where she lived. From the moment he walked in he had been struck by the decor, the refinement and good taste that abounded in the entrance hall and here.

Now, as he sat on the sofa near the fire, he glanced around, thinking how charming and well appointed the room was. There were some lovely landscapes on the walls, and the entire ambience was pleasant and restful.

Gideon sighed and stretched out his long legs. He was feeling a little weary. It had been a trying week at the newspaper. The only good thing was that Christian Palmer was becoming more amenable about working for the *London Evening Post* again. It was all a question of negotiation, and settling the time off Christian needed. His book was practically finished, and after that he would be at liberty to work for them. Possibly it would have to be part-time, but Gideon and his father knew this was better than not having him onboard at all.

His thoughts swung to Evan. He could hardly believe his luck. That he had found her was something of a miracle to him. He had fallen heavily, and he knew she had, too; he had laughed the other day when she called their coming together a *coup de foudre* because he had thought the same thing earlier. When he told her this, she, too, had been amused. "Well, great minds think alike," he had murmured, squeezing her hand. She was not only lovely to look at but charming, and bright and intelligent, and they always had fun together. He never felt bored with her, as he had with so many other women, and they were compatible on every level.

There was one thing that worried him about her, and this was her occasional sadness. It seemed to him that a strange melancholy overtook her at times, and he couldn't help asking himself what caused that change in her. Though they had not discussed it, Gideon thought it had nothing to do with them but came from another area of her life.

A moment later she was walking into the sitting room, her cheeks dimpling prettily as her smile grew wider.

Gideon jumped to his feet as she stopped. She kissed him on his cheek and then said, "I'm sorry I kept you waiting. I was late at the store."

"That cousin of mine is a genuine slave driver!" he murmured, squeezing her arm.

"She is a bit, but I don't mind," Evan replied. "I'm inclined to be a workaholic, as you well know. I'm late because I decided to change after all, even though you said it didn't matter."

He smiled, glanced at her appraisingly. "You look wonderful, but then you always do. Come on, I'm starving. I can't wait to get a knife and fork into some wonderful roast lamb."

"Where are you taking me?" Evan asked as he led her out of the sitting room, through the hall, and out into the street.

"The Dorchester. They have the best roast leg of lamb and roast beef in London." Gideon raised his hand, flagged down a taxi, and helped her in. After giving the cabbie the name of the hotel, he took her hand in his and kissed it. "I've missed you."

Evan turned to him, raising a dark brow. "But you saw me yesterday."

"I know. But I've still missed you in the meantime."

Smiling to herself, she leaned back against the leather seat, wondering if she should tell him she had missed him, too. She missed him whenever they were not together; it was, in fact, a state of affairs that was entirely new to her. But she remained silent.

Within a few minutes they were pulling up in front of the hotel, and the doorman, dressed in green with a tall hat, was opening the cab door and helping her out. "Evening, madame," he said in a friendly voice.

"Good evening," Evan answered and went up the steps, stood waiting as Gideon paid for the taxi.

Inside the hotel, he guided her to the coatroom, and once they had checked their coats they went across the hall to the Grill Room. Instantly, they were seated, and Gideon looked at her and asked, "What would you like to drink?"

"A glass of white wine would be nice, thank you."

Beckoning to a waiter, Gideon ordered her white wine, and a vodka and tonic for himself. When they were alone he confided, "I've had such a heavy day, I need a good strong drink. But I'm happy to say I think Christian Palmer is now seriously thinking about coming back, if only part-time. We'll be glad to have him."

"Oh, that's wonderful. I'm so pleased for you, Gideon. You've wanted this so much."

"And Dad has, too. We're kind of chuffed about it . . . that means, well . . . *pleased,* in case you didn't know."

"But I did. My grandmother often used that word, especially when I was growing up and did something she deemed wonderful. That's when she would tell me she was *chuffed.*"

Their drinks materialized; Gideon lifted his

glass, touched hers, and said cheers. So did Evan.

The Grill Room was busy. Gideon glanced around, but there was no one there he knew. Turning to Evan, he said, "The trolleys over there have the best roasts. Are you going to join me in the roast leg of lamb?"

"I think I will."

"And to start?"

"Oysters."

"Snap. I'm having the same."

Now it was Evan's turn to take in the surroundings. She liked this room, with its dark wood furniture, large tapestries on the walls, its sense of timelessness, its very Englishness. "You come here a lot, don't you, Gideon?"

"Yes, I do. I like the tasty English food they serve, the roasts, the wonderful soups, the potted shrimps and the oysters. But quite aside from the food, it's sort of . . . well, a family hotel. I don't mean it belongs to the O'Neill hotel chain that Shane owns and operates, but *family* in the sense that we've all favored the Dorchester for donkey's years."

"Oh really, why is that?"

"From what I understand, it goes back to the years during the Second World War. My great-grandmother used to come here all the time, as did most of the elegant upper-crust Londoners. My father told me that it was considered the safest hotel in London because of the way it was built. In any event, she came often, and so did her brothers, and the O'Neills. It's kind of —"

"A home away from home," she suggested.

"That's right," he answered with a laugh.

The waiter came, and Gideon ordered for them both. Then he turned to Evan and said quietly, "There's something I've wanted to talk to you about, Evan, but I haven't really dared. Now I think we know each other well enough, and it *is* something that troubles me."

"But what is it? And of course we can discuss it, Gideon." She stared at him intently, a worried expression settling in her eyes. When he remained silent she touched his hand lightly and said, "I've felt right from our first date that we could talk about anything, tell each other anything. . . . Say what you're thinking, Gid."

"There are times when I seem to lose you, Evan," he began, taking her hand in his. "What I'm trying to say is that there are occasions when you become pensive, melancholy really, and you seem to drift off to a faraway place. I don't seem able to reach you for a while. In fact, it's only when you come out of it that we're normal again. I was wondering . . . well, is there something worrying you?"

"Not about us, or you, if that's what you mean," she was quick to reassure him. Clearing her throat, she added, "I do worry about my mother quite a lot. Perhaps that's what you're detecting in me."

"Possibly." He looked puzzled. "Why do you worry about your mother? Is there something wrong with her?"

Taking a deep breath, Evan answered, "My mother suffers from depression. Actually, she's been diagnosed as a manic-depressive, and she's on medication all the time."

"Oh, Evan, I'm so sorry," he murmured, his voice sympathetic. "Is this a recent ailment?"

"No, it isn't. Mom's been depressed for as long as I can remember, from when I was a small child. It was after my parents adopted Angharad . . . that's when her mood swings began. At least that's how I remember it. And that's why my grandmother Glynnis used to come and stay, to look after us and look after my father. I worry about him a lot, too."

"I'm sure you do; that kind of illness is really hard on a family."

"Do you know something about it?" she asked, a brow lifting questioningly.

"Not really, but I do know a couple of people who are manic-depressives, old friends of mine, and of course I've read about famous people who were sufferers. Sir Winston Churchill for one. He called his depressions Black Dog. He fought against them all of his life . . . that's why he had such a rigorous routine, kept himself extremely busy, hoping to sidestep his depression, I guess."

"I understand." Evan shook her head, looked away for a moment, then said in a low, confiding voice, "I often worry that I might get to be like my mother. Do you think that's why *I* keep myself so terribly busy, why I'm a workaholic?"

"Out of fear?" he asked. "Fear that you might have inherited it, that you might become a manic-depressive, too?"

"Yes."

Gideon made a face, shook his head. "I've got to admit I don't know the answer. But my family are all workaholics, overachievers, and none of them suffer from depression. I don't, and I'm just like you when it comes to work." He squeezed her hand. "Try not to worry so much about your parents. They have each other, and presumably take care of each other. Your mother's not in hospital, is she?"

"Oh no, she's at home. And there are days when she's much better —"

Evan broke off as the waiter arrived to serve their plates of oysters. When they were alone again Evan murmured, "I hadn't realized I was drifting off like that when I was with you, Gid, I'm sorry."

"No need to be sorry. Anyway, talking about it has cleared the air. Now that I understand it makes everything easier."

Between swallowing the delicious Colchester oysters they talked about other things, but at one moment Gideon said, "Is Tessa still being difficult with you?"

Evan shook her head. "It's not that she was ever difficult. Well, to be honest, she was snotty, a bit uppity. These days she just sort of . . . ignores me." Evan began to laugh. "I don't care. It worries India at times, and Linnet also, but I told them her attitude is not important. I don't work directly with her. And Linnet and India are both wonderful to me."

"I know. Tessa's like that with everybody. She has a sense of superiority that is most annoying," Gideon explained. "It doesn't mean anything, so don't *personalize* it. Mind you, I bet she's a bit jealous that Linnet has another assistant."

"That's what India said the other day."

"I'm glad you're enjoying working at Harte's, enjoying my cousins." He grinned at her. "They're the best — kind, loving, nice to be around, aren't they?"

"I'll say! And we have a lot of fun together when we're working. They've made me feel at home. I hope Linnet's going to keep me on after the retrospective's finished. It would be hard for me to work anywhere else after being with them at Harte's."

"I'm sure you don't have to worry," Gideon said.

Twenty

Toby Harte sat listening attentively to everything his cousin Tessa Fairley was saying. He always thought of her as Fairley rather than Longden, and he suspected this was because he was not a huge fan of her husband.

When she finally paused for breath, Toby asked, with a frown, "Why are you suddenly so interested in drugs? You of all people, Miss Goody Two-shoes. Do you have a suspicion Mark is on something? There can't be any other reason."

Although she was taken aback by this question, she realized she ought not to be. Toby was one of the shrewdest people in her orbit, and he knew her better than anyone. Clearing her throat, she said, "I'm not sure that he's on drugs, to be honest, Toby. But he could be. He came home a couple of nights ago in a very strange state. Glassy eyed, erratic, trying to pick a quarrel. He'd been drinking, I knew that. He was quite drunk, I'd say —"

"*In vino veritas*, eh?" Toby cut in, raising a dark brow.

"Perhaps. And yet I was suspicious because he was somehow . . . well, *different*."

"Did you question him about his behavior the next morning?"

"Oh yes. He said something about having taken cold pills, and that he had then had several drinks on the train. He suggested the combination must have created a problem. I certainly didn't believe *that* story."

"I don't blame you. Neither do I." Toby stood up, walked across Tessa's office, stood looking out the window which fronted onto Knightsbridge far below. After a moment he swung around and said, "You mentioned he'd had drinks on the train. Where had he been?"

"To see a new client. In the Midlands. He sounded rather chuff about that; it's a big job for him. A grand house apparently. The client's filthy rich, so Mark said."

"What's his name?"

"William Stone. Some sort of tycoon, I think."

"Never heard of him." Toby shrugged. "Not that that means anything. There's a lot of wealth around these days that nobody knows anything about." He strode back to the chair opposite Tessa's desk, sat down, and continued, "If he *was* on something, it was more than likely a designer drug. Probably Ecstasy, that's still very popular."

"What exactly *is* it?" Tessa asked.

"Ecstasy's a party drug, and popular because it creates a rush, a high, and very quickly, so I'm told. But it can be hallucinogenic, and even creates paranoia in some people. Basically, it's a stimulant."

"Is it hard to get?"

"Not if you know where to go."

"Mark doesn't seem a likely candidate for drugs. . . . He does work very hard, and he's made the firm a success."

Toby nodded, then smiled at her. "Perhaps he was just very, very drunk, darling," he suggested, wanting to make her feel better.

"Maybe you're right. Nevertheless, he was awfully weird."

Gazing across the desk at her, Toby thought that she did not look well this afternoon. Her face was drained of color, and in combination with the halo of silvery blond hair, her pale skin made her look like a ghost. But perhaps it was the black suit she was wearing; the color certainly emphasized her pallor and delicacy. Yet there had always been a certain fragility about Tessa; it was one of the reasons he had fallen so easily into the role of protector when they were children. Despite this physical frailness, she was strong mentally.

Toby knew how tough Tessa could be. He admired his cousin, and he had always loved her. To him her *only* fault was her inability to disguise her true feelings, most especially when it came to her sister Linnet. She was competitive with her and seemed to have no idea how to conceal this. The art of dissimulation, apparently one of their great-grandmother's most important assets, had seemingly escaped Tessa.

"You're suddenly very quiet, Toby."

"I was thinking about Mark. He wasn't abusive, was he?" Toby sounded worried, and his dark eyes reflected a sudden fierceness.

"Oh no, nothing like that!" she lied. It would embarrass her to tell Toby the truth. She was aware he would seek Mark out, take him to task or worse, beat him up. Toby had always defended her.

"Now *you're* suddenly quiet," he remarked, staring hard at her.

Tessa gave him the benefit of a wide and loving smile. "You know how mad you get when someone reminds you that you don't look like a Harte?"

"Oh yes, the changeling, that's me," he muttered sarcastically.

"I saw a photo recently of Emma's father, Big Jack Harte, and *that's* who you look like, Toby."

Startled, he said, "I do? Are you sure?"

Tessa didn't answer. Instead she opened her desk drawer and took out an ancient photograph of a tall, well-built, darkly handsome man standing next to a younger man in Royal Navy uniform. It was obviously father

297

and son. She handed the picture to Toby.

He stared down at it with interest, then lifted his head, looked at her. "Where did you get this?"

"I took it out of an old album in the library at Pennistone Royal a few weeks ago. I was up visiting the Leeds and Harrogate stores, and I spent the night there. I was alone, except for Emsie, who was doing her homework, and I went to the library to browse. Actually, I was hoping to find a few pictures of Aunt Edwina when she was young; that's when I came across that particular photograph. I was instantly aware of the striking resemblance you bear to the older man in particular."

"How do you know it's our great-great-grandfather?"

"Look on the back."

He did as she suggested and read out loud the words written in now-faded black ink. "My father, Jack Harte, and my brother Winston when he was in the Royal Navy."

"That's certainly Grandy Emma's handwriting, Toby."

"So I see." He offered her the photograph.

Tessa shook her head. "I don't want it. I brought it for you. Please keep it."

"Are you sure? After all, it might be missed."

"Who's going to look through an old album? There are a lot of them in the library. They're all covered in faded red velvet or fancy tooled leather with big brass clasps. Anyway, I think you ought to have it because it absolutely proves you look like a Harte." She began to laugh and went on, "Like the founding father, actually. Isn't that one for the books."

"Let's have tea," Tessa said to Toby, as her secretary, Claire Remsford, came into her office carrying a laden tray. Tessa rose and crossed the room to the small seating area near the windows.

"Thanks, Claire," she murmured. Then she exclaimed, "Oh that's so nice! You ordered some chocolate fingers. Toby loves them."

"Yes, I know," Claire replied as she went toward the door.

Toby grinned at her, remarking, "You certainly know how to get to a man's heart, Claire."

Laughing, blushing, Tessa's secretary exited, and Toby joined Tessa, sitting down in one of the armchairs. "No milk for me," he told her, "and I'll have a sweetener instead of sugar. I'm on a diet."

She gave him a surreptitious glance. "But I bet you'll guzzle all of those chocolate fingers."

"Not all of them, I'll save a few for you," he shot back, laughing.

"I spoke to my mother the other day,"

Tessa confided as she poured the tea. "About who her successor will be." And she told him about their conversation.

"The one good thing is she didn't say Linnet was going to inherit. In fact, she said it might not be either of us but someone else in the family."

"There isn't anyone else," Toby asserted, putting his cup down with a clatter. "And I know it's going to be *you,* Tessa. Aunt Paula wouldn't cheat you out of your right, just as Dad won't cheat me. I'm the eldest, and I'm going to inherit the Yorkshire Consolidated Newspaper Company and its subsidiaries. Gideon will continue to run the papers, but *I'll* be the head of the media company in Dad's place. My baby brother will be working for me, just as Linnet will be working for you. That's if she's still at Harte's."

Tessa frowned, looked at him curiously. "What're you getting at? Of course she'll be at Harte's. She's very ambitious."

"And very involved . . . in love with Julian Kallinski. She might well be married and the mother of a brood of bairns by the time Aunt Paula steps down."

"She and Julian broke up —"

"They're back together, my sweet," he interrupted.

"How do you know? Oh, I might well ask. . . . Gideon told you."

"No, he didn't. I saw Linnet and Julian having dinner at Harry's Bar the other night. Mind you, Gideon was with them, along with the dark-haired girl —"

"Evan Hughes! I heard on the store grapevine that she's having an affair with Gid. She works fast, doesn't she? She met him in January, it's only the end of March, and they're already bedding down together. My, my."

Toby nodded. "It looks as if they're very tight. Gideon hung on her every word. I've never seen him so . . . well, captivated. It's always been love 'em and leave 'em with him. I used to call him the champion of one-night standers, don't you remember?"

"Yes, I do. What do you think of Evan?" Tessa asked.

"I've only met her briefly, so I can't really pass judgment."

"Do you think she looks like Mummy? A lot of people do."

Toby sat back, his expression turning thoughtful, sipping his tea and then munching on a chocolate biscuit. After a moment, he answered her. "At first glance Evan is the spitting image of Aunt Paula, but when one studies her for a few minutes one realizes it's all an illusion. The same exotic, dark coloring, the same height, the same figure, even similar clothes, but there it definitely stops. Because her face isn't at all like your mother's; the shape is different, and she doesn't have violet eyes, or the famous Harte widow's peak."

"Shane himself did a double take," Tessa announced, giving him a pointed look.

Toby pursed his lips, shook his head. "I bet he did exactly what I did, looked quickly, registered surprise, then realized it was only an illusion."

"*I* think she might be related to us."

"You *do*? But how could she be?" Toby sounded surprised.

"I've figured it out. . . . Through Paul McGill, Mummy's grandfather. He spent a lot of time in America and Australia, and without Emma. He could easily have had an affair with someone else, probably in America, and that woman could have given birth to a child, and Evan could be an offspring of Paul McGill's American child. His grandchild." After this explanation, Tessa sat back. "Well, what do you think?"

"It's a possibility. I hadn't thought of the Paul McGill side," Toby answered, "I must admit that."

"Maybe she came here to try to get something, you know, some kind of inheritance."

"Don't be daft! It's all lashed together with steel ropes. Emma Harte saw to that, and then your mother, my parents, and Aunt Amanda followed her lead and her instructions to the nth degree. In fact, they took many more precautions, as you know. That's

302

why it's a bit of a joke the way the seniors are upset because the notorious Jonathan Ainsley has returned to England. He can't get anything either — well, maybe a few shares of Harte Stores that are traded on the London Stock Exchange."

Tessa nodded. "I overheard my mother talking to your mother yesterday. She'd come over for a meeting with Linnet and Mummy about the birthday party in June. Apparently Mummy put a private investigator on him, but nothing untoward has been turned up so far."

"And perhaps it won't. Maybe he's just come back to live here because he prefers London, and to be near his father. Uncle Robin's quite frail, I hear. Of course Jonathan will inherit his father's money, and that's a fortune."

"But Uncle Robin was a Member of Parliament all his life, a politician. I didn't know he had a *fortune*."

"Emma loved him, despite his misdeeds at certain times. He *was* her favorite son, and I happen to know she not only created a trust for him but gave him quite a lot before she died."

"You obviously know more than I do."

"I do know one thing, Tessa darling. It's going to be you and me running this show one day. You'll be head of the stores, and I'll be at the helm of the media companies. We'll

rule the Harte empire and dynasty together."
He smiled broadly, full of confidence.

Rising, Toby went to join Tessa on the sofa. He put his arms around her, pulled her to him, kissed her lightly on the cheek. "Everything's going to be ours, Tess. Trust me."

"I do. But my mother's not going to retire as soon as you think, I just told you that. I'll be an old lady when I inherit."

"Tessa, life is full of surprises. Nobody knows what's in store. Anything can happen, and when we least expect it. Your mother might retire in a few years, for reasons we don't know now, reasons she herself doesn't know now. People suddenly run out of steam, or want to retire after all, want to enjoy life. They might want to have a bit of fun. God knows, our parents have worked like dogs all of their lives, so there are many reasons why they could change their minds. As Ma always says, the only thing that's permanent is change. I feel that way about Dad. He could decide he's fed up and pass the mantle to me overnight. *We don't know anything.* So stay cool, my sweet, and for God's sake stop being mean to Linnet. When she marries Julian her life will change, and so will yours."

"*If* she marries him."

"Oh, she will, take my word for it. The grandfathers O'Neill and Kallinski are going to push it for all it's worth now that those two lovebirds are back together. They want the three clans to be forever bound. So please, give Linnet some slack, and stop complaining about her endlessly. It makes you look bad."

"She irritates me," Tessa responded, not daring to confide how much she loathed her half sister.

"I know she does, but it gets other people angry with you, and then they favor her, and you can't afford that. You don't need any enemies in the family. You must learn to be like our sainted great-grandmother. You must learn to dissemble the way Emma did."

"I'll try," she answered, knowing he was right.

"Good girl." Toby tightened his grip on her, hugging her warmly.

Tessa flinched.

He pulled away, giving her a puzzled look. "What's wrong?"

She shook her head. "It's just my shoulder, Toby, I hurt it last week." She forced a smile. "In the gym," she added swiftly when she saw that fierce, protective look enter his eyes. Leaning into him, she kissed his cheek. "It's just a bit sore."

"Are you sure he hasn't hurt you?" Toby demanded, the look he gave her full of concern.

"No, no, he wouldn't do that."

"I wish you hadn't married him," he muttered when they drew apart, smoothing his hand over her silver-gilt hair. He cared about her very much, loathed the idea that anyone could hurt her in any way. "I can't imagine why you had to make it legal."

Tessa sighed. "I wonder sometimes why I did . . ."

They were silent, their arms wrapped around each other, for a moment lost in their thoughts. They had once been childhood sweethearts, and some of those feelings remained, however much they both denied them. But there had never been a sexual relationship between them. When Mark had suggested otherwise, Tessa had spoken the truth in denying it.

"How's Adrianna?" she asked, breaking the silence.

"Fine. She's still in Hollywood making that movie."

"Why did you marry her?"

"It seemed like a good idea at the time," he replied with a rueful laugh.

At the low buzzing of the phone, Tessa jumped up, hurried over to her desk, lifted the receiver. "Hello?"

"It's me, Tessa," Linnet said. "I wonder if you can spare me a few minutes, please."

It was on the tip of her tongue to say no. But looking across at Toby, Tessa decided to take his advice. "That's fine, Linnet. When do you want to come to my office?"

"Well, more or less now, if that's all right."

"I'm here with Toby. He came in to ask my help about choosing birthday gifts for our fathers, and I suppose he'll be leaving soon."

"Thanks," Linnet said and hung up.

"How did I do?" Tessa asked, staring at her cousin, then sitting down at her desk.

"You did good, kid!" he said, adopting an American accent. "Real good."

Twenty-one

Toby's manners were bred in the bone, and he rose when Linnet came into the office, moved swiftly across the floor. They met in the middle of the room, and he gave her a light kiss on the cheek and asked, "How's the retrospective coming along?"

"Very well, thanks, Toby." Linnet smiled at him, then swung around and walked over to Tessa's desk, where she sat down and looked across at her sister. She said in a friendly voice, "The reason I wanted to see you, Tessa, is actually to do with the retrospective. I was wondering if you'd lend us some of your couture clothes."

"But I don't have much couture!" Tessa exclaimed, almost too sharply. Catching herself, she adopted a milder tone. "Hardly any at all, Linnet, and anyway I don't think the things I have are in good enough condition to be put on display. I've worn them to death."

"I was thinking of those two evening coats you own. We're still a bit thin on the vintage stuff, and you have that gorgeous coral silk coat with a shoulder cape attached designed by Norman Hartnell. You once told me it was from the 1960s, and there's the Balmain coat Mummy gave you, which belonged to Emma. I think that's from the mid-fifties. Could we borrow those two things, do you think? They would fill a gap."

Tessa's first instinct was to refuse. She had genuinely been against the retrospective from the beginning. She had believed it to be a waste of time, effort, and money. But Toby was watching her like a hawk. Anyway, he had been right earlier. She must be more diplomatic, not so obviously competitive and seemingly against Linnet. She was definitely going to have to watch herself, keep a rein on her temper, and be much more patient. The problem was she found it hard to pretend, thought doing so was two-faced, even though Toby called it dissimulation and admired anyone who had the ability.

Pushing a pleasant smile onto her face, Tessa said, "Of course you can borrow them, but I don't know how pristine they are."

"Oh, thanks very much, Tess!" Linnet said, then continued, "I really appreciate it, and don't worry about the condition of the coats. Evan's wonderfully talented when it comes to restoration, and she's very clever at hand-cleaning, repairing, steaming and pressing, that kind of thing. Your coats will come back to you looking like new. You'll be impressed with her work, everyone is."

"Really," Tessa murmured, and she understood immediately that her sister admired and liked Evan. I bet she's given Evan Hughes her stamp of approval as far as Gideon's concerned.

Linnet, in her usual businesslike manner, rushed on. "Look, I'm very sorry there was a misunderstanding between us about the use of the auditorium. I hadn't realized you had planned a management meeting that morning I'd arranged for the space planning company to measure the areas where the platforms are to be built. I just couldn't stop them from coming. It was already too late."

"I understand, and it's no problem," Tessa answered, endeavoring to appear nonchalant, although at the time she had been furious.

Watching them from the sofa, Toby was fascinated, and it struck him that whatever Tessa lacked in the technique of dissembling her sister more than made up for. No one will ever know what *she's* thinking when it comes to business, he decided. Linnet was being charming and friendly, and she had even apologized to Tessa. *Very clever,* our Linnet, he thought. She had never been his favorite, but he couldn't help admiring her handling of Tessa. He suddenly understood why he had long been wary of her. She was not only crafty but shrewd, not to mention a splendid actress. She ought to get an Oscar for this performance, he thought.

Although he had never recognized it until this moment, Toby admitted that he was actually a bit afraid of Linnet. She was everything their great-grandmother had been at her age: ambitious, driven, hardworking, and calculating. A tough cookie. He must warn Tessa to watch her back.

Linnet was looking across at him and saying, "Would you like to come, too, Toby?"

"Er, er, sorry, Linnet, I was preoccupied. Come with you where?"

"Down to the storage room where we keep the clothes. We've started to put some of them on the mannequins. I thought Tessa might like to see our progress, also look at the really beautiful clothes we've assembled so far. And you could come, too, Toby."

"I'd love to, but I've got to get back to the office. Thanks, though."

But in the end Toby did join them, wanting to have another look at his brother's current paramour. She must have something special to have held Gideon's interest all these weeks, he decided.

Toby had been coming to the Knightsbridge store since he was a child, but he had never been into the famous storage room. As he walked behind Linnet and Tessa, he was stunned by its size. It was an airy space almost the length of a football field, and it was filled with clothes. They hung on racks aligned side by side, from rods affixed to parts of the ceiling, and some were laid flat on white sheets on top of long trestle tables running the length of one wall.

He could see at a glance that all of the clothes were beautiful and costly; the other thing he noticed immediately was the perfect order. No sign of mess or chaos here. It struck him that somebody on this team, more than likely India Standish, had good organizational abilities. She had been annoyingly neat and tidy as a child, he suddenly recalled.

"Why are these dresses laid out on tables?" he asked Linnet as they walked to the far end of the storage area.

"Because they're beaded. Gowns with beading are never hung on hangers. The weight of the beads pulls the dress out of shape. Also, it's easier to check for loose beads and damage when the dresses are laid flat. We have a specialist in this kind of beaded embroidery who checks and does repairs."

"I thought Evan did that," Tessa said, a blond brow lifting quizzically.

"Some of it, but Miriam Flande is the expert who helps out when we need her," Linnet responded with a small smile.

Glancing around, Tessa suddenly said, "There're so many clothes here, I can't imagine why you want my poor bits and pieces."

Toby grabbed her arm and squeezed it. She glanced at him, saw his warning expression, and added, "But of course you're welcome to them as I said, and naturally I'm flattered."

Linnet looked at her sister oddly but made no comment.

"Oh, hello, India," Toby exclaimed as his cousin appeared from behind a rack, wearing the white cotton coat favored by couturiers to protect the clothing, part of an outfit in her hands. For once he was glad to see her; Tessa could be aggravating at times.

"Hello, Toby," India answered, then turning to Tessa she went on, "I'm so glad you came to visit us. This is all quite something, isn't it?"

Tessa simply nodded, fully aware of Toby's presence right behind her. But inside she was seething with envy. They were going to pull it off, damn it; the retrospective was going to be a big hit. But she made an effort to keep her irritation in check, her face neutral.

India hung up the jacket she was holding, then said, "Come and look at Emma's clothes. Evan's been working on them for the last few weeks, and they look as if they'd been bought yesterday, not fifty years ago."

"That's great," Tessa muttered and fell into step with India behind Linnet.

Toby followed the three women. He couldn't help thinking how much Tessa and

India resembled each other, at least in their features and coloring. That they were related was transparent. The Fairley strain runs through them both, he thought; from Jim to his daughter Tessa, and from Aunt Edwina to her granddaughter India. He sighed under his breath. What a muddled up mixture his family was.

These thoughts fled when he came face-to-face with Evan Hughes. Suddenly she was standing in front of him, dressed in the white couturier's coat like India. In fact, he'd almost run into her, pulled back just in time, quickly apologizing.

"My fault, suddenly appearing like that," she said, and thrust out her hand. "I'm Evan."

He shook her hand, nodding, then found himself smiling at her, thinking at once that she was a true beauty. "Nice to meet you, Evan. Linnet's just been singing your praises."

"That's kind of her, but she's the one who's responsible for all this, she and India, that is. I haven't done all that much. I've only been here a few months."

"I know the planning of the retrospective has been under way for a year, but Linnet obviously values your contribution," Toby told her.

She nodded, then explained, "Today we've been putting some of Mrs. Harte's clothes on the fiberglass mannequins. I think that's where Linnet's leading Tessa. Shall we join them?"

"That's a good idea," he answered, and together they headed down the center of the room. Toby still held to his opinion that Evan Hughes resembled his aunt only at first glance. Up close, as he was now, he could see they were quite different. But she *was* a knockout, and extremely well put together. Just as Paula O'Neill was; yes, that was part of the illusion, the stylishness. They had that in common, he realized.

Linnet, India, and Tessa were waiting for them at the bottom of the storage area. It was here that the team had created a makeshift office with desks, lamps, and telephones. A lot of charts, sketches of the auditorium, lists and photographs of clothing were pinned on several bulletin boards, and in general there was an air of high efficiency.

Tessa realized at once that they were going to give a show. Linnet and India had always been good at that; both rather theatrical, they reveled in presenting projects as if they were entertaining an audience. She sighed. Well, she supposed they were this afternoon. But it was an audience of two, herself and Toby.

She stole a look at him. He was watching the three young women attentively, or rather, he was watching Evan Hughes. He was obviously fascinated by her, although she knew this was mostly because of Gideon's involvement with the girl. Her cousin had a deserved reputation for being flighty, so not unnaturally the family were intrigued by his unexpected steadfastness with the American. They all wondered how long it would last.

Linnet, India, and Evan were now moving the racks around to reveal five mannequins, each displaying some of the loveliest clothes she had ever seen. Tessa knew at once that these were her great-grandmother's clothes, and she was stunned by their stylishness, taste, and elegance.

Stepping forward, Linnet explained, "Tessa, Toby, these are just a few of Emma's outfits. We're going to be displaying fifty altogether, maybe even a few more; her collection is actually the main feature of the retrospective . . . *she* was the real inspiration behind it." Linnet looked at India and said, "Tell them about the ball gown, India."

India walked over to the mannequin, explaining, "We're showing this gown with the back facing out, because it is the most spectacular part of the gown."

"It's beautiful," Tessa said, moving forward to inspect it closer.

"It is," India agreed and continued. "It's made of cotton tulle, masses of it in the skirt, as you can see, and it's a peculiar sort of grayish green I would say. It's from Christian Dior's 1947 collection, created just after

World War II, which became known as the New Look." India turned and beckoned Evan to come forward.

Evan explained, "You can see that the narrow, pale green silk belt defines the waist, then comes around to the back and essentially grows into the huge bow. This is a kind of bustle, with the ends falling to the hem. And it's the trail of pale, creamy, slightly pink cabbage roses that give the gown its great style. It was in almost perfect condition," Evan now remarked, looking directly at Tessa. "As were most of Mrs. Harte's clothes. Very few needed real cleaning or repairs. She took care of her things."

"Well she would, wouldn't she?" Tessa said. "Since she came up the hard way, from nothing."

Whatever Tessa had intended by the remark, it fell into the group like a lump of heavy lead.

Linnet looked appalled, Evan appeared embarrassed, but India took it in stride. With a huge smile, her expression one of immense pride, she said in a smooth and loving voice, "Our great-grandmother was known to be a perfectionist, Tessa, and it was her nature to take care of things well. Just as I do. I am thrilled I inherited that trait from her. Emma loved beauty and beautiful things, whether they were clothes, jewelry, antiques, or furnishings. Paintings were her joy, as we all know from her many homes. So naturally she took care of all of those things . . ." India stared at Toby, who seemed as embarrassed by Tessa's remark as Evan was.

Tessa flushed scarlet. "You don't have to reprimand me in that way, India my dear! I didn't mean anything rude by the remark . . . actually, I was being complimentary."

"It didn't sound that way," Linnet muttered, filled with disgust. "Well, let's get on with it. We don't want to be here all day, and Toby's got to get back to his office. This emerald green cocktail dress is also by Dior, from the fifties. It has a bouffant skirt, shorter at the front to show the legs, and Emma seemingly selected it to wear with her emerald collection."

Moving to another outfit, Evan said, "Here is a Balenciaga cocktail dress from 1951. Mrs. Harte liked bouffant skirts, and this is made of black tissue taffeta with a ballooning sash."

It was now India's turn, and she walked over to yet another mannequin and pointed to the jacket. "This is Schiaparelli, 1938. It's from her Circus collection. See the pattern of prancing horses? The pink jacket particularly stands out because it is partnered with a narrow black skirt."

Linnet came forward, saying, "This is one of Emma's most famous evening gowns. Your mother found it stored away in the attics at the Belgravia house a number of years ago, Toby. Aunt Emily pointed us in the right direction, and India and I finally found it up at Pennistone Royal. Look at the beading, Tessa, all these green and blue bugle beads. The gown is the color of the sea in the south of France. She also wore this with her emeralds, and we even found emerald green silk shoes from Pinet of Paris to go with it. Evan, come and explain about the restoration of the beading."

Evan joined Linnet and took over. "At first glance, the gown seemed to be in perfect order. But on closer examination I discovered some of the bugle beads were hanging by a thread, and others were missing. It was Madame Flande who did the repair work, and she made a beautiful job of it. The shell of the gown is composed of silk and chiffon, and it was designed by Jacques Heim in the 1940s."

"Such a lot of evening clothes," Tessa said. "She must have led quite a social life, even after Paul McGill was dead."

Again the three women exchanged startled looks but said not one word. It was Toby who jumped into the breach, exclaiming, "This is all wonderful. I'm sure the retrospective will be a smash. Thanks for showing it to me, to us, but I've got to go, I'm afraid."

"Yes, thank you, it's been very interesting," Tessa added quietly. "I have to go, too." Inclining her head, looking at the three of them, she took Toby's arm and led him away, saying, "I'll take you down to the David Morris shop. I know you'll find interesting watches there for Shane and your father. They have a great selection."

"Thanks for your help, Tessa," Toby murmured and hurried her away. Once they were outside the storage room he turned to her and said in a quietly vehement voice, "My God, Tessa, sometimes you say the worst things! I don't know what gets into you!"

"I wasn't being critical when I said she came from nothing," Tessa protested, sounding very earnest.

"But it came out that way, and that comment about Emma leading a big social life after Paul's death was just awful. Your mouth is always open and your foot's always in it. You've got to learn to be more diplomatic."

"I'm trying," she answered, sounding on the verge of tears.

After introducing Toby to the manager of the David Morris watch shop on the first floor, Tessa went back to her office. In the elevator she thought about the presentation the women had given, and envy surged through her again. But it was envy of their relationship with each other rather than anything else. What she had seen was their easy way of working together. Also she had picked up on the camaraderie between them. Linnet and India, who had been close all their lives, and Evan, a comparative stranger, were obviously on the same wavelength. She had witnessed their knowing glances, their affection, and their devotion. They were a team, and this made her angry.

But the most upsetting thing of all was their obvious happiness with their lives. She had wanted to be happy with Mark, to have a good marriage. But both seemed to be eluding her right now. Her bitterness was like a sharp pain in her chest.

Twenty-two

Sarah Lowther was irresistibly drawn to Harte's of Knightsbridge when she was in London. Today was no exception. She felt its pull as she hurried toward the greatest emporium in the world, founded by her grandmother Emma Harte long ago. She had worked at Harte's before taking over Emma's fashion business, Lady Hamilton Clothes, which she had run with great success.

But Sarah had always believed that retailing was in her blood, and over the years she had opened six stores of her own in France. They were actually boutiques selling antique furniture, objects of art, paintings, porcelains, and fabrics of all kinds. She specialized in lovely old silks and brocades, antique toile de Jouys, and the finest of tapestries, and she had become quite well known for her taste and style in home design and decor.

In fact, the boutiques were a huge success, and she was very proud of the busy little company which she had created all by herself. It was apparent to her that her talent for selling had been inherited from her grandmother; she was even noticing that trait in her twenty-five-year-old daughter, Chloe, who was currently running the boutique in Paris, where they lived. Yves, Sarah's husband and the father of Chloe, had recently remarked about this tendency himself, laughingly adding, "She takes after you, *chérie*, not I."

Sarah had had to agree with him. Although Chloe had an artistic bent and a very good eye, she had not inherited her father's brilliance as a painter. Today Yves Pascal was one of France's greatest living artists, renowned throughout the world for his contemporary Impressionist paintings, and in Sarah's eyes he was a true genius.

She glanced around as she walked along Knightsbridge making for the store. It was a beautiful day, surprisingly mild for early May and sunny, with a pale blue canopy of a sky shimmering overhead.

Although she loved Paris, where she had lived even before her marriage to Yves some twenty-seven years ago, Sarah was happy to be back in the country of her birth, if only for a short while. Everything was familiar, and so many fond memories abounded, particularly happy memories of her grandmother, her father, Kit, who was Emma's eldest son, and her mother, June. All three of them were dead, but they lived forever in her heart and were frequently in her thoughts.

As she approached the main doors of

Harte's, she felt a rush of anticipation, and once she was inside, standing in the middle of the cosmetics department, she experienced a marvelous sense of coming home. It was a combination of excitement, relief to be back in the store, and an awareness of belonging to a greater whole. Walking through her grandmother's emporium was the next best thing to being part of the family.

Leaving cosmetics behind, entering jewelry, Sarah's thoughts as usual focused on Paula O'Neill. She had no doubt that her cousin was sitting upstairs in her office, if she was not at one of the stores in Yorkshire. Sarah had to resist the temptation of going up to the executive suite to see her. Better not, she cautioned herself as she generally did and walked on, admiring everything she saw. The store looked wonderful. Nothing had changed . . . except perhaps for the better. It was the greatest in the world, and Paula was obviously carrying on the tradition of excellence started by their grandmother.

For years now Sarah had wanted to write a letter to Paula, not of apology but of explanation. She had long needed her cousin to understand that *she* hadn't done anything wrong all those years ago, that *she* hadn't been treacherous to the family.

What she had done was simply invest some of her money in a company called Stonewall Properties, following the advice of her cousin

Jonathan Ainsley. He had not told her that Stonewall was his own company, run by his straw man, Sebastian Cross. Nor had she been aware that Jonathan was cheating the family, diminishing their property interests by funneling deals which belonged to Harte Real Estate to Stonewall instead.

Nonetheless, she had been blamed along with Jonathan, kicked out of Lady Hamilton Clothes most unceremoniously and out of the family, by Paula and her father, the late David Amory. That had been the worst part; it had broken Sarah's heart, and in many ways she had never recovered. It had been, and still was, a most painful banishment.

But she was not a Harte for nothing, Sarah had reminded herself at the time, thinking of her grandmother's favorite line, which Emma had applied to so many situations. And she had managed to draw on her considerable inner resources to steady herself. Taking strength from the spirit of Emma Harte that lived in her, she had started her life over again and made it work for her.

She had moved to France and built herself a career in the world of Paris fashion, working as a *directrice* at a top haute couture house. It was during this time that she had met and married Yves Pascal, a young artist rapidly gaining recognition. They had started a family almost at once; today she had a good marriage, a very special daughter, a good life in general. She was content. And yet . . .

There was a hole in Sarah's heart, a sadness, an awful emptiness at times. Very simply, she longed to be back in the fold, to be friends with her cousins with whom she had grown up and had spent so much of her life: Paula, Emily, the twins Amanda and Francesca, and Winston. And those two dashing characters from the other clans, Michael Kallinski and Shane O'Neill. *Shane* . . . She had been enamored of him once, but he had only had eyes for Paula.

Each and every one of them had been part of her existence, her world, and she missed them very much, particularly Emily and Paula. They had had their quarrels, but then what large families didn't have their disagreements from time to time? For the most part, they had got along and had never really held any grudges. Linking them was their love for their extraordinary grandmother, their shared background, upbringing, and experiences. They knew where they belonged . . . they were part of the Hartes, and to be that was special indeed.

Jonathan Ainsley had ruined all this for her when he had involved her in his schemes without her knowledge. Sometimes she wondered why she still bothered with him. But then there was no other family member left in her life, and she knew she needed that connection to her past, to her heritage. It made her feel whole and special and different from the rest of the world.

Yet it was true that she was frequently troubled by their relationship; she thought of Jonathan as something of a loose cannon. She never knew what he was up to, what he was going to do. But then weren't these very good reasons to stay close to him?

Jonathan could not help admiring Sarah as she walked toward him down the length of the Grill Room in the Dorchester Hotel. She was an elegant woman, tall, slender, and as good-looking as ever. Sarah was fifty-nine now, and he thought she wore her years well, looked so much younger. Her lovely auburn hair was the same vibrant color it had been when she was younger, but it was obviously touched up discreetly. She had the Harte coloring and looks, and was proud of this.

The thing that struck him was her chicness; she had always been stylish, and this was most apparent tonight. Sarah was wearing a black wool suit, so beautifully cut it could only be haute couture from a top French designer. On one shoulder she had pinned two flower brooches made of black and white diamonds, and added matching earrings.

Jonathan stood up as she drew to a standstill, kissed her cheek, and greeted her warmly as she took the other chair, which had been pulled out by the waiter.

"You're as chic as always, Sarah darling," he murmured, squeezing her arm. "Nobody holds a candle to you."

"Why thank you, Jonathan, it's nice of you to say so."

"A drop of the bubbly, or what?"

"Champagne would be nice, thanks. I see you're having a martini." She smiled. "Too strong for me these days. Anyway, it's nice to see you."

He inclined his head, still smiling. "And you, too. Have you had a busy day?"

"Not so bad. I met with an antiques dealer this morning and got a good price on a Georgian desk, and then this afternoon I took a stroll around Harte's."

"Is it falling down? I hope," he said dryly, giving her a long, pointed stare.

Although his comment irritated her slightly, she decided to play it lightly, and so she laughed before saying, "Don't be so silly, of course it isn't. In fact, it's looking fabulous. Paula's doing a great job."

A blond eyebrow shot up, and Jonathan gaped at her. "Good Lord, a kind word for Paula! Things *are* looking up."

"What do you mean?"

"You were always such rivals, for Grandy's approval and love, and position, power, and Shane O'Neill. I can't imagine what's brought about this change in attitude."

The waiter arrived with her glass of Dom Pérignon, and after they had toasted each other, clinked glasses, Sarah murmured, "I'm a retailer myself these days, and I know what it takes, a great deal of hard work, back-breaking work, not to mention a huge amount of truly smart buying. I suppose I sort of admire her. . . . Anyway, all that was long ago. Isn't it better to forget those things?"

Jonathan merely smiled, toyed with the stem of his martini glass, then took a sip. After a moment he glanced up, gave his cousin a very direct look. "I'll never know why you go mooching around Harte's. I think it's positively . . . *morbid*."

"No, it's not! I enjoy roaming through the Food Halls and cosmetics, the other departments. It's Grandy's store, and I used to work there, and I feel — well, I feel rather at home there."

He sighed, shook his head, threw her a reproachful look, but he was wise enough not to respond. He knew she was in one of her mawkish, sentimental moods, living in the past. Much better to remain utterly silent, at least about Harte's and the family. After a moment he asked, "How long are you staying in London this time?"

"Only a couple of days, I'm afraid. I have to go up to Scarborough, or rather, just outside. The outskirts. There's an estate sale coming up, and I understand there's going to be some wonderful eighteenth-century French furniture on the block, as well as French silver. Apparently there was a French wife aeons ago, somewhere in the late seventeen hundreds, and she brought a lot of things with her. Part of a big dowry, I suspect. Anyway, it's the kind of stuff that's hard to come by, so I'm going up to Yorkshire for a couple of days, hoping to bid on some of it, then I'm back here for one day before returning to France."

"Do you think you'll have time to go and see my father?" he asked.

"I might, Jonny, I'll certainly try. And how is Uncle Robin?"

"Not so bad. I was in Yorkshire myself last weekend, staying with friends in Thirsk, and went to see him. He's much better; fortunately he's recovered well from that awful fall."

"I'm glad." She took a sip of champagne and asked, "Are you going to look for a country house near Uncle Robin? You said you were thinking about it the last time I was here."

"Don't know. Not awfully keen anymore. My work is suddenly keeping me busy. I have to be in London most of the time, you know."

"You mean your property company is finally up and running well?" she asked swiftly, although she wasn't surprised. He'd always been a good businessman.

"It is indeed! Are you interested in investing?" he asked, the blond brow lifting again.

Sarah shook her head. Not bloody likely, she thought, but said, "Thanks, but not really. I've got my hands full with my own company. I need lots of ready cash to buy antiques. Actually I do have to carry a lot of stock, make sure I have a big inventory with six boutiques to supply."

"What do you feel like eating?" he asked, reaching for the menu.

Sarah did the same, murmured, "Nothing too heavy. Fish maybe. I prefer something light at night."

They were halfway through dinner when Jonathan suddenly looked across the table and said, "One of these days you'll run into one of those damned cousins of ours when you're flitting about the store, and then where will you be? What on earth would you do?"

"I'd say hello, Jonathan, what else? I'm sure much of the animosity has dissolved by now. It probably did years ago. There's no reason we can't be civil with each other."

He put down his fish knife and fork, and leaned back in his chair, studying her for a moment.

Sarah stared back at him, thinking that he was better-looking now, in some ways, than he had been when he was younger. In her opinion he had been a bit too pretty in his early twenties and thirties. Blond, with light eyes, not blue but not gray either, a sort of mixture of the two. Tall, slender, dashing, and the spitting image of his grandfather Arthur Ainsley, Emma's second husband. Now in his mid-fifties, he had acquired a certain distinction, the blond hair touched with threads of silver, the bland and handsome face etched with the lines of a life well lived.

She wondered suddenly why he had never remarried. Perhaps the ghastly end of his horrific marriage to Arabella Sutton had scared him off matrimony. Once bitten twice shy, especially since he had inadvertently married a questionable woman. A shady lady, she called her; Yves, more blunt, dubbed her a *putain*, French for whore, once a Madame Claude girl, high-priced and going to the highest bidder. How terrible for Jonathan to learn this from Paula, and then to discover that his child was fathered not by him but by his partner, Tony Chiu.

"You're staring at me, Sarah!"

She laughed. "Admiringly so, cousin dear. I was thinking how really handsome you look these days. And much more distinguished than when you were merely a pretty boy, a sort of poor woman's matinee idol."

He grinned at her. "You do have a quaint way of putting it, Sarah. Now, I haven't asked, but how're Yves and the delectable Chloe?"

"He's painting madly, and he sends his best, by the way. He's in the south, at our house in Mougins for a few months. He has a big show coming up, and he needs to complete a number of canvases. As for your god-daughter, she's just wonderful."

"You've been lucky, Sarah darling," he said and made a face, then added ruefully, "Luckier than I."

"No one special in your life, Jonny?"

"I have a nice girlfriend in Yorkshire —" He broke off. "I don't think I'd better say another word about Ellie. Every time I boast about a woman, she turns out to be a dud."

"You've just had one bad experience," she answered and pushed her plate away, leaned against the back of the chair, patting her mouth with her napkin.

"Getting back to the store and the inhabitants therein," Jonathan said. "I do want to remind you that they're all as mad as hatters. So you mustn't become entangled with them ever again."

Sarah stared at him, her auburn brows pulling together in a jagged line. "I don't think I quite understand what you're getting at."

"They're bonkers, darling. Just think about it, cousins marrying cousins ad infinitum.

Relatives committing suicide, or covering up murders in the bogs of Ireland —"

"My God, Jonathan, that's not true!" she interrupted him, her voice rising shrilly. Sarah shook her head. "Your imagination's getting the better of you."

"Then there's that tendency toward immorality . . . Aunt Elizabeth and her *six* husbands, not to mention all of her lovers, most of them members of the bloody British government."

"I'm not really sure the latter is true," Sarah protested.

"It is! Dad told me all about it, and don't forget he was a Member of Parliament most of his adult life."

"Yes, I do remember," she murmured, suddenly wondering what had started him off on this rampage about the family.

"Do you want a pudding?" Jonathan asked after their plates had been cleaned away, glancing at the dessert trolley nearby. "Gosh, they've got bread-and-butter pudding. *Ugh*, not for me. Reminds me of my school days at Eton."

Sarah nodded. "I think I'll just have herb tea. I'm off coffee, especially in the evening."

"I still like a cup of coffee after dinner, sort of settles me down." Jonathan threw her a small smile, motioned to the waiter, and ordered for them both. Then turning to face Sarah again, he went on, "Then there's the

tendency the Hartes have for vendettas . . .
first Emma had one with the Fairleys for
years, then Edwina had one with her for
years. And only God knows who they've got
a vendetta with at the moment."

"Probably nobody," she shot back suc-
cinctly, her eyes narrowing.

"Maybe you're right, but there's a lot of
gossip about a new employee."

"Who?"

"Her name's Evan . . . Evan Hughes. And
she's —"

"Really a boy," Sarah cut in, smiling.
"Evan is a Welsh boy's name."

"We all know that, my dear. This Evan is
an American. And she amazingly resembles
our dear cousin Paula McGill Harte Amory
Fairley O'Neill, to give her her full name."

"She *does?*" Sarah looked at him curiously.
"Is she a relative?"

"Nobody knows. She arrived as if from nowhere, was taken in by Linnet when she
came looking for a job at Harte's, and now
everyone's saying she's a McGill."

"A McGill! That's . . . preposterous!"

"No, it's not, Sarah. Think for a moment.
What if the sainted Paul had an American
mistress, who gave birth to his child, who
grew up and gave birth herself to . . . Evan?
Or it could be a boy who was Paul McGill's
son, who married and had a child. It's a real
possibility. After all, he spent a lot of time in

New York without Emma when he was building Sitex Oil into a major corporation."

"How do you know all this?"

"I have a . . . *source,* shall we say?"

"Don't you mean a spy?"

"Call it what you will, my dear."

"Why are you digging up all this old family history tonight, Jonathan, and then relating the current gossip at the store to me? To what purpose?"

His face was bland as he smiled at her offhandedly, then shrugged. "I don't know. . . . Frankly, I thought you'd be interested to hear about the new employee who looks so much like your old rival."

"You're not planning to make any crazy moves against Paula, are you, Jonathan?" Sarah asked, giving him a piercing look through her intelligent green eyes. "Because if you are . . . I wouldn't, if I were you."

"How can I do anything to Paula? She's got the business buttoned up like the vicar's little sister's knickers. And you know that from twenty years ago, when I almost sneaked the stores out of her grasp."

"I know she's made everything very secure. But you and I still get treated properly when it comes to Harte Enterprises. We get our dividends on time, and Emily's run the company very well. We make a lot of money."

"Ah yes, she has indeed, and yes we do," he acknowledged.

Sarah sat back, studying him quietly as he waved elegant fingers at a nearby waiter, who came hurrying over to take an order for Calvados. Her gut instinct told her that Jonathan was plotting *something* against Paula. Since business didn't come into it, it had to be personal. Unexpectedly, Sarah felt slightly bilious.

Twenty-three

Paula O'Neill sat at the small, kidney-shaped Georgian desk in a corner of her bedroom at Pennistone Royal. Her face was thoughtful as she turned the pages inside a manila folder, studying them carefully. After ten minutes she closed the folder and set it to one side, knowing that she would find nothing of any consequence there, even if she read it ten more times.

Sitting back in the chair, she gazed out of the bay window, her eyes on a wooded hillside opposite. In spring it was covered with daffodils, which gleamed in golden streams rippling under the trees in the morning sunlight.

Wordsworth's poem leapt into her mind:

When all at once I saw a crowd,
A host, of golden daffodils;
Beside the lake, beneath the trees,
Fluttering and dancing in the breeze,

she said out loud to the empty room. It had been her grandmother's favorite poem, and it had been Grandy who had planted the hundreds of daffodils under the trees on the hill. She herself had kept them going over the years. Now, in early May, the bluebells were out, creating another stunning carpet of color.

Paula let her thoughts drift for a few minutes, then she pulled herself back to the present. Opening one of the drawers in her desk, she placed the folder inside, then locked it. There was no evidence in the papers she had been reading that Jonathan Ainsley was plotting against her, yet she knew he was. Even though the private investigator had turned up nothing, it was an instinctive feeling lodged in the marrow of her bones. And she trusted it implicitly. What he would do, when he would do it, she did not know, but he *would* move against her. Since he could not strike at her through the Harte holdings or the chain of department stores, it was obvious to her that he would strike at her through her personal life. But she could not conceive in which way.

Life has a funny way of coming at you, she thought. Who could have imagined that Jonathan Ainsley would return to England to live after all those years in Hong Kong and Paris? She did not believe he had come back out of concern for his father; it wasn't in his nature to play the devoted son, therefore there had to be an ulterior motive. In the inner recesses of her mind, Jonathan's voice echoed back to her. "I'll get you, Paula Fairley. I'll bloody well get you for this," he had threatened. She had never forgotten his words.

Rising, Paula walked across the room, paused at the large chest of drawers to look in the mirror which hung above it. But she did so absently, her thoughts still focused on her vindictive cousin, who had been her sworn enemy for so long.

As she half-turned away, lost in her reflections, her glance fell on the casket which sat atop the commode, and automatically she smoothed her hand across its lid as she had done so many times in the past, just as her grandmother had done before her.

It was a beautifully made antique box of highly polished fruitwood the color of aged cognac, intricately chased with silver scrolls and interlocking circles. In the center of the lid there was a silver heart with the initials E. H. engraved upon it. It had been sitting on this chest for as long as she could remember, from the time she had been a young girl visiting her grandmother here.

The box was locked, and there was no key. It seemed that Emma had lost the key long ago, but since it was empty she had not bothered to have the box prised open for fear of damaging it. Because it had been thus for fifty years or more, Paula had never seen a reason to tamper with it.

Turning away, Paula walked on into the upstairs parlor which adjoined the bedroom, crossed to the fireplace, and stood with her back to it, warming herself.

A few moments later, when she felt less chilled, she turned around and looked up at the portrait of her grandfather Paul McGill, which hung above the fireplace. He wore an officer's uniform; it had been painted in the middle of the First World War, when he was in the Australia Corps. She couldn't help thinking how dashing and debonair he looked. And very handsome with his black hair, mustache, and bright blue eyes. She had inherited his coloring, his eyes, and also the cleft in his chin and his dimples. There was no mistaking who *she* was descended from.

In the picture he was smiling, and Paula knew that this painting had been her grandmother's favorite . . . perhaps because he had looked exactly like this when they had met and fallen immediately and madly in love. Her grandmother had once told her that he had been irresistible, and Paula could well imagine it.

He had had the world in his arms, or so he believed, Paula now thought. But he hadn't really, because he had not been able to marry Emma Harte, the love of his life. And so after years of living with Emma in London, he had returned to Sydney to ask his wife, Constance, for a divorce, determined to legitimize his daughter Daisy by Emma. By some terrible misfortune he had been in a head-on crash with a truck on a wet, stormy night, and when the truck driver had extracted his mangled body from the wreckage, he was paralyzed from the waist down, his handsome face badly scarred, one side ruined beyond recognition.

Paula sighed, thinking of those awful events. Because there was no way to treat paraplegics in 1939, he knew that he would not live long, that he would inevitably die from kidney failure. So he had taken his own life. And Emma had never seen him again.

Paula's mother had told her that Emma had almost been broken by Paul's death, that it had taken her a long time to recover from her grief. But she had managed to pick herself up and go on, for Daisy's sake, hiding her sorrow behind a brave front, finding comfort in her daughter by Paul.

Grandy had taught Paula that life was hard, that it always had been, and that the important thing was to keep going no matter what, to fight back, to win in the end, to triumph over adversity.

Paula had not had a lot of adversity in her own life, just those horrible problems with the venomous Jonathan Ainsley, and a truly bad marriage to Jim Fairley. And of late things had been running fairly smoothly, both in the business and in the family. There had been that great disappointment last autumn when Linnet had made the decision to "cool it with Julian," as she put it. But now they were back together and all was well between them.

Her daughter Tessa worried her. There was something amiss in her marriage, Paula was certain of that; she was also rather concerned about the bruised arm and shoulder. She had believed Tessa when she said she had fallen at home. But how had that happened? Had she been pushed? Or had she and Mark been in a fight? On the one hand, maybe it really had been an accident. Nevertheless, Mark Longden had long caused Paula worry. She found him too obsequious by far. As Emily put it, he was "a bit of a Uriah Heep."

That Jonathan had unexpectedly returned and been seen with Sarah was really upsetting. They had plotted together ever since their childhood. I wish Jack Figg were around, Paula suddenly thought, remembering how talented and fearless the former head of security for the stores had been. But Jack had retired, more or less, and was enjoying his new home by the sea, where he sailed, fished, and in general led a happy life. She sighed again and went and sat on the window seat, picked up their newspaper, the *Yorkshire Morning Gazette*, casually leafed through the pages.

A door slamming in the distance made her

sit up with a start, and she listened attentively, wondering if Shane had arrived. He was driving up from London this morning, and he had told her he would be there in time for lunch. She looked at her watch . . . it was almost noon. A look of expectancy settled on her face as she sat staring at the door, but when Shane did not appear she went back to the newspaper, focusing on the national news. But quite soon thoughts of Jonathan Ainsley began to infiltrate her mind. She laid the paper on the padded cushion of the seat and gazed out the window toward the moors.

It was still a brilliantly sunny morning, the arc of the sky the color of speedwells, those tiny blue flowers she loved so much. It was such a pretty spring day, yet she began to shiver involuntarily when an unexpected sense of foreboding swept through her. Paula jumped to her feet, hating this feeling, and hurried over to the fireplace; she stood warming her hands over the flames flying up the chimney back, still shivering.

Deep within herself she was convinced that Jonathan's return signified trouble. He can't *do* anything, not really, she told herself and then thought, But I do have five children and a grandchild, and a husband, not to mention many other family members I am close to . . . accidents *could* be arranged, couldn't they? She had long been aware that he would stop at nothing to wreak his revenge on her for *twice* bringing him to his knees.

Years ago her grandmother had said that there was a dazzle to Shane O'Neill, an intense glamour, adding that this sprang not so much from his extraordinary good looks as from his character and personality. Paula remembered Emma's words now as Shane came into the room. He had a bright smile on his face as he walked toward her.

Paula watched him, thinking that Grandy's pronouncement, made when he was about twenty-seven years old, still held. And next month he would be celebrating his sixtieth birthday. What a wonder he was, hardly aged, tall, broad-shouldered, with a barrel chest; a fine figure of a man, as his father was wont to say. Shane's jet-black hair was tinged with gray these days, and there were a few lines around his eyes and his mouth, but otherwise he looked much the same as he had when he was that dashing young man her grandmother had so admired.

Even though he was wearing his Saturday casual clothes, he was impeccably dressed. Well-tailored gray gabardine slacks were teamed with a red cashmere turtleneck and a black blazer. He looked as smart as ever, right down to his highly polished brown loafers.

His presence filled the room, and she felt

that rush of excitement she always experienced when she had not seen him for a while. She went to meet him, wanting to touch him, to hold him close. A wide smile enlivened her normally serious face, and he smiled back at her lovingly as he swept her into his arms. After a moment he held her away, kissed her lightly on the lips, and said, "Sorry I'm late, darling. Heavy traffic on the way up from London."

She nodded. "But you're here now, and it's just wonderful to see you, to have you home at last. I do hate it when you're in London and I'm not."

He glanced down at her, a small, puzzled frown pulling his dark brows together. "I've only been gone a few days. And someone has to run O'Neill Hotels International, you know."

"But I always miss you so much, Shane. It seems to get more acute the older I get."

He chuckled as he walked with her to the sofa, where they sat down. "I would have thought that by now you'd have had enough of me . . . all these years we've been together."

"All these years indeed! Thirty years married, and the time that went before when we were growing up."

He smiled and took her hand in his, looked into those unique violet eyes, and murmured, "You sound a little tremulous,

346

Paula darling. Is something bothering you?"

She was not at all startled by his perception; he knew her far too well, and she realized there was no point in denying it. "I had an awful premonition of trouble brewing, to do with Jonathan Ainsley."

Twenty-four

Shane listened attentively. He always paid attention to his wife; he both admired and respected her, and he knew she never made rash statements, nor did she exaggerate. Nonetheless, he was alarmed by what she was saying, and when she finally sat back on the sofa and gave him a questioning look, he exclaimed, "But Paula darling, Jonathan Ainsley wouldn't be stupid enough to hurt any of us physically. He'd be in serious trouble with the law if he did."

"I know, but he could hire somebody to do it."

"He'd still be in trouble, as an accessory to the crime. No, I don't think you have to worry about any of us being harmed, I really don't."

"He's capable of anything!" she cried.

"Oh, I know that only too well."

Paula shifted slightly, gave her husband a hard stare, and said, "I suppose I'll have to try to relax, about Jonathan, I mean. Maybe I'm being overly imaginative because of the past."

"Perhaps you are, sweetheart." He touched her face tenderly. "Jonathan may be vengeful and devious, but he's by no means stupid, we all know that. He wouldn't do anything to put himself in jeopardy with the law. And personally, I think he came back because he wanted to come home to England, to be close to Uncle Robin, amongst other things."

Paula shook her head and said quietly, "I don't agree. He doesn't have a decent bone in his body, not even when it comes to his father. But looking at it objectively, as you are doing, I'm sure he would be careful." She went on, "Did you see Philip when you arrived? Was he anywhere around?" Her brother was visiting England from Australia. Whenever he came, he stayed at Pennistone Royal.

Shane shook his head. "But when I spoke to him the other night, he said he wanted to go riding on the moors this morning. That's why he decided to come to Yorkshire last night, and —"

"But I didn't see him," Paula cut in. She went on, "I felt very tired. By ten, when he hadn't arrived, I left him a note and went to bed. And I haven't seen him this morning. So perhaps he did go riding. Margaret thought she saw him crossing the yard a couple of hours ago. I bet he went up to the moors."

"I think so. But come on, darling, your

baby brother will show up eventually, and I think you and I should go for a walk. It'll do you good, and it's such a lovely day."

Half an hour later, Philip McGill Harte Amory walked into the Great Hall, his riding boots making a loud clatter against the stone floor. He made straight for the huge stone fireplace and stood warming himself. There was a cold wind blowing across the moors. Even though he had been warmly dressed, with a Barbour over his riding jacket and sweater, he had felt the chill up there under the high fells.

The ride had done him good, and he was feeling more refreshed than he had been since he'd arrived from Sydney at the beginning of the week. Back home in Australia he was on the move a lot, between the city and Dunoon, the family sheep station in Coonamble. There he rode every day and spent a lot of time outdoors.

He loved Dunoon more than any place on earth; it was his true home, where he felt the most comfortable and at peace. Perhaps this was because there were many wonderful memories of his beloved Maddy there, although he had made it his safe haven when he was a boy, had become unusually attached to it early in his life.

The other place where he felt totally at ease and relaxed was this house. Pennistone

Royal had been the center of gravity for Paula, himself, and all their cousins when they were growing up; they had congregated here around their grandmother. He, in particular, had spent a lot of time with Emma, learning everything there was to learn about the great McGill empire, which he and Paula had inherited and he now ran from Sydney. "I learned at the knee of the master," he would tell anyone who asked him about his business training, and then sing the virtues of the renowned Emma Harte.

Tall, slender, dark haired, with the most startlingly blue eyes, Philip resembled his grandfather Paul McGill. And while he had inherited many of Paul's traits, he was also very much a grandson of Emma Harte, and he was exceptionally proud of this. His adored Grandy had been his mentor until the day she died. His life was lived on the principles she had taught him.

Philip walked over to the table set against one of the end walls. Here Margaret had earlier put out a bottle of white wine in an ice bucket, a jug of tomato juice, a bottle of vodka, and a variety of soft drinks. Philip poured himself a glass of tomato juice and went and sat down on the sofa next to the fire, his thoughts veering to his daughter Fiona, who was an undergraduate at Oxford. She was the light of his life, and now, at nineteen, she had become a unique young woman in his opinion. Bright, intelligent, and mature beyond her years, she made him very proud. He always came to England in the spring to see her. He was a single parent, having never remarried after Maddy's death in childbirth.

At the sound of footsteps, Philip rose from the sofa, smiling at his sister as she hurried toward him, looking anxious.

"There you are, Pip!" Paula exclaimed, embracing him. "We wondered where you were."

After hugging her and shaking Shane's outstretched hand, he told them, "I went riding. There's nothing like a good gallop across the moors to blow the cobwebs away. It was great but a bit chilly, I've got to tell you. Now can I pour you a glass of wine or make you a Bloody Mary?" He glanced from Shane to Paula.

"I'll have an orange juice, please," Paula said and went and sat down on one of the straight-backed chairs.

"Are you having a Bloody Mary?" Shane asked, eyeing Philip's drink.

"No, it's just plain old tomato juice."

"I'll have the same, thanks. I don't feel like drinking today. Well, maybe a glass of red wine at lunch." Shane walked across to the sofa.

Philip poured their drinks and carried them over to the fireplace, where they were sitting, retrieved his own glass, then joined them. They spoke about a few inconsequential things; then Philip turned to his sister and said, "I'd like to discuss something with you, something that's troubling me, Paula."

"Oh dear, Pip, is there something wrong? It's not Fiona, is it?"

"No. It's Evan Hughes."

As he spoke the name, Paula knew at once that he had heard the gossip and was put out by it. She didn't blame him, she herself was annoyed. She wished she knew who had started the unfortunate story. Taking a deep breath, she said, "I know, I know. The story is that she's somehow related to us, that she's a long-lost McGill, and that she's after *something*. I wish I knew who'd started this, I'd make mincemeat out of them. And I believe this came about because some people actually think she looks like me."

Philip instantly picked up the denial in her voice and exclaimed, "But she *does*, and very much so."

"No, she doesn't. We're the same type, that's all. We have the same coloring, somewhat exotic looks," Paula protested. She shook her head vehemently.

Philip, his expression negating what she had just said, remarked, "You're wrong, sweet'art. I know you're right about most things, but this time you're *wrong*." He glanced at Shane. "Well, she's your wife, and you've known her as long as I have, what do *you* think?"

"When I first saw Evan, I was struck by a likeness, but on second glance I realized I was quite mistaken."

"You've seen her then?" Paula asked, giving her brother a long, penetrating look.

"You bet! I went over to the store on the pretext of talking to Linnet about something, and I was introduced to Evan in no time at all. She's wonderful-looking, no denying that, and personable. And I can understand why people might think she's a McGill."

"Is that when you heard the story?" Shane asked.

"No, it's not. I heard the gossip on Tuesday, and I heard it in my *own* office."

"Good God, the gossip stretched across London to McGill Holdings!" Paula was astounded.

"You know what they say, gossip travels fast. I also hear she's engaged to Gideon." Philip looked from Paula to Shane.

Shane began to laugh. "She's dating him, that's all. And I think things have become overly exaggerated, Philip, I really do."

"Seemingly so. Nonetheless, I would like to know more about her. Have you had her background investigated?" Philip now asked Paula.

"Of course not! I had no reason to, and I still don't," she retorted, looking at her brother askance.

"I do think we ought to know more," he insisted.

"And when we know more, so what? She can't plunder the McGill empire, or ask for anything, for heaven's sake. Like Emma, Paul McGill tied everything up in trusts and foundations." Paula shook her head. "Let's leave things alone, Pip, otherwise there's going to be a real storm flaring up around here. Gideon's very involved with her . . ." Paula let the words drift away, dismayed by the conversation.

Shane said, "I think I have a solution. Paula, why don't you talk to Evan next week when you're back in London? Ask her a few questions about her parents, her grandparents. You can do that nicely; you might even want to have Linnet in the room with you. That may make the girl feel more at ease."

"I don't have to wait until next week, Shane," Paula murmured, her heart sinking slightly at the thought of confronting Evan. "She's here," she added in a low voice.

"What do you mean by *here?*" he asked, eyeing her curiously.

"In this house. She came up with Linnet and India late on Thursday. I'd promised them a weekend here, a bit of R and R. They've worked so hard on the retrospective, I thought it would be nice for them to be pampered a bit by Margaret. And me. They went to Harrogate for lunch. Linnet wanted

Evan to see the store there. So I can talk to Evan later. Diplomatically, of course," she ended on a sigh.

"Excellent idea," Philip said.

"I hope it's not going to create undercurrents," Shane muttered and gave Paula a questioning look.

"It won't, I promise you," she reassured him.

Twenty-five

It was just four o'clock when the three young women came bursting into the upstairs parlor, looking for Paula. She saw at once that they were already full of energy and exuberance again; obviously their trip to Harrogate had been successful. They look *happy*, she thought, and they're such good friends, a wonderful team; this pleased her enormously.

Linnet and India were both shrewd, clever girls, and they would not have taken to Evan Hughes in the way they had if she was at all questionable. Paula also trusted Gideon's judgment, and he was smitten with her, wanted to marry her, according to Emily. She was obviously first class.

"Hello, all of you!" Paula greeted them with a broad smile.

"Hello," they answered in unison, and Linnet bounded over to the sofa and flopped down next to her mother, kissed her cheek with great affection.

"How was lunch?" Paula asked, warmth echoing in her voice.

"Great," Linnet replied, laughter in her

green eyes. "Thanks for the treat, Mums."

"We took Evan to Betty's Café," India volunteered. "She was astonished."

"I loved it, Mrs. O'Neill," Evan said, "such a quaint place. It reminded me of an old English movie. Oh, and the store is just beautiful."

"Thank you, Evan. I'm sure Linnet told you we redid it from top to bottom last year."

Paula poured the tea, Linnet passed the cups around, and then they all sat back, filling her in on their morning and afternoon. India explained how they had given Evan a full Cook's tour of the lovely old spa city.

As they talked to her, Paula surreptitiously studied Evan, and the more she scrutinized her, the more she recognized that the American girl was not really like her facially. At the same time, she understood why some people thought otherwise. Evan, albeit unwittingly, gave the impression she was a younger version of Paula, because their style of dressing was so similar.

At one moment, Evan flushed slightly when she realized Paula's eyes were trained on her. Haltingly, she asked, "Is there something wrong, Mrs. O'Neill?"

Paula shook her head, offered the young woman a quick smile. And seeing the opening she needed to launch into a conversation about Evan's background, Paula said,

"I'm staring at you, aren't I? That's so rude. I'm sorry, Evan . . . You see, a number of people think you look like me, and I was endeavoring to spot a few similarities."

"We're the same type physically, but that's all there is to it," Evan replied, relieved that Paula O'Neill had brought the matter up. She had heard the gossip at the store, and it both troubled and dismayed her. It also cast a cloud over her, which now worried her because of Gideon.

Linnet said, "At first glance Evan does have a look of you, Mummy, but she's right, basically you're the same *type* . . . but there the resemblance *stops.*"

"I agree, Aunt Paula," India volunteered.

"Nevertheless, I would like to . . . well, sort of clear the air, Evan, if you wouldn't mind answering a few questions. I think we would all feel happier if we could put a stop to these silly rumors about you being a long-lost McGill."

Evan nodded. "I agree, and to be honest, Mrs. O'Neill, I'd never heard that name before, not until I came to work at Harte's."

"Why *did* you come?" Paula asked, leaning forward slightly, once again focusing on Evan. "I mean, what made you choose *Harte's* above all the other stores in London?"

Evan knew there was no point fibbing, as she had to other people. In many ways her future hung on this conversation, and only

359

the absolute truth would do.

Taking a deep breath, she said, "I came to Harte's because of my grandmother. She died last November in New York. I was with her, we were waiting for my father — her son, Owen — to arrive. He was driving in from Connecticut, and he was late because of the heavy traffic. Anyway, Gran and I talked a little as I sat and held her hand. At one moment she became revitalized, and she told me to leave New York, go to London to see Emma. She said Emma Harte had the key to my future. That's all she said. Then my father arrived, a few minutes too late to see his mother alive, and in all the upset and grief that followed, I forgot about Gran's words. Until later, that is. When I repeated them to my father, he seemed truly baffled. A short while after, he remembered that my grandmother had met Mrs. Harte during the Second World War, and he told me a bit about the store. But he didn't know much of anything."

Paula nodded. "I see. So apparently there *is* some sort of connection between your grandmother and mine."

"I don't think it's a very important one," Evan answered, her honesty reflected on her face.

"What was your grandmother's name?"

"Glynnis. Glynnis Hughes. But before she married my grandfather she was called

Jenkins, and she came from the Rhondda Valley in Wales. My grandfather Richard Hughes was a GI stationed near London. They got married during the war, here in London, where my father was born. As I was later."

"What year was your father born?" Paula probed, realizing that Owen Hughes's birth date would clarify a great deal.

"In 1944, Mrs. O'Neill."

Paula felt the tension sliding away, and she exclaimed, "So he can't possibly be the son of Paul McGill, my grandfather! Because Paul McGill was already dead then. *He died in 1939.*"

Evan nodded, answered in a low, subdued voice, "I told you, I've never heard that name mentioned in my family. Nor did I ever hear Gran mention Mrs. Harte. Perhaps they had only a passing acquaintance. I know Gran lived in London during the war, my grandfather told me that. He'd met her at a canteen for the troops, where she was working with her girlfriends in the evening, entertaining the GI's, he said. And they connected because his forebears had gone to America from the Rhondda Valley. That's where they fell in love, he said."

"I think we've managed to clear the air rather quickly, Evan," Paula exclaimed, smiling at her. "At least I'm satisfied, and we —"

"But, Mummy, why did Glynnis tell Evan to come and see Emma?" Linnet interjected. "Why did she tell her that her future was with Emma Harte? Doesn't that strike you as odd?"

"No, it doesn't," Paula shot back impatiently, wanting this matter finally closed.

"But, Aunt Paula, it *is* a bit strange," India murmured, giving her a hard stare. "I mean, why would an old lady on her deathbed suddenly tell her granddaughter to seek out a woman in London? *Why?* Think about it. I bet Glynnis and Grandy *were* friends, and that there *was* a connection between them, something important. Perhaps there's something here we're not aware of . . . a secret maybe?"

"If that's the case, why didn't Evan's grandmother explain in more detail, give her the proper information?" Paula asked, first looking at India and then swinging her eyes to Evan, raising a dark brow.

It was Evan who answered. "She was dying, Mrs. O'Neill, and she was very weak. I don't think she had the strength to say another word. I was surprised she'd spoken at all. By then she was on her last breath."

"Obviously your grandmother didn't know Emma Harte was dead, and had been for thirty years," Paula murmured, "so tell me, what did *you* think when you discovered this?"

"I was really shocked, Mrs. O'Neill. Staggered, actually, and to be truthful I felt a bit foolish that I'd listened to Gran. When I told my father on the phone, he said perhaps his mother had been delirious or rambling. And I sort of accepted that."

"But you still came up to the management offices, to apply for a job," Paula pointed out, her steady gaze fixed on Evan.

"Eventually. I went and had coffee, and thought about what I'd do, and I realized I wanted to stay in London. After all, I'd given up my job in New York. And I was very taken with the store, impressed by it, and I thought, Why not go and apply for a position? And so I did."

"I think everything has been satisfactorily explained," Paula announced, looking at each of the young women, again wanting to move on.

Linnet glanced at Evan and asked quietly, "How old was your grandmother when she died?"

"Gran was seventy-nine."

"So, during the Second World War she would have been in her twenties. And she *must* have been a young woman since she gave birth to your father. Correct?" Linnet said.

"Yes," Evan answered, wondering what Linnet was getting at.

Paula had been thinking the same thing

and asked, "What's your point, Linny?"

"At the beginning of the war, Emma Harte was forty-nine, fifty, anyway thereabouts, and from what I know about her, she didn't have time for a lot of girlfriends, not the way she worked. Besides, there was the age difference between Emma and Glynnis. Could it be that Glynnis Jenkins worked at Harte's during the war?"

Paula was startled, but after a moment's thought she said, "Yes, she could have worked at the store, that's quite true."

Linnet now turned to Evan. "What did your grandmother do before she was married to your grandfather? Do you know?"

"I'm not sure . . . but she could have been a secretary, because she did do all the paperwork for my grandfather's antiques business when I was growing up."

India sat up straighter and cried, "That's it! I agree with Linnet. I think Glynnis worked as one of Emma's secretaries during the war."

"But what does that mean, India?" Paula asked, sounding puzzled. "We've eliminated the McGill connection because of Owen Hughes's birth date. We can put a stop to the stories and forget it all."

"I'm not so sure," Linnet began slowly, a little hesitantly. "There's more to this than meets the eye, Mums. I just feel *that* in my bones, and I'm a true Celt like Dad, remember, so listen to me. Anyway, Aunt Emily said —" Linnet instantly broke off, regretting these words. She knew that bringing Emily into this discussion could cause trouble.

"What exactly did Emily say?" Paula probed, concerned as well as surprised.

"I shouldn't have said that, Mummy. Aunt Emily will be angry with me."

"We can't worry about that right now. Just tell me what she said, Linnet," Paula demanded, staring at her daughter.

Linnet cleared her throat and explained in a low, steady voice, "Aunt Emily never thought Evan had a connection to the McGill side of the family, nor does she really think she looks like you. But she does believe there might be a connection . . . to *the Hartes*. She says she can't put her finger on it, but at the edge of her memory there is a face that won't come into focus. I guess it's like having something on the tip of your tongue."

Paula was taken aback. "She thinks Evan could be related to the Hartes, and she never told *me*."

"Don't get excited, Mums," Linnet said in a placating tone. "Aunt Emily only mentioned it in passing to me. You see, she didn't want to worry you. That's the reason she didn't say anything, I'm sure."

Paula sat back against the cushions on the

sofa, for once rendered speechless.

Linnet now said swiftly, "Mummy, don't look like that, let's try to get to the bottom of this . . . *mystery*. Where are the old employee records kept? I bet they're in the basement storage rooms at the London store."

"I doubt they still exist. They may have been destroyed when we went to computer," Paula muttered, feeling slightly put out with Linnet.

"I've just had a brainstorm, Aunt Paula!" India sprang to her feet and went to sit next to her aunt on the sofa. "The diaries! Grandy's diaries, the ones we found in the clothes storage attics months ago, written in the war years. If there *is* some sort of secret, or something about Evan's grandma, I bet you'd find it in one of those."

"Perhaps," Paula agreed, remembering her reluctance to plunge into such a personal area of her grandmother's life. Diaries were always so intimate, meant only for one person's eyes . . . the writer of them.

Evan took a deep breath and began slowly, carefully. "I really do think my father *is* who he *is*. He's Owen Hughes, the son of Glynnis and Richard Hughes. He looks like my grandfather, and he's like him in so many other ways . . ." She broke off, gazed at Paula, her eyes reflecting her sadness and hurt.

Paula did not fail to miss this, and she was

instantly filled with chagrin. "Oh, Evan, my dear, how thoughtless we've all been! So unkind, impugning your grandmother's reputation the way we have. How cruel of us to suggest she might have had a relationship with someone else, a man who was the father of her child rather than your grandfather. I think we've been quite . . . *unconscionable.* I'm so very sorry. I apologize," she finished softly.

"It's all right, Mrs. O'Neill, I haven't taken offense. I think you all meant well, and that you do want to stop the silly gossip, and it *is* silly. It's all conjecture. But I just want to say this. . . . I know I'm not related to any of you. I'm neither a McGill nor a Harte. My grandmother loved Richard Hughes, and she would never have cheated on him. My grandmother helped to bring me up, and she was . . . well, she was true blue, as Linnet would say."

After the girls had left, Paula brought out the suitcase which contained her grandmother's diaries. Placing it on the coffee table, she opened the case and stared at the small black leather books lined up side by side.

She could not bring herself to look at the one for 1939, for her mother had told her that Emma spent hours writing in her diary that year, and Paula could not face reading what she knew would be heartbreaking passages about her grandfather and his untimely death.

So she picked up the volume for 1940 and began to leaf through it, still a trifle reluctant to read her grandmother's very private thoughts.

The diary fell open, and Paula read:

I had dinner tonight with Blackie O'Neill. He made me laugh for the first time in months. He is my dearest friend . . .

Paula heard a slight noise, and as she looked up there was Shane, standing next to her. She said, "Here is my grandmother writing in her diary that your grandfather is her dearest friend."

Shane smiled down at her. "So you finally had the courage to start reading them. Maybe she wanted you to do that, Paula. Perhaps that's why she left them for you to find. She could have destroyed them, you know." Lowering himself onto the sofa, he asked, "What year is that?"

Paula glanced at him and said, "Nineteen forty. She wrote this when she was fifty-one years old. I knew her only when she had become an old woman, and I can't help wishing I'd known her back then. . . . I wonder what she was like, Shane."

He put his arm around her and drew her

close to him. There was a moment of silence before he spoke. "I bet she was . . . simply bloody marvelous!"

PART TWO
Legend

1940

She possessed, in the highest degree,
all the qualities which were required in
a great Prince.

> GIOVANNI SCARAMELLI,
> VENETIAN AMBASSADOR
> TO THE COURT OF
> ELIZABETH TUDOR,
> QUEEN OF ENGLAND

Be not afraid of greatness: some are
born great, some achieve greatness, and
some have greatness thrust upon them.

> WILLIAM SHAKESPEARE,
> *TWELFTH NIGHT*:
> ACT II, SCENE V

Twenty-six

Emma Harte stood in front of the cheval mirror in the spacious, elegant bedroom of her Belgrave Square house, regarding herself thoughtfully.

And she hated what she saw.

Her reflection was of a thin, almost wraith-like woman, deathly pale, with a mass of red hair surrounding a tired, sorrowful face like a fiery halo. The contrasts were stark.

And she hated the dress she wore.

It was a good dress, couture, but it was black, funereal and depressing, and it did nothing for her except underscore her un-precedented lack of physical appeal. In gen-eral her appearance disturbed her as she studied herself objectively. She had never looked like this before.

Glancing at the dressing table nearby, her eyes settled on the photograph of Paul McGill. "It just won't do anymore, will it, darling?" she said out loud, talking to his picture as she had done every day for months. Instinctively shrewd, and an extraor-dinary judge of people, Emma was aware that the staff thought she was slightly mad these days, the way she talked to herself, and quite loudly. But she wasn't crazy, and she was actually talking to Paul. She knew she would for as long as she lived. It gave her such comfort, made her feel less alone, less lonely. They had lived together here for sixteen years, and his presence was everywhere.

"Nothing for it but a radical makeover," she continued, and as she walked past the dressing table she let her hand rest for a split second on top of the gold photograph frame that held his picture. In the incandescent light from the lamp, the great, square-cut McGill emerald ring Paul had given her after Daisy's birth shone like bright green fire on her small, capable hand.

Moving across the floor rapidly and with the lightest of steps, she took off the black dress and laid it on the bed, put on a silk robe, and hurried into the adjoining bathroom. She found a pair of large scissors in a drawer of the vanity, and with a burst of energy she began to cut off her hair. She did so with precision and skill, and she did not stop until she was left with a sleek, slightly wavy pageboy, a style that was all the rage.

Peering at herself in the mirror, she saw that she suddenly looked ten years younger, and much less sorrowful. Stepping off the bath mat, she bent down and folded it over to trap the discarded hair, then put it to one side for Grace, her maid, to remove later.

Returning to the bedroom, Emma sat down at the dressing table, regarded her face for a moment or two, then picked up a large powder puff and swept it across her cheeks and brow. Next she added a trace of pink lipstick, smoothed her eyebrows with her fingertips, and brought the black mascara brush to her lashes. Finally sitting back, she saw how her appearance had undergone a swift change for the better. She no longer looked like a demented Ophelia en route to the asylum.

Within minutes Emma had put on a navy blue dress and stepped into a pair of navy blue, high-heeled court shoes. Again she regarded her reflection in the cheval mirror in the corner near the window, this time nodding in satisfaction. Falling to her ankles, the dress was beautifully made of matte wool crepe. Designed by Jean Patou, it was narrow and elegant, with long sleeves and a long stole. She had bought it in Paris in 1935 because Paul had loved it, and now she understood why. It was extremely flattering to her slender figure and made her seem taller than she was.

Moving back to the dressing table, she put on Paul's square-cut emerald earrings that matched her ring and an emerald bracelet, and pinned Blackie's lovely emerald bow on her shoulder. After spraying Chanel No. 5 at her throat, she went to find a navy blue bag to match her dress, stole, and shoes.

A moment or two later she was ready to go to the Dorchester to meet the boys, as she called them. As she walked toward the door, she decided they would be pleased that she had put away her mourning black at long last.

Emma stood at the top of the steps for a moment before going down into the street, where her car and driver were waiting. She could not help marveling yet again at the extraordinary weather. It had been glorious all week, and the week before, and it was still the same, a truly gorgeous spring evening, the air balmy, and warm, the sky a perfect cerulean blue and without clouds.

The worse the news was of a devastated Europe crumbling under Nazi jackboots, aggressively goose-stepping into countries too defenseless to withstand them, the more splendid the weather in England.

And to Emma, now walking down the steps, there was something terribly poignant, almost heartrending, about the radiance of these lovely days and nights when everything seemed so normal and all was tranquil under an English heaven. She could not help wondering how long it would be so . . . asking herself when the Nazi assault on her beloved country would begin in earnest. And she knew it would . . . and soon.

Her driver hurried to open the car door for her, touching his cap. "Evening, Mrs. Harte."

"Good evening, Tomkins, I was just admiring the weather. Isn't it a beautiful night?"

"It is, madame, an' a blinkin' miracle, it is that, this luverly warm spell. It's usually still a bit nippy in May."

After helping her into the backseat, he went around to the front, and a moment later the Rolls was smoothly pulling away from the curb.

"I'm going to the Dorchester," Emma murmured, settling back against the leather seat.

"Right you are, madame," Tomkins answered as he circled Belgrave Square and headed up toward Hyde Park Corner, making for Park Lane.

Emma thought about her destination as the car pushed through the early evening traffic. The Dorchester Hotel had been opened in April 1931, and from that moment it had been a favorite spot to rendezvous for royalty, the denizens of high society, politicians, and the rich and famous. Those who frequented it affectionately called it the Dorch; now it was more popular than ever because it was considered the safest hotel in London. This was because it had been built entirely of reinforced concrete, according to Blackie O'Neill, who knew the builder, Sir Malcolm MacAlpine. Blackie loved it as much as everyone else did, herself included.

It was Blackie's favorite place to dine, and she was on her way to meet him there now, and very much looking forward to seeing him. He had been absent for several weeks, and she missed him when he was out of town. He was her true and dearest friend.

Blackie had come up to London earlier in the day and had brought with him their old friend and longtime companion, David Kallinski. He had been depressed since his wife, Rebecca, had died, and his emotional state had scarcely been alleviated when he had discovered that his sons, Ronald and Mark, had joined the armed forces without conferring with him. Blackie had told her only last week that David was filled with a deep conviction his sons would be killed in battle on foreign soil.

I'll have to do my very best to pull David out of his black mood, Emma told herself. He meant a lot to her, and she could not bear to think that he was suffering. They had been in love with each other once, long, long ago, but she had walked away from the relationship because he was married. "I won't build my happiness on another person's unhappiness," she told him. David had eventually accepted her decision, and they had managed to preserve both their friendship and their business partnership in Lady Hamilton Clothes.

Quite suddenly his father's face flashed before her eyes, and she thought of Abraham Kallinski, her good friend in Leeds when she was a young girl, alone, destitute, and pregnant by Edwin Fairley.

One day when she had first lived in Leeds, she had been tramping along North Street looking for work at one of the clothing factories. It was near there that she had seen a couple of street hooligans throwing stones at a man, jeering at him, calling him a dirty Jew. Injured and bleeding, he had fallen down and lost his spectacles and his loaves of bread, called challah, she had found out later.

Without thought to her own safety, she had run to his aid, shaking her fist at the young thugs, saying she would call a bobby, yet ready to take them on single-handedly, forgetting momentarily that she was carrying a child in her womb.

After she had helped the man to his feet and picked up his glasses, she had dusted off the challah loaves and put them back in the paper bag, which contained several other items. He had asked her name and introduced himself as Abraham Kallinski, all the while thanking her profusely.

And then she had helped him to his house on Imperial Street. "A most unfortunate name for that poor little street, considering it is hardly royal in any sense of that word," he had told her, and she remembered his wry smile even to this day. He had gone on to explain that the street was in the Leylands, and only then had she been afraid, for she knew that this was the ghetto and dangerous. But she had taken him home anyway, wanting to be sure he would be safe, and now she recalled the way Janessa Kallinski, his wife, and their two sons had welcomed her. They had taken her under their wing, she, a stranger, and Abraham had given her a job at his little clothing factory and treated her like one of his own.

Having just run away from Fairley village on the Yorkshire moors, she had not known the ways of the big city, nor had she really known what a Jew was, and it was Abraham who had explained about their religion, their customs and their ways. Yes, she remembered all of the Kallinskis with great affection, and she owed them so much for their kindness to her some thirty-five years ago. . . .

"Here we are, Mrs. Harte," her driver announced, interrupting her thoughts as he brought the Rolls-Royce to a standstill in front of the hotel.

"I'll be a couple of hours, Tomkins," Emma informed him. "So if you'd like to go and have supper that will be perfectly all right."

"Thank you kindly, Mrs. Harte. But I'll just hang around in the vicinity. I'll be about when you come out."

Emma nodded and stepped out of the car, assisted by the doorman in his dark green uniform and tall top hat. She walked toward the wall of sandbags, which had been built around the front entrance of the hotel after war was declared on September 3 last year. This offered protection, as did the shingles which had been added to the roof at the same time, according to Blackie, who seemed to know everything about his beloved Dorch.

Making her way across the elegant front hall, Emma was instantly struck by the activity; people were milling around, others standing chatting, bellboys and porters were rushing about their duties, and telephones were ringing insistently. The Dorchester lobby appeared to be busier than usual. But then the whole of London was hectic these days, teeming with troops, both enlisted men and officers, American war correspondents, and the rather forlorn-looking refugees who had flooded in from Europe. Many of them were Jews fleeing persecution, and her heart went out to them.

Inclining her head, smiling at the head concierge, with whom she was acquainted, she walked on through the larger hall, making for the restaurant, unaware of the eyes that followed her progress with great interest.

At the restaurant entrance the maître d'

greeted her pleasantly, then escorted her to the table where Blackie was seated with David. Both men rose as she approached, and each kissed her on the cheek.

Once the maître d' had seen that she was seated, he departed discreetly. Now Emma looked from Blackie to David and said in a loving voice, "It's wonderful to see my boys. I've missed you both."

They beamed at her, and Blackie cocked his head to one side, his black eyes narrowing slightly as he said, with a small, delighted chuckle, "Well, mavourneen, I can see you've been titivating yourself up a bit, and all I can say is that you're a sight for sore eyes. And a mighty bonny one at that, my lass."

"My lass indeed! Some lass," she shot back dryly, but her expression was warm and her deep green eyes were merrier than they had been in a long time. "Thank you, Blackie darling. You're a sight for sore eyes, too, and so are you, David. It's been weeks since *you* were in town." Emma laid her hand on his arm affectionately. "You have to come to London more often, so I can pamper you a little bit."

"I will," David replied. "And I've missed *you*, Emma. Blackie's right, you know." He cast an appraising eye over her and added, "You're bonnier than ever."

"Sounds to me as if you've kissed that famous stone in Ireland Blackie O'Neill embraced so enthusiastically donkey's years ago," Emma murmured. "But it's a nice compliment, and I thank you. I decided tonight it was time to put away all the black mourning clothes, cut my hair, and titivate myself a bit, as Blackie so aptly calls it. I suddenly realized I had to come back to the land of living, because life *is* for the living. Paul would be the first to say that, David, and so would Rebecca."

He nodded and forced a smile. "I agree with you, and before my wife died she said something similar, so I've managed to bring my sadness to heel . . . at least I hope I have." He threw Blackie a questioning look.

"David's been wonderful today, Emm. The best I've seen him in a month of Sundays."

"Your hair is as beautiful as always," David now said, gazing at her, and when he smiled it was a natural smile, full of love. He had always adored her.

And so had Blackie, who asked, "And now, me darlin', what would you be wanting to drink?"

"Oh, Blackie, I think I'd like a glass of champagne. Yes, that would be nice."

"Right away. David and I are enjoying a drop of good Irish, but we might partake of the bubbly later, so I'll order a bottle. What would you be preferring?"

"Pol Roger is my new favorite, thanks, Blackie."

He nodded, motioned to the waiter, who was by his side in an instant. After Blackie had given the order and the waiter was out of earshot, Emma asked, "How's Bryan? Is he all right?"

"Aye, Emma love, he is, although as I keep telling you, I'm not too happy he joined up so quickly. But these young lads are in such a hurry, wanting to do their bit for their country, full of patriotism, itching to fight the Jerries, just as we were in the Great War."

"I don't think you were all that keen," Emma murmured thoughtfully, throwing him a knowing look. "If I remember correctly, you and Joe were quite late joining up. You both waited to be *called* up, as a matter of fact . . . married men *last,* that was the rule of the day. I'm positive you and Joe joined the Seaforth Highlanders in 1916, after the Compulsory Service Act was passed. I've a good memory, you know."

"I don't be doubting," he said, "and aye, you're quite right about this year. Nineteen sixteen it was."

Turning to David, Emma said, "Ronnie and Mark will be all right, David, try not to worry so much about them."

"I do try, but it's awfully hard," he answered, making an effort to sound more cheerful for her. She was so brave and strong, he didn't want to appear weak in her eyes.

Blackie, meanwhile, was suddenly flooded with memories of the Great War. Yes, she was right, he and Joe *had* gone only when they had to, sent to France and the Battle of the Somme. He thought of the rain. And the mud; he had been knee deep in it in the trenches. He could almost smell the cordite, and the sound of the cannonade seemed to reverberate in his head. Pure hell it had been. The kind of hell he prayed his son would not have to face. *The Battle of the Somme . . .* where Joe had been killed. Emma's first husband, Joe Lowther, the father of Kit. And now Kit was with the British Expeditionary Force fighting another war with Germany after the last one had barely ended only twenty-odd years ago. He prayed that Kit and Bryan, and David's sons, did not become cannon fodder. He prayed for all of the boys at the front . . .

"Don't you agree, Blackie?" Emma asked.

Rousing himself from his introspection, Blackie muttered, "I'm sorry, Emm, I missed that."

"I was just saying to David that when you look around this restaurant you'd never know there was a war on. The women are elegantly dressed and bejeweled, very glamorous, and the men are smart, too."

"That's true," he replied. "On the other hand, those somewhat weary-looking Royal Air Force officers over at that end table give the game away, don't you think?"

After the waiter had poured a tasting of champagne, Emma took a sip and nodded; he then filled the flute and departed.

Blackie picked up his glass, touched it first to Emma's and then to David's, and said, "Cheers! Here's to old friends."

The two of them responded in unison, and after a sip of the icy cold sparkling champagne, Emma announced, "I will never forget the date." She looked pointedly at Blackie and then at David. "It will go down as one of the most memorable dates in the history of England. Wait, I'd like to amend that . . . the most *momentous* date in the history of our country."

"Now which date are you talkin' about?" Blackie asked, peering across the table at her, frowning. "I'm afraid I'm not following you, Emm. Are you, David?"

David shook his head, also puzzled. "I'm sorry, Emma."

Emma gave them both the benefit of her incandescent smile, that famous smile not seen by either of them for a very long time. She explained, "Friday May the tenth, 1940. *Yesterday's date,* to be exact. You know as well as I do that something truly wonderful happened last night. Winston Churchill walked into Number Ten Downing Street as the new Prime Minister, and at long last. Now I am positive we are going to win this war!"

"Aye, Emma, you're quite right, Winston's the best man for the job, and some job he's got, to be sure. We are in great peril. And we are facing a long road, and it's going to be a bumpy one, but he'll pull us through. We'll beat the Jerries, so long as Churchill is our leader. The country's behind him, even if the politicians in Westminster are not."

"I endorse that," David remarked with a quiet authority. "I must admit, I thought we'd be stuck with Neville Chamberlain and his ridiculous talk of appeasement. Who can appease Hitler? He's voracious for power and world domination."

Blackie nodded. "He wants all of Europe. And England as well. I'll tell you this, and you mark my words, the two of you, he'll invade our little island home . . . at least he'll give it a try."

"He will never succeed!" Emma cried. Picking up her champagne glass, she added, "Let's drink a toast to our savior . . . the savior of Western civilization. Here's to Winston Churchill!"

Crystal clinked against crystal, and the three of them repeated his name with genuine enthusiasm. Like Emma, Blackie and David had wanted Churchill back in power for years. He was the only man they trusted in the British government, the only man they believed could lead them to victory against the Nazis.

After a moment, Blackie said slowly, "To think how they've ignored Winston, all those bloody idiots in the government. He's been warning them about the threat of Hitler for years, and not one of them paid any attention. He was a voice in the wilderness, and all the bloody politicians did was cling to the coattails of Chamberlain, who would have led us all to doom if he'd remained in office much longer. Just think on this, he makes a pact with Hitler, whose armies have *already* trampled down half of Europe. It's not believable. And there's another thing, nobody here has done a bloody thing about rearming the country. We're not prepared for war at all. We have no arms, well very few, not many bombs, and certainly not many planes. In truth, we don't have much to defend ourselves with. I suppose because we've been led by a blind man backed up by his sycophants."

David nodded vigorously, looked across at Emma. "Hitler's armies are marching into France at this very moment, and the Gestapo will hotfoot it behind them, in order to persecute and murder Jews." He shook his head sorrowfully, anguish entering his blue eyes. "And Chamberlain believes Hitler wants peace! The man's unconscionable! Thank God he's left office."

Emma said in a low voice, "There's none so blind as those who will not see."

Twenty-seven

"Do I look all right, Mummy?" Elizabeth said, walking into Emma's bedroom.

Emma swung around to face her daughter. Elizabeth stood staring at her mother openmouthed.

"Whatever's wrong?" Emma asked, peering across the room at the nineteen-year-old.

"Nothing's wrong, Mummy, you look absolutely and impossibly *gorgeous!* Whatever have you done since last week?" As she spoke Elizabeth floated into the room on the most beautiful legs Emma had ever seen, adding, "Well, it's perfectly obvious you've cut your hair, but there's something else . . . you look so *glamorous.*"

Emma began to laugh. "It's just the suit. I dug it out from the back of my wardrobe. And yes, I did cut my hair, but that's all I've done, darling, I promise."

"No, it's not, you've stopped wearing *black*. And so perhaps it is *partially* the suit. Pale blue has always been your color, it looks wonderful with your red hair. And it's perfect for today, it's like the middle of summer outside. Tony says the worse the news the better the weather."

"I thought that myself on Saturday night when I went to dinner with Blackie and David. Anyway, darling girl, to answer your initial question, you don't look *all right,* that's the understatement of the year. You look positively beautiful, and if anyone's gorgeous it's you, Elizabeth."

Emma spoke the truth. Elizabeth Barkstone, who was Robin's twin, had movie star good looks. A cloud of shining black, wavy hair surrounded an exquisite, delicate face, with high cheekbones, a slender nose, and a smooth, wide forehead. Black brows arched above clear blue eyes, which were large and set wide apart. She had a slender but shapely figure and those long legs that drew masculine whistles of admiration on the street.

Until last year she had been studying at the Royal Academy of Dramatic Art, having long wanted a career in the theater; Emma had always thought she would succeed, considering her somewhat wayward daughter the consummate actress.

But this past January, Elizabeth had dropped out to become a Red Cross nurse. "I feel I must be part of the war effort, Mummy," her daughter had told Emma at the time. "I want to do something worthwhile, especially with Tony up there in the air, fighting the German Luftwaffe."

Emma had fully understood and endorsed this move. In December 1939, Elizabeth had married Tony Barkstone, a great friend of Robin, who was also in the RAF, from Cambridge. They had met through her twin brother and fallen madly in love. Even though Elizabeth was only eighteen at the time, and Tony not much older, Emma had not had the heart to stop them marrying. As Blackie had said, "If he's old enough to be sent up into the skies in a Spitfire to defend our country, then he's old enough to get married. And so is she."

The wedding had been small and quiet, because of the war, but lovely, and all of the family had been present except Kit, who couldn't get leave. Edwina, who was still estranged from Emma, had remained in Ireland but had sent a wedding gift. Emma had long wished there was a way to heal the breach. But Edwina was nothing if not stubborn, and she would not bend. The fact that she was illegitimate troubled her to the point of loathing her mother.

Emma said, "I'm glad you're wearing your uniform; it suits you very well, and you do it justice. But aside from that, I think it's appropriate for this afternoon. It strikes just the right note."

"I would have felt a bit odd not wearing it, Mummy. I'm proud of being a nurse, doing something worthwhile for the war. It's a good feeling, being able to help others."

"Yes, it is. Now, I just have to put on my jewelry, and then we can leave."

"I think you should wear blue stones today," Elizabeth ventured. "The aquamarine pin, perhaps, and the earrings to match."

Emma paused on her way to her dressing table, glanced over her shoulder at her daughter. "I'm going to wear my string of pearls and pearl earrings, Elizabeth, I want to keep everything simple."

"Oh yes, I understand." Elizabeth strolled to an easy chair and sat down. "I spoke to Tony yesterday. He called from the RAF station in Yorkshire, where he's gone for special training . . . Topcliffe. He sends his love."

"Give him mine the next time he phones," Emma murmured. "I wrote to him the other day, to all of the boys, in fact. Kit, Robin, Bryan, Randolph, Mark, and Ronnie . . . the whole gang."

"You're just amazing. I don't know how you do it all. Running the stores, Paul's companies, and everything else that's under your control. By the way, I forgot to ask, how's the Little Tadpole?"

Turning around again, Emma said softly, "She's fine, and I do wish you wouldn't call Daisy that. You know it's not really a very nice name, and I'm surprised she doesn't resent it."

"Oh, Mummy darling, don't be so silly!

She knows it's a joke from the days when she loved to play with the frogs in the pond at Pennistone Royal. Anyway, it was Paul who started calling her that, not I."

"I know." Emma smoothed her hands over the immaculately tailored Lanvin suit, picked up her handbag, and said, "Well, let's be off, we don't want to be late for the House of Commons. Aunt Jane wanted us to arrive by one-thirty, no later than one-forty-five. This is Winston Churchill's first speech in the House as Prime Minister. We must not miss a single word."

They sat together in the gallery. Three beautiful women: Emma Harte, Elizabeth Barkstone, and Jane Stuart Ogden, wife of William Stuart Ogden, Conservative Member of Parliament for South-East Leeds. Quite a few pairs of eyes swiveled to stare, and all of those long stares were full of admiration.

When Jane had heard from her husband earlier in the day that Winston Churchill was to speak in the House that afternoon, she had telephoned Emma to invite her to hear him. It was May the thirteenth, Whitsun bank holiday Monday, and the House of Commons was packed.

Emma was amazed at the reception Neville Chamberlain, the outgoing Prime Minister, was given when he came in. It seemed to her that *everyone* was cheering and applauding.

How can they? she asked herself. This man has led us into an abyss with his policy of appeasement, his reluctance to rearm, his blindness to events in Europe. He has been a disaster for this country and for its people.

These dire thoughts were replaced with the utmost admiration when she spotted Winston Churchill entering the Commons chamber. Emma waited for an even greater acclamation than Chamberlain had received, but it was not forthcoming. Later Jane would tell her that the cheers for him emanated mostly from the Labour and Liberal benches, not from his own Conservative Party.

It infuriated Emma that Churchill was being treated in this shabby and mean-spirited way. They just didn't understand. Did not understand either this man and what he stood for or the mood of the country. The people wanted Winston back, and thank God, now they had him.

When Churchill began to speak, Emma leaned forward eagerly. That marvelous, mesmerizing voice rang out:

"I would say to the House, as I said to those who have joined the Government, 'I have nothing to offer but blood, toil, tears and sweat.' We have before us an ordeal of the most grievous kind. . . . You ask, what is our policy? I will say: It is to wage war, by sea, land and air, with all our might and with all the strength that God can give us: to wage war against a monstrous tyranny, never surpassed in the dark, lamentable catalogue of human crime. That is our policy. You ask, What is our aim? I can answer in one word: Victory — victory at all costs, victory in spite of all terror, victory, however long and hard the road may be; for without victory, there is no survival."

Tears filled Emma's eyes, and it took her a moment to bring her emotions under control. This man, whom she instinctively understood was a great man, perhaps even the greatest man in England today, never failed to touch her with his words and sentiments. No wonder the ordinary man and woman in the street loved him, believed in him, wanted him to lead them.

Much later that evening, just before Emma went to bed, she took out her diary, and recorded the events of the day. In her neat and gently sloping handwriting, she gave the details of her visit to the House of Commons to hear Winston Churchill speak. And then she wrote:

Parts of his speech moved me to tears. He has such a command of the English language. He convinces. And he inspires; he is the inspiration of this country. He has come to power in the most dangerous of times, and he has inherited an unholy mess, but somehow he will prevail. He makes me feel safe. And very proud.

She finally closed the diary. Then she went to bed, and she knew that tonight she would sleep because at last they had a valiant and determined leader. And a promise for the future.

Twenty-eight

Over the years Emma had mostly walked to Harte's in Knightsbridge, weather permitting. But of late walking had become mandatory. She needed to traverse these familiar streets to reassure herself that all was well in this great metropolis, a city in which she had lived half her life, and which she loved.

It comforted her when she saw the smiling faces of the Londoners as they went about their daily tasks. The bobbies following their beat, the newsboys on the street corners yelling the headlines; the cabbies, the milkmen, the window cleaners, and the char ladies, all of them stalwart and full of good cheer.

Also out on the streets these days were the Home Guard and the ARP wardens, their presence reassuring but underscoring the fact that England was at war. Sometimes it did not seem like it to her; there was a normality to daily life, and London was peaceful, still unscarred. There had been no invasion; nothing had happened since war had been declared last September. That was why so many people now called it the Phony War.

On this Friday morning in late May, Emma crossed Belgrave Square at a brisk pace, once again marveling at the weather. It was a blessing to have these warm, sunny days without clouds and even the merest hint of rain, but there were moments when she felt there was a terrible beauty to this unusual spring. It was . . . *unreal,* that was the only word to describe it. As her daughter Elizabeth kept saying to her, "The nicer the weather the worse the news gets."

And the news was very bad indeed.

At this very moment thousands of British and French troops were in retreat, falling back to the coastline as the Wehrmacht divisions progressed from the Low Countries into the middle of France. The German army, millions strong, was pushing the Allied troops into Calais and Dunkirk, and RAF bases in France had been attacked once again.

Only last night the BBC had broadcast the latest and most dire bulletin: Allied troops would soon be trapped between German artillery and the sea. They would be sitting ducks on the beaches; the Luftwaffe would be in the skies in full force.

Emma's eldest son, Kit, was in France, and so was Robin, who spent most of his time in a Spitfire, flying over France. As did her son-in-law, Tony Barkstone, and Bryan, Blackie's son. He was her surrogate son in a sense, since she had brought him up after Laura's death, when Blackie was away fighting in the First World War.

Ronnie and Mark Kallinski were over there, and so was her nephew Randolph Harte, her brother Winston's son. Her heart sank when she considered what could happen . . . the youth of the three clans could so easily be killed. Just like that, in a flash.

France is going to fall, Emma suddenly thought, with a clarity that stunned her. Her step faltered for a moment, and then she took a deep breath and walked on determinedly. England will have to go on alone . . . because we have no alternative. It will be a fight to the death, though. Churchill will see to that.

Yesterday Blackie and David had come up to London, and she had invited them to dinner at the Belgrave Square house. Because he had business to discuss with her, David had arranged to come a little earlier. At one moment he had expressed his worries about their sons and Blackie's, and they had commiserated with each other.

They had moved on after that, mostly talking about Lady Hamilton Clothes, currently producing uniforms for the armed forces instead of ladies' fashions. Emma had not been surprised when David told her that they had, just the day before, received another large order for winter overcoats for the army and air force.

"As we both knew, Emma, the government is expecting the war to continue into next spring," he had pointed out. And Emma had swiftly answered, "Yes, we're in for a long siege, I'm afraid. We must face that now, not have any pipe dreams about the conflict being over soon." She had sighed and gone on. "Despite rationing and the blackout, and everything else we're having to put up with, the war hasn't really hit us yet. At least not here."

Once they had finished talking about their joint business ventures, which went back years, David had exclaimed that she was looking more like her old self, even better than she had when he had seen her at the Dorchester.

"You've put on weight, filled out a bit. Yes, you look just wonderful. All you need is a bit of color in those pretty cheeks of yours, Emma. Perhaps you should come to Yorkshire for a while, get out on the moors. It would be nice for me if you spent more time at the Leeds and Harrogate stores."

She had not given much thought to his compliments or his affectionate embraces last night, because Blackie had suddenly arrived and taken over in his inimitable way. And she had been busy helping Grace and Mrs. Coddington, the cook, get dinner onto the table. Podges, her butler of several years, had left to join the Royal Navy, and Rita, the other parlor maid, had joined the ATS. And so she was short of staff. But they had managed very well, the three of them, and her two boys had enjoyed the dinner, relishing the home-cooked Yorkshire pudding and roast beef.

Then this morning, when she was reviewing the evening in her head, she had suddenly wondered if David's interest in her was no longer fraternal. Did he see her as a potential lover now? After all, he was a widower. She had no interest in rekindling their old relationship, which had died a natural death thirty-odd years ago. However, she knew she must be careful. She must not hurt him; still, she didn't want to give him the impression she was encouraging him.

Emma sighed as she pushed open the side door of Harte's and went inside. The last thing she was interested in was an involvement with a man. Those days were over. *Absolutely.*

Emma spent the morning at her desk going over balance sheets. But at one moment she opened a folder which held the inventories of the store's goods. Everything was listed, from clothes to foodstuffs.

As she scanned the first few pages of the overall appraisals, she was relieved to see that they were in good shape, at least for the time being. But as the war continued she knew most things, especially food, would be difficult to obtain.

The Food Halls of Harte's had been impressive from the day she had opened the store. They were renowned the world over, and they had always been stocked to the hilt, especially with fresh produce, baked and boiled hams, meat pies, pâtés, a variety of cheeses, cold meats and sausages, a selection of game pies, smoked salmon, smoked trout, and the like. But she realized these items would soon be in short supply.

I'll just have to cope, she muttered to herself, leaning back in the chair, staring off into space for a moment. Rationing had been enforced some time ago.

The phone shrilled, cutting into her thoughts, and she picked it up. "Hello?"

"Mrs. Harte, it's Mr. O'Neill," her secretary told her.

"Oh yes, put him through, please."

A moment later Blackie's voice boomed over the phone. "Hello, Emma. Now, shall we have lunch today? Or dinner, whichever you prefer."

"Just the two of us?" she asked, a lilt of laughter in her voice.

"Sure an' just the two of us! I couldn't get a word in edgewise last night. I thought David would never stop talking. I love the lad, but —" Blackie cut himself off, chuckled. "I'd like to have you to meself a bit, mavourneen."

Emma smiled into the phone. "I think it *will* have to be lunch, Blackie, if you don't mind. I promised Elizabeth I'd spend the evening with her. She's so worried about Tony because of the latest news."

"Understandable, understandable. So, lunch it is then. How about the good old Dorch? Unless you're getting bored with it."

Emma laughed. "Bored with it! I haven't been there since we had dinner together at Whitsuntide. I've not been out, actually, I've been working round the clock."

"That's your problem, Emm. You're always at it, and you always have been. You've got to slow down," he told her, his tone chastising.

"Don't be daft," she exclaimed. "You should know better than to say that to me of all people."

"Aye, I should, considering the length of time I've known you. So, the Dorchester at one o'clock. Can you make it by then?"

"Yes. I'll be there on time."

"Well, there's certainly no evidence of rationing or food shortages here," Emma murmured when she had joined Blackie in the hotel's restaurant and scanned the menu. "Smoked salmon, smoked trout, cold lobster,

Morecambe Bay potted shrimps, roast beef, shoulder of lamb, beef patties, steak-and-kidney pie, and roast quail."

"Aye, you wouldn't think we were living in dire times," Blackie agreed, nodding his great leonine head. "All the luxury hotels are still serving three-course meals, and the food is as good as it's always been. But for how long, I wonder? We might as well enjoy ourselves whilst we can. Do you know what you fancy, Emma?"

"I think I'll have the potted shrimps, and then grilled sole, thank you, Blackie."

"Sounds good to me, I'll have the same." He gave her a broad smile and motioned to the waiter.

Once they had ordered lunch, the two of them talked about the war, mostly focusing on what they had heard on the radio last night about the plight of the troops in France.

At one moment Emma said, "I don't know how we can get them off the beaches, Blackie. Surely the water's too shallow for the destroyers to get in close to the shore."

"It is, and you can bet your bottom dollar that the sea is mined." He shook his head again, his face grave, and then, after glancing around the restaurant, he leaned closer to her. He said in a voice that was almost inaudible, "But we're going to start doing something —" He broke off as a couple walked past their table.

"Doing what?" Emma asked, drawing closer, her eyes riveted on his.

"I can't go into details right now," he muttered. "Let me just say this, we'll be using the little boats —" Again he broke off as two army officers sat down at a table nearby.

"How do you know?"

"Oh, Emma, *lass*," he said quietly, "you know I can't tell you that. And I wouldn't even if I could. Better you don't know who my" — he dropped his voice and finished — "government sources are."

"But what's the plan?" she probed, unable to let go.

Blackie realized she would pester him until he gave her more information, so he said, "I'll walk you back to the store, after lunch, and we can have a chat then."

Emma nodded. "That's a good idea." She went on, "How long are you staying in London?"

"Just for a few days. I have to get back to Leeds. We still have a couple of buildings under construction, and I want to get 'em finished as soon as possible. But I really don't know what's going to happen with my business. A number of contracts have been canceled because of the war."

"You're not going to close down, are you?" she cut in swiftly, worry settling on her face. She had always been concerned for him.

"Oh no, no, lass, it's not as bad as that.

Tell you the truth, I have enough put away to carry the business for quite a long spell."

"I'm glad to hear that," Emma murmured. She was about to say that he should never worry, that she would always be there for him, but then she changed her mind. He was so proud; she didn't want to upset him. Anyway, she was well aware he was a millionaire many times over because of the success of his building company, his ownership of several office buildings and shops in Leeds, and other buildings in Harrogate and Sheffield. He was a fine builder, a brilliant businessman.

After this short silence, Blackie asked, "Any news from Edwina?" As he spoke he wondered if he'd asked the wrong question.

Emma grimaced, then shook her head. "I never hear from her, although Winston sometimes does. She always loved her uncle, you know, and she did invite him to the wedding. . . . The trouble with Edwina is that she's stubborn, Blackie, as you well know, and that stubbornness sometimes gets in the way of her better nature. I hope she comes around one day."

"She will, to be sure." He looked at her and began to chuckle, his black eyes merry.

"What is it?" she asked, staring back at him quizzically.

"I remember the day we christened her, in the kitchen sink at Laura's house in Upper

Armley, because you were afraid to go to the church —"

"I *wasn't* afraid! I've never been afraid of anything," Emma exclaimed. "I simply didn't want the embarrassment of the vicar knowing she was illegitimate. And you *know* that, we discussed it at the time," she finished snippily.

"Aye, I expect we did. And such a little itty-bitty thing you were in those days, Emma, a sprite. You were thin as a rail but so full of vim and vigor. I did admire you."

"I was strong, Blackie, and that was the most important thing of all."

He nodded and said nothing, thinking of their early days in Leeds, when he had been a navvy, at times building canals, at others working on the railway lines, occasionally doing private jobs for the likes of Squire Adam Fairley. That's when he had met her, on the way to Fairley Hall. He had come across her hurrying over the moors to that miserable house on a wintry morning. It was there she worked as a maid. Skivvy, more like, he added to himself, the way they treated her. They'd turned her into a drudge, and she only fourteen.

Blackie O'Neill glanced around the rather grand restaurant of the Dorchester Hotel, marveling to himself that she and he had come so far, she more than he, in many ways.

Emma said, "A penny for your thoughts, Blackie, you're looking so faraway."

He grinned at her. "Thinking about our early days, that I was, and who would have imagined that you would have become such a grand and elegant woman, a real lady." He winked at her and added, "Even though most of the time you're still a drudge, as you were then, working like the navvy I used to be."

"Nobody ever died of hard work, Blackie."

"Aye, Emma, I've heard you say that many times, for the last thirty years, in fact. But sometimes I think you're too hard on yourself. You should take it a little easier; after all, you are fifty."

"Fifty-*one* on April thirtieth, Blackie. But I don't feel it. I feel like a young woman inside, like a twenty-year-old."

"And that's what you look."

"It's *me* sitting here, Shane Patrick Desmond O'Neill. And please remember that I am fully aware you did your teething on the Blarney Stone."

"Only too true, mavourneen. Ah, here comes the waiter with our Morecambe Bay potted shrimps." He threw her a long, old-fashioned look and winked.

The following evening Blackie and David came to Emma's house in Belgravia, again for a home-cooked supper. Afterward, they adjourned to the library for coffee and cognac, and at one moment Blackie volunteered, "I was told last night by one of my government friends that we're assembling quite an armada to get our boys off beaches in Dunkirk. If anyone can do it, the Prime Minister can."

David and Emma agreed with him wholeheartedly, and later Emma turned on the radio so that they could listen to the nine o'clock news on the BBC. And that night, Saturday, May 25, they learned that the British army was completely isolated; it had been separated from the French. The Germans occupied Boulogne, and the other French ports in the English Channel were falling one by one.

The three old friends sat in silence for a short while after the broadcast was finished, filled with dismay.

It was Emma who finally roused herself and said, "They're all alone out there, targets for the enemy, I know that. Nonetheless, we must believe they're going to be all right . . . somehow. We can't give up hope. That would be defeatist. No, we must believe all of those boys are coming home. They're young and they're tough and they *are* going to make it."

It was an armada the likes of which the world had never seen. But it was an armada with an implacable will to succeed. Its aim: to get the British troops off the beaches of

Dunkirk and back to England before they were annihilated by the German onslaught.

The motley assemblage included an amazing assortment of vessels, and they had made the hazardous journey across the Channel from every corner of England to assist the British destroyers and light battleships anchored off Dunkirk. The bigger ships were making desperate efforts to evacuate the men on those wide open beaches, but because of the shallows they could not move in close.

However, the little vessels could, and they ferried the troops to the safety of the Royal Navy ships, which in turn transported them to Deal and Ramsgate.

These little boats were owned and manned entirely by civilians. Volunteers from all walks of life, and none of them would rest until the sons of England were safely home.

And so they came . . . in their little rowing boats and yachts, in sailing boats and fishing trawlers, pleasure steamers and even barges from the canals of England. Anything that could float, and was seaworthy, set sail. There were over a thousand vessels in all. It was the most daring rescue ever known.

The evacuation went on under heavy enemy fire, and fierce bombardment from the Luftwaffe circling the skies above. But the RAF was up there, too, ensuring that the enemy planes did not have supremacy in the skies.

The whole of Britain waited in suspense.

On Sunday, May 26, the weather broke, and it poured rain for the first time in weeks. Like everyone else, Emma was more than ever worried because of the weather, believing it might slow down the rescue mission. But the BBC reported that the seas were calm, and this reassured her somewhat. Also, her confidence in Churchill did not wane, and this helped to keep her spirits up.

At work as well as at home, Emma was glued to the radio. On Monday evening she was thrilled to hear on a BBC news bulletin that 7,000 men had been evacuated by the end of that day, and on Tuesday night she learned that 17,000 soldiers had been rescued. The rest of the week, as the boats and navy ships plowed the Channel, 50,000 troops were lifted off the beaches every day. In the end, 200,000 soldiers were evacuated in those four days alone, stunning a nation that was suddenly and unexpectedly joyful.

The rescue surpassed anything the Prime Minister and his War Cabinet had thought possible. The epic of Dunkirk gripped the imagination of Britain and her Allies. Out of hell came all the little steamers and rowing boats and pleasure steamers, bringing back the living and the wounded. The evacuation had taken eleven days, and some 335,000 Allied troops, including 26,000 French soldiers, had been brought to safety by the time

411

the Germans captured the sea town. Their equipment had been abandoned, but the men were safe, and that was all that mattered. Only 40,000, mostly French troops, were left behind.

Emma was thankful that she was one of those who could rejoice. On June 3 her son Kit stepped off the barge that had transported him to Deal across a choppy Channel jammed with wreckage and vessels. Many of the small boats, in a hurry, simply ferried the troops across to the coast of Kent, bypassing the destroyers and bigger ships, anxious to get the boys home without delay. Then they turned around and went back for more.

David was euphoric when he telephoned from Leeds to tell her that both Ronnie and Mark had been among the troops who landed at Ramsgate, and she soon learned from Blackie that Bryan was safe. And so, fortunately, were her son Robin and Elizabeth's husband, who had survived the air battles over Dunkirk and were back at the RAF station at Biggin Hill.

Later, when he came home on leave, Kit told her: "I made it by the skin of my teeth, Mother. I must have a guardian angel watching over me." He embraced her tightly, and Emma choked up, thinking of his father, Joe Lowther, who had died in France in 1916, apparently in vain.

Twenty-nine

"I'm sorry to bother you, Mrs. Harte, but I wonder if I could have a word with you."

Emma looked up from the papers on her desk and smiled at her secretary standing in the doorway. "Of course, Anita, come in and sit down."

The young woman gave her a tentative smile, stepped into the office, and closed the door. Then she walked across to Emma's big partners' desk and took the seat opposite her.

After studying Anita for a second, Emma said, "You've got a face like a wet week, as my brother would say. Now, Anita, my dear, it can't be all that bad, can it?"

Anita shook her blond head and forced a smile. "It's not, not really. But I think you're going to be upset, Mrs. Harte, and the last thing I'd want to do would be to upset you, you've been so good to me, but —" Anita paused, took a deep breath, and finished in a rush, "I'm leaving, Mrs. Harte, I want to give you my notice."

Startled though she was, it took Emma only a moment to catch on, and she exclaimed, "Well, I certainly don't want to lose you, Anita, but I think you're going to tell me that you're joining one of the services. Is that it?"

"Not exactly. Well, what I mean is, I'm not going into the ATS or the WAFs. I'm joining the *Land Army,* Mrs. Harte. I am going to be one of the land girls working on farms, helping out because the men have gone to war."

"I see. That's very worthy of you." Emma smiled, put down her pen, and leaned back in the chair. "I must admit, it had crossed my mind that you might want to do your bit for the war effort, and of course I think it goes without saying that I'm sorry to lose you. You've been an excellent secretary and worked very well here."

"Thank you, Mrs. Harte. I love the store, you know. But I just don't feel right, what with my three brothers in the forces and my sister working in a munitions factory. I want to . . . well . . . pull my weight, so to speak."

"I understand, I really do. All of the young people feel as you do, Anita."

"I hate to let you down, I know what a lot of work you have."

"Yes, and I shall miss you, you've been a godsend over the last couple of years. Actually, I don't quite know what I'll do without you." Emma brought her hand to her chin, her eyes suddenly growing thoughtful.

"What about one of the junior secretaries who work out there with you? Either of them a possibility for me?"

"I think Fanny might be . . . in a year. Both she and Lois *are* juniors, Mrs. Harte. I give them a lot of the filing, letters to type, small things. Honestly, I don't think they could handle what I've been doing. Not that I want to blow my own horn, Mrs. Harte, but, well, they just haven't had my experience."

Emma nodded and sighed heavily as she thought of what faced her. "I suppose you're leaving immediately?" She raised an auburn brow as she spoke.

"Well . . ." Anita stopped, and leaning forward from the waist, she focused on Emma intently and said, "Look, Mrs. Harte, I hope I'm not doing the wrong thing saying this, but I think you should talk to Mr. Harte's junior secretary. He's not in London much these days, since he's been running all the Yorkshire stores, and I don't think she has all that much to do because Brenda Small is the senior secretary. She's a very competent junior from what I've noticed."

"Perhaps I should talk to her, and I doubt Mr. Harte would mind, because he *is* away a great deal these days."

Anita sat up straight. She beamed at Emma, pleased that her idea had been received so well. "Shall I go and get her, Mrs. Harte?"

415

"I think I'd better speak to my brother first. He's here in London this week, and he'll be coming to the store today. If he's not already here. And thank you for your suggestion, Anita. By the way, when will you be leaving me?"

"I'd like to give a week's notice, but I can stretch it to two if necessary, Mrs. Harte."

Ten minutes later Winston Harte was sitting in the chair just vacated by Anita Holmes.

He listened closely as Emma spoke, nodding from time to time, paying strict attention to her words as he always did. He adored his sister and thought she was the most brilliant person he had ever known.

When she had finished repeating Anita's conversation, he said at once, "No problem, Emma. It's true, I'm hardly here these days, and one of the other juniors in my office can help Brenda if there's any spillover."

"If you're sure, Winston. She would be a great help until I can find someone else, a permanent secretary."

Winston chuckled. "I doubt you'll want anyone else."

"Oh, she's that good?"

"Yes, she is, as a matter of fact."

"Glynnis . . . Glynnis Jenkins. Isn't that her name?"

Winston nodded. "She's Welsh, from the

Rhondda, and quite aside from being a good secretary, she's straightforward, a very nice young woman altogether, Emm."

Emma's relief was reflected on her face; her vivid green eyes suddenly looked less worried. "It's nice of you to do this, Winston."

"Anything for you, love, and I know you're a bit overwhelmed at the moment. The McGill Holdings to handle on top of everything else is a hell of a load for you."

"Yes, it is, and it's awfully time consuming. But you'll never hear *me* complain, Winston. When Paul left me everything, he made me one of the richest women in the world, and Daisy a great heiress, as you well know. I do my best to look after McGill Holdings properly because the company will go to her one day, and to her progeny . . . that's what Paul wanted, you know. He wanted Daisy and any children she might have to be safe, and properly taken care of financially. Just as he took care of Constance and Howard in Australia. Those are lifetime trusts he created for them. He was very good that way."

Unexpectedly, a look of sorrow fell across her face like a dark shadow, her eyes turned cloudy, and Winston heard her imperceptible sigh. He asked softly, leaning forward, "Are you all right, our Emm?"

She stared across her desk at him and blinked several times, then swallowed hard.

"Yes, I'm fine, Winston . . ." Another sigh escaped, and she went on, "I wish he'd never gone back to see Constance about the divorce. He might still be alive if he'd come here from New York with me last year."

"He had to go, because he knew war was coming and he wanted to put his affairs in order, and make sure his companies would run properly without him. You know very well he did think he would have problems going back and forth to Sydney," Winston pointed out gently.

"You're right. And yet I can't help thinking if only . . ."

"Oh, Emma, darling, life is full of if onlys, you know that better than anyone else. And we all think *if only* we hadn't done that, or this . . . it's human nature to react in this way. But what about this? If only you hadn't married Arthur Ainsley, you'd have had a few extra years with Paul, have you ever thought about that?"

"Of course I have. But if I hadn't married Arthur, I wouldn't have had Robin and Elizabeth, now would I?"

"No, you wouldn't." Changing the subject, Winston now said, "Is Henry Rossiter all right? I haven't heard you mention him lately. He is working out well, isn't he?"

Quite visibly Emma cheered up, and she exclaimed, "It's one of the best things I ever did, making him my financial adviser on a

418

permanent basis. He's been extremely smart with McGill Holdings, and he works very well with Mel Harrison in Sydney. Long-distance business relationships are not always successful, but this has been wonderful, and continues to be. As for Harry Marriott in Texas, he and I work well long distance, too. He's running Sitex Oil the way Paul did, and since he's a partner I know he has the company's interests at heart."

"I'm glad to hear all this, but it's still a burden for you at times. I wish I could help lessen the load."

"Oh, Winston, you do. You run the Yorkshire stores, and help me with Harte Enterprises. Very frankly, I don't know what I would do without you. Which is why, right now, I'm wondering how I could be so selfish and take one of your secretaries."

"It doesn't present a problem, Emma." Winston rose, smiled down at her. "I'll go and have a word with Glynnis and Brenda, of course. And then I'll bring Glynnis in so you can talk to her."

"Thanks, Winston." Emma's eyes followed him, and she could not help thinking how handsome he was. Like her, he was all Harte in looks and coloring; there was certainly no mistaking that they were brother and sister. His devotion to her meant a lot, and she realized, as he closed the door softly behind him, how much she relied on her older brother.

★ ★ ★

Within fifteen minutes Winston was back in her office, bringing with him Glynnis Jenkins. As Emma went to greet her, she found herself marveling at the young woman's looks. She had forgotten how beautiful the Welsh girl was. She wasn't beautiful in a classical way; she was too voluptuous for that. But she had a certain sultry glamour about her even though she wore a plainly tailored black cotton dress with a white collar and cuffs. Her thick, glossy brown hair, worn in a pageboy style, fell around a full face that was superbly sculpted, and she had a wide forehead, a pert nose, and dimples in her cheeks. Her eyes, large and thickly lashed, were blue and luminous.

"Here's Glynnis," Winston said, leading the young woman across Emma's office.

"Hello, Glynnis," Emma said, giving her a warm smile.

"Good morning, Mrs. Harte," Glynnis answered rather shyly, trying not to appear nervous.

"Now, let's go and sit down over there on the sofa," Emma went on, "so that we can have a little chat. I'm sure Mr. Harte has explained that Anita is leaving to join the Land Army."

"Oh yes, he has."

"Would you like to work for me, Glynnis?" Emma sat in a chair next to the sofa.

"Very much, Mrs. Harte." Glynnis cleared her throat and added, "I think I'll be able to do the job. I've learned a lot from Brenda . . ." She let her voice trail off and sat down on the sofa, looking first at Winston, who remained standing, then back at Emma. "I'll certainly try very hard, Mrs. Harte."

"I'm sure you will."

Moving toward the door, Winston said, "You'll be just fine, Glynnis. And if you'll excuse me, Emma, I'll leave you two alone to talk."

"I realize you've things to do, Winston, I'll see you later," Emma murmured and turned to the young woman sitting opposite her.

"Let me tell you a little bit about Anita's job, Glynnis. Naturally I realize you know what being a secretary means, and the only difference really, if you work for me, will be the hours. They're a bit longer, but you would be properly compensated for any overtime. Also, I often work at home, so I would need you to be there with me at certain times. I give a lot of dictation. You do know how to take shorthand, don't you?"

"Oh yes. As I said, Brenda has trained me for the last year, and I'm a good typist as well. Brenda says I'm a fast learner when it comes to office work."

"That's good to know. Anita wants to give a week's notice. Today is Monday, so I expect she'll leave on Friday. That gives you only four days with her, Glynnis. However, I might be able to persuade her to stay an extra week. That's up to you."

"If I can start working with her this morning, Mrs. Harte, I believe I can be ready by Friday to take over —" Glynnis stopped and gave Emma a worried look, biting her lip.

Emma said, "Is something wrong?"

"It's the other two juniors who work with Anita. Do you think they'll be upset? I mean about me being brought in."

"I'm sure not, but you can leave me to handle things. Now tell me a little bit about yourself, Glynnis. How old are you?"

"I'm nineteen, Mrs. Harte, and as you can guess, I'm Welsh. Mr. Harte's always said there's a bit of a lilt in my voice, a bit of the Welsh there. Anyway, I came to work in London in 1938, when I was seventeen. I live with my cousin Gwyneth in Belsize Park Gardens; she's got a little flat there, and I'm sharing with her. My younger brother, Emlyn, is in the RAF, and my older brother, Dylan, is in the army. So we're all gone from home at the moment, except for my little sister Elayne, who's back in the Rhondda with my parents." Glynnis cleared her throat again and then finished, "Oh, and I'm single, Mrs. Harte."

Emma nodded. "Thank you, Glynnis, for filling me in. Now perhaps we'd better talk to Anita, get you started. The sooner the better."

Thirty

By the end of Tuesday afternoon, Emma knew how right her brother had been about Glynnis Jenkins. Aside from the fact that the Welsh girl was willing and efficient, she had a way about her that was most appealing. This had a lot to do with her personality, which was warm and outgoing, and Glynnis had a great deal of natural charm.

Emma found her pleasing to have around. She was lovely to look at, and a person of depth and sincerity, with nice manners and a gentle, rather quiet demeanor. It seemed to Emma that she was brighter than average, and certainly not afraid of hard work or long hours. "Glynnis is quite a find," she said to her brother on the phone. "And unless I'm very mistaken, she's going to be around here for a long time."

Winston laughed knowingly. "I told you, Emma, I knew you'd want to keep her. There's something about her that's quite . . . irresistible, that's the only word I can think of, to be honest. I used to believe she was too good to be true, but I discovered she's the real thing, a genuinely *nice* young woman."

"She has a lot going for her," Emma murmured. "I'm grateful to have her, Winston, thanks so much." Then she asked, "Would you like to come to supper?"

"I would. But on one condition."

"Oh, and what's that?"

"I don't want you faffing around in the kitchen with Mrs. Coddington. Let her make the dinner and I'll come."

"Don't you like my cooking anymore? You used to," she shot back.

"I do, but you work too hard to start preparing meals when you get home. Anyway, what I'd like for dinner is a very simple dish. Cottage pie and peas, which Mrs. Coddington can make by herself."

Emma laughed. "That's it? Nothing to start with?"

"Whatever you like as long as it's not soup."

"I'll see you around six, Winston, and the rest of the dinner will remain a surprise."

After she had hung up, Emma stacked her briefcase with reports and balance sheets, and walked across her office. As she emerged into the secretarial area adjoining, Glynnis instantly jumped to her feet, and said, "Is there anything I can do for you, Mrs. Harte?"

"No, no, but thank you, Glynnis. I'm a

little tired today, and so I decided to go home early. I can easily do some work there."

"Shall I come with you, Mrs. Harte?"

"That's very sweet of you, but there's not much you could do for me, to be honest. I'm taking home a pile of reading. But thank you for offering."

Glynnis gave her a shy smile. "You just have to say the word, and I'll be there."

"Thanks again, Glynnis." Emma smiled in return and left.

Tomkins was waiting in front of the store, and as she got into the Rolls she picked up at once on his gloom. "Hello, Tomkins."

"Good afternoon, Mrs. Harte."

"I'm going straight home."

"Yes, madame."

"The news is not too good today, is it?" she said, settling back against the seat.

"Never been worse, Mrs. H. The whole bloomin' country's been knocked back on its ar—" He coughed and swiftly corrected himself. "Knocked on its behind. Nobody thought the Frenchies were going to . . . collapse the way they did. We're on our own now, madame. It's just us against the Nazis."

"We'll be all right, Tomkins."

"We don't have much choice, Mrs. H. It's beat them afore they beat us."

"Are you thinking of leaving me, Tomkins? Joining up, maybe?"

"Oh no, Mrs. Harte. I'm not A-one fit,

otherwise I might go in the army. Act'lly, I've got flat feet, Mrs. H. Not serious when it comes to driving a car and life in civvie street, but they don't like flat-footed soldiers. Oh no."

"I understand," Emma murmured, trying not to laugh. There were times when Tomkins was quite droll.

But he was correct. The news was not just bad, it was disastrous. The French High Command had fled Paris several days ago, and the Germans had captured the city without one shot being fired.

They were indeed on their own, and the whole of England was traumatized by the news that their only ally was no longer fighting alongside them.

"Hello, Mummy darling!" Elizabeth exclaimed as Emma came through the front door of the Belgravia house. Running across the marble foyer, she embraced her mother enthusiastically, then said, "I hope you don't mind, but I've decided to move in with you. I've come *home,* Mummy."

"So I see," Emma replied, smiling as she glanced at the suitcases scattered across the hall. "What about your little flat in Chelsea?"

"I've given it up. It was all right for one person, but Tony can hardly *fit* into it, and anyway, he's not likely to get any leave soon, not with what's going on in France." Elizabeth blew out air and continued in a rush, "Besides, he'll be much more comfortable *here* when he does get leave, don't you think? And anyway, Mummy, I didn't want you to be lonely."

Emma glanced away to hide a smile; Elizabeth was so transparent, and at times so without guile. "I'm happy you've come home. And you're always welcome, darling . . . you're a tonic to have around. Let's ask Grace to help us upstairs with your luggage."

"Oh, she's up in my room already, unpacking for me, Mummy. I'll carry some more of the cases, don't you worry. We can do it together, Grace and I." Hurrying to the bottom of the curving staircase, Elizabeth picked up two bags and started to climb the stairs. Halfway up she stopped and turned around. "I forgot, Uncle Frank called. He's invited himself to sups, and he hopes that's all right. He said Uncle Winston had told him about the cottage pie and peas and he couldn't help but come."

"I see. I'd better go and talk to Cook, explain about the guests and the cottage pie."

"Oh, I already did that!" Elizabeth cried. "I thought I'd better alert her. I hope you don't mind, but Uncle Frank said you'd left the office and I didn't know where you were. I didn't realize you were on your way home. You're usually so late at the store."

"I felt a bit tired," Emma explained.

"Are you all right? You're not ill or anything, are you?" There was a surprised note in Elizabeth's voice, and her expression was worried. She remained on the stairs, gazing down at her mother.

"I'm not ill, Elizabeth. Only a bit tired. Now scoot, get unpacked and settled in. Are you sure you don't want me to help you?"

"No, you go and have a rest, I can manage."

Frank Harte was thrilled to see his sister looking so well tonight. He watched her closely, with much love as she moved around her small library.

Emma was wearing a white silk shirt, man-tailored with long, full sleeves, and a pair of well-cut black linen trousers, and he thought she looked superbly elegant. And glamorous, with her new shorter hairdo and subtle makeup.

When he had last seen her, two weeks ago, he had noticed the new hairstyle and that she had put away her mourning clothes, and both had made a vast improvement in her appearance. But this evening she was finally back to looking like her old self, he decided.

He had worried about his sister for the last nine months, ever since he had been the one to break the news to her about Paul McGill's unexpected death. He would not forget that night as long as he lived. She had gone into shock, and at times seemed so demented he wondered aloud to Winston whether she would ever come out of it. The two of them had kept vigil over her for hours, until she had fallen into a drugged sleep.

But Emma was implacable, and after weeks of searing grief she had suddenly taken total control of her feelings. "I have Paul's child to look after, to bring up," she had said to him one afternoon. "Our daughter needs me, and I mustn't fail her, Frank, I'm all she has." From that moment on she had displayed nothing but self-discipline, unselfishness, and practicality. Of course the last came easily to her, Frank knew that well. Emma was an absolute pragmatist, had been since they were growing up together in Fairley village on top of the Yorkshire moors.

Fairley village . . . good God, he hadn't thought about that place in years. A series of grim pictures flitted through his head, and he shivered involuntarily. But he knew that the village hadn't been quite so dreadful as he sometimes liked to imagine. It was the circumstances of their life there that had been so disheartening at times. Not inside the cottage, where they had all lived so happily, but the troubles outside somehow always affected *them*.

And then there were the memories of the terrible things that had happened to the family . . . so vivid, so heartbreaking: their mother's untimely death, Winston running away to join the navy when he was underage, then Emma's strange disappearance, and finally his father's tragic and unnecessary death.

Frank remembered with total clarity the day his father had rushed into the burning woolen shed at Fairley mill . . . to rescue Edwin Fairley, trapped beneath fiery bales of wool and a fallen beam. Big Jack Harte, their father, had thought only of rescuing the young master. He had pulled Edwin out of that wreckage and been badly burned in the process. Their father had died a few days later from his burns and smoke inhalation. And Frank had been left on his own, well, not actually alone, since there had been Auntie Lily to look after him. Nevertheless, Frank often thought of the worthless Edwin, who had seduced Emma when she worked at the hall. He had taken advantage of her, made her pregnant, then repudiated her. He hadn't even given her any money, only an old suitcase so she could run away.

Deep within himself Frank could not abide the name Fairley, and he had, over the years, secretly and silently cheered Emma on as she had ruined the Fairleys and acquired everything that had belonged to them. She had even bought that hideous mansion, Fairley Hall, where she had once been employed as the kitchen maid. But wisely, Frank had always thought, she had torn that house down until there was nothing left standing and all the memories were expunged. And eventually she had turned the grounds of Fairley Hall into a park for the villagers and named it in memory of their mother, Elizabeth Harte. Today Emma owned Fairley village in its entirety, the Fairley mill, the Fairley brickyard. . . . Everything that had once been theirs was now hers.

"Champagne, Frankie?"

He stared at Emma, a brow lifting. She hadn't called him Frankie since he was a boy. Had she somehow zeroed in on his thoughts? "I'd like that, Emma," he said at last. "Do you have any of the Pol Roger left?"

"I certainly do, and it's sitting over there in the ice bucket." She smiled at him and glided across to the console where bottles of alcohol and crystal glasses were kept. She opened the bottle carefully. "And I think I know who got *you* into the habit of drinking Pol Roger," she murmured and popped the cork.

"You like it, too."

"I do, Frank. But I was referring to the great man. Didn't he start you on this particular brand?"

"By great man I am assuming you mean the Beaver?"

"Not actually, Frankie, although I'm the first to agree with you that Lord Beaverbrook is a great man and a wonderful newspaper publisher-proprietor. I think the *Daily Express* gets better every day."

Frank grinned knowingly. "Now that the Beaver's back in government, the Churchill government to be exact, the slant of the paper is powerfully for Winston rather than against him. I think that's what *you* mean, isn't it?"

Emma simply smiled again and carried two flutes of Pol Roger over to Frank, who was sitting next to the open window on this warm June evening. He took one and raised it to her. They clinked glasses and said "cheers" together, then Emma sat down in the chair opposite her brother. "I *was* referring to the Prime Minister when I mentioned Pol Roger, that's true. You told me he had served that at lunch the day you went to interview him over two years ago, when he was still in . . . *limbo,* I suppose one would call it."

"He did serve it, yes, and I did acquire a taste for it. You're right . . . what a great man he is, Emm. For six years, no, longer even, he *warned* us, and the world, that Germany was rearming and dangerous. Nobody listened —"

"But they certainly do now!" she interjected.

Frank nodded. "Do you like the way the paper's looking?"

"I do, Frank. It's very modern, very clean.

That's Arthur Christiansen's doing, isn't it?"

"That's correct. He's a wonderful chap, we all like him. He's a fine editor, and he has certainly given me my head, with the blessing of the Beaver, of course, who gets to read every piece I write before Chris can let it go. Control, wouldn't you say? But it doesn't bother me, we're all of like mind these days. Just let's win this bloody war."

"What's the feeling in Fleet Street . . . about Churchill?" Emma now asked, looking at Frank carefully, always keen to get his opinion.

"He's damned popular these days, Winston is."

"Are you talking about me?" Winston Harte asked as he came into the room, grinning from ear to ear.

"I was talking about Winston as in Churchill, not as in Harte," Frank said, jumping up and going to shake Winston's hand. The brothers half-embraced quickly, and Winston went to sit in one of the chairs near a small end table.

Watching him walk slowly, leaning on his stick, Emma decided that his limp was more pronounced than it had been for quite a while. When he was in the Royal Navy he had lost his leg toward the end of the Great War; he had fought to keep it, but he had lost the battle in the end. Shrapnel had been embedded in his left calf, and even though the shrapnel had been removed, gangrene had set in, and it was only because of Emma's intervention that he had lived. She had forced him to agree to the amputation. She thought now of his long recuperation and how he had learned to wear an artificial leg made of aluminum, to endure the pain and the torturous hours of learning to walk on it. Long after those endless months, she had thought of her brother as one of the bravest men she had ever met. He had mastered the artificial limb, and most people thought he merely had a stiff leg.

Now she said, "Is your leg troubling you, Winston?"

He shook his head. "Not really, our Emm. Sometimes it's a bit sore . . . the heat in the summer. It gets to me." He paused, then added, "But I'm all right, really. However, I would like a drink, love, I'm rather thirsty. It's very close tonight."

"Winston, I'm sorry, darling! Champagne? Or a Scotch?"

"I'll have a bit of the bubbly tonight, it's lighter than Scotch. Not that there's anything to celebrate, with the current war news. France has evaporated as our ally. We are truly alone now."

"The Prime Minister is going to broadcast tonight," Frank announced. "He gave a magnificent speech in the House this afternoon, and he's repeating it later, on the BBC. He wants the whole country to hear it."

"Oh, but we *must* listen," Emma exclaimed.

Elizabeth said, from the doorway, "Yes, Mummy, it's just been announced again. Mr. Churchill is going to be on the radio tonight. At nine o'clock, I think."

"Come in, darling, and say hello to your uncles."

Smiling, Elizabeth entered the library, and Emma's brothers greeted her affectionately.

Grace served plates of smoked salmon with lemon wedges, and thin slices of brown bread and butter, and Frank poured white wine in the tall ruby-tinted crystal goblets. Once Grace had disappeared into the kitchen, the family began to eat the fresh Scottish salmon as Emma talked about food shortages and rationing, and ate very little.

"Mummy, you sound like the voice of doom," Elizabeth said at one moment, looking across the table. "Things seem fine in some areas . . ."

"I'm afraid the difficult days are coming, Elizabeth, and we're going to have to tighten our belts all around. I spoke to Mr. Ramsbotham today and suggested that he plant a few allotments at Pennistone Royal. Everybody's starting them, you know, and they're growing vegetables. I also suggested he use the three greenhouses to grow tomatoes and perhaps some soft fruits, rather than orchids and exotic flowers. Much more useful, don't you think?"

"It's amazing, you know, how people *do* pull together," Winston murmured. "I know that half the women in the Leeds store have started knitting scarves, mittens, and balaclava helmets for the troops in their spare time. I think it's quite remarkable the way everyone has become less selfish."

"I do, too," Emma agreed. "And you've been very unselfish, Winston, letting me have Glynnis."

"Who's Glynnis?" Elizabeth, always curious, asked.

"She's my new secretary."

"What happened to Anita, Mummy?"

"She's going to join the Land Army. She's leaving the store on Friday, and I think it's most commendable of her."

"Anita in the Land Army! She'll never be able to lift a shovel, she's so delicate!" Elizabeth cried.

Emma chuckled. "There's a certain truth to that, Elizabeth, but she's very determined, and that can go a long way."

"So you've discovered Glynnis's qualities in just two days," Frank murmured, glancing at Emma.

"I certainly have. She's going to be very good for me, and we have a lot of traits in common."

This remark startled Elizabeth, who asked

swiftly, "Such as what?"

"She's quick, to begin with, and very willing. Not afraid of hard work. Determined, punctual, well organized, tidy. All the things I am." Looking across at Frank, she raised a brow and asked, "Do you know Glynnis, Frank?"

"I don't actually *know* her, Emm. But I've met her a few times when I've gone to pick Winston up, and he told me that she was now working for you when we spoke this afternoon."

"Oh, I see. She's very —" Emma shook her head. "Appealing . . . no, *beguiling,* that's a better word."

"I'll say!" Winston exclaimed.

Emma stared at him but made no comment, although she was surprised at the overtones of admiration echoing in her brother's voice.

The four of them talked about things in general, and Grace removed the dirty plates, served the cottage pie, and accepted, on behalf of Cook, the praise offered by Emma's brothers. "Tell Mrs. Coddington it's as good as the one Mrs. Harte usually makes," Frank said, once they had all finished.

"I will, sir," Grace murmured as she hurried out.

"It's jam roll with custard for pudding," Elizabeth announced, looking at her uncles. "I know you like it . . . Mummy told me."

"A perfect choice," Winston replied, smiling at her warmly. Like his brother, he tended to spoil his niece, who bore such a striking resemblance to their mother before she had fallen ill with consumption in 1904. This was how Mam would have looked if she had been well cared for and well off, Winston thought, as he quietly studied Elizabeth. Poor Mam, she never had a chance, what with the poverty and the hard work. Winston pushed aside the sadness, suddenly not wanting to dwell on the past.

"I think we should have coffee in the den," Emma said. "After the pudding, of course. We can relax and wait for the broadcast, it's comfortable in there."

And so as soon as dinner was finished, they trooped into the den, just beyond the library. It was a pleasant room of medium size, decorated in shades of dark red and a rich, deep green, furnished with comfortable armchairs and two love seats, plus a small Georgian desk, where Emma sometimes worked. Silk-shaded brass lamps, and a few lovely paintings and decorative objects gave the room coziness and charm.

Emma turned the radio on as everyone sat down, drinking coffee. They fell silent as the BBC announcer introduced the Prime Minister. His eloquent voice boomed out. Emma, sitting next to the radio, concentrated on every word. It was a long and detailed speech, and there was total silence in the den as everyone listened closely.

As he came to the end, Emma leaned forward slightly, clasping her hands, waiting for his final words.

The Prime Minister paused for a split second and then finished: "What General Weygand called the Battle of France is over. I expect that the Battle of Britain is about to begin. Upon this battle depends the survival of Christian civilization. Upon it depends our own British life, and the long continuity of our institutions and our Empire. The whole fury and might of the enemy must very soon be turned on us. Hitler knows that he will have to break us in this Island or lose the war. If we can stand up to him, all Europe may be free and the life of the world may move forward into broad, sunlit uplands. But if we fail, then the whole world, including the United States, including all that we have known and cared for, will sink into the abyss of a new Dark Age made more sinister, and perhaps more protracted, by the lights of perverted science. Let us therefore brace ourselves to our duties, and so bear ourselves that, if the British Empire and its Commonwealth last for a thousand years, men will still say, 'This was their finest hour.' "

After a long silence, Frank said softly, "Well, he's said it all, as he always does. And he's made it very clear . . . Britain does stand alone."

"I think what he just said is inspiring, and comforting in a way," Emma remarked, flicking the tears off her face with her fingertips. Clearing her throat, she added, "He's told us what we have to do. We have to stand up and fight with all our might . . . and I know we will all do that."

"Yes, I agree," Winston interjected. "And you can bet the entire country listened to him tonight, just as we did. He's all we've got. To inspire us, to lead us, to show us the way."

"We do have the troops we rescued from Dunkirk," Frank pointed out, "they will help to defend us, all two hundred fifty thousand of them. In the meantime, we'd better prepare."

"For the Battle of Britain," Emma said. "And some battle it's going to be."

Thirty-one

Later that night Emma was unable to sleep, and she finally got up, put on a dressing gown, and went down to the den. She sat at her desk for a short while, reading some of the balance sheets she had brought home with her, but other thoughts soon intruded.

The war and the invasion were uppermost in her mind for a few minutes, and then, quite unexpectedly, an image of Paul danced before her eyes. She sat back in the chair, staring into space, seeing him much more vividly than she had in months. It seemed that he was actually in the room with her, coming toward her. She sat very still, waiting. Then the image was gone, just like that, as if it had never been there.

"Paul," she said out loud and rose, glancing toward the open door. She was quite alone, she knew that, but she still hurried out to the corridor, looked up and down. Naturally it was empty. Yet she could not shake off the feeling that he had been there with her, if only for a brief second. Nothing like this had ever happened to her, and she leaned against the doorjamb, wondering suddenly if she were losing her mind. But of course she wasn't . . . perhaps it was her imagination playing tricks on her.

Almost against her volition, she walked down the corridor, opened a door that led to a small foyer and the elevator that went down to Paul's bachelor flat. On the ground floor, it had its own entrance at the side of the house. The front door in Belgrave Square led into the grand foyer of Emma's maisonette, built on the three floors above the self-contained flat.

Going down, Emma thought of when Paul had bought the mansion, given her the deeds, then set about creating the two apartments. It had been 1925. "It's much more discreet," he had explained, and then he had grinned at her in that rather cheeky little boy fashion of his and added, "Naturally, I'll be living in the maisonette with you and Daisy. My bachelor flat is for appearance's sake." She remembered smiling to herself at the time, wondering who on earth he thought he was fooling. Everyone knew they were together.

But he had used the flat from time to time, mostly when he wanted to work long hours or entertain business colleagues. She had gone down rarely, and only once since his death. But tonight, somehow, she had a compulsion to be in these rooms. It would not bring him closer, because he had mostly been in the upper portion of the house, and that was where she felt his presence most. And yet . . . something pulled her there . . .

Stepping out of the elevator, she turned on the lights in the little foyer and was instantly struck by the wonderful masculine look of the wood-paneled walls, the dark burgundy carpet, the mahogany console table set between two straight-backed Georgian side chairs.

His favorite room had been the library, with its dark green brocade walls and French Empire antiques. He had always worked there, and she walked in, switched on a lamp, and stepped across to his desk. She ran her hand along the highly polished mahogany surface and stared for a moment at a photograph of her and Daisy with Paul. Then she sat down in his chair. Leaning back, she closed her eyes and thought of him. For a few minutes so much of the past came rushing back . . . remembrances of little things, forgotten things . . . and the tears came then. She put her head down on the desk and let them flow unchecked. She wept in a way she had not wept since Frank had rushed to this house from Fleet Street nine months ago, bringing with him the UP wire story which told of Paul's suicide . . .

"Mummy, are you all right?"

On hearing Elizabeth's voice, Emma lifted her head and looked toward the door, where her daughter was standing. For a moment she could not speak.

Elizabeth came into the library hesitantly, staring at her mother's tearstained face. "Oh, Mummy, you're grieving for Paul."

Emma simply nodded. She was racked by dry sobs.

Elizabeth murmured softly, "I woke up, I felt so alone, and worried about Tony. And Kit and Robin, and so I came to your bedroom. . . . I didn't know where you were until I saw the door in the corridor wide open." She put her hand on Emma's shoulder gently and whispered against her hair, "I wish I could help you. . . . I love you so much, Mummy . . ."

Turning, Emma put her arms around her daughter's body and held her tightly, trying to control her swimming senses, her emotions. Eventually the sobs subsided, and she pulled away and said in a choked voice, "I don't usually let go like that. I'm sorry, darling."

"You mustn't be sorry. You must grieve, you've got to get it out . . . that's what Uncle Winston said to me months ago. He said I was trying to be far too brave about Paul's death."

Emma looked up at Elizabeth, standing there in her pale blue dressing gown, exactly the color of her eyes, and she nodded slowly. "I know you loved him."

"I did. He was like a father to me. And to Robin. Certainly more of a father than Arthur Ainsley ever was."

"I know, and Paul loved you and Robin, thought of you both as his own."

"Perhaps we'd better go back upstairs." Elizabeth looked at Emma, her expression puzzled. "What were you doing down here?"

"I don't really know. I felt I had to come to the library, but there's really nothing here." She took a deep breath and said in a voice that suddenly faltered, "All of the memories are upstairs . . . that's where we lived together."

"Then come on, let's go back."

Emma nodded and stood up, and Elizabeth led her out, turning off the lights as they left the library and then the little foyer and stepped into the elevator.

Once they were back in the maisonette, Elizabeth said, "Go up to your bedroom, Mummy, and I'll make us some hot chocolate. Don't you think that would be nice?"

"Yes, darling, thank you," Emma replied, suddenly feeling ice cold.

A short while later Elizabeth hurried into Emma's bedroom carrying two beakers of hot chocolate on a silver tray. After giving one of the beakers to her mother, Elizabeth took the other for herself, put the tray on the floor, and climbed into bed with Emma.

"The hot chocolate's going to warm you up. You felt very cold downstairs," Elizabeth told her, sinking back into the pillows. "I'm so glad I moved in here today, Mummy. We'll be able to keep each other company when I'm not working at night."

"It's nice to have you here," Emma said softly and took a sip of the hot chocolate. She was considerably calmer but still puzzled about why she had felt impelled to venture down to the ground-floor flat.

After a small silence, Elizabeth said in a tentative, rather nervous voice, "Mother, can I ask you something?"

"Of course you can." Emma glanced at her, frowning. "You sound very serious."

"It's a serious question," Elizabeth replied quickly, "and perhaps I ought not to ask it." She cleared her throat several times. "Actually, Mummy, I don't think you're going to like it at all."

"Well, you'd better ask it, and then we'll see, won't we?"

Elizabeth bit her lip, made a small grimace. After a pause and a sigh, she said slowly, "It's very personal. . . . Perhaps I'd better not."

"Come along, darling, he who hesitates is lost. What is it you want to know?"

"Well, it's about Daisy."

"*Oh*. What about her?" Emma looked at her daughter alertly.

"She's not my *full* sister, is she?"

Emma gaped at her.

Elizabeth, seeing Emma's startled expression, hurried on, "She's not Arthur Ainsley's child, is she?"

It was Emma's turn to hesitate, but only for a split second. "No, she's not, even though she bears his name. And you're right, she's your half sister," Emma answered in a steady voice, knowing only the truth would do now.

"She's Paul's daughter, isn't she, Mother?"

Emma nodded.

"I've thought so for quite a long time, and so has Robin. But we never dared ask you."

"And what gave you the courage tonight?" Emma stared at Elizabeth, her vivid green eyes narrowing slightly as they grew flinty.

"I felt very close to you downstairs, Mummy, and I know I'm much more grown-up these days. And the world's falling apart around us, and the boys are in danger, actually everyone's in danger. And, oh what the hell, Mummy, why does it matter that her father's Paul?"

"I know what you mean, Elizabeth, the times have suddenly been turned upside down, and the world seems to be in chaos. Suddenly we all know what our real priorities are. However, I do think it matters to me, and more important, to Daisy, because she doesn't know Paul is her father. And you mustn't tell her."

"Are you sure she doesn't know?" Elizabeth sounded skeptical.

"*Positive.* Why are you staring at me like that?"

"But she *looks* so much like him, don't you think she realizes that, Mother?"

"No, I don't. Now you must promise me that you will not betray my confidence in you by telling her," Emma insisted.

Elizabeth exclaimed irately, "I would never break a confidence, Mother! You always taught me to be honorable. And I won't tell Robin if you don't want me to."

"I'd prefer to tell him myself when the time is right," Emma replied.

"You *are* going to tell Daisy who her father is, was, I mean, aren't you?"

"Yes, when she's older. She's only fifteen, Elizabeth. Sometimes I think you forget that."

"Well, she seems a lot older, perhaps because she was always with you and Paul, and never with children her own age."

"That's silly, she was with you and Robin a great deal of the time."

"But we were mostly away at school."

"That's true. And of course I will tell her, how could you ever think I wouldn't? Any child would be proud to claim Paul McGill as her father."

"I am," Elizabeth said and squeezed her

mother's hand. "He was so good to us . . . Robin feels the same way."

"Yes . . ." Emma's voice trailed off, and she put the beaker down on the bedside table, leaned back against the mound of pillows, closing her eyes.

Mother and daughter were lost, for a while, in their own thoughts. It was Elizabeth who broke the silence when she said, "I think Edwina is being rather beastly, the way she's hiding herself away in the bogs of Ireland, being incommunicado with us. I do think she could have brought her husband to meet us, and brought the baby over, too. After all, you're the child's grandmother. Don't you agree, Mummy?"

"It would have been nice, Elizabeth, but Edwina's rather angry these days, and most especially with me. I don't think we'll be seeing her soon, I really don't."

"It's her loss, she's such a fool. I don't think she has a right to be angry. You've been a wonderful mother to all of us. We've been lucky."

"I'm glad you think that, darling."

"Why did Paul kill himself?"

This question, coming out of the blue, shocked Emma, and it took her a few moments to recover. "This is the first time you've ever admitted you knew that. . . . I thought you all believed Paul had died of his injuries."

"Not really, Mummy."

"He knew he wouldn't have long to live," Emma began. "There is no way to treat paraplegics. They invariably die of kidney failure in a few months. . . . He knew he couldn't get back here in time to see us. I suppose he wanted to take control of his life again . . . his destiny."

"I see."

Emma was silent, thinking about Paul's last letter, wondering if she should show it to Elizabeth. She was a married woman now, and living with the dangers of war. Yet Emma hesitated. The letter was so personal, meant for her eyes only. And perhaps one day for Daisy's. No, she would not get it out of the casket. Not yet . . .

But later, when she was alone, Emma got out of bed and went to her dressing room. She unlocked the fruitwood-and-silver casket which stood on a chest, took out the letter that had arrived from Australia just after Paul's death, and returned to the bedroom.

Sitting down on the bed, she took the letter out of its envelope and read it again, as she had so many times before:

My dearest darling Emma:
You are my life. I cannot live without my life. But I cannot live with you. And so I must end my miserable existence, for there is no future for us together now. Lest you think

450

my suicide an act of weakness, let me reassure you that it is not. It is an act of strength and of will, for committing it I gratefully take back that control over myself which I have lost in the past few months. It is a final act of power over my own fate.

It is the only way out for me, my love, and I will die with your name on my lips, the image of you before my eyes, my love for you secure in my heart always. We have been lucky, Emma. We have had so many good years together and shared so much, and the happy memories are alive in me, as I know they are in you; and will be as long as you live. I thank you for giving me the best years of my life.

I did not send for you because I did not want you to be tied to a helpless cripple, if only for a few months at the most. Perhaps I was wrong. On the other hand, I want you to remember me as I was, and not what I have become since the accident. Pride? Maybe. But try to understand my reasons, and try, my darling, to find it in your heart to forgive me.

I have great faith in you, my dearest Emma. You are not faint of heart. You are strong and dauntless, and you will go on courageously. You must. For there is our child to consider. She is the embodiment of our love, and I know you will cherish and care for her, and bring her up to be as brave and as stalwart and as loving as you are yourself. I give her into your trust, my darling.

By the time you receive this I will be dead. But I will live on in Daisy. She is your future now, my Emma. And mine.

I love you with all my heart and soul and mind, and I pray to God that one day we will be reunited in Eternity.

I kiss you, my darling.

Paul

Emma sat for a moment, holding the letter in her hands . . . such small hands, Paul had always said to her. The tears rolled down her cheeks, and she thought her heart was breaking once again. But deep within she knew she had been correct to read yet again his last letter to her. It had reminded her of her duty to Daisy, and to her other children as well. And it had also reminded her of the stuff she was made of . . . steel.

Once she had returned the letter to the casket, locked it, and pocketed the silver key, Emma went to the desk in a corner of her bedroom. She took out her diary and opened the page for June 18, 1940.

She made a short entry:

The Prime Minister spoke tonight. He reiterated that France has fallen, and warned us that the Battle of Britain is about to begin. We cannot allow ourselves to be broken by Hitler. We must not be defeated. Those were the sentiments he expressed. And so we must be courageous, stalwart, dauntless. Paul's last letter to me reminded me of that when I re-read it tonight.

My beautiful Elizabeth moved back home, so that we can share our loneliness, help each other in these difficult times. She is a good daughter. I am lucky to have her. I have decided Daisy must stay at boarding school. She is safer in the country. Winston and Frank came to supper. What would I do without my loyal and loving brothers? We must pull together now that we are about to be invaded.

Emma closed the diary and put it away. Then she went to bed. But she did not sleep. Her mind was too preoccupied with thoughts of the days ahead, the plans she would have to make for her family, her employees, and the stores. Everyone and everything had to be protected. The defense of Britain was about to begin.

She tossed and turned all night, and fell asleep only as dawn broke.

Thirty-two

"Come on, Glynnis, we'd better make a run for it!" Emma cried. "They're going to start dropping their bombs any minute." As she spoke Emma rushed across Belgrave Square, heading for her house on the far corner.

Glynnis followed, her high heels clattering against the pavement as she raced to catch up, marveling at Emma Harte's fast sprint. Her boss was quite extraordinary.

The sirens were wailing, warning them of an imminent air raid, but in fact the Luftwaffe was already overhead, the planes roaring across the skies of London on one of their daylight raids. The ARP warden on the corner caught sight of them both and shouted out, "Hurry up, Mrs. Harte! Go inside as quick as you can. Get down in your cellar! It's the safest place."

"We will, Norman, you can be sure of that," Emma called back. "And if you need to shelter, please come and join us."

"Right, I will, Mrs. H." The warden shooed them on before turning away, his attention suddenly caught elsewhere.

Glynnis hurried after Emma up the steps and through the front door, closing it behind her. They both stood for a moment in the marble entrance foyer, catching their breath.

"I think we made it just in time," Emma muttered at the sound of a loud explosion not far away and then the shattering of glass. A split second later there were several more explosions, and Emma and Glynnis exchanged apprehensive looks. "They've made several hits," Emma said, shaking her head. "But so far they've managed to miss us. Keep your fingers crossed."

The foyer was devoid of furniture, except for an ornate French console table, set against a side wall under a French gilded mirror, and a Louis XV bench on the opposite wall. A crystal chandelier dropped down from the slightly domed ceiling, and the curving staircase led up to Emma's maisonette.

Aside from the front door, there was only one other door in the foyer, and this was set in the wall underneath the staircase. Emma now hurried to this door, opened it, and went down a steep flight of steps, followed by Glynnis; the stairs led them to the small hallway of Paul's bachelor flat.

"From here we take the lift to the cellar," Emma said and beckoned to Glynnis. Together the two women rode down; when the elevator stopped they stepped out into Paul

McGill's extensive wine cellar.

Glancing at the walls of wine racks, Emma said, with a small sigh, "I think I'd better have my brothers come for some of this; it's all vintage, much of it very rare. I'd much rather they and their friends drank it than have the Germans drop bombs on it. Now . . . we go through this arch, Glynnis, and here we are in the air-raid shelter."

"Is that you, Mrs. Harte?" a voice called out nervously, and there was Grace peering at them from behind a pillar.

"Yes, it's me, Grace. I have Glynnis with me." Emma hurried through into the air-raid shelter, which had recently been built by Blackie O'Neill. It was completely reinforced with steel girders and concrete-and-steel pillars; sandbags had been stacked against all of the walls as an extra precaution. "Are you alone?" Emma asked, looking at Grace.

"Yes, Mrs. H. Wot 'appened is this. Mrs. Coddington never come in today. The docks was bombed again last night, ma'am, and parts of the East End, and 'er sister Ethel's gone and got bombed out. So she went to 'elp her," the maid explained. "She phoned, but you was gone . . . to the shop." Stepping aside so that Emma could walk over to the desk she had recently brought down to the cellar, Grace continued, "Cook'll be in termorrow, so she said, ma'am."

"I understand, and I do hope her sister's

family is all right. Nobody's been hurt, have they?" Emma asked anxiously.

"No, her sister was there with their mother, and they're both all right, Mrs. H. Ethel's five sons are in the army, the navy, and the air force, and her two daughters, Flossie and Violet, are in the Land Army, so they wasn't there to be 'urt, was they?"

"That's true, Grace. And certainly that's one family which is truly doing its bit for the war effort. Most commendable. Goodness, yes!" Emma glanced around, and turning to Glynnis, she said, "It's not too bad down here, you know."

"I think it's very nice, Mrs. Harte," Glynnis responded swiftly. "Air-raid shelters are usually sort of . . . *dismal*. Certainly this is a lot more comfortable than those Anderson shelters everyone's building in their back gardens. My da has copied the neighbors'. Mum's quite chuffed about it." Surveying the cellar a little more thoroughly, Glynnis sat down in a chair and added, "You've certainly thought of everything. A Primus stove for cooking and boiling a kettle. Electric fires for the winter months, plenty of chairs, a rug underfoot, and lots of blankets and pillows."

"I've also ordered a number of camp beds," Emma told her.

"And there's a big stock of tinned stuff," Grace interjected in a proud voice. "Baked beans, sardines, red salmon, corned beef,

Spam, tomato soup, and a lot of candles, just in case the lights go."

"Did you get a first-aid box?" Glynnis asked, glancing across at Emma, who was already sitting behind the rather ugly, very utilitarian desk.

"Yes, we have a couple down here, but perhaps I'd better order some more. You never know."

"I'll make a note of it," Glynnis murmured and took out a shorthand pad.

In her usual businesslike way, Emma took a stack of papers out of her briefcase and was soon absorbed in them.

Grace picked up the ladies' magazine she had been reading before, and Glynnis pulled out her knitting; she was making a khaki scarf, her second in a week. The two young women focused on what they were doing, knowing better than to waste their time with idle chatter in front of Emma Harte.

As she knitted, Glynnis thought about the war. Mrs. Harte had told her it would last for quite a few years, and although she hoped that was wrong, Glynnis believed her boss was probably right. Emma was a genius about everything else, so how could she be wrong about the duration of war?

The Battle of Britain had begun in June, just after France had fallen, but so far not a lot had happened. The bombing raids had been rather sporadic, and during June and

July the whole country had been working hard to ensure the safety of Britain. People were building air-raid shelters in their gardens and reinforcing their cellars, piling sandbags in front of exposed entrances. Candles were bought in case of electrical shortages; tinned food was stacked in homes from Dover to the Hebrides. People thought of everything they might need in emergencies and went out and bought it if it was available. Already there were shortages. Gas masks were issued to every citizen, and many people made sure they had tin helmets to protect themselves from falling rubble.

Not many civilians had been killed in either June or July, but in August the figures had started to rise as the Luftwaffe stepped up its efforts, flying in from its northern French bases to bomb London and the surrounding counties of Kent, Surrey, and Sussex. Hitler's aim was to destroy the RAF, now Britain's only real defense, and to demolish the factories where production of Hurricanes, Spitfires, and bombers was already in full swing. Daylight raids had been relatively infrequent, the German air force preferring to bomb under cover of dark.

But things had begun to change, and Emma kept telling anyone that would listen that they were going to get worse. In the next few days she was to be proven right.

After two and a half hours, the all-clear siren sounded, and they heard it, albeit somewhat faintly. "That's it!" Emma exclaimed and immediately put her papers back in the briefcase. "We'd better go up and see what the damage is. Glynnis, Grace, come along."

Emma was relieved that her house had not been hit, and she was fairly certain that Belgrave Square remained undamaged. Nonetheless, it was with trepidation that she opened the front door and looked out. The square was intact, although the air was acrid and filled with smoke, and there was the sound of falling rubble from the streets beyond.

"I'd better phone Harte's," Emma said to Glynnis as she stepped back inside. She hurried upstairs to her den; within seconds she was talking to the operator at the store. "It's Mrs. Harte, Gertie. Is everything all right?"

"Oh yes, Mrs. Harte. The Jerries missed us this time, thank God."

"I'm glad to hear it. I'll see you on Monday. Have a nice weekend, and a safe one."

"Thanks, Mrs. Harte, and the same to you." Emma turned to Glynnis, who had followed her into the small room, and nodded her head. "The store's still standing, and that's a plus. But there must be an awful lot of damage out there, especially on the docks."

"Yes, and perhaps some of the factories were hit. We know the Germans are hell-bent on slowing down the production of planes," Glynnis said, looking as worried as Emma.

"I wonder if there is anything we can do to help," Emma murmured, but before Glynnis could answer the phone rang. Emma picked it up. "Hello?"

"Hello, Emma, it's Jane."

"Jane darling, how are you? I hope everything's all right with you. You haven't been bombed, have you?"

"No, no, we've escaped again, thank goodness. But Bill just heard that the docks and the East End have taken a terrible beating. It seems there's a massive cleanup starting, but he thinks those poor people are going to need help tomorrow."

"What about right now?" Emma asked swiftly.

"I believe they're going into the tube stations soon to take shelter for the night, and the Red Cross, the St. John's Ambulance Brigade, and several other agencies are doing quite a lot. But I can't help thinking about tomorrow. It's Sunday, and it seems to me they will need food."

"Jane, you're right! And I'm onboard, if that's what you were going to ask."

"Well, yes, I was, Emma. I'm going to start making sandwiches tonight, and I thought you could do the same."

461

"Of course, but we'll need more than sandwiches. I'll phone Harte's and have the manager of the Food Halls bring over a few hampers of food. Now, what time are you setting off tomorrow? And where should I go?"

"I'll come around at nine o'clock in the car, and Tomkins can follow me. And, Emma, thank you for this, you're a good woman."

"I'm glad to help," Emma murmured and glanced at her watch. "I'd better go, Jane, I need to arrange for the food."

An hour later, Jack Field, the manager of the Food Halls at Harte's and a favorite of Emma's, stood in the middle of her kitchen, explaining what the collection of wicker hampers contained. "Every kind of pie, Mrs. Harte. Game, chicken, veal, and ham, and a lot of the individual pork pies we sell. Cornish pasties, sausage rolls, cold meats for sandwiches, cold chickens, tea biscuits, eggs, mayonnaise, like you requested, and bags of fresh sausage as well as sausage meat."

"That's excellent, Jack. Now let's unpack the sausages and the ingredients for the sandwiches first. Oh, and the eggs. I want to make a big batch of egg salad."

As she moved across the kitchen, Emma beckoned to Glynnis and Grace. "Let's get to work. You can get the eggs boiling, Grace, and Glynnis, why don't you help me to fry the sausages? Jack, you can assist with the sandwiches, if you don't mind."

"Mrs. Harte, it's a pleasure to do anything I can, and I'll be here tomorrow morning with the van and driver, to go with you to the East End."

"Thanks, Jack, I appreciate that very much." Emma, who had earlier put on a shirt and trousers and flat shoes, now donned an apron and handed one to Glynnis. "Thank you for staying," she said to her secretary. "It's very good of you, especially on a Saturday night."

"Oh, Mrs. Harte, I'm pleased to be of help. I'd nothing to do that was special. My cousin and I talked about going to the pictures, but we can do that another night."

Emma was always focused and fast, but in a crisis she became a dynamo. And such was the case on this September Saturday night, as she and her helpers fried sausages, made Scotch eggs, and prepared hundreds of sandwiches, which they wrapped in dampened white linen napkins to keep them from going stale overnight.

"These 'ere napkins'll be ruined," Grace muttered at one moment, looking at Emma reproachfully.

"For heaven's sake, that doesn't matter, there's a war on, Grace! I can't worry about napkins at a time like this!" Emma exclaimed, shaking her head and rolling her eyes. "Just let's keep going, and once we've finished you should all sit down and eat some of the sandwiches and sausages, or the Scotch eggs. And Grace, you must make a pot of tea."

"That sounds grand, Mrs. Harte," Jack said with a laugh. "I must admit, I'm getting a bit peckish meself."

Emma glanced at her watch. "I'm not surprised, it's turned eight o'clock already. Well, we've almost finished, and you've all done a wonderful job. Thank you very much."

"We want to help, do our bit," Glynnis said, smiling at Emma.

"Yes, we must do everything we can to help those who've been bombed out," Emma answered. "And Glynnis, please take a taxi home."

"I will, Mrs. Harte. Will you need me tomorrow?"

"It's nice of you to offer, but you must have a rest, it's been a very busy week. I can manage with Jack and Tomkins, I'm quite sure."

"I can bring one of the chaps from my department," Jack volunteered. "Dennis Scott's a good lad, he'll be happy to oblige."

"That's a good idea, Jack. And now I'll say good night to you all."

"Don't you want a bit of supper, Mrs. Harte?" Grace asked.

"Not right now, thanks. I have some work

to finish." She smiled at them and made her way across the kitchen.

"Good night, Mrs. Harte," they chorused.

The following morning Emma set off with Tomkins following Jane and Bill Stuart Ogden in their car. The green Harte van, stacked with hampers and carrying Jack Field and Dennis Scott, was at the rear.

When they arrived Emma was speechless, as were the rest of their group. The Luftwaffe had done its work well. The streets were leveled, rubble piled everywhere, and it was the worst carnage any of them had ever seen. They picked their way slowly over the rubble, passing out the food, saying comforting words to the men and women who were working in the piles of bricks and dust which had once been their homes.

"Thank you, thank you," a woman said to Emma. "It's right good of you to come and help us."

Emma's eyes filled, and unable to speak, she simply touched the woman's arm gently and walked on.

Despite the suffering they had endured, there were cheery smiles on many of the Cockney faces, and a frequent disparaging quip about the enemy would ring out, causing much laughter.

"How strong our people are," Jane said.

"And brave," Emma added. Suddenly she

came to a halt and grabbed hold of Jane's arm. "Look! Over there! Everyone's cheering. Isn't that Winston Churchill?"

"Oh my God, it is. Bill, it's the Prime Minister. Look! Look! He's standing on that pile of rubble, wearing a funny-looking hat and smoking his cigar."

Bill followed Jane's gaze and saw for himself that it was the man he had been devoted to for many years, always supporting him in the House of Commons.

"Come along, ladies," Bill said. "I shall take you over there to have a word with him."

A few minutes later Bill was greeting the Prime Minister, who smiled and shook hands with Bill and Jane. Then Emma was introduced. She was awestruck, but after shaking his hand she managed to say, "Thank you, Mr. Churchill, for inspiring us."

"And thank you," he answered, realizing what their mission was this morning.

Later one of the air-raid wardens told Bill that Churchill had had tears in his eyes when he first viewed the devastation. Emma nodded, knowing that everyone loved him that much more because he was not afraid to display his feelings.

That night, when Elizabeth got home from the hospital, Emma saw how tired her daughter looked, and she fussed over her for a while. "There have been a lot of casualties," Elizabeth explained, as she and Emma sat down to eat sandwiches and drink a cup of tea in Emma's den. "And this is just the beginning of the Blitz, Mummy. You've been saying it was going to get worse, and you were right."

"*Unfortunately.* I wish I'd been wrong. Our boys are up there in the air every night, and now they'll have to be up there during the day as well."

"Yesterday's raid was catastrophic," Elizabeth murmured. "But we're going to win, Mummy, you've instilled that in me."

"No, Winston Churchill has. And our fighter pilots are very brave."

"I'll never forget what Mr. Churchill said last month, when he spoke about the fighter pilots. You won't either, will you, Mummy?"

"No, I won't. Actually, I wrote it in my diary for posterity. He said, 'Never in the field of human conflict was so much owed by so many to so few.' As always, he got it exactly right."

"They will be all right, won't they?" Elizabeth now asked, looking at Emma intently. "Tony and Robin and Bryan?"

"Yes, they will. I believe that, I truly do, darling. I must believe it, Elizabeth, because if I have any doubts about them surviving this war I'll fall apart." Tears sprang into Emma's eyes, and she blinked them back.

"Years ago I taught myself to be positive in the worst moments. That's what kept me going when I was a young girl, out on my own, struggling to make a living. I couldn't afford to have any negative thoughts then . . . and *we* can't now."

"It's nice to see you, Frank," Emma said, smiling at her brother as he came into her office. "But you look awfully tired, and pale."

"I've always been pale, Emma, even as a child. Don't you remember how you used to fuss around me and wrap me up in scarves. And send me out onto the moors to 'get some color in your cheeks,' you used to say."

She laughed. "I know I did, and you used to get very upset with me. But you *are* all right, aren't you, Frankie?"

"It's *Frankie* again, is it? Do you know you hadn't called me that for years until quite recently?"

"Because you told me not to when you were young. You said our mam had told you that you were a big lad, and Frankie was a baby's name. But I like it, perhaps because it's affectionate."

Frank gave her a long, loving look but said nothing. He had always believed that his sister could read his mind; she was certainly on the same wavelength as he was. "I am a bit tired, Emma, you're right about that. Mostly because I've been working hard at the *Express*."

"How's the great man?"

"Which one? Beaverbrook or Churchill?"

"Either. Both." Emma leaned forward now, her face lighting up as she exclaimed, "Frank, I met Winston Churchill. Finally and at last."

"When? And where?" he asked. He knew it must have been a thrill for her.

"I met him last Sunday, September eighth . . . four days ago, to be precise. In the East End. I'd gone with Jane and Bill Stuart Ogden to take food to those poor people who were bombed out, and he happened to be there. Bill introduced me. He's just extraordinary."

"That he is, and he often goes out to inspect the bomb damage, to talk to people. They love him for that. He reaches out to common folk, and he moves them in a way few politicians can. And, of course, Bill has always been a supporter of his, so no doubt the P.M. was glad to see him, to see all of you. Especially since you were being so kind, and helping. We're all going to have to pitch in now the Blitz has started."

"I was so overawed I could hardly speak," Emma admitted with an embarrassed laugh.

"I know what you mean. It's easy to be overwhelmed by him these days. He's a monumental man. And you'll see, one day in the not too distant future, he'll be thought of as a legend, Emm."

"To me he's a legend now. He is well protected, isn't he, Frank?"

"Oh yes, of course he is, and he spends most of his time in his various bunkers."

"What do you mean *bunkers?*"

"He's got a lot of sort of . . . underground bolt holes, where he works and lives and sleeps. He's not really at Number Ten Downing Street, you know. I think he pops in and out, but it's far too dangerous for him to stay there. He could so easily be bombed there. Mostly he's in the War Cabinet Rooms. When he saw the room which was to be his he apparently said, 'This is the room from which I will direct the war.' And that's what he's doing."

"Where are they, these Cabinet War Rooms?"

"Only the most privileged know that, Emma, but making a guess I'd say they're somewhere in Whitehall."

"I'm glad to know the Prime Minister is in a safe place. But getting back to you, Frank, why do you have so much work at the moment?"

"That's a daft question for someone as smart as you, Emma. Because a lot of our young journalists have left to join the army, the navy, and the air force. So I've been writing more than usual. I enjoy it, though. I suppose the reason I'm also a bit more tired than usual is I'm writing another novel and —"

"Oh, Frank, that's just wonderful!" Emma interrupted enthusiastically. "I love your books. What's this one about?"

"The war. What else?" he said and smiled at her. She was his biggest fan.

"Do you think America's going to come in to help us, now that we stand alone?" she asked, changing the subject.

"I'm not sure. I hope so. President Roosevelt's a good man, and he and Churchill do seem to have a certain rapport. But he's answerable to the American people, and they don't want to go near this war." Frank bit his lip. "Incidentally, the daylight bombing's going to get worse, so be alert, Emma."

"You know I always am."

"How's Elizabeth doing?"

"She's working hard. Thousands and thousands have been hurt, you know, in the last few days, and she's run off her feet at the hospital. Now she's talking about helping out at the London Bridge tube station, where eight thousand people gather every night for safety."

"You can't let her do *that!*"

"I don't know how to stop her. So I think perhaps I'd better go with her, to keep an eye on her and to help."

"Oh, our Emma, you're too much!"

"Come on, Frank, let's go to lunch." As she spoke she rose, and together they left her office at the top of the store. "I think it's a no-choice lunch today in the café."

"What on earth is that?"

"Exactly what it says. No choice. Tomato soup followed by bangers and mash with fried onions. Not bad really, when you consider there's a war on."

Thirty-three

Winston Harte nodded when Emma had finished speaking and said swiftly, "I think you're absolutely correct, we do have to make changes at Yorkshire Consolidated, and this is what I propose. Let's promote Martin Fuller to managing editor, and Peter Armstrong to managing director."

"But *you're* managing director, Winston!" Emma sat up straighter on the sofa and stared at her brother, frowning. "Please don't tell me you want to leave the running of the newspaper company to someone else."

"No, not at all. Sorry, I don't think I made myself quite clear. I ought to move up too, become cochairman with you, if that's all right. I'll still supervise, be on top of everything. But I'd feel much better knowing we had a managing director sitting at the main office in Leeds, and a managing editor alongside him. Both of them handling the day-to-day stuff right on the spot."

"Then we'll do it, Winston. And frankly I've been worried about you lately. You're burdened down between the Yorkshire stores, the Fairley mill, and the newspapers. And there's also your involvement with Harte Enterprises. It's too much."

Winston began to laugh. "Listen who's talking. There's nobody busier than you, and on top of your work, you volunteer for so much war work. You're running yourself ragged."

"When I think of what our troops are doing to keep us safe and win this war, my burdens seem light." As she spoke Emma picked up the silver Georgian teapot and poured another cup of tea for her brother and herself.

The two of them were sitting in front of the fire in the upstairs parlor at Pennistone Royal. It was 1942, and a freezing afternoon in the middle of December. Emma had been in Yorkshire for a week, reviewing her business interests with Winston and checking out the situation on her estate.

Leeds, Bradford, and Sheffield, and many of the other industrial cities in the north had been bombed, but Ripon and the Dales remained mostly unscathed, although some Royal Air Force bases at Topcliffe and Dishforth had been near misses when the Luftwaffe had flown over. At Pennistone Royal things were relatively normal except for the food, gasoline, and other shortages affecting everyone in Britain.

As he sipped his tea, Winston went on,

"Marty and Pete are good chaps, talented and hardworking, and devoted to you and Consolidated. It's going to be fine, Emma."

"As long as you're sitting on top of them, I feel secure about things, although I do agree with you that they're *both* smart and dedicated." Emma shook her head and made a small moue. "I always hoped Frank would take over the running of the newspaper company, but it's just not for him, is it, Winston?"

"No, it's not. He's never been interested, not even when you bought up the Sheffield papers in 1935 and started Consolidated. You offered him the top job and he said no. So that's that. He's a journalist, not a manager, and to each his own, Emm."

"He loves the *Express* and working for Lord Beaverbrook, and let's face it, Winston, Frank is the golden boy on that paper, a favorite of the Beaver and of Arthur Christiansen as well." She put her cup down in the saucer and gave Winston a long, thoughtful stare. "I suppose Edwin Fairley will try to cling to the *Yorkshire Morning Gazette* until the day he dies."

Winston nodded. "That newspaper's been in the Fairley family for three generations. You don't think he'll ever let go of it willingly, do you?"

"No, I don't suppose he will. But it's lost a lot of its circulation."

"That's because we've been giving it a run for its money. We've taken a lot of readers away."

"I know," Emma said with a small, satisfied smile. "But Edwin Fairley should stick to the law. He's a much better barrister than he is a newspaper owner, don't you think?"

"Remember, that plays in our favor. He'll have to sell one day, and you'll be able to buy it . . . for a song."

"Let's hope you're right. Speaking of Frank, he said he and Natalie won't be able to spend Christmas with us in London because of her family. Do you think you can talk him into it?"

"I do," Winston responded, but he looked slightly puzzled. "However, I don't think I'll have to, Emm. Frank told me only the other day that he has to be in London. He said Beaverbrook needs him for something special during Christmas, and that it's mandatory."

"Oh, I'm glad. Then he will be able to come on Christmas Day after all. He's probably not got around to telling me yet."

"Perhaps that's so."

"You and Charlotte are coming, aren't you? And Randolph?"

Winston's face lit up at the mention of his only child. "We're keeping our fingers crossed that he'll get leave, if only for a few days. His battleship's up at Scapa Flow at the moment. But yes, we're coming. What about your boys?"

"I think Robin will be getting a two-day pass, and hopefully Kit will, too. I know he's anxious to see June and the baby."

Winston's expression changed yet again, and he almost chortled as he said, "And what a smashing little redhead Sarah is . . . there's no mistaking that she's a Harte and *your* grandchild. She looks just like you, well, at least her coloring is the same."

"I can't believe I have a second grandchild —" Emma stopped abruptly, and sadness settled on her face as she looked at Winston and asked, "Have you heard from Edwina lately? How's her marriage, and how's my first grandchild?"

"I did get a short letter recently," Winston admitted quietly. "But she didn't say very much. Little Anthony is flourishing, and Jeremy is fine. I thought he was a splendid chap, Emma, when I went to the wedding. Please don't worry about Edwina, I'm sure she's happy, and she'll come round one day."

"I don't know about that. Maybe it's wishful thinking on my part." Unexpectedly, her face lit up with the radiance that had always captivated everyone. "Just think, Winston, I've got a grandson who's a lord . . . Lord Anthony Standish."

He smiled, enjoying this flash of pleasure in his sister. Wanting to prolong it, he moved away from the discussion of Edwina and said, "How's Daisy?"

"She's just a miracle! Of course, even though she's seventeen, there's no way she can go to a finishing school in Switzerland, as Edwina and Elizabeth did. But she doesn't seem to care. She's perfectly happy living at home with me and Elizabeth, and thank God they've always been the closest of friends. The house is very harmonious."

He nodded, relieved that her other two daughters were so devoted to her. Edwina irritated him at times; her grudge about being illegitimate was ridiculous, he thought, and made up his mind to write a stern letter to his niece. Or perhaps he would phone her at Clonloughlin. He would talk to Frank about it.

"Blackie's also coming on Christmas Day," Emma said, interrupting Winston's thoughts. "And hopefully Bryan will get leave."

"What about David? Is he coming up to London, too?"

"Naturally. He's always attended my Christmas Day lunch, you know that, Winston. The three clans are always together; it's the one day we celebrate our friendship. Blackie O'Neill, Emma Harte, and David Kallinski. The Three Musketeers, that's what Frank used to call us. Such a long time we've been friends. Blackie and I met when I was only fourteen and a half, almost fifteen . . . in 1904. And I met the Kallinskis about a year later. Thirty-eight years or more . . ."

"Of great devotion, loyalty, and love between the three of you. Do you know how remarkable that is, Emma?"

"Yes, I believe I do."

After her brother had left to drive back to Leeds, Emma remained in the upstairs parlor, enjoying a time of repose and reflection. She had not been in this house for some time, caught up as she was with the store and her worldwide business enterprises. And the war.

She had missed Pennistone Royal, and she had missed this room. It was understated and not at all pretentious, yet she knew only too well that its simplicity was deceptive. It had been achieved by a great expenditure of money when she had decorated it in 1932; she had also been both skillful and patient when she sought out furniture, knowing that only the very best antiques would do.

Now, she saw how beautiful everything still looked after ten years. Pale yellow washed over the walls, giving the room a truly sunny feeling even on the dullest of overcast Yorkshire days. A dark, highly polished wood floor gleamed against the antique Savonnerie rug that splashed its pale colors into the middle of the room. She had always loved beautiful crystal and silver, and her favorite pieces sparkled against the rich, mellow patinas of the Georgian tables, consoles, and chests.

Two long sofas faced each other in front of the fireplace of bleached oak and were covered in a colorful floral chintz with a white background. Emma smiled to herself, knowing how right she had been to buy numerous bolts of this fabric. Every few years she had the sofas reupholstered, so that the same pink, yellow, blue, and red floral pattern literally bloomed afresh. Once she had created a decorative theme for a room, she rarely changed it, simply refurbished it when required.

Her eyes roamed around, noting how fine the Rose Medallion china looked in the elegant Chippendale cabinet; then she focused for a moment on the priceless Turner landscape above the fireplace. It was redolent with misty greens and blues, a poignant, bucolic setting that never failed to stir her. Yet she had decided only the other day to hang it elsewhere in the room. Certainly there was plenty of wall space, and she wanted to put a painting of Paul over the fireplace. It was the perfect spot. She wondered which to hang there and decided it should be the one of him in his officer's uniform. He had sat for it after the Great War, and she had always thought this one bore the greatest likeness to him, the way he looked when they first met.

Rising, she walked across to the leaded windows and stood looking out. The hillside opposite was covered in snow, but in spring the daffodils bloomed, always evoking in her mind that lovely Wordsworth poem. Sighing, she turned away and walked over to the large Queen Anne chest. It needed something, some sort of decorative object, to give it a completed look. The fruitwood-and-silver casket, she suddenly thought. I'll bring that up here the next time I come. It will look beautiful on top of the chest.

She sat down at her large desk, took out her diary for 1942, found the day's date, and wrote a few lines about her meeting with Winston and the decisions they had made about the Yorkshire Consolidated Newspaper Company. Then she put the pen down and sat back, thinking about the *Yorkshire Morning Gazette*. She had always wanted that paper, and one day she *would* own it. Edwin Fairley did not have the financial resources to keep it going. It had had staggering losses over the last few years; she was using her own Yorkshire newspapers to run Edwin Fairley's into the ground. It was the only Fairley business she did not own . . . once she did own it, her revenge would be complete.

All of a sudden she heard Blackie's voice in her head; he was quoting the Bible to her. " 'Revenge is mine, sayeth the Lord,' and that's the truth, Emma." At the time she had laughed and answered, "And someone once wrote that revenge is a dish best served cold." She had shaken her head and laughed hollowly again, then added, "I want to enjoy my revenge. I'm not leaving it to the Lord or anyone else. And I'm certainly not going to serve it cold."

Emma knew deep within herself that Edwin knew she had deliberately set out to ruin the Fairleys, and he did not care. Because he knew they deserved it, and that his brother Gerald had been as responsible for their downfall as she had. Edwin had prospered as a barrister, specializing in criminal law. The newspaper was his great folly . . . and he was playing into her hands, just as Gerald had done before him.

Edwina was the fruit of their brief union when Emma had been a servant girl at Fairley Hall and Edwin the son of the squire, Adam Fairley. She had always done her best for Edwina, even gone that step further, yet Edwina hated her because she had not been able to give her daughter the one thing she had always wanted: legitimacy and the name Fairley. Emma longed to see her firstborn child and her first grandchild, little Anthony Standish . . .

The jangle of the telephone interrupted her thoughts.

"Hello? Pennistone Royal."

"Hello, Emma. It's Frank. I just spoke to Winston, and he asked me to let you know about Christmas. We'd love to come, all of us. Is that all right?"

"Of course it is! Oh, Frankie, I'm so pleased you're able to make it after all. This means the family will be together . . . well, almost all of us. If the boys get leave."

Thoughts of Edwin Fairley and his betrayal vanished. Bleak memories of her painful past were expunged. And a rush of real joy at the prospect of spending Christmas with those she loved galvanized her. Emma jumped up, almost ran out of the upstairs parlor, down the stairs, through the Stone Hall, and into the kitchen. "Hilda! Are you here?" Emma called out, glancing around.

A split second later her devoted young housekeeper hurried out of the stone storage larder at one end of the kitchen, carrying two bottles of preserved plums and pears.

"That's just what I need," Emma exclaimed, laughter echoing in her voice.

"Bottled fruit, Mrs. Harte? Whatever for?" Hilda looked slightly puzzled as she put the bottles down on the large wooden table in the center of the kitchen. "Do you mean you'd like some for supper? With custard?"

Emma shook her head. "No, Hilda, not for supper. I've just had the most wonderful news! Both my brothers and their wives are coming to dinner on Christmas Day. It looks as if I'll have the whole family with me, if the boys get leave, of course. Hopefully Mrs. Lowther will come with baby Sarah. And there will be Mr. O'Neill and Mr. Kallinski, and with a bit of luck their sons, too. So you see, Hilda, I'm afraid I'm going to have to raid your larder."

Hilda beamed. "Oh, Mrs. Harte, that's luvely to hear! I sort of hoped you'd be having a family gathering this Christmas. It was awful for you the year of the Blitz, and last year as well, what with the boys away fighting. So I did prepare some nice things for you to take back to London with you, on the off chance you'd need them." Hilda paused, then finished. "Would you like to come into the stone larder? You can look at everything."

"I would indeed. And I might have known you'd be thinking ahead to Christmas in the summer. Did you bottle a lot of fruits?"

Hilda nodded. "Pears, damsons, plums from the orchard. Gooseberries and blackberries, we had some luvely ones in the garden this summer. I also bottled some of the tomatoes Mr. Ramsbotham's been growing in the greenhouses." Hurrying over to the larder, Hilda added, "And I've made things like chutney, and done a lot of pickling. Onions, beetroot, gherkins, and your favorite, piccalilli, Mrs. Harte."

Following Hilda into the stone larder, Emma said, "Thank you. And you made some Christmas cakes and Christmas puddings as well, didn't you?"

"Oh yes," Hilda answered, beaming at her. "Christmas wouldn't be the same without a bit of your fruitcake, would it, Mrs. Harte? I always use your recipe." Hilda indicated the large round tins stacked on one of the many shelves. "These are the cakes. I put lots of fruit in, just the way you like, and sherry, plenty of that. And down there are the puddings in the white basins tied with cheese-cloth. I've also got jams and jellies made, all your favorites, madame, and lemon curd as well."

"Thank you for preparing all these wonderful things, Hilda, I really appreciate it." It was cold in the larder, and Emma was shivering as she hurried back into the big family kitchen. She went and stood in front of the fire blazing in the hearth.

"Cook taught me well before she retired, Mrs. Harte," Hilda murmured, walking over to the table.

Emma's face changed slightly, her eyes turned anxious. "How *is* Mrs. Walton doing? Is she any better?"

"Yes, a bit. It's the gout, a'course, in her right foot. Too much uric acid. Anyways, it makes standing and walking right there difficult for her."

"Give her my best, Hilda, when you see her."

"Oh, I will, madame, she always asks about you." Hilda sighed, and giving Emma a long, pointed stare, she said, "I do wish you could all spend Christmas here at Pennistone Royal, that'd be luvely, it would."

"I'm afraid it's quite impossible."

"But it's right dangerous in London, what with all the bombing, madame. If you don't mind me saying so, I was thinking only the other day that it'd be right nice for Miss Daisy and Miss Elizabeth if they were in Yorkshire. *Safer,* madame." Her voice faltered, and she wondered if she had spoken out of turn.

"I agree with you, Hilda, that it's safer up here, and calmer." As she spoke Emma was reminded of the screaming sirens, the deafening antiaircraft guns in Hyde Park, the bombs exploding, the searchlights at night, and the general air of chaos, although things were becoming a bit better.

Returning Hilda's steady, questioning gaze, she felt the need to explain. "The problem is they want to be in London with me. As you know, Miss Elizabeth is very committed to her nursing. Also, her husband is stationed at Biggin Hill, which is much closer to London than it is to Yorkshire." Emma shook her head. "Not that he's been on leave lately. Those boys are always up in the air, in combat."

"Perhaps things'll get a bit better now that the Americans are in the war," the young housekeeper suggested.

"Let's hope so, Hilda, let's hope so. And speaking of the Americans, what have you planned to do for Christmas for the American pilots stationed around here?"

"Well, I was going to speak to you about that before you left," Hilda replied. "Joe and I thought we'd do a nice buffet for them in the Stone Hall, with your permission, that is. It'd be luvely for the young lads to have a bit of Christmas fare, sort of remind them of home, don't you think, madame?"

"I do, Hilda, and naturally you have my permission. Don't skimp either, make sure it's a proper treat for them. I remember how much they enjoyed the July Fourth party we gave this summer."

"And the bowling on the lawn," Hilda reminded her. "They enjoyed that. And the dancing later with the girls from the village. *You* were a big hit, Mrs. Harte, you really were. Especially with that nice young major."

"Come along, Hilda, don't be so silly," Emma murmured and changed the subject.

Thirty-four

Blackie O'Neill stood with his back to the fire in the drawing room of Emma's Belgrave Square house, waiting for her to come downstairs.

"Mrs. Harte'll be down in a minit," Grace had told him, after she had ushered him into the room. "Wot she said was to fix yerself a drink. Do yer want me ter do it for yer, Mr. O'Neill?"

He had declined. Now, as he glanced at the clock on the mantel shelf, he saw that the minute had stretched into ten. He was just about to fix himself something after all when he heard Emma's high heels clicking against the parquetry floor of the hallway outside. He swung around to greet her and just stood there staring at her, speechless for a moment.

"What's the matter, Blackie?" she asked, walking into the room. "You're gawping at me."

"Aye, I am that, Emma Harte. And everybody else that comes here today will also be . . . *gawping* at you." He chuckled. "I do love that funny Yorkshire word of yours."

Coming to a standstill in front of him, she smiled a little coquettishly for her, stood on her tiptoes, and kissed him on his cheek. "And why will they be doing that? Why are you doing it, Blackie darling?"

"Oh, Emm, you know very well *why*. You know exactly how you look this afternoon," he answered, chuckling again. "And if you don't, mavourneen, then it's a new pair of glasses I'll have to be buying you."

"My eyesight's perfect," she shot back.

"Aye, I know it is, so you must know that you look positively beautiful. In all the forty years I've known you, I've never, ever seen you look bonnier. And that's the God's own truth, me darlin' girl. You've outdone yourself, Emm."

"Thank you, Blackie. It's an *old* dress, you know. I've had it since 1937. You like it, do you?"

"Aye, I like it. Very elegant it is."

Emma had spoken the truth when she had said it was old. It was a cocktail dress from Paris, designed by Lanvin, made of black cobweb lace mounted on emerald green silk, the silk showing through the lace. It had a V neckline and long sleeves, and was sashed in emerald silk. The full skirt and tight bodice flattered her youthful figure and long, shapely legs. She wore very high black silk court shoes by Pinet, her favorite shoemaker.

Still eyeing her with the utmost admiration, Blackie said, with a huge smile, "I'm glad to see that you're wearing my emerald brooch. It goes well with your frock."

"Yes, it does, doesn't it? I've always loved my emerald bow. Do you know, Blackie, I still have the original one you gave me."

"You *do?*" He sounded surprised yet pleased. "I can't believe it . . . all these years you've kept it, since you were a little sprite of a girl, only fifteen. My little green glass bow?"

"That's right. And by the way, I've known you since I was fourteen and I'm now fifty-three, so actually I've known you only thirty-nine years, not forty."

"Splittin' hairs are we now, mavourneen?" he asked, his black eyes narrowing.

"No, I'm just teasing you, my dearest friend. Now, would you like champagne? Or a drop of Irish?"

"I think I'll be having a drop of whiskey, Emma love. And I can fix it meself, you know."

"No, I can do it for you. But perhaps you can open the bottle of champagne."

"It'll be my pleasure, Emma. And isn't it grand Bryan got leave, and the other lads. It's a jolly Christmas night we'll be havin' with our families."

A few minutes later he was handing her a flute of champagne, and she gave him his Irish whiskey in a crystal glass.

"Here's to you, me darlin' Emma, the most beautiful woman I know."

"And to you, Shane Patrick Desmond O'Neill, the young spalpeen who became a great gentleman and a toff and who has always been my best friend." She laughed. "You used to say to me years ago . . . 'I'm going to be a toff one day.' And you are. And I'm so proud of you."

They touched glasses, and Emma hovered next to him in front of the fire as they waited for her children, his son, and her other guests to join them.

After a short silence, Blackie said, "I'm glad Frank could come after all. He might have some news about the war . . . you know, inside stuff."

"He might, but I doubt very much he'd tell us," Emma murmured. She knew Blackie liked to pick her brother's brains, as she did herself, but Frank could be extremely closemouthed. Above everything else he was discreet and trustworthy, as his boss, Lord Beaverbrook, knew very well.

Emma looked toward the hallway as she heard running feet, and suddenly there was her daughter Daisy, rushing into the drawing room like a young colt, flying to her uncle Blackie, who was one of her favorites.

"A little decorum. Walk don't run, Daisy," Emma admonished gently, but her eyes were loving, her smile benign.

"And if it's not me darlin' little Daisy, the prettiest flower in the world," Blackie said, hugging her close, then holding her away. "You've sprung up in the last week, little one," he murmured with a frown.

Daisy, dark haired and blue eyed like her father, Paul McGill, laughed uproariously. "Oh, Uncle Blackie, don't be silly! I'm wearing high heels." As she spoke, she spun around, her dark blue velvet dress billowing out like a bell.

"Aren't I the foolish man!" Blackie laughed and then looked at the door as Elizabeth came in clutching the arm of her young husband, Tony Barkstone. She wore a red silk dress and pearls, and he was resplendent in his blue Royal Air Force uniform. Blackie couldn't help thinking what a handsome couple they made, Elizabeth, a stunning dark beauty; Tony a blond, blue-eyed Englishman, the bloom of youth still on his handsome face. Why are they always so young, those who defend us? he wondered.

After greetings had been exchanged all around, Elizabeth went over to Emma and said, "Mummy, you look gorgeous." She stood staring admiringly at her mother's red hair and perfect pink-and-white complexion, the vivid green eyes that matched the matchless emeralds at her ears, on her shoulder and hands, and she found it hard to believe she was gazing at a woman of fifty-three.

Leaning into her mother, Elizabeth whispered, "Mummy, you don't look a day over thirty-nine."

Emma threw back her head and laughed. She was happy this afternoon. In fact, she had not felt this happy since Paul's death, four years ago. She knew it was because her children and family and friends would all be with her today. They gave her such joy and comfort, and she was proud of them.

She heard the faint cry of the baby, and she hurried to the hallway as Kit and June came toward her. June was carrying the newest redhead in the family, Sarah Lowther, not yet a year old but making her presence felt.

Emma kissed her baby granddaughter, touched her fat little cheek, then kissed her daughter-in-law June, and finally turned to her elder son, Kit, son of Joe Lowther, her first husband. She thought he looked a lot like Joe today, blond, fair, gray eyed, a solid-looking young man wearing his army captain's uniform proudly, grinning from ear to ear and showing his perfect white teeth and dimples.

Taking hold of Emma's arm, Kit drew her toward him and hugged her tightly. He had always adored his mother, and now he said against her auburn hair, "I'm thrilled the baby looks like you, Mother, just in case you didn't know."

Emma drew away from him, touched his cheek. "So am I, Kit darling."

"I'm not the last, am I?" Robin cried, running down the stairs and walking swiftly across the parquetry floor to join the small group in the hallway.

"No, no, we're still waiting for a few others," Emma murmured, smiling up at Robin. He was her favorite, but never once had she shown this; she had not believed in playing favorites in the family, had treated them all equally.

As she watched Robin shaking hands with Kit and kissing June, Emma could not help thinking that Robin resembled her brother Winston more than he did his father, Arthur Ainsley. He was tall and dark haired like Winston and his twin, Elizabeth. Tonight he appeared more dashing than ever in his air force blue. He was a pilot, something of an ace flyer, and had recently been promoted to captain. She suspected he might be a daredevil, and she worried when she thought of him in his Hurricane over enemy territory. In order to keep her sanity, she endeavored not to think about what Robin did in the air.

Grasping her hand, Robin twirled her around, almost but not quite jitterbugging, and whistled. "Wow, Ma, you look like . . . a film star. If some of our chaps could see you now, they'd be fighting over who got to be your escort."

"Indeed they would," David Amory said as he came down the stairs. "Good evening, Mrs. Harte," he said, as he joined them.

"Good evening, David," she responded, steeling herself, trying not to stare too hard at him. It would take her a while to get used to this young man who bore an odd likeness to Paul McGill. She had been floored last night when he had arrived with Robin and Tony, and two other young pilots, all members of the 111th Squadron stationed at Biggin Hill.

"They're going to bunk in here with us, Ma, is that all right?" Robin had asked, and she had been happy to acquiesce. For several years now Robin had been bringing his squadron mates home, and she had willingly opened her door and her heart to these dauntless young men.

But throw her off balance he did. Yet David was not as outrageously handsome as Paul had been as a young man, nor did he have his massive size and audacious personality. Last night David had charmed her at once. However, she was already concerned about his presence. . . . Daisy had not been able to take her eyes off David, who was twenty-four and something of a war hero already. He had seemed taken with her also.

"Well, let's not stand here," Emma now said, taking hold of David's arm. "And where are your friends?" she asked, looking up at him.

"They'll be down in a few minutes, Mrs. Harte," he replied, and bending closer, he added softly, "They're enjoying the luxury of your bathrooms, Mrs. Harte. They're rather different from those in our billets."

Emma laughed as they went into the drawing room together, where she introduced David to Blackie, then watched as Daisy glided toward him looking as if she were floating on clouds.

June went to sit on a sofa with Sarah, and Kit helped Robin pour champagne while Blackie engaged in a conversation with David, whom he had instantly taken to.

Emma swung around as Winston and Charlotte came into the drawing room. She was disappointed to see they were alone, but kept her expression neutral. After kissing first Charlotte and then her brother, she stepped back and said to her sister-in-law, "How lovely you look, Charlotte, the deep burgundy velvet is so becoming on you."

"Thank you, Emma, and I must say you're as elegant as always." The two women, who were good friends, smiled at each other warmly, and then Winston said, "But where are Randolph and Georgina? Haven't they arrived yet?"

"No, they haven't," Emma answered, relieved to hear her nephew had been given leave after all; Winston would have been glum company otherwise, and so would Charlotte.

Frank and Natalie, with their daughter, Rosamund, and son, Simon, arrived on the heels of Winston, and once more greetings were exchanged, compliments given. Emma then led her brothers and their wives into the drawing room and said to Frank in a low voice, "I did manage to get extra staff today, but not really enough. So could you help Robin and Kit with the drinks, darling?"

"No sooner said than done," Frank murmured and went to join his nephews at the console.

Emma took hold of Natalie's arm and led her over to the fireplace to introduce her to David Amory. Frank's wife was lovely, rather ethereal-looking, with a finely drawn face, swanlike neck, and slender figure. Her hair had turned color years ago; she was prematurely white, but the tone suited her and somehow did not age her.

"I would like to introduce you to my sister-in-law," Emma said, smiling at David, who turned to greet Natalie.

Blackie drew Emma away from the fireplace and said in a worried voice, "I can't imagine what happened to Bryan and Geraldine. I told them to be here by five, and it's almost twenty past."

"Since he's already in London, you know they're coming, so do relax, darling. It's not as though he had to come from Scapa Flow, like Randolph."

"I believe Randolph got here in the early hours of the morning," Blackie informed her. "So Bryan told me." Once again Blackie looked toward the hallway and suddenly began to laugh. "And speaking of the two young devils, here they are," he added, clasping her hand in his, leading her out into the hallway.

"There you are, lads, just in time for a drop of the Irish before dinner," Blackie said, throwing his son an affectionate look and embracing Randolph, of whom he was exceptionally fond. He then went to kiss his daughter-in-law Geraldine, who had baby Shane in her arms. Turning to Randolph's wife, Georgina, he kissed her also and glanced at the little boy in her arms . . . Winston the second they called him.

"Now come along, ladies, and you, too, Bryan, Randolph. You all look a bit nithered. What you be needing now is a drink and your backs to the fire for ten minutes. It's hellish cold out there today."

"I'm just going to pop into the kitchen to make sure everything's all right," Emma murmured to Blackie and glided away. He watched her go, his adoration of her written all over his face. Then he marched across to the console table and filled two crystal glasses with Irish whiskey, saying to Frank as he did, "What's happening in the world today?"

"Not a lot, thank heavens," Frank answered. "And I hope it stays that way . . . at least for Christmas Day. Oh, look, Blackie, here's David and the boys."

As soon as they spotted Blackie and Frank, David and his sons came over to greet them, and a moment later Robin was dashing across the room to welcome the two young pilots from Biggin Hill whom he had invited to spend Christmas with them. He introduced Matthew Hall and Charlie Cox to everyone present before going to get them both glasses of champagne.

A few minutes later, when Emma returned to the drawing room, she went first to greet David, Ronnie, and Mark Kallinski, then floated over to make the two young pilots feel at home.

Frank, watching from the sidelines, could not help admiring her. His sister was charming and gracious this afternoon, not to mention staggeringly beautiful. To Frank, Emma was, at fifty-three, a great lady . . . soigné, sophisticated, exceedingly intelligent, a fountain of information about everything from haute couture and jewels to great art, eighteenth-century French furniture, porcelain and silver, and Georgian antiques.

When he thought about their early years, so poverty stricken and isolated in Fairley, it was miraculous to him that she had become this woman. She was also a tycoon par excellence, and a power to be reckoned with in international business circles. She was, to him, a phenomenon.

He shifted his eyes from Emma and let them roam around the drawing room. Frank thought it was one of the most beautiful rooms he had ever seen. The walls were a funny sort of color, not quite blue, not quite pale green, but a mingling of both shot through with a hint of gray. The billowing silk taffeta draperies at the three tall windows were the identical color, and this shade was repeated in French chairs and a sofa, while a love seat was covered in pale blue; another series of four French chairs were in pale green. Jade and crystal lamps, shaded in cream silk, stood on various eighteenth-century French tables and chests, and the whole was pulled together by the faded antique Aubusson carpet underfoot.

Emma had acquired any number of beautiful objects, but the art was perhaps the most stunning element: two Renoirs, a Sisley, and a Monet, all in pale pastel colors that added to the soft quality of the room.

Emma had taught herself everything, he reminded himself. But she always had great taste.

Thirty-five

Jack Field and Dennis Scott, both single, with no immediate family in London and nowhere to go on Christmas Day, had been willing and happy to help Emma with her holiday dinner, flattered to be asked, in fact.

Promptly at six o'clock, Grace came into the drawing room and whispered to Emma that the buffet table in the kitchen had been completed and the helpers were waiting to serve.

Emma, who was standing next to Blackie, asked him to announce that dinner was ready, and he did so, his deep voice booming out across the room. Of course he used his own words: "Ladies and gentlemen, our Christmas fare awaits us in the kitchen. Emma has had everything set out on a grand buffet table, but you will take your places in the dining room once you have your food. Now, let's be going into the kitchen before everything gets cold."

Jack, Dennis, Grace, and Mrs. Coddington, the cook, all stood behind the buffet table, which was grand indeed. Covered in a white damask cloth, it had silver candelabra holding red candles at each end and was groaning with food: two large, delicious-looking boiled hams from Yorkshire, three roast turkeys, and three roast chickens, all browned to perfection and steaming; a selection of vegetables, also from Pennistone Royal; a huge platter of roast potatoes; bowls of sage-and-onion stuffing; smaller crystal bowls of relishes such as piccalilli and chutney, as well as the pickled beetroots and onions, all from Hilda's larder, and several gravy boats of Emma's special gravy.

Once all had been served, they followed Emma into the dining room, which was filled with seasonal touches. Again she had used red candles in the silver candlesticks on the long mahogany table, and in the center was a large crystal bowl filled to overflowing with red, silver, gold, and green ornamental balls instead of a floral arrangement. On the sideboard were matching crystal vases filled with red Christmas berries, sprigs of holly and mistletoe, flanked by more red candles in silver sticks, and standing on a chest was an artificial Christmas tree glittering with gold and silver ornaments and big gold bows. Next to the chest Emma had placed a double crib for the baby boys, Winston II and Shane, and Sarah was nearby.

Everyone found their seats, thanks to Emma's table plan. Kit, Robin, Bryan, and

Randolph were assigned the task of serving the red and white wines. Once they had finished and were seated, everyone began to eat.

As always, Emma ate sparingly, and she was gratified to see that all of the young men were tucking in, relishing the home-cooked meal. Her eyes settled on each of them in turn . . .

Tony, sitting next to his beloved Elizabeth, his face so easy to read, without guile, blessed with blond good looks, very English in his appearance.

And *Kit,* on the other side of his sister Elizabeth, adoring of June and their baby, Sarah, who gurgled in the small crib Emma had placed against the wall, just behind June. He was true blue English.

Bryan, alongside Geraldine, also in air force blue. He was the spitting image of Blackie. Tall, broad of chest and shoulder, he had the same merry black eyes and a fine head of curly black hair. He looks *exactly* the way Blackie did the day I met him on the moors above Fairley, Emma thought, smiling inwardly.

There was her darling *Robin,* handsome as the day was long, dashing in his uniform, his sensitive face quick and alert as he listened to everyone, and talked to everyone, as usual the genial and articulate host. Robin sat between his sister Daisy and his aunt Charlotte, who was drawn to him because of his similarity in appearance to Winston.

For a moment her eyes rested on her elder brother, and her heart overflowed with love for him. He had always been her right hand, devoted, loyal, and hardworking. How happy he looks tonight, she thought, because Randolph, Georgina, and baby Winston are here.

Now it was her nephew's turn to undergo a moment of her scrutiny. *Randolph,* sitting next to his wife, was tall, a little broader in the chest than Winston, and good-looking; it was obvious he was a Harte from the shape of his face and his coloring. He had eyes only for Georgina. A lieutenant in the Royal Navy, he wore his uniform with great aplomb.

And so did *Ronnie* and *Mark* Kallinski, David's sons, who were both in the army and seated on either side of Natalie. Handsome young men, dark haired, with lively, intelligent blue eyes inherited from their grandmother Janessa Kallinski.

David caught her studying his sons, and he smiled at her and winked. She was seated at the head of the table, and he was on her left, Blackie on her right, as usual.

"Quite a gathering of the clans, Emma," David murmured. "We're all enjoying this meal, it's delicious. And just look at the boys . . . they're practically smacking their lips. I bet they haven't had food like this in a while."

She laughed, her green eyes sparkling. "I'm quite certain it's a bit different from their usual fare," she murmured, and hearing Daisy's sudden lilting laughter she looked down the table, saw the fervent happiness on her daughter's face, and her heart sank. Daisy was sitting next to David Amory, and she was totally absorbed in the young RAF pilot. I fully understand why, Emma thought, for a moment concentrating on him.

David Amory was undoubtedly a charmer, and his looks were guaranteed to make him a target of women. Robin had described him as "a real pinup boy, Ma, but he's genuine, very sincere." He had grinned at her and added, "It's Daisy you should watch." Slowly she was growing accustomed to his uncanny likeness to Paul. It struck her again that he was as interested in Daisy as she was in him, and she wondered if he knew her daughter was only seventeen. She would make sure Robin pointed that out to him later. David was quite obviously well bred, with impeccable manners, and Robin had told her he was from an old Gloucestershire family.

Matthew and Charlie, the other two pilots from Biggin Hill, were having a wonderful time, she could see that. Matthew had made her laugh uproariously when he had given her a rave review of the bathroom adjoining his bedroom on one of the upper floors. He kept exclaiming about the size of the tub, and the *hot* water. Not to mention the *heated* towel rail. "A bit different from our billets," he had explained.

Matthew Hall, a lanky young fellow with brown hair and a sensitive face, seemed much more serious than the others. Yet he had that lovely sense of humor, a wicked grin, and a somewhat wry approach to life. She had taken to him immediately.

Emma's eyes swiveled to his friend. *Charlie,* who was seated next to her niece Rosamund, was obviously an experienced raconteur, and he was engaged in a long story to which Rosamund was listening with obvious interest. He was a pleasant-looking, clean-cut young man, with the same fair English coloring as Kit and deep brown eyes, rather soulful. Emma decided that his quiet looks belied a fatal charm.

Her attention was caught by Jack Field, who had appeared in the doorway, inviting them to come back to the buffet table to select their desserts.

"There's quite a lot to choose from," Emma told Blackie and David Kallinski as they escorted her to the kitchen. "Hilda's bottled fruits with hot custard, Christmas plum pudding with a brandy sauce, Christmas cake, full of sultanas, currants, candied peel, and sherry." She threw Blackie a quick glance and added, "Just like those fruitcakes Mrs. Turner used to make in that other life of ours."

Blackie looked down at her and put his arm around her shoulder, almost protectively, as thoughts of their past came flooding back to him. "I think I'll be having a bit of each. . . . I won't be able to resist, and neither will David."

"Only too true," David agreed. "But I've always loved your fruitcake."

After dinner, when everyone was satisfied in a way they had not been for several years, Robin ushered the party into the drawing room. "For a singsong, Mother," he told Emma and thought to add, "Oh, and by the way, I invited some other chaps over for drinks later, Ma, some American pilots I got to know recently. I hope you don't mind."

"Of course not, Robin," she said, well used to the way her younger son did things on the spur of the moment. Long ago she had decided it was part of Robin's charm, that spontaneity of his. He had an outgoing personality, a friendliness about him, and he enjoyed making new friendships.

Coffee was served in the drawing room by Grace; Georgina, Geraldine, Elizabeth, and Daisy passed the cups around; Kit stoked the fire; and Blackie walked over to the baby grand, lifted the lid, and tinkled on the keys for a few seconds.

"It's in fine tune," he announced, then realized, much to his embarrassment, that this was rather a silly comment. Anything to do with Emma Harte was always in fine tune, exactly the way it should be.

Robin, Bryan, and Randolph acted as bartenders, pouring cognac for Blackie, Winston, and Frank, and a crème de menthe for Charlotte. The other ladies declined and stayed with the coffee.

"There's quite a lot of sheet music in the piano stool," Emma began and stopped as the doorbell pealed loudly.

"It's my Yanks!" Robin exclaimed, hurrying out into the hall and down the stairs three at a time.

He came back escorting the three young American pilots, who entered the drawing room rather shyly, Emma thought. Her heart went out to them as they came over to be introduced. They were just boys.

"Gee, thanks for having us, Mrs. Harte," Harry Trent said, shaking her hand enthusiastically. He was so tall she had to crane her neck to look him in the face.

"It's great to be with a family for Christmas," Phil Rodgers murmured, glancing around. "Beautiful place you have, Mrs. Harte, and thanks for having us. It's just like being at home."

"It's kind of you to have us over, ma'am," the third pilot, Harvey Wilson, said. "This is better than the officers' club any day."

Emma smiled, nodded, ushered them to various chairs, and asked them if they wanted anything to eat. None of them was hungry, but they did accept the drinks Bryan and Randolph offered and jumped up when Elizabeth, Daisy, and Rosamund came to speak to them.

"Would you be excusing me, mavourneen?" Blackie murmured, bending over Emma, who was now seated with Winston on one of the sofas. "I think it might be a good idea for me to get this singsong of Robin's going, sure an' I do."

"Oh yes, do do that, Blackie darling. It'll be lovely. . . . I know everyone's going to enjoy it."

Striding over to the piano, Blackie made himself comfortable and announced, "I'll start this singsong off then, and you must all join in . . ."

"Go for it, Uncle Blackie!" Kit called out, grinning.

"I will, I will, lad, just give me a moment."

Blackie looked through the sheets of music and then sat back and began to play. It was a haunting melody, and everyone fell silent, touched by it.

In an instant Emma recognized it, and as Blackie started to sing, her throat tightened with emotion and she leaned into the cushions and closed her eyes, letting herself be carried back to the day she had met him.

She remembered what a shabby, starveling little creature she had been as she had hurried over the windswept moors. And how he had come across her as he walked out of the mist, asking the way to Fairley Hall. He had frightened the wits out of her. . . .

Blackie's wonderful baritone rang out, filling the room.

The Minstrel Boy to the war is gone
In the ranks of death you will find him.
His father's sword he has girded on,
And his wild harp slung behind him . . .

The drawing room was totally silent as they listened to his wondrous voice, so he sang another verse then moved on quickly, thinking perhaps this Irish ballad had been overly poignant. So he sang an Irish jig full of tongue-twisting names, and once again Emma recognized it immediately. He had also sung this jig that long-ago day, and he had made it his second one then. After the jig he sang "*Danny Boy*," a ballad that was one of her favorites, and apparently everyone else's, since they sat listening raptly, not moving.

Finally, changing the mood, Blackie launched into one of the most popular songs of the day.

As he started the next verse, Blackie lifted his right hand, motioning to the others to join in. Elizabeth leapt to her feet and ran to the piano, and Daisy immediately followed. A second later David Amory was standing next to her, his arm around her waist, Emma noticed.

Others came, too, Harry and Phil, Robin and Kit, and then Bryan walked over and stood behind Blackie, his hands on his father's shoulders.

They all sang along as Blackie started another verse, then they repeated it since everyone loved this wartime song.

When Blackie paused for a moment, Elizabeth bent down and said, "Uncle Blackie, could we have a Vera Lynn favorite? I know all of them, and I can sing, too."

"That I know, me darlin'," Blackie said and began to play the song he heard her singing all the time, and Elizabeth accompanied him, her voice quite lovely, just as he knew it would be.

The room had listened attentively without joining in, and now there were shouts for more and clapping, but Elizabeth simply smiled and demurred, all the while looking across at Tony.

Phil began to sing "Paper Doll"; Blackie picked out the tune, and many sang with him. Then Matt asked Blackie to play "There'll Always Be an England," and everyone sang enthusiastically, that song and many more tunes that Blackie and then Bryan played.

As she listened to them, and watched them enjoying themselves, Emma's heart was full to overflowing. How handsome the boys look in their different uniforms, she suddenly thought. It had often struck her that there was something rather glamorous about uniforms, and a man wearing one was usually lethally appealing to women. But there was nothing glamorous about their jobs; what they did was terrifying. And they're all so very, very young. Why is it always the flower of a nation that has to go to war? she asked herself. Her heart clenched as her eyes swept over them, knowing what they would be doing tomorrow and the day after. And she looked at Blackie and her brothers and thought: The young *have* to go, it's always been so, because our other men are too old, they could not stand the rigors of war.

It was Charlotte who suddenly said, "Blackie, can we have a Christmas carol?"

"Sure, me darlin', and why not?" he answered, smiling broadly. "Come on, Bryan, me lad, and you, too, Randolph. I know you two have often sung together . . . let's have a bit of harmonizing here."

Bryan and Randolph came around the piano and stood together facing the room, and the others moved back a little. And as Blackie struck a few chords, Emma recognized the first strains of the carol he had chosen:

Silent night, holy night,
All is calm, all is bright

Round yon virgin mother and child.
Holy infant so tender and mild,
Sleep in heavenly peace
Sleep in heavenly peace . . .

Thirty-six

It was a glorious Indian summer day in early October 1943, the kind of day Emma could not resist. Golden sunshine streamed in through the leaded windows of the upstairs parlor at Pennistone Royal, flooding the room with incandescent light.

Emma had been writing in her diary, as she did each day, and now she put down her pen and closed the black leather book. Locking it in her desk drawer, she pocketed the key and stood up, walked across the room, stood gazing out of the soaring window that faced toward the moors.

The sky was a lovely cerulean blue, filled with puffy white clouds, an unusual sky for October. Even in the summer months it was frequently overcast, bloated with dark clouds, as rain blew in from the North Sea. Such was the Yorkshire weather; today was special.

The heather's still lingering, she murmured to herself, noting the purplish tinge on the rim of the hills. How they beckoned her; she was a child of those stark, implacable moors, had grown up amongst them under the high fells and great black rocks that rose like monoliths to touch the heavens. It had been her world, her most beloved world, and she always yearned to be up in that desolate country.

On an impulse, she hurried downstairs to the Stone Hall. After changing into a pair of flat walking shoes she kept in the armoire, she slipped into a loden green wool coat and headed toward the office at the end of the hall.

As she went in Glynnis looked up from her typewriter and gave Emma a small smile. "I was just going to come up and see you, Mrs. Harte. I have your letters ready to sign, and —"

"Would you mind if I did it later, Glynnis? I need a breath of air to clear my head. I'll only be gone a short while, a quick walk on the moors."

"That's fine," Glynnis murmured, turning back to her typewriter.

"Is everything all right?" Emma asked, staring hard at her secretary. "You seem a bit wan today."

"I'm fine." Glynnis smiled at her once more.

Emma noticed at once that it was another faltering smile, but she made no reference to it. Glancing at her watch, she said, "Why don't you go to the kitchen, Glynnis dear? Hilda will make you a little lunch, a cup of tea. It's almost one o'clock, you know."

"Thank you, Mrs. Harte, I think I will."

Nodding and smiling at her secretary, Emma closed the door behind her as she went out. She walked off in the direction of the moors, passing the beautifully designed parterres. She paused for a moment to inspect them, they were perfect today. She had always loved their geometrical designs, which did need intense care and weeding. As she moved on she saw Mr. Ramsbotham, the head gardener, in the distance. He was with his young nephew, Wiggs, who one day would take over from him. She waved to them. They both waved back, and Mr. Ramsbotham, who was wearing a cap, doffed it to her.

Within minutes Emma was heading up the steep path, making for her favorite spot under the monoliths, as she always called them. Although she had not been up on the moors for several months, she did not find the climb hard. At the end of April she had been fifty-four, but she knew she did not look it, and she certainly did not feel it. Thank God I'm so fit and healthy, so strong, she thought as she pushed on up the steep incline. She was anxious to reach the summit, where she felt she could touch the sky if she stood on tiptoe and reached up a little bit.

She smiled inwardly, thinking of her

brothers and Blackie, and how the three of them had always teased her about the moors and her unwavering passion for them. Long ago she had stopped trying to explain what they meant to her. How could she put into words this almost mystical feeling she had about them? Sometimes she felt as though they belonged to her and her alone; they were a safe place, her haven. Whenever she was troubled she came up here to think; sometimes she came just because she loved to walk across them. There were times she craved the solitude that abounded here.

After a twenty-minute climb she reached the huge pile of black rocks which looked as if they could topple over on a windy day. But they had been here for aeons and aeons, she knew that.

It was windy, and she quickly slid into the niche between two rocks and sat down on the stone she had had a gardener place there as a seat for her. That had been in 1932. Eleven years ago now, she thought . . . how time flies, like those birds on the wing soaring into the sky. They were in a V formation. *V* for victory, she murmured to herself, and no sooner had that thought entered her mind than she spotted the bombers coming in, flying low across the blameless blue sky in the same V formation. *V* for victory, she thought yet again, filled with relief and joy. They were coming back to their airfields, Dishforth or Leeming, or perhaps Topcliffe, where Tony had been stationed for special training at the beginning of the war. As they droned overhead, she stood up and found herself saluting them . . . the sons of mothers just like her. She swelled with pride.

Then Emma sat for a while, staring out at the panorama that spread itself in front of her: the valley below, and beyond the continuation of the endless moors, empty, solitary, and without life. Except for the larks and linnets with their joyous songs, the tender little birds of her childhood days.

It seemed to Emma that time had sped by since Christmas. So much had happened in the last nine months. The war was progressing quite well; it had become a world war in 1941 after Germany had invaded Russia and the Japanese had bombed Pearl Harbor. The Americans had been fighting alongside them for some time now, in Europe, North Africa, and the Far East. There had been defeats but triumphs, too, for the Allies, and everyone was optimistic.

Emma believed they would win the war, just as Winston Churchill had always predicted, especially now that they had the Americans on their side. She thought of the young pilots she had met through Robin, and here in Yorkshire; she had been impressed with all of them. Her sons were still unharmed, as were all the sons of the three clans, and for that she was thankful.

The spring had passed quickly this year, with Robin coming and going, bringing his comrades in arms to bunk in with them, as he called it, and with David Amory always tagging along. There had been much laughter and gaiety, the gramophone playing constantly, the clink of glasses, the peals of laughter, the songs around the piano. She had loved those months; the youth and high spirits had drowned out the wail of the sirens, the harsh fire from the antiaircraft guns in Hyde Park, the deafening sound of exploding bombs.

She had taken them all, most especially David, under her wing, loving them, spoiling them.

It had come as no surprise to her when he had approached her in May and asked her permission to marry Daisy when she became eighteen. "But that's next week!" she had exclaimed, and he had answered, "Yes, I know, Mrs. Harte, but there's a war on." She had been unable to refuse them, they were so much in love. And she approved of young David, with his boundless charm and sweet nature. Besides that, Emma knew that she had set her own precedent by allowing Elizabeth to marry Tony at eighteen. There was no way she could say no to her most beloved child, the love child of Paul McGill. And their wedding had turned out to be the happy event of the summer of '43.

She herself had been bogged down with work since the beginning of the year, as she invariably was. But she refused to give up her war efforts, even though Winston was always telling her she was exhausting herself. Emma felt honor bound to do her bit, that was her nature. She often went with Elizabeth to the London Bridge tube station to bring food, kind words, and comfort to the Londoners who were sheltering there, and Daisy was a willing volunteer as well. Emma gave money to various causes, and raised money for them, and ran a canteen for the troops.

Suddenly she began to laugh, remembering how Jack Field had protested when she had decided to use the basement of Harte's for the canteen, asking her if she had a permit to do such a thing. His objections, albeit uttered in mild tones, had surprised her. She had glared at him ferociously and snapped, "*Permits? Who needs permits? There's a war on. And anyway, in case you've forgotten, this is my store. If I want to have a canteen in the basement, I'll have one!*"

Within ten minutes she had been filled with remorse at the way she had spoken to Jack, one of her most loyal and devoted employees. And she had run down to his office and apologized profusely; he had been relieved that she was so forgiving. "There's nothing to forgive, Jack," she had told him softly. "Well, let's put it this way, *you* have to forgive *me* for speaking to you so harshly, and so very rudely. I value everything you do for me. I'm so sorry."

He had nodded and smiled and explained, "I was just worrying about things like fire regulations, Mrs. Harte, and the number of people we are allowed to have there, and whether the canteen would affect store security in any way."

Emma now understood that he had only been doing his duty. She had listened to him carefully as he outlined the inherent problems, and of course he was right; she had been carried away in her desire to help the fighting forces. Instead of using Harte's basement she had bought a warehouse just off Fulham Road. It had become a great success, and she and Jack had remained good friends and colleagues. He even worked at the canteen once a week, as she herself did. They both enjoyed it.

A sudden smile illuminated Emma's face, and in an instant she was transported to a memorable evening at the canteen, not so long ago that she didn't remember the details. The weeks and months fell away . . .

"Mummy, look, over there, at Glynnis dancing with Bryan," Elizabeth said, tugging at her arm. "Isn't she a wonder, the way she's jitterbugging? Gosh, they're like Ginger Rogers and Fred Astaire. They ought to be in the pictures together."

Emma followed the direction of Elizabeth's gaze, and she had to agree. Glynnis really was a fantastic dancer, whirling around on her high-heeled wedge shoes, her dress flaring as Bryan spun her around and out, then pulled her back to him and twirled her again. It was obvious they were enjoying themselves.

"My goodness, I've never seen anyone dance together the way they do, except on the silver screen," Emma murmured. "They're a perfect team, just as you said."

Emma and Elizabeth were standing near the bar, watching the young Englishwomen and servicemen of various nationalities jitterbugging. Earlier the two of them had made stacks of sandwiches and served them to the boys along with cups of tea and coffee, lemonade, Tizer pop, and beer. And quite a few glasses of Paul McGill's vintage wine; Jack Field had managed to get Emma a liquor license for the canteen. "And what better way to dispose of some of that wine?" she asked her brothers, who had agreed with her wholeheartedly.

Frank and Winston were with them tonight, along with Robin, who had been given a two-day pass unexpectedly, as had Elizabeth's husband, Tony. Emma liked coming to work at the canteen, to talk to the boys from the different services, to give them a bit of mothering and encouragement. And it warmed her heart to see how much they enjoyed having a little fun.

Tony, who had been playing darts, now came over and joined them, putting his arm around Elizabeth's waist. Suddenly the jitterbug music came to an end, and Emma noticed Frank was at the gramophone putting on another record. Within seconds "Moonlight Serenade" was filling the canteen with the captivating swing music popularized by Glenn Miller's big band.

Bryan began to lead Glynnis around the floor at a slower pace, obviously reluctant to release her, but he had to when Frank tapped him on the shoulder, cutting in. Emma smiled to herself when she saw Robin making a beeline for them; she knew her son was about to cut in just as Frank had done a moment before. "I must say, Glynnis is very popular," Emma said to Elizabeth and Tony. "I bet she'll dance with almost every serviceman tonight, she's such a good sport."

Tony agreed and added, "Anyway, she happens to be the best dancer who comes to work here. She's as light as a feather on her feet."

"Have you heard her sing, Mummy?"

"No, I haven't, Elizabeth."

"She's got a golden voice, very lovely."

"The Welsh are wonderful singers," Tony

informed them. "They have very special vocal cords."

Emma stared at her son-in-law in surprise. Tony was always full of tidbits of information. But there was some truth to what he had just said. "Yes, the Welsh choirs are renowned," she murmured, looking past him at Frank, who was strolling over to join them.

A moment later Winston came over, too. Placing an arm around Emma's shoulders, he whispered, "That's the one thing I miss, Emm. Dancing. I used to love it so before I lost my leg."

Slipping her arm through his, she whispered, "Yes, I know. But let's just remember that if you hadn't had it off when you did you wouldn't be alive."

"That's true." Winston was staring at Glynnis and Robin on the dance floor together, and he suddenly said, "She's turned out to be the best secretary you've ever had, hasn't she?"

"Indeed she has," Emma answered and then laughed as she watched an American flyer cut in on Robin. Her son loped over and exclaimed, "Why are you standing, Mother? Let's all sit down, shall we?" He pulled out a chair for Emma, and they seated themselves at a table near the edge of the dance floor.

Jack Field was standing at the gramophone now, and he changed the record this time.

The strains of Glenn Miller's band playing "Fools Rush In" floated into the air, and Emma leaned back in the chair, her mind focused on Paul McGill. She had not ceased to miss him, and now she felt a pang, understanding that there would never be another man in her life. Paul had been her great love, and would remain so always.

When the music stopped, Glynnis glided across the floor, and Emma said, "Do sit down, Glynnis dear, and catch your breath."

"Thanks, Mrs. Harte. I am a bit puffed. But it was lovely. I'm crazy about dancing."

"Would you like a glass of lemonade, Glynnis?" Bryan asked, hovering around her solicitously.

"Oh yes, I would, thanks, Bryan." Turning to Emma, Glynnis went on, "I was hoping my nice GI friend Richard Hughes would be here, but I haven't seen him. Have you, Mrs. Harte?"

"I haven't, I'm afraid, but it's early. Also the canteen is full tonight, it's hard to spot everyone."

Winston said, "How's everybody in the Rhondda, Glynnis? Family all right, are they?"

"Oh yes. Mum worries a lot about my brothers, off in the war. But then we all worry these days, don't we?"

Winston nodded, lit a cigarette, sat back and relaxed, sipping his glass of red wine.

Robin asked Glynnis if she'd like another turn around the dance floor, but she declined. She also said no to Bryan's invitation when he returned with her lemonade. "I'm just a bit tired right now," she murmured, smiling at them in turn, her eyes full of sparkle, her cheeks flushed from exertion.

Watching the men ogling Glynnis, trying to win her favor, Emma saw her in quite a different light than she did at the office. There had never been any question about Glynnis's good looks, but studying her intently tonight, Emma had become acutely aware of her sexuality. Glynnis was *luscious,* as well as sultry and glamorous. She had long, very beautiful legs, an ample bosom, a small waist, and the most luxuriant dark hair.

She's definitely a knockout, Emma thought; no wonder they all want to get her in their arms on the dance floor. But that's the only place they will get her. She's such a nice girl, not a flirt, not coy, not coquettish. Glynnis is a good girl. I hope her nice American GI comes tonight. She'll be disappointed if he doesn't.

No sooner had Emma thought this than Richard Hughes appeared, striding over to the table. He nodded to everyone, stretched out his hand to Emma. "Good evening, Mrs. Harte."

"Hello, Private Hughes. It's nice to see you."

Glynnis looked up at him, her large blue eyes shining, full of laughter. "There you are, Richard. I've been wondering where you were."

Richard gave her a long, intense look, obviously smitten with her, and stretched out his hand. Glynnis took it, and he pulled her to her feet.

"Please excuse us," he said to the group at large, nodding politely, and then he led her to the dance floor.

"He seems like a nice chap," Frank observed, lighting a cigarette. "She deserves only the best, she's a special girl."

"Yes, she is," Emma agreed, her gaze following them. The dance floor was now crowded. There was a happy feeling in the air, a low, excited buzz below the sound of the music . . . laughter, voices in conversation. She was filled with gratification, pleased that she had started this canteen. It did such a lot to boost the morale of the troops, troops of all nationalities. British, Canadian, Australian, American, French, Polish . . . young men of spirit, courage, and daring.

Now on the moors, feeling the wind biting into her bones, Emma pushed the past away and stood up, casting a lingering glance at the high-flung fells, then began to make her way back down the path to Pennistone Royal.

"Have you seen Glynnis?" Emma stood in

the doorway to the kitchen, looking across at Hilda, who was scraping parsnips at the sink.

Her housekeeper swung around and exclaimed, "Oh, Mrs. Harte, you did make me jump! I didn't know you were standing there. And yes, I saw her about half an hour ago. She had a sandwich, here at the kitchen table. And a cup of tea."

"Was she all right, Hilda?"

"I think so," Hilda began and stopped, bit her lip, looking suddenly hesitant. "Well, madame, as I say that I realize I don't rightly know. Glum she was, and well, I thought she seemed to be a bit downhearted . . . perhaps even troubled."

"I see."

"Why do you ask, Mrs. Harte? Isn't she in that there little office at the end of the Stone Hall?"

"No, Hilda, she's not, and there's a half-typed letter in her machine. I came to the kitchen thinking she might be here, still having lunch. Although it's not like her to leave a letter in the typewriter." Emma paused, threw Hilda a baffled look.

"I asked her about her boyfriend, the nice GI she told me about the last time she was up here, and she gave me such a funny look. Right queer it was, madame." Hilda shook her head and announced, "The's nowt sa queer as folk, Mrs. H."

Smiling knowingly, Emma exclaimed, "I

know all of those Yorkshire sayings, Hilda, don't think I don't. There's nowt so queer as folk, except for thee and me, and thee's a bit odd. You should have finished it, you know."

Hilda just laughed, thinking you never knew what Mrs. Harte was going to say, and put the parsnip down. She wiped her hands on the teacloth and said, "Speaking of lunch, madame, I noticed you haven't had anything to eat since that bit of toast for breakfast. You'll not get fat on that, madame, you knows."

"You can make me a cup of tea, Hilda, that would be nice, but just at the moment I'm not hungry. Now, getting back to your mention of the boyfriend, do you think perhaps there's trouble between him and Glynnis?"

"Ooh, I just don't know about that. But she did act a bit queer."

"Perhaps she's not feeling well. She looked a little peaked earlier. I'll just pop up to her room. In the meantime, you can put the kettle on, Hilda."

"Oh, right away, madame."

Glynnis was occupying a guest room on the floor above the upstairs parlor, and as Emma climbed the stairs she couldn't help wondering about her secretary's boyfriend, the nice American she had met at the canteen. He had appeared to be pleasant. Had they broken up? she asked herself as she came to the door of the Blue Room.

Before she even knocked Emma heard the muffled sobs, and she hesitated, wondering what to do. Then she rapped on the door, deciding that perhaps Glynnis needed help of some kind.

A moment later Glynnis was staring at her from the doorway. She was white as bleached bone, her eyes red-rimmed from crying.

"Whatever's the matter?" Emma asked in a gentle voice.

When Glynnis did not respond, Emma went on, "May I come in? I can't bear to see you like this, so very upset."

Still Glynnis did not speak. She merely opened the door a little wider and stepped back so that Emma could enter.

Emma saw that the bed was rumpled; apparently Glynnis had been laying on it, crying. Moving toward the seating area in the bay window, Emma lowered herself onto the sofa and said, "Come and sit with me, my dear. You don't have to talk if you don't feel like it, but at least I can try to give you a bit of motherly comfort."

Glynnis immediately burst into tears, covered her face with her hands, and just stood there, shaking and sobbing.

Emma was on her feet at once, and she guided Glynnis across the room, helped her to sit down, then took the armchair opposite. "Take your time, my dear, try and calm down. Would you like a glass of water? A cup of tea?"

Glynnis shook her head and groped in her pocket for her handkerchief, pressed it to her swollen eyes. After a moment or two she took a deep breath and said in a choked voice, "I'm so . . . so . . . sorry to break down like this. I've tried to be brave, but it just got to me today."

"What did?" Emma asked quietly.

Glynnis shook her head, bit her lip, looking worried.

Emma said, "Is it something to do with your nice GI boyfriend? *Richard?* Have you quarreled or broken up?"

"Oh no, Mrs. Harte," Glynnis whispered between dry sobs.

"But there is something that's disturbing you, Glynnis dear, and I don't want to pry, but I do want to help. I can assure you no one will ever know what you tell me. I would never break a confidence."

Glynnis inhaled deeply and tried to get her heaving breath under control. Finally, in a tearful voice, she blurted out: "I'm going to have a baby, Mrs. Harte. And I don't know what to do."

For a second Emma was speechless. Far away in the past she heard a poor little servant girl saying, "I'm going to have a baby, Edwin, and I don't know what to do." Her chest tightened as memories of that day in the rose garden at Fairley Hall swamped her. But then, shaking off the past, she took Glynnis's hand in hers.

"Oh, Glynnis, no wonder you're so upset," Emma consoled. "But what about your friend, Richard? Surely he's going to do the right thing by you. I thought he seemed quite taken with you the night you introduced him to me, and I've noticed subsequently how lovely he is with you. He seems very caring, very protective."

"Yes."

"Doesn't he want to marry you, Glynnis? Is that the problem?"

Glynnis bit her lip, looking suddenly flustered.

Emma frowned. "You have told him, haven't you?"

Glynnis couldn't speak. She just shook her head, her face whiter than ever, and there was a stricken look in her lovely eyes.

"But, Glynnis, you must tell him, my dear —"

"It's not his," Glynnis whispered.

Emma sat back suddenly, staring at her secretary, her expression troubled. "Then have you told the man who *is* the father?"

Glynnis nodded and began to cry, tears gushing down her cheeks.

"He doesn't want to marry you, is that it?"

"Yes. He can't."

"Is he married?" Emma asked, giving the

young woman a long, knowing look.

When Glynnis remained silent, Emma murmured, "Oh, Glynnis, my dear, getting involved with a married man only spells trouble. They rarely, if ever, leave their wives —" Emma broke off, realizing she was giving this poor girl a lecture when she needed comfort and guidance.

Glynnis began to weep once more, and Emma went to sit next to her on the sofa. She held her close, and eventually, as Glynnis calmed down a little, Emma told her firmly, "We must make a plan, Glynnis. I will help you in any way I can. I don't suppose you want to go home to the Rhondda Valley?"

Glynnis pulled away with a jerk. "No, no, Mrs. Harte, I can't! My da will kill me, or he'll die himself. For one thing, he couldn't stand the shame, me giving birth out of wedlock."

"Sssh, my dear, I understand what you're saying," Emma murmured, and she did, for hadn't she said the selfsame thing to Edwin Fairley when she was fifteen years old?

"Would you like me to speak to the man in question?" Emma asked softly.

"I don't think it would . . . make any difference," Glynnis said in a low, choked voice.

"Who *is* the father, Glynnis dear?"

There was a moment's hesitation, and then Glynnis told her.

Emma stared at her, flabbergasted. I'm

facing a disaster, she thought, and closed her eyes.

But quickly recouping, she opened them, took hold of the girl's hand, and said in a steady voice, "I think perhaps you'd better tell me all about it."

And Glynnis did.

It was an old, old story, as old as the world, of a man and a woman, and Emma Harte was only too familiar with its many interpretations. An instantaneous attraction — the French called it a *coup de foudre* — a falling in love so obsessive it obliterated everything else. A kind of insanity, a love so intense it transmuted the ordinary into the sublime . . . for a time. She knew all the words and phrases Glynnis was uttering. And then heartbreak and pain, as the man cooled when she told him she was carrying his child. His bastard was the way Glynnis had just put it.

Yet Emma now noticed that speaking about it seemed to have calmed Glynnis. The tears had ceased to flow, her voice no longer quavered, and her trembling had stopped.

Emma had been attentive to every detail of the overcharged romance now gone wrong. And she fully understood that nothing was going to change. The man had vacated Glynnis's life; he would not come back. And Emma was quite certain that Glynnis was aware of this, for she was both intelligent and smart.

When the young woman finished, she sat back, paused for a second, then murmured in a subdued voice, "Now you know it all, Mrs. Harte. You know my terrible predicament."

"Indeed I do, Glynnis," Emma answered and thought, Only too well do I know what you are facing. But she said, "Basically, you are on your own. At least that is what you believe. But you're not, in fact, because you have me, and I am going to help you through this tough time. I'm going to make sure you have a proper doctor, wages while you take maternity leave, a job waiting for you after the baby's born. This I promise you."

Glynnis, taken aback by Emma's sympathy and generosity, was silent, an uncomprehending expression in her eyes. At last she said slowly, "Why would you do this for me, Mrs. Harte? Don't think I'm not grateful, because I am. But *why?*"

"Because I'm fond of you, Glynnis, and because long ago, when I was much younger than you, I was in a similar position. I had no one to help me, and so all I craved was money. I knew money would protect the baby, protect me, and I strove hard to acquire it. A lot of it. So you see, I *know* firsthand that money is the most important thing to a single mother, as well as a little understanding and kindness from others, if it's available. But it isn't always, you know. Most people turn a blind eye, or treat you like a leper."

"That's true, I'm sure." Glynnis took a deep breath. "I don't know what to say, Mrs. Harte. *Thank you* doesn't seem quite enough."

"Oh, it is, Glynnis, of course it is. I just want you to try not to worry now."

"I do worry, I'm afraid, it's my nature." Glynnis stopped, bit her lip, and said in as steady a voice as she could summon, "Mrs. Harte, a while ago you spoke about Richard. You said he seemed attentive and caring, protective even . . ."

"Yes, I did say that. And it was my honest observation, Glynnis."

"Richard loves me, and he wants to marry me, and I was thinking that perhaps . . . well . . . actually, I wondered what *you* thought about it. I mean about me marrying Richard. Wouldn't it be a solution . . . to my *predicament?*"

Emma kept her face neutral as she sat back, giving Glynnis a somewhat appraising look. "Do you have any feelings for him? I thought you were so madly in love with the other man you couldn't see straight."

"That's true, Mrs. Harte, I just told you, I loved *him* too much. But I like Richard a lot; you can't *not* like him, he's so kind and good natured. And he's crazy about me, so I suppose I could grow to care for him in a *good way* . . ." Her voice trailed off when she saw the stern look settling on Emma's face. "What's wrong, Mrs. Harte? Why are you looking at me like that?"

"I was thinking that you cannot possibly deceive a man as good and kind as Richard apparently is, according to what you're saying anyway. It would be dishonest, and dishonorable. You cannot let him think this child is his."

"Oh, but I wouldn't do that!" Glynnis cried, her voice rising. "Anyway, it couldn't be his, because we . . . well, we haven't, you know, done anything like that." Glynnis stopped abruptly, her face now scarlet with embarrassment. "I'm not promiscuous."

"Forgive me, Glynnis, I didn't mean to imply that you were. However, you did appear to be rather close to him when I saw you together at the canteen, so I made an assumption. That was totally wrong of me, and I apologize. I would never cast aspersions on your morals, my dear. I understand life too well to do that."

"It's all right, Mrs. Harte, please don't get upset." Glynnis swallowed hard and added sotto voce, "I was a virgin until I fell in love with *him*. . . . He was the first man I . . . knew." Her voice was lower as she added, "You *know* what I mean."

"I see." Emma rose, went to look out the window at the parterres. Best seen from above, the young Wiggs was always telling her. He was such a sweet little boy . . . they were all sweet when they were boys. Returning to the chair, Emma continued: "So . . . how will you go about this, Glynnis? Are you simply going to accept Richard's proposal and then tell him you're pregnant?"

"I don't know," Glynnis said quietly, looking more subdued and downcast than ever. "Perhaps I should just tell him the truth, say that I'm pregnant, that the man's not standing by me, and ask him if he still wants to marry me. That *I'd* be willing if he is."

Emma turned this over in her mind, her eyes narrowing imperceptibly.

"What do you think, Mrs. Harte?"

"I think it's the only way to approach it, I really do," she replied finally. "I think in this instance honesty is your best policy." Leaning forward, she explained: "You have nothing to lose. If Richard turns you down, then you have your fallback position. *Me.* You know I won't break my word to you, Glynnis. I will help you all I can, and for as long as you need my help. I promise you that."

"Thank you, thank you very much. And will you promise me something else, Mrs. Harte?"

"If I can keep the promise, then of course I'll make it. What is it?"

"Whether I marry Richard or not, I don't

want anyone to know who the father of my child is, not ever. You must promise me that you'll never tell a soul."

"I promise I won't tell anyone *ever*, Glynnis, not as long as I live."

Glynnis sighed in relief. "You see, if Richard doesn't marry me, I'll figure out a story about the father of the baby. It's 1943, there's a war on, and there are a lot of dead heroes already. . . . I'll invent a good story to protect my child . . ."

Emma nodded but remained silent.

"Perhaps it doesn't sound very nice, but it's only a sort of . . . well, a white lie, isn't it? You see, I wouldn't want the world to know that *he* had . . . abandoned me. It would be humiliating. Do you understand that?"

"I certainly do. However, remembering how beautifully your nice GI treats you, I feel certain he'll marry you. Why wouldn't he? You're lovely, Glynnis, and a very nice girl. He'd be a fool not to marry you."

Thirty-seven

Emma picked up the silver-framed photograph of Daisy and David, taken at their wedding in May 1943, and breathed on the glass. Then she rubbed it with the yellow duster she held, removing the fingerprints.

There, that's better, she murmured, staring down at the picture, thinking how lovely Daisy looked in her wedding dress. It was made of pale blue silk, and she wore a matching picture hat and carried a nosegay of spring flowers. Almost two years ago. Now she was a mother, having given birth to a baby girl in January of this year . . . 1945.

Stepping closer to the long library table in her Leeds office, Emma put the photograph back in its place and picked up the latest one of her newest granddaughter.

Paula McGill Harte Amory. How surprised Emma had been the day of her birth, when she had gone to the London Clinic to see her daughter. "I've chosen the baby's first two names, Mummy," Daisy had announced. "I'm going to call her Paula McGill. After my father." Daisy had simply laughed at her mother's reaction and said, "Don't look so *shocked.* Honestly, Mummy, for a woman as sophisticated as you are, you can be awfully naïve sometimes. Did you think I didn't know Paul was my father?"

Emma had not known what to say. Daisy had gone on to explain that she had worked it out for herself when she was quite a small child. "And anyway, I realized how much I resembled him physically. And when I was twelve he told me himself." Emma had gaped at Daisy, who had laughed again, but very gently this time. Then Daisy had told her how much she loved her and Paul, that they had been the best of parents. But now Emma recalled that she had remained a little flustered all that day.

His heiress, she thought as she put the picture back on the table and reached for the one of her second grandson, Alexander Barkstone. Elizabeth had given birth to him in February 1944. He was a handsome little devil, gurgling at his christening, the spitting image of his father. She set the photograph down and leaned closer to the table, now focusing on Robin's wedding picture. He had married Valerie Ludden, a nursing friend of Elizabeth's, in January 1944; Elizabeth had been their matron of honor. They look well together, Emma decided, and she'll be perfect for him, good for his career. She stared at her favorite son; how good-looking and

541

clever he was. Recently he had told her he was going into politics after the war.

After the war, she thought, moving away from the table; how glibly we say that these days. But the end *was* near. Churchill kept saying it. They *were* winning the war, with the help of the Americans. Thank God the Yanks had come in to fight alongside their troops. They might not have made it without them. And certainly not without Winston Churchill, the greatest leader their country had ever known. Deep in her heart Emma believed that it was Churchill who would bring them to a victory hard won and honorable.

Walking back to her desk, Emma suddenly thought of Glynnis Jenkins. Eventually Glynnis would go to America as a GI bride. She was Glynnis Hughes now, having married her nice GI boyfriend in December 1943. The wedding had been at a chapel in her hometown in the Rhondda Valley, and everyone had had a grand time, Glynnis had told her. Especially the Jenkins family. They had discovered that Richard's forebears had lived in that part of Wales before emigrating to America a century before.

Glynnis's son had been born in April 1944, and they had called him Owen, a favorite Welsh boys' name. He was a year old this month. Emma made a mental note to send him a card and an appropriate present. She and Glynnis had stayed in touch; there was a deep friendship between them. And without knowing it, perhaps, Glynnis had averted a disaster.

Marriages and births, they are what makes the world go around, Emma thought, then looked at the door as it burst open.

Winston hurried in, moving so rapidly she prayed he wouldn't trip with his artificial leg. She thought something dreadful must have happened, perhaps to one of their boys. His face was drained of color, and his eyes were dark with pain.

She jumped to her feet. "Winston, whatever is it? You look . . . *demented.*" She took a deep breath and steadied herself for bad news. "It's not one of our boys, or Blackie's or David's, is it?" she asked, her voice faltering slightly.

"No, no," he was swift to answer, seeing the fear in her eyes.

"But what is it? You seem so distressed."

"I am. And so will you be. It's hard for me to explain here. You have to *see.* You have to come across the street to the *Evening Standard.* They're waiting for you. We have some important decisions to make. About what to put in the next edition today. The first one's already on the street. I want you there because the decisions will be yours ultimately. It's your newspaper, and you've got to call the shots today, Emma." He grabbed her arm and started to pull her away from her desk. "Come on, it's urgent!"

"But for God's sake, Winston, tell me what's wrong. What is this all about?" She struggled to free herself from his grip and stared into his face, endeavoring to understand. "Please tell me before we go over to the paper. You owe me that."

"I do." Winston took a deep breath. "American troops marched into Buchenwald yesterday . . . Thursday, April 12, 1945. Don't forget the date. What they found boggles the mind. Prisoners in such appalling condition the Americans thought they were *dead*. But they weren't. Just tortured beyond belief. It's been wholesale murder for years. The Nazis have committed the most vile atrocities imaginable. They've murdered millions. It's genocide . . ." Tears were running down Winston's face, but Emma was sure he didn't know, so disturbed was he. He stared at her, then brushed his face with his hands absently. "David Kallinski was always right, Emma, when he told us the reports were toned down. *Millions and millions.* The Nazi have murdered millions of Jews . . ."

She was looking at him almost uncomprehendingly; then she said, very slowly, "But, Winston, they wouldn't dare."

"They dared," he replied.

Emma and Winston left Harte's and

walked across Commercial Street to the back entrance of the newspaper company, which faced the front of the store, entering the building through the circulation department. Here the vans waited to be loaded with the latest edition, which was distributed throughout the city and suburbs as well as outlying districts and other nearby towns.

The familiar smells of damp newsprint and ink hit them as they went in and made Emma feel instantly at home. These were her newspapers, and she loved them; she nodded to the men who turned to greet her, wished them good morning.

As they went up the back stairs to the offices of the *Yorkshire Morning Standard* and its sister paper, the *Evening Standard*, Winston suddenly drew to a halt and took hold of Emma's arm. They had barely spoken since leaving the store. Now he said, very quietly, "Brace yourself, love. You're in for a shock."

She simply nodded, and they continued on up the stairs, through the linotype room, where the typesetters waved to her or called out greetings. Finally they came into the corridor of editorial offices and hurried down to Martin Fuller's office. It seemed to Emma that an air of gloom pervaded the newspaper company. Usually she was energized by the activity and excitement of news gathering; today that energy was oddly absent.

Just before entering Marty's office, Emma

straightened her black jacket, adjusted the collar of her white silk shirt. Then she nodded to Winston. They went in.

Only twenty-seven, Marty was a boy genius in Emma's eyes, very much from the same school as Arthur Christiansen, editor of the *Daily Express*, where her brother was the leading columnist. Chris, as he was called by everyone, had changed the look of the *Daily Express*. Marty had done the same with the *Yorkshire Morning Standard* and the *Evening Standard*.

Marty was on the phone, but he instantly hung up at the sight of Emma and Winston.

After they had greeted each other, Emma said, "Winston tells me the news is horrendous."

Marty nodded but said nothing.

She noticed the strain on the managing editor's face, his pallor. "We'd better get to work on the next edition, hadn't we?" she said.

"I had to let that one roll, Emma. It's got to be on the streets at ten o'clock, and it's already nine-twenty. It's printing as we speak. If we make some quick decision, I can revamp the front page, maybe more, for the noon edition."

"Let's go to the newsroom then," Winston said.

"I've got everyone working at the conference room table. The editor, the chief sub, the news editor, the pictures editor, my layout man, several of our top reporters . . . it seemed easier to have them all together, Emma."

Emma sat in the midst of Marty's team, hardworking newspapermen with their sleeves rolled up ready for action, their eyes on her but also occasionally glancing at the big clock on the wall opposite. The deadline for the next edition was creeping closer.

"Some of the national dailies have carried stories this morning but not too many pictures. Remember, they were going to press last night and in the early hours of the morning, when the story was breaking," Eric Knowles, the editor of the *Evening Standard*, reminded her. As he spoke he pushed the papers toward her, but she barely glanced at them.

"Are you telling me we have much more information already?" she asked, pinning her eyes on him intently.

He nodded and turned to the news editor, Steven Bennett. "Tell Emma what we have."

"Loads of stuff has been rolling in all night, from Reuters and the other wire services and our own correspondents. We have a lot more information now than was available last night. It's still coming in. And we have the pictures."

Jack Rimmer, the pictures editor, interjected, "They're horrific, Emma. Almost unbearable to look at."

Swallowing hard, she said, "I'd better see them, Jack."

He pushed a pile of wire service photographs toward her, and she began to shuffle through them. Horror spread across her face, and her eyes held a stunned expression as she looked up and stared for a moment at the pictures editor. She couldn't bear to look again at the photographs spread out before her, but she knew she had to. The decision about what went in the paper was, in this instance, her responsibility.

Finally she focused on the pictures once more. Naked and half-naked people, emaciated beyond recognition as human beings, hollow eyed and without hair, living skeletons, stared out at her from tiered bunks and from behind barbed-wire fences. The images were chilling.

There were more photographs, equally disturbing, of gas ovens and torture chambers and dead bodies dumped like so much rubbish in mass graves. All victims of the highly efficient and relentless Nazi death machine . . .

Emma could not stop trembling, and her eyes filled with tears. She compressed her mouth and snapped her eyes shut for a moment, not wanting to break down in front of these tough newspapermen. But when she opened her eyes a moment or two later, she saw the horror and pain in their eyes also. Groping for a handkerchief, she wiped her eyes and blew her nose, but the tears started again.

Then, taking a deep breath, she said, "This has to be the most barbaric crime against humanity that has ever been committed."

"It is," Marty agreed. "Millions have been killed. And the wire service stories now coming in are predicting a lot more dire news. Other camps are being liberated by American and British troops as we are speaking. They're starting to go into Dachau, Belsen, and Ravensbrück, to name only a few. God only knows what further atrocities they'll find."

Winston glanced at his watch and said, "Do you have some front pages for us to take a look at, Marty?"

The managing editor nodded and beckoned to Johnny Johnson, his layout man. "Bring those front pages over here, Johnny, for Emma and Winston to see." As he spoke Marty also looked at the clock on the wall. "Time is ticking," he muttered.

The layout editor spread out the first mock-up.

Emma stared down at it and shuddered. There was a large photograph of the skeletal prisoners staring out from behind barbed wire and a banner headline of one word only: GENOCIDE.

The next three mock-ups were similar: a graphic photograph with a damning headline. She read: CRIME AGAINST HUMANITY, MASS MURDER, and NAZI DEATH MACHINE.

Emma did not have to ask anyone's opinion. Swiftly she said, "I think we must go with this one. *Genocide*. It says it all. Now what are you carrying inside, Eric?"

The editor told her, "We've a number of stories, very detailed, about the camps, and we can keep updating them for later editions as the news breaks."

"Good." She took another deep breath and continued, "I don't think you should pull any punches, either in the text or in the pictures. Our readers have to be told about this in detail. Unflinching detail."

"Leeds has a big Jewish population," Marty remarked. "They'll want to know."

Emma looked at him and nodded. "That's true. But even if there were no Jews living in Leeds, I'd still play this to the hilt. The whole world must know what was perpetrated by Nazi Germany. We're in the business of news, so let us do our best to present this most . . . heartstopping story —" Her voice broke, but she recovered and finished, "In the most dignified way we can, but without minimizing it to protect people's feelings. The pictures are harrowing to look at. *But we must show them*. One picture is worth a thousand words, so I'm told. We have to give this our all. Cut down on local news if that's necessary."

Eric Knowles jumped up and exclaimed, "You're right, Emma! And I'd better go with Johnny and get things rolling. 'Genocide' it is, then? That's the headline you want?"

"Yes. It says it all in one word." Emma then asked, "Will we make the noon edition?"

"Just about." He ran out, followed by the news editor and the reporters.

Emma stared at Winston, then focused on Marty. "I want a special edition devoted entirely to this story."

"When for?" Marty asked, staring at her worriedly.

"Can we get it out today?"

"Not if we want to do the story justice. There's a lot more coming in on the wires, not only from Reuters but from the Associated Press. And we have our own reporters on the job in London. Let's face it, it's the biggest story of the century."

"Of any century," Winston murmured. Turning to Emma he said, "Let Marty and his team do the story *right*, Emma." Addressing the editor, he suggested, "Why not do a special edition for the weekend?"

"Good idea," Marty exclaimed.

Emma said, "I concur."

Later, Emma wept in the privacy of her office at the store. The images kept floating in front of her eyes, and she would begin to weep again.

But eventually she gained control of her swimming senses, picked up the telephone, and dialed David Kallinski at his office.

"David, it's Emma."

"Hello, Emm. How're you?"

"So-so. Can I come and see you?"

"Is something wrong? You sound upset." His voice echoed with sudden concern.

"David, some of the national papers carried stories this morning . . . about the Americans liberating the concentration camps in Germany. Did you see any of them?"

"No, I left for the office very early, and the paper hadn't arrived." There was a small silence, then he said, "It's . . . bad, isn't it?"

"Very bad. Worse than bad. *Horrendous.*" Her mouth had gone dry. "Let me come and see you, David darling . . ." With one hand she flicked the tears from her cheeks.

"Yes, I'd like that," he said in a voice that was suddenly hoarse. "You've always been a comfort to me, Emma."

Thirty-eight

It was Monday, May 7, 1945. That morning, at exactly 2:41 a.m., General Alfred Jodl, the representative of the German High Command, and Admiral Hans von Friedeburg, empowered by the Grand Admiral Karl Doenitz, the designated head of the German state, signed the act of unconditional surrender of all German land, sea, and air forces in Europe to the Allied Expeditionary Force and simultaneously to the Soviet Union. The war with Germany was finally at an end.

Walking with Emma to the small seating area near her library table of family photographs, Winston went on, "Marty called me a few minutes ago. Apparently it's now official. It's been declared V-E Day in Europe . . . tomorrow, May eighth. So we can all celebrate. I thought it might be a nice idea to throw a little party for the boys over at the newspapers. I tested the waters with Marty, and he reacted in a very positive way."

"Then do it, Winston. Let's show our appreciation. Have Marty arrange it." She frowned. "But where will they have it? In one of the pubs?" She shook her head. "No, it wouldn't work. Perhaps a private room in a restaurant?"

"That sounds better, but don't worry about it, Emma. Marty will handle it. I just wanted to be sure the idea had your approval."

"Of course it does. They all deserve it. They've worked like demons through these war years, done a terrific job even though they've been understaffed. And the special editions they did in April when the death camps were liberated are masterpieces of twentieth-century journalism. I'm very proud of the staff, and of the specials."

"Yes, they were very successful," Winston agreed. "Are you staying in Leeds for the rest of the week, Emm?"

"Yes, I am, Winston, why?"

"Well, since it's V-E Day tomorrow, I thought you might like to celebrate with me and Charlotte."

"There's nothing I'd like better. Thank you."

It seemed to Emma that Leeds went crazy on V-E Day night. The red, white, and blue Union Jack hung out of every window, fluttered from every flagpole, and was waved in the hands of most children and adults as they crowded into the streets. The air of festivity was beyond belief.

People danced, and sang, cheered each

other and laughed; they hugged and kissed, strangers as well as friends; and they shouted out their pride and happiness at their victory over tyranny.

Rivers of light from windows no longer blacked out against enemy bombers illuminated the streets like sunshine. Bonfires blazed on every corner, as if it were Bonfire Night in summer, and effigies of Hitler were sacrificed to the flames.

The pubs were filled to overflowing, the customers spilling out into the streets, and everywhere there were patriotic songs and toasts to the brave boys in blue and khaki and navy, and cheers for Winston Churchill. "Long live Winnie!" they cried, affection in their voices. "He's brought us through. Our British bulldog has brought us through. Long live Winston Churchill!"

Charlotte had cooked a wonderful dinner, and when Emma arrived at their lovely house in Roundhay she felt hungry for the first time in weeks. After Winston had opened a bottle of champagne, they toasted each other and their sons, and finally Emma said, "Here's to our Prime Minister, the greatest leader we've *ever* had."

The following morning she experienced the same sentiments as she opened the *Yorkshire Morning Standard* and saw the Prime Minister's speeches printed on the front page. She had asked Marty to make sure the paper carried them in full, and the managing editor had obliged.

As she began to read the report, she truly wished she could have been there. Thousands had assembled near the House of Commons, and they had roared their approval of the Prime Minister as he appeared with some of his colleagues on the balcony of the Ministry of Health in Whitehall. He made two brief speeches to the vast crowd. After the words "This is your victory," the crowd had roared back, "No — it is yours." According to the *Morning Standard,* this response had signified an unforgettable moment of love and gratitude.

She read on, savoring every word Churchill had said:

"God bless you all. This is your victory! It is the victory of the cause of freedom in every land. In all our long history we have never seen a greater day than this. Everyone, man or woman, has done their best. Everyone has tried. Neither the long years, nor the dangers, nor the fierce attacks of the enemy, have in any way weakened the independent resolve of the British nation. God bless you all."

Emma sat for a few moments on the sofa under the leaded window in the upstairs parlor, thinking about the past six years. Last night everyone had celebrated, but her uppermost emotion had been relief. Relief that her sons had not been killed, that her son-in-law and her nephew, and the sons of Blackie O'Neill and David Kallinski, had managed to cheat death also. They had their futures ahead of them, and that was something to celebrate, wasn't it?

Walking over to her desk, she clipped the speech from the newspaper, put it in an envelope, and stowed it safely away in the fruitwood casket scrolled in silver. It was worth keeping.

It had been sunny all day, remarkably balmy for May, and to Emma's surprise it stayed warm well into the early evening.

She sat on the long terrace at Pennistone Royal, waiting for Blackie O'Neill to arrive. He had been in London on business on V-E Day, so he had not been able to celebrate with them in Leeds. But now that he was back in Yorkshire, they would have their own celebratory dinner, just the two of them.

Her thoughts drifted. Events of the last seven years sped through her head like a reel of film. Paul's death, her overwhelming grief, the perils of war — the Blitz, the V-1s, those pilotless bombs that had devastated London. Their young at risk in the air and on land and sea. But the triumphs, too. Dunkirk and other victories. So many good things mixed in with the heartache, her children's marriages, the birth of three grandchildren.

How time passes, and so swiftly as we get older, she thought. She had been fifty-six at the end of April; it didn't seem possible to her. In a few years she would be sixty. Yet she felt so *young*. Young at heart and in spirit, and her strength and energy were the same as they had been when she was ten years younger.

I have been lucky, she thought suddenly, her mind turning to the mothers and fathers who had lost sons in the conflict: young Matthew Hall, Robin's friend from the 111th Squadron at Biggin Hill, shot down over France. A smile touched her mouth when she thought of him, but her eyes were moist. So young, too young to die.

A fragment of Rupert Brooke's famous poem ran through her head:

If I should die, think only this of me,
That there's some corner of a foreign field
That is forever England. There shall be
In that rich earth a richer dust concealed,
A dust whom England bore, shaped, made
    aware,
Gave, once, her flowers to love, her ways to
    roam,
A body of England's, breathing English air,
Washed by the rivers, blest by suns of
    home . . .

★ ★ ★

She heard his step and then his familiar voice calling, "Are you out there, mavourneen?" and she quickly brushed the tears from her cheeks before she stood up and went to meet her longest friend.

Blackie put his arm around her, and they walked back down the terrace and sat together on the wrought-iron garden seat. He said, "I'm sorry I missed all the excitement in Leeds. Winston told me it was quite something to behold."

"It was, the town went mad."

"Aye, the whole of Britain went mad with joy." He looked into her eyes. "We've been lucky, you and I. And Winston, And David Kallinski. Our sons are safe. Some not so lucky, eh?" He touched her damp cheek with a fingertip. "You've been crying, lass."

"I was thinking of that nice young man Matthew Hall. Robin's friend, and Bryan's, from the 111th Squadron."

"It's a tragic thing, the loss of our young. Bryan's been devastated that Matt didn't make it."

"I spoke to David today, Blackie. He was so sad about his cousin Ruth. She married a Frenchman, if you remember, and went to live in France. She just vanished during the war, and he has worried about her so much. Poor Ruth, whose fate he'd never known but now surely does."

"There are a lot of broken hearts around these days, me darlin', but we must not dwell on sadness this evening. You and I have such a lot to be thankful for . . ." His eyes grew warm and loving as he asked, "And how's the bairn?"

Emma's face lit up. "She's just wonderful. Daisy was concerned that her eyes would change color, but they haven't. They're still that lovely deep blue, so deep they're almost violet, like pansies."

"Aye, I noticed that when we saw her two weeks ago. And she has Paul's black hair. She's a McGill, all right."

"I have a good feeling about Paula. She's going to be my girl."

"Nay, lass, you can't be taking her away from her mother," he admonished, looking at her askance.

"I didn't mean that she'll be mine *physically*, to bring up. I'm leaving that to Daisy and David for a few years. Rather, I meant she would be mine *spiritually*. Neither Elizabeth nor Daisy wanted to come into my business, but I'm hoping Paula will."

Blackie began to laugh, shaking his head. "There you go again, thinking about business, as you have done all of your life. But then a leopard doesn't change its spots, I suppose. Still, she is only five months old, Emma. Give her a chance, let her have a childhood." He continued to laugh, highly amused.

Emma joined in his laughter, and then, sobering, she said softly, "Paula is my future, Blackie, she surely is. Mind you, I suppose we *will* make an odd couple, the little girl and the old lady . . ."

"You're not *old*, Emma Harte! Why, you'll never be old, me darlin'. You'll always be *my* young colleen of the moors, that little sprite of a girl with her big green eyes and bright red hair shot through with gold. I can see you now, Emma, in my mind's eye . . . such a powerful *being* you were, even then."

Emma sat back. "Thank you, Blackie, for always being here for me, for being my very best friend, my dearest friend."

"And I thank you, Emma, for the same. It's been a privilege to know you, mavourneen."

They sat together in silence. After a moment Emma looked up at the sky. It was a deep pavonian blue, turning deeper as twilight descended, tinged with gold on the rim of the moors. A gentle sky tonight. She took hold of Blackie's hand. He looked across at her, and she gazed back at him for a long moment; then she smiled her incomparable smile, which illuminated her face with radiance.

"Hearts at peace, under an English heaven," she said.

THREE

Legacy

2001

The legacy of heroes is the memory of a great name and the inheritance of a great example.

> BENJAMIN DISRAELI,
> BRITISH STATESMAN AND
> TWICE PRIME MINISTER

I charge you to hold my dream.

> EMMA HARTE

Thirty-nine

"I didn't find any secrets," Paula said, leaning against the doorjamb, watching Shane change in his dressing room, which adjoined their bedroom in the Belgrave Square maisonette.

"Nothing?" he asked, a surprised look on his face as he buttoned his fresh shirt.

"Well, let me amend my statement. There is definitely a secret to do with Glynnis Hughes, and it's a name. But that name is not in any of the diaries. Grandy never wrote it down."

"Who is it the name of?"

"The real father of Owen Hughes."

"Oh, so Richard Hughes wasn't his biological father after all?"

"No." Paula adjusted her stance and went on. "While you've been out of town, I've done nothing but read Emma's diaries in the evening, well, I skip-read some of them. And interesting reading they do make. Emily agrees. She had to help me out at one point. As I mentioned on the phone, Glynnis was Emma's secretary during the war years. She mentions her a lot in the diaries, but she was awfully close-mouthed about her private life, *protective*, I'd say."

"But do you think Emma knew the name of the man involved?" Shane asked, his curiosity getting the better of him.

"Oh yes, I'm certain she did. Emma wrote something in her diary the day Glynnis broke down in tears and told her about her little predicament. It was at Pennistone Royal, she used to take Glynnis up there with her from time to time. Actually, Shane, she promised Glynnis she'd never reveal the name of the baby's father as long as she lived, and she didn't. You knew my grandmother. Integrity was her middle name."

"So was honesty. Grandfather always said she was the most honest person he had ever known, man or woman. But getting back to Glynnis, she and Grandy must have been quite friendly."

"I believe there was a deep affection there. I think Glynnis hero-worshiped Emma, and my grandmother was certainly exceedingly fond of Glynnis."

"So the mystery man made Glynnis pregnant, probably refused to marry her, so she married Richard Hughes. . . . Do you think that's the true story, Paula?"

"More or less."

Shane threw her a questioning glance and frowned. "You sound doubtful."

"From what I gather, Glynnis knew Richard for some time. They'd met at Grandy's wartime canteen for the troops —"

"Emma had a canteen for the troops?" he cut in. "Well, I'll be damned!" A surprised but pleased expression crossed Shane's face. "Why am I sounding surprised? That's just like Emma. I wonder why Grandpops never mentioned the canteen to me?"

"It was so long ago, darling, water under the bridge to them. Grandy never mentioned it to me, either. Anyway, Richard was crazy about Glynnis and had proposed, according to Grandy's diary for 1943. She told Glynnis to tell him the truth and suggest marriage. If he walked away, Grandy said she had her for a backup position. That she'd help Glynnis financially."

"That was generous . . ." Shane threw Paula a pointed look and raised a brow suggestively.

"Just Grandy remembering Edwin Fairley, and her own predicament. That's all, I'm sure. Anyway, the reason I looked a bit doubtful is this. . . . I'm not certain the man involved *could* marry Glynnis."

"Oh, I get it. A married man?"

"Possibly."

"You've got a funny look on your face, Beanstalk," Shane said, reverting to his childhood nickname for her. "Come on, spill it."

"It's only a thought . . . but maybe Uncle

Winston was the father. Emma's brother was awfully high on Glynnis, singing her praises constantly. Grandy even remarks about it in her diary."

"You can't be serious!" Shane exclaimed, reaching for a blue silk tie.

"It's just a thought that crossed my mind, because Grandy mentions Winston making extremely flattering remarks about Glynnis."

Shane swung around to face Paula. "But why would Emma give the game away? If her brother was the culprit, why make comments about him liking the girl? Isn't that like . . . spelling it out?"

"I suppose you're right."

"So Glynnis married her GI and went off to America. End of story."

"Not quite. As you well know. On her deathbed Glynnis instructed her grand-daughter Evan to find Emma Harte because Emma had the key to her future."

Shane took his jacket off the hanger and slipped it on, then opened a drawer looking for a silk handkerchief for his breast pocket, saying, "The dying meanderings of an old lady most probably." Then he suggested, "Look, we established Evan Hughes is not a McGill. Your grandfather had been dead for several years when Owen was conceived. Let's just assume she's not a Harte either. Case closed."

"I agree, and so does Emily. She went

through some of the diaries, as I told you. She came across no reference to the mystery man. She thinks I'm wrong even to consider Winston the first. She says it's well known in the family that he adored Charlotte and would never have so much as glanced at another woman. So, case closed it is. And naturally I'm not going to mention a word about Glynnis to Evan. There's no reason for her to know about her father's illegitimacy."

"You're right, darling. All you have to do is kill the gossip about Evan being a long-lost McGill."

"Philip and I will do that, don't you worry. Now, are you ready? We don't want to be late for the retrospective."

"That's right. How do I look?"

Paula smiled at him. "Not bad for a man who's spent half a day on a fast plane and in a fast car, trying to get here on time."

"But I did make it in one piece."

"And some piece it is." She laughed, winking.

Shane pulled her to him and held her in his arms for a moment. Then he held her away, looking into her eyes, which were truly the color of pansies. "You're beautiful, and I love you. And I think we're going to be very proud of our daughter tonight."

"I agree with you." Paula slipped out of his arms and went to pick up her black silk evening purse, then turned to look at him. "I'm very worried about Tessa, Shane. I think she's being abused by Mark."

His mouth dropped open.

"She has all the symptoms of an abused woman, and I've always thought Mark caused that problem with her shoulder. I think that psychologically she's unbalanced."

"If it's true, then she'll have to leave him! I won't allow a man to beat up on her, you can be damned sure of that." His face had turned grim, and there was a hard glint in his black eyes. "We're going to have to get to the bottom of this, Paula!" he exclaimed. His rage matched hers.

"It won't be easy. Women who are being abused don't always want to talk. Or leave a dangerous situation. I thought we could take her to dinner with us tonight, Shane, after the retrospective. In fact, I invited her already."

"Isn't Mark going to be there?"

"Apparently not."

Shane nodded. "Perhaps we'll find *something* out; we can certainly try. Anyway, who else is coming to dinner?"

"Winston and Emily. Uncle Ronnie and Michael Kallinski. India and a boyfriend of hers, nobody serious, I understand. Linnet and Julian. Evan and Gideon. Lorne and Mummy. Your father. Aunt Elizabeth and Marc Deboyne. And Amanda."

"We won't really be able to have a serious

talk with Tessa, but we can try to glean something from her, and certainly we can ascertain her state of mind, her mood. How has she been at work?"

"That's just it, Shane, she's not been particularly well, in my opinion. Impatient, irritable, and not cooperative. Linnet said she's been very moody, combative, worse than ever."

"This is a priority . . . we must get to the bottom of it and as soon as possible."

India Standish glided down an aisle between two fashion displays, looking stylish in a multicolored chiffon dress with a narrow torso, bell-like sleeves, and a flattering skirt that fell to her ankles. Some of the pink, yellow, and pale blue flowers in the chiffon's pattern were lightly embroidered with tiny bugle beads. The stunning summer evening dress emphasized her slender figure and height.

"You look fabulous, India," Evan said admiringly, walking over to join her. "And I love your Manolo Blahniks. I almost bought the same pair."

India grinned. "I know, Linnet told me, and you could've, you know, I wouldn't have minded at all. And Evan, you look really beautiful. What a lovely color this delphinium blue is on you."

"Thank you. It was Linnet who made me

buy the dress, but to be honest, I'd fallen in love with it anyway. I've never had anything quite as stylish before." Or as expensive, Evan thought, but she did not say this. Her dress was slightly off the shoulder, with tiny cap sleeves and horizontal pleats of chiffon from the neck to the midcalf hem. It was by Chanel, and only someone of Evan's height and willowy figure could have carried it so well. She wore silver strap sandals with high heels and a pair of diamond stud earrings from Gideon.

The two young women walked around the auditorium, looking at the haute couture clothes on mannequins standing on slightly raised platforms. Some sections were devoted to famous designers and their clothes from the 1920s to 2000, with blowup portraits of the designers on the walls behind the platforms. There was a section featuring Fashion Icons, the stylish women who had lent some of their couture pieces. Their large photographs were displayed on easels in front of their clothes. And finally there was the biggest display, devoted to the clothes of Emma Harte, the collection dating from the 1920s to the late 1960s.

Silk banners bearing the words eighty years of fashion: a retrospective hung from the ceiling. The entire space was designed to allow the maximum of people to walk around comfortably without impeding the view.

"Those space planners from Yorkshire did a really great job!" Evan exclaimed. "Gee, India, I sort of hate to say this, but I think the whole auditorium looks smashing. Congratulations to you, to us!"

"I agree. You know, we've really pulled it off," India murmured in a pleased voice.

"Oh look, here's Linnet with one of the press people." As she spoke Evan waved, and Linnet hurried over. She was wearing a black-lace dress with green silk showing through the cobweb lace, and when India stared at her, frowning, she said quickly, "It's a *copy*. The original's still over there somewhere in Emma's collection."

India and Evan both laughed, knowing she was making a reference to Emma's Lanvin, and Linnet said, "I'd like to introduce you to Ms. Barbara Fitzpatrick. She's the editor of *Chic* magazine, and she wrote that lovely story about the retrospective that appeared last month."

After the three women had exchanged greetings, India and Evan moved on, leaving Linnet to escort the editor around the show. "It was really nice of you to come back to see the retrospective finally finished," Linnet said, smiling.

"I wouldn't have missed seeing this," Barbara answered. "I think you've done a superb job. In fact, I don't think I've ever seen anything quite so well mounted before."

"Thank you again for saying so, and I must say we've had some really talented people working on it. Anyway, you'd said on the phone that you wanted to see the Emma Harte Collection again, now that it's really and truly in place."

"Yes, I would. I've always been a great admirer of your great-grandmother. I think she blazed the way for women in business, in the boardroom, so to speak. In fact, my mother told me she knew her vaguely in the Second World War, they worked at some charity together. In any case, she was a legend in her time, everyone knows that. So naturally I'm interested in the clothes she chose and wore. Apparently with great aplomb."

"It's just over here," Linnet murmured and ushered the fashion editor, renowned in London for her style, down one of the aisles. They came to a stop at the largest display, composed of a dozen or so platforms. Laughing all of a sudden, Linnet said, "My cousin India was startled a moment ago when she saw me in this cocktail dress. She thought I'd nicked Emma's Lanvin. But as you can see, Ms. Fitzpatrick, there it is in all its glory."

Barbara Fitzpatrick followed Linnet's gaze, then stepped closer to look at the black lace dress on the mannequin. Glancing back at Linnet, who stood behind her, she said, "Someone made you a wonderful copy of this, I must say."

"I know. I couldn't get over it myself. The person who made it copied it right down to the last little detail. The emerald bow on the shoulder of the dress on the mannequin is costume jewelry, of course. But my great-grandmother had a real emerald bow."

"Yes, I've seen photographs of her wearing it. In fact, there it is on that blowup of her. Oh my goodness! You do look like her, don't you? You're the spitting image."

"That's what everyone says."

At five-fifty exactly, a cadre of good-looking young women, all wearing identical tailored black pantsuits, moved discreetly through the exhibition. Approaching those who were attending the Press Preview, they explained that the cocktail reception was about to start in the adjoining area.

Once the exhibition hall was empty, Linnet went out and locked the glass doors herself, then gave the key to her secretary, Cassie Littleton. Then she asked one of the Harte's security guards to put the red rope in place. Turning to Cassie she said, "A little later you can have them put the no food, no drinks signs outside these doors, which can be opened again at exactly seven-thirty, so that the public can view the clothes. That's what they paid for, after all."

"And the cocktail reception, too, Linnet," Cassie said. "The evening's a total sellout.

We could easily have sold two or three hundred more tickets."

"But then it wouldn't have been *exclusive*, it would've been a bun fight," Linnet answered, laughing. "Limiting the event to four hundred people at a thousand pounds a ticket means that Breast Cancer Care benefits to the tune of four hundred thousand pounds, because Harte's is absorbing all the costs, don't forget. It's going to be a good evening, with a celebrity-ridden crowd. *Hopefully.* They did all finally accept, didn't they?"

"Oh yes, and Lorne helped with the actors and film stars. We've got a whole lot coming, big names, too."

"I knew he wouldn't let us down." Glancing around, Linnet nodded. "Thanks, Cassie, for working so closely with the floral people. I think the reception area looks beautiful with all the orchids and the orchid trees."

"Everybody's really gone behind the retrospective, Linnet." Cassie turned her head when she heard her name being called and said, "Oh, that's the reporter from the *Mail* who's assigned to cover the evening, I'd better go and help him. Excuse me."

"Fine, I'll see you later. Oh, and you said I'm to go to the podium at about seven-twenty, to announce the opening?"

"That's right."

Cassie hurried away, and Linnet meandered

around for a few minutes, checking on last-minute details. Then, spotting India and Evan on the other side of the room, she went to join them. Over the last five months they had become inseparable friends as well as colleagues, and she wanted to be with them now, to savor the success.

Forty

Jonathan Ainsley considered promptness on social occasions plebian; he preferred to be late by at least fifteen minutes. And so it was six-twenty when he sauntered into the charity cocktail reception in the auditorium at the top of Harte's.

He had not been inside his grandmother's store for years, and he was here tonight only because of his rampant curiosity. He wanted, no needed, to see his nemesis, his cousin Paula O'Neill. And her family. After all, he *was* in the process of destroying them, her husband, Shane O'Neill, included, and he had the irresistible desire to gloat.

After a moment or two, moving around the periphery of the room, he realized it was a smart, indeed very fashionable crowd, quaffing champagne and nibbling on hors d'oeuvres of all nationalities, including a large variety of Asian tidbits. That was one of the things he missed about Hong Kong . . . the food. And certain other aspects of that notoriously tantalizing city of limitless pleasures.

Jonathan now slipped his hand into the pocket of his dark blue suit jacket, his long fingers curling around the Imperial jade disc. His talisman. Good joss, he thought, *this* piece will bring me good joss.

Long ago he had had another favorite talisman, a smooth pebble of mutton-fat jade. But in the end that had brought him only bad joss, and twenty years ago he had flung it out the car window as he had sped through the London traffic to Heathrow on his way back to Hong Kong. And bad trouble.

He rubbed the Imperial jade piece between his fingers, almost sensually, and he knew in his bones that this disc was lucky. It had been blessed in a very unique way by an extraordinary woman.

A waiter passed by, and Jonathan took a glass of champagne, murmured a thank-you, but declined a miniature spring roll offered by a delectable girl in a black cheongsam. He loathed getting his teeth messy at cocktail parties; one never knew who one was going to run across. His eyes lingered on the Chinese girl as she proffered her tray to other guests; he wondered what different wares she might offer later and considered getting her number, then dismissed the idea. He had better fish to fry.

Glancing around, seeking Sarah Lowther and her daughter, Chloe, who were his guests tonight, he realized they had not arrived yet. Suddenly his eyes fell on a tall, handsome young man standing only a few feet away. Jonathan recognized him at once as a well-known and much-loved young actor who trod the boards regularly in the West End. *Lorne Fairley.* Paula's son by Jim, once a friend of his. And there was no question that the woman clinging to his arm was his twin, Tessa Fairley, Mark Longden's wife. No mistaking her; she resembled her twin too much for that.

Appears a bit wan tonight, the beautiful Tessa does, he thought. Pale, nervous. Poor girl. Was she having marital problems? He'd heard that Mark Longden was a bit of a devil, and on the fast track these days. *Pity.*

Now who's this? Jonathan asked himself as another blond young woman joined Lorne and Tessa. He peered at her over the rim of his glass, his eyes narrowing. It took a moment before it hit him. She looked a bit like the other two, had the Fairley genes. So she had to be India Standish, the daughter of his cousins Anthony Standish and Sally Harte, Winston's sister.

Disgusting, he thought, all this intermarrying. He was surprised they weren't all bonkers by now, stark raving mad.

And here was the famous Linnet Harte O'Neill arriving. Jonathan had no trouble recognizing her. She was the reincarnation of

Emma Bloody Harte, his sainted grand-mother. And by God the resemblance was terrifying. It wasn't just the red hair, it was everything about her, and the cut of her jib. He was close enough to see the vivid green eyes, the perfect complexion, the shapely figure. *She* must have looked like this at her age, he thought. And he had to admit that Linnet O'Neill was beautiful. But then his grandmother had been beautiful, and also the devil incarnate.

So focused was he on his relatives, Jona-than did not see Sarah Lowther approaching him.

But Sarah noticed Jonathan. In fact, she paused, her eyes widening as she followed the direction of his intense gaze. Immediately she saw Paula's three children with India Standish, the four of them obviously enjoying themselves. What fine-looking young people they are, Sarah thought, smiling. Rather like my lovely Chloe. She wished Chloe knew her cousins; that was something her daughter had always missed, siblings and an extended family.

Sarah took a few steps toward Jonathan and then unexpectedly faltered. The expres-sion on his face was one of pure malevo-lence. She felt a chill run through her, and suddenly she knew how he would seek re-venge on Paula. He would hurt her children somehow.

So sure was Sarah of this she wanted to leave. But that would be cowardly, she told herself. No, she must stay, play him at his own game. Be his friend. That was the only way she could help her cousin Paula. And help her she would. More than anything else she wanted to be accepted back in the family, not only for her own sake but also for Chloe's. Besides, Paula's children were innocent . . . in a way so was Paula.

"Hello, my darling Jonny," Sarah said a moment later, touching his arm, smiling up at him.

Instantly his face changed. The hard and dangerous expression was replaced by a warm smile. "Sarah, my dear, as beautiful and chic as always. I like this cocktail dress. Whose is it?"

"Balmain."

"The royal blue flatters you. Where's Chloe?" he asked, looking beyond her, as he sought out his goddaughter.

"She couldn't come, Jonathan, I'm so sorry. She sends her apologies. And where's Uncle Robin?"

"Dad wasn't well enough to come up to town. He's stuck in Yorkshire. Pity I bought all those tickets to this event. His ticket was a waste of money, and apparently so was Chloe's, unless you've given it away."

"No, I haven't, and I'm so very sorry about this. Look, I'll reimburse you."

"Don't be silly, I don't want your money."

"Oh, and I thought you did. I was under the impression you wanted me to invest in your new company, Jonny." She pouted. "I guess I was mistaken."

His face lit up, and he exclaimed, "If you want to, I'd be glad to have you invest, Sarah. You'd be on to a good thing, too, have a very profitable return."

Smiling back, she took hold of his arm affectionately. "Then we must talk about it over dinner. After all, I was a very good partner in the past, wasn't I?"

"Certainly. Mind you, I'd only let you in on this deal because you're family."

"I understand, and I'm very grateful. I've always been grateful to you, Jonathan, for letting me into these little deals of yours." She wondered if he'd forgotten all the money she'd lost with him.

He half-smiled, then drew her attention to the family members nearby. "See that group over there . . . Paula's little gang. And look at the flaming redhead like you . . . that's Linnet O'Neill."

Sarah merely nodded and took a glass of champagne from a passing waiter.

"She's going to be the one to inherit it all," he whispered, leaning closer. "Even Pennistone Royal."

Startled, Sarah looked at him intently. "How do you know that?"

"A little dickey bird told me," he answered with a laugh.

Sarah shook her head. "I wouldn't be too sure of that."

"Well, well, well!" Jonathan exclaimed, suddenly grabbing hold of her arm fiercely. "Enter a blaze of princes!"

Sarah stared at him, frowning, then swung her head toward the entrance. Coming through the double doors were her cousins Paula, Emily, Amanda, and Winston. And Shane O'Neill accompanied them, looking more handsome than ever to her. Well, she had loved him once.

She heard Jonathan sniggering. "Who the hell do they think they are?"

But Sarah paid no attention. She felt a surge of love for them all, and a sudden, long-absent sense of absolute pride. Four of those five people entering the room with such dignity, such elegance, were Hartes. Just as she was a Harte. And she felt herself standing a little taller. A blaze of princes indeed. Emma Harte's princes.

"Just look at bloody Paula O'Neill, dripping in Grandy's emeralds!" Jonathan muttered angrily. "A bit overdone isn't it, rather vulgar."

"No, not vulgar at all, Jonathan. I think Paula looks beautiful in the white satin jacket and black skirt. That outfit also happens to be a Balmain, and the emeralds are fabulous on the white satin."

"Oh God, are you getting all sentimental on me, Sarah? Bloody mawkish again?" he growled.

"No, not at all," Sarah answered quickly and reminded herself to be careful. She wanted to get as much information as she could from him.

The moment Paula saw Evan Hughes, she excused herself from the others and hurried over. "Good evening, Evan," she said, smiling warmly.

"Hello, Mrs. O'Neill. You look *fantastic*. If you don't mind me saying so, you'll be the star of the show tonight."

"Thank you, Evan, that's nice of you, but I think there are *three* genuine stars here. You, India, and Linnet. You've done the most extraordinary job, all of you. And I'm proud of you."

"We've tried very hard . . . I'm glad you're happy."

"Evan, I've got some wonderful news for you. There's no mystery, no secret in my grandmother's diaries. I've read most of them, and Emily helped me by reading some of the others. Yes, your grandmother Glynnis did work for Harte's during the war. She was Emma Harte's favorite secretary. My grandmother was very, very fond of her."

"And that's all? There really is no terrible

secret buried in those pages?" Evan asked, her eyes on Paula.

Paula shook her head. "Just mentions of them working together, at the store, at the house in Belgrave Square, and up at Pennistone Royal. Actually, what I thought was really interesting is that your grandmother met Richard Hughes, your grandfather, at the canteen for the troops Emma started in Fulham Road."

Laughter flooded Evan's face, and she exclaimed, "That's what grandfather told me! That they'd met at a canteen. Just imagine, he must have known Mrs. Harte, too."

"I believe he did."

"So I can relax, Mrs. O'Neill. I'm not a McGill. And I'm not a Harte either."

"That's correct," Paula replied. "Now, if you'll excuse me, Evan, I see my mother standing over there, with Grandfather O'Neill. I need to speak to them."

"Thanks so much for going to all that trouble, Mrs. O'Neill," Evan said, and then she exclaimed, "Oh, there's Gideon, I think he must be looking for me."

Evan stepped away from Paula still smiling, headed for Gideon. But she was intercepted by a tall, elegantly dressed man. "Excuse me," he said, his voice very upper class. "You're Paula's daughter, aren't you?"

Evan looked up at him, frowning, and shook her head. "No," she said finally.

"But a relative, surely," Jonathan Ainsley went on. "Your resemblance is quite remarkable."

"We're not related," Evan answered, beginning to edge away.

"You do work at Harte's though."

She nodded.

"With Tessa? Or Linnet?"

"Please, I must be going," Evan exclaimed, her voice rising slightly, and she hurried away. It was only then that she realized the man had not introduced himself; she had no idea who he was or why he had been so interested in her.

Forty-one

Evan walked along the beach, kicking a stone, feeling miserable. She had never been one for confrontations, and she endeavored to avoid them whenever she could. But Gideon had been in a terrible mood, not only last night but this morning. Sighing, she walked over to an ancient stone wall and sat down, wondering how to bring their relationship back to an even keel.

Even keel, she thought, and suddenly smiled to herself. She hadn't thought of that phrase for years. Her grandfather had often used it. He had loved boats and frequently taken her out on his sailboat when she was a child; she had thoroughly enjoyed every moment of sailing with him.

The wall she was sitting on overlooked the Irish Sea, and she realized that was why the phrase had popped into her mind. The view was beautiful, and it was a lovely sunny day, pleasantly warm. Not a day for rows or upsets.

It had all begun last night, at the retrospective. Toward the end of the evening, a strange man had come up to her and engaged her in conversation. He had wanted to know who she was, if she was related to Paula O'Neill, and he had tried to ask a lot of other questions.

Startled, she had resented the intrusion, had excused herself and hurried away. A moment later Gideon had been by her side asking her what the man had been talking to her about. He had been upset. She had explained everything to him, but he hadn't seemed satisfied, and the incident had cast a pall over the dinner later.

Even this morning, on the private jet flying to Douglas on the Isle of Man, he had been curt with her, and moody. After they had checked in at the hotel, he had disappeared almost at once, telling her he had to meet with Christian Palmer. She had fully understood, that was the reason they had flown over to this little island, yet it had upset her because he was so . . . *cold.* Yes, that was it, that's what bothered her. His coldness. Until last night he had always been warm, loving, and considerate.

She wondered if he wanted to break up with her, then dismissed that thought at once. After five months, almost six, she knew him well. He was too open to play games. If he wanted to end the relationship, he would. He would tell her in his usual frank way, which she had found refreshing and disarming. Some men were devious. Not Gideon Harte. He was almost too honest at times.

He had told her he would be back after lunch and would meet her at the hotel. It was called the Nunnery, and if she hadn't been so upset she would have teased him about the name. After all, he had signed them into a suite as Mr. and Mrs. G. Harte.

Did she want to be Mrs. Gideon Harte? She wasn't sure. Yes, she wanted Gideon, the man, but her father had tried to put her off him, telling her she wasn't in his league. It struck her again that her father had been strange on the phone over the last few months, especially when it came to the Hartes.

Jumping up, Evan shrugged into her cotton windbreaker and, shoving her hands in her trouser pockets, walked along the pretty beach, wishing they could stay on the Isle of Man for the weekend and work things out. But they had to go to Yorkshire.

She glanced up. The blue sky was filled with hazy clouds, and out on the bay there were sailboats and several yachts. It was a charming spot. There were quaint little houses and shops, and ancient-looking pubs, and the surrounding landscape was quite breathtaking. Did it remind her of Nantucket? Or somewhere else? Somewhere she had been with her grandfather when she was young? Somewhere in France, she thought.

Paula O'Neill had been so nice last night, and Evan was relieved that those now-famous diaries contained nothing odd or unpleasant about her darling gran. Glynnis Hughes had been the center of her world when she was a child, and she had loved her deeply. She couldn't bear it if there was something wrong about her gran.

The sunny weather, the pretty surroundings helped to calm Evan, and soon her morose mood fled. Blown away by the Irish wind from across the sea, she thought, and taking a deep breath she decided she was going to be *on an even keel* when Gideon returned from his meeting. She hoped that the brilliant newspaperman would agree to come back to work for the Hartes. Certainly that would put Gideon in a better mood.

Leaving the beach, Evan wandered up into the town and soon found a charming little café for lunch. After ordering a bottle of nonfizzy water, she looked at the menu, and when the waitress arrived she asked for fish and chips.

Gideon found Evan sitting in the garden of the Nunnery. She was reading a magazine but put it down when she heard his step. Looking up at him, smiling, she said, "I hope everything went all right, Gideon. Is Christian coming back?"

"Yes and no," he said, sitting down next to

her in one of the garden chairs. "It's a kind of compromise."

"What do you mean?" she asked.

"He's coming back part of the time. It's not exactly what my father wanted, but it's better than nothing, I suppose. He just loves it here in Douglas so much. What we've agreed is that he works for three weeks and then gets a week off. Also, quite a few free months in the summer. He loves sailing, the beach life." Gideon sighed. "I'm going to have to cover us by finding a really bright young journalist who can fill the gap when Christian's away."

"Yes, I understand."

Gideon fell silent, lost in thought.

Looking across at him, Evan said, "Can we talk about last night, Gideon? *Please?*"

"If you want to, yes," he agreed in a neutral tone.

"I do. Not that there's a lot to talk about. . . . I just don't understand why you were so angry . . . about that guy speaking to me." She shrugged, half-laughed. "He didn't mean any harm."

"How do you know?" Gideon asked, sitting up straighter, giving her a hard stare. He didn't want to tell her how angry his father had been when he had seen Jonathan Ainsley and Evan chatting. Ainsley's presence at the retrospective had infuriated Winston, and then he had grown suspicious, asking if Evan knew Ainsley from somewhere. Deep down, Gideon knew it was an innocent encounter on her part. On the other hand, a Harte didn't talk about a Harte to somebody who wasn't a Harte. Family rule. Emma's rule. So he didn't mention his father being upset, just fudged it a little. "The man who came over to chat to you is a somewhat disreputable member of our family. His name's Jonathan Ainsley, and I was upset he was . . . *accosting* you, Evan. And curious to know what *actually* he talked to you about."

"But, Gideon, darling, I *told* you," she responded, being careful to keep her voice soft, very low. "He asked if I was related to Paula O'Neill, who I was, did I work at Harte's, what I did there. And so I told him, but then I began to think he seemed a bit . . . *creepy*, you know, so I edged away. And then suddenly you were at my side and steaming."

He nodded, realizing he had been a little out of line. Forcing a laugh he said, "Hasn't it occurred to you I might have been jealous?"

Evan stared at him askance and grinned. "But he's old enough to be my father! This Jonathan Ainsley guy is easily sixty! Really, Gid!"

"Ainsley's not a nice man. If you ever run into him again, walk in the other direction. And walk fast."

"I won't run into him again."

"You never know."

Evan decided he was goading her again, and she said quietly, "Enough of this relative of yours. Are you angry about something else?"

"Not angry. No. Just disappointed," he admitted.

"In *me?*" she asked, her voice suddenly rising an octave.

"No, not actually in you. I'm disappointed that you seem to be pulling away from me. . . . I've never been in a serious relationship before, Evan. *I am serious about you. . . .* I'd hoped that you would have been able to commit to me, as I have to you . . . but you're so *elusive.*" He sighed. "Don't you feel the same way anymore?"

"Oh, Gideon, yes, yes, I do. I just want to be sure. We've only known each other five months . . ."

"Sometimes you can know someone all of your life, and never *truly* know them . . . then again, you can know someone totally in only a few days."

"I do love you, Gideon . . ." Her voice trailed off.

"But there's a *but?*"

"Not really. It's my father —" She cut herself off, shocked that she had mentioned him, and stared at Gideon, unexpectedly lost for words and furious with herself.

"Your father doesn't even know me. Are

you saying he objects to me?"

"No, no, not at all!" she cried, her expression earnest, seeing the color flooding into his face. She knew he was a very proud man. "He thinks that we're from different worlds, that it might not work out in the long haul."

"That's your father. What do you think?"

Evan did not speak for a moment; she sat looking at him, loving him, knowing that if she wasn't careful she would lose Gideon Harte. And that she did not want to risk.

"I don't think it matters at all that we're from different worlds." Reaching out, taking hold of his hand, she smiled at him.

He stood up, went over, and tilted her face to his, kissed her cheek. "Let's go inside so that I can kiss you properly."

Forty-two

A shaft of bright light suddenly cut through the dim grayness of the bedroom, and Tessa blinked and endeavored to sit up. She saw Mark silhouetted in the doorway, and instinctively she knew he was in one of his hostile moods. Over the last few weeks she had grown more and more attuned to him.

Taking a deep breath, she said in a steady voice, "Hello, darling. We missed you last night."

"Where were you?" he asked in a dull, low tone, coming into the room, closing the door behind him.

Tessa turned on the little brass lamp she used for reading. But it cast only a small pool of light near the bed, and she could not make out the expression on his face. He remained standing near the door.

"It was the retrospective at the store," she explained. "The fashion retrospective. I kept thinking you would arrive."

"I told you I wouldn't be able to make it," he muttered.

He had done nothing of the sort, but Tessa

ignored this and said, "Never mind. We did miss you at dinner, though. My mother was asking for you."

"I left you messages."

This wasn't true either. However, she went along with it, exclaiming, "Oh dear, and I never got them. Were you working late again, Mark?"

"Yes, at the office."

"Do you want me to make you something to eat?" She pushed herself up in the bed, her eyes riveted on him. She was suddenly wary.

"No, I've eaten." He slouched into the room, undressing as he did. Then he went into the adjoining bathroom and closed the door.

After a moment, Tessa heard the toilet flush, the water running. She stared at the door, her mind racing. He hadn't been drinking, she was fairly certain of that, but there *was* a strangeness about him. He'd spoken in a mumble, and he had moved in slow motion. Was he on something again? Suddenly feeling vulnerable in bed, Tessa threw back the bedclothes and got up.

At that moment the bathroom door flew open, and Mark stepped into the bedroom. There was an aura of anger around him.

They stared at each other across the bed.

Mark spoke first. "Why did you get up? Don't you want to sleep with me anymore?"

Tessa forced a faint laugh before saying, "Don't be silly, Mark, of course I do." She laughed again, even more weakly, and added, "I was just going to check on Adele."

"Why?"

"I thought I heard a noise."

"No you didn't! You just want to leave my bed. Who are you screwing these days? Is it Toby Harte? Are you still having it off with your cousin?"

Tessa tensed up, but she kept control of herself, edged toward the door.

"Answer me!"

"You know there's no truth in what you suggest," she replied, keeping her voice low, taking a few more small steps.

"I don't trust you, you bitch!" Mark rushed to the door, locked it, and then moved in on her, his fury finally bursting out.

Tessa backed away, but he suddenly had his hands on her shoulders. Pulling her toward him roughly, he brought his mouth down hard on hers. She struggled, trying to avert her face. He gripped her even tighter and pushed her up against the wall, then slammed her back as she tried again to push him away. But he was stronger than usual. Now he flattened his body against hers, brought his mouth to hers, pushed his tongue in it, then with one hand sought her breast. She tried harder to extract herself and almost did, but he lunged at her, snatched at the neck of her nightgown, and ripped it to the hem. Grabbing her arm, he dragged her to the bed, threw her on it, and flung himself on top of her. As his face came down to hers, he mumbled, "You're not going to get away from me."

"Please, Mark, don't do this. I don't want us to have sex like this. You're hurting me. Please, Mark, calm down. I'm saying no to you, Mark. No. No. *No.* Please stop!"

"It's Toby you want. I know that. The whole world knows that. But you can't have him. I won't let you. You're mine, bitch. And you're going to submit to my will!"

"No, Mark, no. Not this way. This is rape, Mark." Tessa began to sob and tried once more to slither out from under him, but he was a dead weight on her body. She could barely breath.

His face, hovering above hers, was engorged, and there was a look of pure hatred in his eyes. Unexpectedly, he threw back his head, and a shout of laughter escaped him. "Rape? You call this rape? Then you'd better get used to it, you little whore. Because this is the way it's going to be from now on."

"Oh please, don't do this," she cried, tears running down her face. She grabbed at his shirt, tried to pull herself upright.

Mark paid no attention to her pleas. Instead he plunged into her, thrusting against her, grunting, his breathing ragged.

Tessa was no match for him, and she finally gave up. She lay still, let him have his way with her, vowing it was never going to happen again. He was raping her for the last time.

Finally he rolled off her and fell into a deep sleep almost immediately.

Tessa waited for a while. Then she turned off the small brass reading lamp, slid out of bed, and crept toward the door. Unlocking it as quietly as possible, she slipped out into the corridor and shut the door softly behind her. After checking that Adele was still asleep, Tessa went down the corridor to her private suite.

She took off her torn nightgown, threw it in the waste basket, then stepped into the shower and let the hot water sluice over her for some time, leaning against the tiled wall and sobbing as if her heart would break. But after a while the tears ceased, and she shampooed her hair and washed herself thoroughly, wanting to remove all traces of Mark. She was thankful that she had started to use birth control pills again . . . the last thing she wanted now was to find herself pregnant by him.

After drying herself and her hair, Tessa got dressed for work, pulling on panty hose, a pair of gray lightweight gabardine trousers, and a white cotton top. Pushing her feet into a pair of comfortable brown loafers, she began to pack a few clothes to see her and Adele through the weekend.

Later, sitting at the desk in her office in the private suite, Tessa racked her brain, wondering where to take her daughter and the nanny. Certainly she did not want to go to Yorkshire; she didn't want her mother and Shane to know about Mark's treatment of her. *I'm an abused woman, and I'm fitting the profile perfectly,* she thought. *Hide the facts. Don't tell a soul. Accept his contriteness and apologies. Until he does it again. And again. And again. Until he kills you.*

Tessa had now read enough about spousal abuse to understand many of the reasons for it. Yet Mark did not exactly fit the profile of an abuser. She knew he was on drugs of some kind. And he was drinking.

Sitting back in the chair, staring blankly at the computer screen, she unexpectedly had a moment of absolute clarity. There was only one place for her to go. *Pennistone Royal.* There was nowhere else she would be truly safe from Mark Longden. For undoubtedly he would come after her with deadly intent.

Anyway, she belonged there, didn't she? Belonged in her mother's house.

It struck her that she knew exactly who she was. She was the daughter of Paula O'Neill, the great-granddaughter of Emma Harte. She was a Fairley in many ways, but she *was* a Harte. And therefore she must stand tall, be strong, take control of her life. And it must be a life without Mark Longden.

Forty-three

Paula stared at her pad, scanning the list of guests she and Shane expected at Pennistone Royal for the weekend. It was more than she had originally thought.

Some of their children would be there. Emsie; Desmond, who was coming home from boarding school; and Linnet. Linnet had invited Evan Hughes, so she wrote Blue Room next to her name and moved on to Julian Kallinski. He would be comfortable in the Gold Room, she decided. Grandfather Bryan came every weekend these days, so he had his permanent suite. He would stay put.

Feeling a sudden surge of happiness, Paula sat back in the chair, thinking about her daughter's forthcoming engagement to Julian. How happy Grandy would be, and David Kallinski, Emma's dear old friend. Emma had longed for the three clans to be joined in matrimony, and finally it was going to happen. She and Shane had elected to announce the engagement and throw a family dinner the night before the birthday party for Shane and Winston two weeks from now.

Aside from Evan Hughes, all the guests at the dinner would be family members. She hoped there would be no family squabbles . . .

There was a knock on the door, and Margaret walked in, looking apologetic. "I'm sorry to disturb you, Mrs. O'Neill, but there's a young woman in the Stone Hall asking to see you."

"Who is it, Margaret?" Paula asked, looking puzzled. "I'm not expecting anyone today."

"She didn't tell me her name. She has a letter for you. She showed it to me, but she wouldn't give it to me. She says she was instructed to put it in your hands and yours only. Very adamant she was."

"I suppose I'd better see her then."

Margaret was staring across the room at the long library table which held a large collection of family photographs, and Paula glanced at the table herself. "What is it, Margaret? What's bothering you?"

"The girl downstairs has red hair. Almost the same color as Miss Linnet's. I think she might be a relative." Walking across the room, Margaret stopped at the library table and touched the top of a silver frame. "She looks a bit like her."

Paula stood up, shaking her head, nonplussed. "It can't be. . . . Why would Sarah Lowther's daughter be here?"

"I don't know, Mrs. O'Neill. But she

is . . . she's downstairs. I'm sure of it."

"Please bring her up. Straightaway."

Margaret nodded and hurried out, and Paula crossed the room to the library table. It was jammed with Emma's collection of favorite pictures, which Paula had never had the heart to put away. Her grandmother had brought the table from the Leeds store over thirty years ago, and the photographs, all in silver frames, had been her pride and joy. She had often held a picture in her hand and talked about the person in it to Paula, always warm, always loving, never critical about any of her children or grandchildren. Except Jonathan Ainsley. Emma herself had removed his photograph just months before her death; she had come to the conclusion he was double-crossing her. And how right she had been.

Focusing on Sarah's photograph, Paula wondered if it really was her daughter downstairs. She knew Sarah had married a famous French painter, Yves Pascal, years ago and had made a success of her life and her business in France.

She wondered if Shane had really spotted Sarah at the retrospective; he had insisted several times that she was present. With Jonathan Ainsley. Winston had definitely seen *him,* and had been outraged. "What temerity he has," Winston had spluttered to her at the dinner. "How dare he show his face to us!" Emily and Gideon had managed to calm him down, but he had really seen red.

Turning away from the table, Paula walked over to the long sofa in front of the leaded window and stood waiting. A moment later Margaret was ushering the visitor into the room. With a slight nod, her housekeeper disappeared.

The young woman walked forward, held out her hand, and said, "Good morning, Mrs. O'Neill. I'm Chloe Pascal, Sarah Lowther's daughter. Please forgive this intrusion, but my mother wanted you to have this. I'm to wait for your answer."

After returning her greeting and accepting the envelope, Paula indicated that Chloe should be seated. Then she walked over to her desk, slit the envelope with a paper knife, and took out the letter.

The stationery was expensive, and it had her cousin's professional name engraved across the top: *Sarah Harte Lowther*.

Paula scanned the letter quickly. It said:

Dear Paula:

I am sending this note by hand with my daughter, Chloe, because I want to get it to you quickly, while I am still in England. I must see you urgently. I have vital information which concerns you. I am nearby, and if you will see me now, Chloe will come for me.

Sarah

Walking back toward the leaded window, Paula lowered herself into a chair and said, "Where is your mother, Chloe?"

"She's sitting in the car further down the driveway. You can't see the car from here."

"I know. Would you please go and get her? From what she says in her note, we have to talk."

Chloe jumped up. "Right away, Mrs. O'Neill."

Paula watched her hurry out. The girl had a good look of her mother, with the burnished auburn hair that was such a Harte family characteristic. Chloe wore a stark black cotton suit and simple gold jewelry, but she had that French chic which was so hard to imitate.

Rising, Paula looked out the window, saw Chloe heading for the driveway. She turned away, went back to her desk, putting the letter in a drawer. She had a gut instinct that her cousin wanted to tell her something disturbing about Jonathan. But why? Had they had a falling out? Or had Sarah had a twinge of conscience? It had to be something of vital concern to *her* or Sarah would never have asked to see her. She felt herself tensing, suspecting bad news.

A few minutes later, Margaret came into the room, escorting Chloe and her mother.

Walking forward, Paula said, "Hello, Sarah. This is a surprise," and stretched out her hand.

Sarah shook hands with her. "Thank you for seeing me. And please excuse the way I've handled this. But I needed to see you before I return to Paris. And I thought if I telephoned you might —"

"Hang up?" Paula interrupted. She shook her head. "No, Sarah, I *would* have taken your call. In fact, I've often thought you would be in touch over the years. . . . I sort of expected it, actually."

This comment startled Sarah, and she exclaimed, "If only I'd known. I've wanted to speak to you, just to explain one thing. And it's this. I never knew Jonathan was cheating the family. I did invest in his company, that's true, but I thought everything was aboveboard. I only found out how wrong I'd been the day your father fired me and you threw me out of the family. I trusted Jonathan and I shouldn't have. I think I was rather naïve, looking back. But I swear on my child's head that I never knew what he was doing."

"I realized that a long time ago, Sarah. I came to understand that you were innocent of any wrongdoing." Paula paused, pursed her lips, shook her head sadly. "What a waste of the years. . . . Well, that's all water under the bridge . . ."

"Yes, it is," Sarah agreed and went on swiftly. "And I didn't come here to explain, or to endeavor to exonerate myself with you. I came to warn you."

"Let's sit down," Paula murmured. "Can I offer you anything? Tea? Coffee? Water?"

"No, thank you," Sarah said, sitting in a chair.

Chloe, lowering herself onto the sofa, simply shook her head.

Focusing on Paula intently, Sarah began: "I've suspected for a long time that Jonathan wanted to hurt you in some way. He has always believed that you destroyed him. He cannot get at you in business anymore, you've seen to that, but he can hurt you through your children. The other night I was at the retrospective, and I saw something that frightened me. It also alerted me. At one moment he was staring very intently at your children, and he had a look on his face of pure evil. I didn't know what he planned, but I made up my mind to find out as much as possible."

"Did you think he would simply . . . *confide* in you, Sarah?" Paula asked, giving her a long, hard stare.

"No, I didn't, he can be very close-mouthed, even with me. But Jonathan likes his wine and he likes to boast. And he has a tendency to boast when his tongue has been loosened by a good French vintage."

"Are you saying you got him drunk?" Paula raised a brow quizzically.

"No. But I had invited him to dinner, and I ordered a very expensive bottle of Mouton

Rothschild, which he loves. And I asked the right questions."

"What's he planning to do?" Paula asked, alarm making her voice sharp.

"He's already hurt one of them I'm afraid, Paula."

Holding herself very still, Paula said, "Tell me . . . tell me the worst. Who has he hurt? And how? Why don't I know?"

"Indirectly he's hurt Tessa, through her husband, Mark Longden. Mark is Jonathan's architect . . . of the house he's building near Thirsk."

"My God, none of us knew *that!*"

"No, you didn't, because Jonathan and Mark invented a phony name for the new client. William Stone."

Sarah shifted slightly in the chair and explained, "Mark told Tessa his new client was a very rich tycoon, that his name was William Stone and he was building a house in the Midlands. Your daughter had no reason not to believe her husband."

"I understand. But how has Jonathan hurt Tessa?" Paula demanded.

Sarah hesitated, then explained in a quiet voice, "I had the feeling the other night that Jonathan is getting Mark hooked on drugs and drink, and other women. And that he's enjoying doing so. I've long suspected Jonathan was a little depraved under that gentlemanly exterior of his. I truly believe Mark

Longden is now in his clutches in the worst way. Jonathan was laughing about Mark and his weaknesses. He made some remark about that marriage going south sooner than anyone had expected. He even commented on Mark's mistreatment of Tessa . . . physical mistreatment."

Paula turned very pale. "No man would boast of abusing his wife."

"I don't think Mark *did* boast, Paula. I'm putting two and two together. Jonathan told me that Mark had said to him he was teaching Miss Moneybags who wore the pants in the family, that she'd feel the back of his hand on her if she didn't behave."

"I've suspected he was abusing her," Paula confided in a shaken voice. "And thank you for warning me, Sarah. I now know what to do."

Nodding, Sarah cautioned, "If I'm to continue helping you, then you must leave my name out of it."

"I understand."

"There's one other thing you must know, Paula. At the retrospective, Jonathan made a comment about Linnet. He said she was going to inherit everything, including Pennistone Royal. I was so taken aback I retorted that I didn't believe it and asked who'd told him. He said a dickey bird, and he had a very smug, knowing look on his face."

"Oh, but he's completely wrong about that!" Paula shook her head vehemently. "Completely." She wondered where the leak had come from.

It was almost as though Sarah had read her cousin's mind when she remarked, "I think you've got a problem in your office. At the Leeds store, I suspect. Jonathan is having an affair with an old friend of his, a woman called Ellie. I think she works there."

"Eleanor Morrison! That's who it must be. She's one of my secretaries in Leeds. But she doesn't have access to my private papers, and anyway, I told you, it's not true."

"Don't give her the sack," Sarah warned.

"I wouldn't dream of it." Paula now threw Sarah a knowing look. "It would only make Jonathan suspicious."

"Just be very careful . . . about anything confidential."

"I always am," Paula answered. But she knew she would have to keep a sharp eye on Eleanor. Sarah was correct, she couldn't sack her. But she could render her useless to Jonathan.

Standing up, Sarah said, "That's it. I've told you everything I know, Paula. I hope it helps you."

Also rising, Paula answered, "It does." She stared at Sarah in the most penetrating way and confided, "I've had an instinctive feeling lately that Jonathan Ainsley would do something to injure me or mine. Ever since he came back to live in London. Even Sir Ronald warned me."

"Uncle Ronnie was always smart. Grandy said he took after his father. Anyway, I'll keep my eyes and ears open. I usually see Jonathan when I come to London —" Sarah did not finish her sentence. She glanced around the room and then addressed her daughter. "This is the upstairs parlor I've often spoken to you about. My grandmother's favorite room . . . everybody's favorite room actually, Chloe. We had wonderful times here when I was growing up."

"Mother, there's your photograph!" As she spoke Chloe hurried to the library table and picked it up. "You look so beautiful. Come and look, Maman." Sarah joined her daughter, and they stared at the photograph together, then Chloe put it back.

Sarah and her daughter now moved toward the door; Paula followed them. Sarah turned around just before leaving and said, "The room hasn't changed. And it's full of wonderful memories for me, especially of Grandy."

Returning her very direct gaze, Paula saw the tears in Sarah's eyes, and she filled with compassion for her cousin whom she had banished so many years ago. Had she been too harsh? Perhaps. But at the time she had truly believed Sarah had betrayed the family.

"I don't know how to thank you for what you've done today, Sarah. I'm so very grateful. As our grandmother used to say, forewarned is forearmed. Now that I'm alerted I'll be on my guard."

"That's wise, I think."

"I hope we'll see each other again soon. I want you to know . . . you're very welcome . . ." Paula's sentence trailed away as she stepped forward and embraced her cousin.

Sarah clung to her, swallowing her tears. "And I don't know how to thank *you*. . . . It makes me so happy to know I'm welcome . . . in the family again." Stepping away, Sarah shook her head. "Just as long as Jonathan Ainsley doesn't know."

Once she was alone, Paula tried to reach Tessa. She rang her at the Knightsbridge store only to discover she had been in her office earlier but had suddenly left. She tried the house in Hampstead and was surprised that there was no answer. Finally, she punched in the numbers of Tessa's cell phone; her daughter did not respond, so she left a message and hung up.

Paula looked at the carriage clock on the desk and was taken aback to see that it was only noon. Tessa was probably out to lunch, and Elvira had more than likely taken Adele for a walk on Hampstead Heath. She must try not to worry; she knew her daughter would call her back as soon as she had her message. In the meantime, she would concentrate on the plans for the weekend. She went to straighten the picture frames on the library table. Chloe had moved them around to pick up Sarah's photograph and now they looked muddled.

It struck her that Sarah had been so proud her picture was still so prominently displayed at Pennistone Royal when she herself had been in disgrace for years. I just hadn't noticed it was there, Paula muttered under her breath as she began to move the frames around. Soon order reigned; Sarah's photograph was back in its given place.

The phone rang, and Paula rushed to her desk, knocking a photograph onto the floor. She heard the glass shatter as she grabbed the receiver.

"Hello?"

"Mummy! It's Tessa."

"Darling, where are you? I've been trying to reach you."

"I know, I got your message. I'm in a limousine. Just leaving London. With Adele and Elvira. I'm being driven to Yorkshire. I'm too exhausted to drive myself. Mummy, I've left Mark."

"Thank God for that!"

"I'm never going back to him. I'm getting a divorce."

"I'm relieved to hear it. When will you arrive here?"

"It'll take us a good four hours, maybe a little bit more."

"I'll be waiting for you, darling."

"Bye, Mummy."

"See you soon, Tessa." Paula hung up, filling with relief. Thank God her daughter was out of that house and away from Mark Longden. And thank God for her cousin Sarah and her sense of decency and duty.

Paula returned to the library table, picked up the photograph frame which had fallen on the floor. The glass was broken. She couldn't slide the pieces out, so she went to her desk and carefully took the frame apart. As she slid the velvet-covered back and then the piece of cardboard out, she noticed two envelopes taped to the inside part of the cardboard. She was surprised, and opened one. Inside was a silver key.

Paula knew at once that it belonged to the fruitwood casket scrolled with silver. It had never been lost, only hidden. She felt a rush of excitement, and opened the second envelope. It contained a photograph, probably taken in the mid-fifties, of a young woman who was holding the hand of a small boy. Her grandmother held the child's other hand. Paula turned the photo over. On the back was written: "Glynnis, Owen, and me."

Paula placed the snapshot on the desk and

finally took the eight-by-ten photograph, one she had looked at so many times over the years, out of the frame. With a small shock she realized at last who the father of Owen Hughes was.

Forty-four

Paula put the snapshot in her desk drawer, then walked over to the Queen Anne chest where the fruitwood casket embellished with silver had stood for her entire life. So many times she had asked her grandmother what had happened to the key, and so many times Grandy had told her it was lost. But it had been carefully hidden, not lost at all.

With shaking hands Paula put the elaborate silver key into the equally elaborate silver escutcheon and turned it. The casket opened easily. Lifting the lid, she looked inside, almost afraid of what she would find. She saw at once that the casket contained a bundle of letters tied with blue ribbon, all of them addressed to Mrs. Emma Harte at Pennistone Royal. Turning one over, she read the sender's name: Mrs. Glynnis Hughes, New York City.

After reading a number of the letters, Paula had a fairly good understanding of everything, and she knew what she had to do. Locking the letters in the casket which had kept them safe for forty-odd years and pocketing the key, Paula ran downstairs.

She put her head around the kitchen door and told Margaret that Tessa, Adele, and the nanny would be arriving in time for tea. "I'm going out, Margaret," she added. "I should be back within an hour or so if anyone calls."

Margaret nodded. "What time will Mr. Longden be arriving? Or isn't he coming tonight?"

"No, Margaret, he can't make it this weekend," Paula replied. Or any other weekend, she thought, as she headed toward her car parked in the cobbled yard near the stables. The bastard, she thought, cursing him under her breath.

Thirty-five minutes later Paula was driving through the tall, wrought-iron gates of Lackland Priory in Masham. She had always liked the appearance of this old stone manor, a priory before the Dissolution of the Monasteries, when Henry VIII had destroyed so much church property because of his anger against papal Rome. Fortunately, Lackland Priory had gone into private hands and so avoided being turned into a ruin like Fountains Abbey.

It was a graceful house made of local gray stone, with a series of windows perfectly aligned across the front facade. She liked its simplicity and its plainness. It stood in the middle of flat green lawns, not surrounded or backed by stands of trees as so many manor houses were in Yorkshire.

After parking near the kitchen, she walked around to the front door and rang the bell. She had only a moment to wait before Bolton, the butler, appeared at the door, staring at her in surprise. "Miss Paula!" he said. "Good afternoon. Are we expecting you?"

"No, you're not, Bolton," she answered, offering him one of her most charming smiles. "I thought it would be nice to give him a surprise. He once told me he had always liked surprises."

"Indeed he does. Come along, Miss Paula. I'll take you to him. He's in the library."

"How is he?" she asked, following the butler across the polished parquet floor.

"I'm pleased to tell you he's a lot better. Still not quite his old self, but he will be in a week or two. He's made wonderful progress." Opening the library door, Bolton said, "Sir, it's Miss Paula, she's driven over to see you."

The man, who had been reading in a wing chair by the window, put his book down and stood. "My dear Paula, what a lovely surprise."

Paula glided across the Savonnerie carpet toward him, thinking how marvelous he looked. He had made a wonderful recovery. She had known him all her life, but now she tried to see him through objective eyes. He was still good-looking; he must have been quite devastating when he was younger.

She gave him a radiant smile, stood on tiptoe, and kissed his cheek. He held her to him for a moment, his face against her hair; then as they drew apart, he said, "Your hair has always had the most lovely smell, ever since you were a child, Paula." He smiled at her and indicated a chair. "Now, to what do I owe this honor, my dear?"

"I haven't heard a word from you about the birthday party for Shane and Winston. You are going to come, aren't you?"

"I do believe I am. I think it would be rather jolly to see all of you. We might even have a turn on the dance floor, you and I."

Paula leaned back in the chair and crossed her legs, studied him for a moment.

Becoming aware of her scrutiny, he said, "Is there something wrong, Paula? You're giving me a rather sharp look again."

"Oh, I'm sorry. I was just thinking about something I recently discovered. I was reading my grandmother's diaries, and I learned she started a canteen during the Second World War. On the Fulham Road."

He nodded, his eyes lighting up. "That's true. She did."

"Did you ever go there?"

"Indeed I did. We always had a lot of fun."

"Did you meet your wife there?" she asked,

her head to one side, watching him closely.

"No, as a matter of fact, I didn't. But why do you ask this, Paula?"

"I know you met a young woman there, and I wasn't sure exactly who she was. This young woman . . . she was beautiful. My grandmother thought she was so glamorous . . ."

He sat back in the leather chair rather suddenly and turned his head. He did not speak, merely stared through the window as if he could see something that was not visible to her.

What a marvelously patrician profile he has, and such a splendid head of white hair, Paula thought. And waited. Waited for him to speak.

At last he turned back to face her, and she thought his face was sad, almost sorrowful. He seemed to ponder for a moment, and then he said, "Her name was Glynnis . . . Glynnis Jenkins. And she *was* beautiful, and glamorous, just as you said, quoting your grandmother's diaries, I've no doubt. But Glynnis was much more than that." He stopped speaking, shook his head. "She was very loving, passionate, sensual."

"You loved her."

"Oh yes, I did."

"And you made her pregnant."

"Yes. That's true, Paula, I did," he answered without hesitation.

"But you didn't marry her."

"No."

"Why not?"

He let out a long sigh. "Our relationship was passionate, but it was also extremely volatile. We could fight as quickly as we could make love. In the vernacular of today, it was over the top. I was aware that a passion like that could easily burn out as fast as it had flared. Or it could consume me. And —"

"You couldn't afford that," she cut in. "You had to protect yourself, didn't you, Uncle Robin? Because of the career you planned." She spoke softly, kindly, and finished, "I do understand."

"You are quite correct in your assessment, Paula. But let me explain. . . . I broke up with Glynnis before I knew she was pregnant. And soon after that I became engaged to Valerie Ludden, a young woman I'd known for a while and of whom I was very fond. Of course, it was not the same kind of relationship I had with Glynnis. It was much calmer, more stable. I loved Valerie in a different way, and we were ideally suited. She was right for me, for my future in politics. Whereas Glynnis and I would have been destroyed by each other."

"But Glynnis was pregnant, and in those days that was a terrible stigma."

"I'm aware of that, and I offered to support Glynnis. But she refused any help from me."

"I see."

There was a silence, and then Robin said, "So you found Emma's old wartime diaries. . . . Apparently she wrote about my affair with Glynnis."

"No, she didn't, Uncle Robin. There is one entry, in October 1943, about Glynnis's predicament. But you are not mentioned as the father. No one is named, actually. Your mother protected you, and she protected Glynnis. Anyway, Glynnis Jenkins never wanted you named as the father of her child either."

"Then how do *you* know?" he asked, giving her a baffled look.

"Because today, utterly by chance, I found some old letters from Glynnis Hughes, as she had become, to Grandy. I read several of them in which you were mentioned as Owen's father. She wrote to Emma for years, you know, and Emma even met your son by Glynnis."

"My mother supported Glynnis for a long time . . . sent her money, even after Glynnis had gone to America," Robin said. "So I'm not surprised Glynnis wrote to her. I'm just surprised my mother kept the letters."

Paula nodded. "I know what you mean."

Leaning toward her, Robin now asked, "Why have you come to tell me about this today, Paula? What's this visit really all about? I know you very well, and there's a reason behind it."

"You have a granddaughter called Evan Hughes . . . she's the daughter of your son Owen. And she's living in London, Uncle Robin. I thought you might want to know that."

"A granddaughter . . ." He was silent for a while, once more staring out the window, his eyes suddenly full of sadness, perhaps even regret.

Watching him, Paula thought of his long career. He had been a popular Member of Parliament, had served in the government several times, and Emma had always been proud of him. He had lived the life he had envisioned for himself, and he had been successful. So perhaps he had made the right choice.

Finally, Robin shifted in his chair and gave her a long, penetrating look. "How do you know this young woman? Did she come looking for me?"

"No, she didn't. She didn't even know about you. Let me explain everything."

Robin listened to Paula attentively, his expression revealing nothing. When she had finished he said, "And so you want me to meet her, is that it?"

"That's up to you, Uncle Robin. *You* must decide."

"I think I would like to meet her. . . . From what you've just said she's very nice. Very appropriate."

Paula laughed. "Indeed she is, and beautiful. Oh, my God! I've just realized who she has a look of . . . Aunt Elizabeth, your twin. And everyone has been saying she resembles me."

He smiled. "Then she must be quite lovely. Elizabeth is a beauty. Perhaps you should arrange a meeting, Paula."

"Whenever you want, at the birthday party perhaps. She will be coming with Gideon."

"Gideon?" He stared at her, puzzlement invading his face. "Why Gideon?"

"Because she has been seeing him . . . they're involved."

"I wonder why it is that Hartes are always attracted to Hartes." He shook his head. "It's like the pharaohs in ancient Egypt, don't you think?"

Paula burst out laughing. "Oh, Uncle Robin, you are a hoot."

"Anyway, that is a good idea. I could meet her at the party for Shane and Winston. Yes, indeed, most appropriate."

Paula leaned closer to her uncle and said in a low voice, "I don't think you should mention anything I've told you to Jonathan. It might upset him. He *is* your only son and heir, and since he's never given you grandchildren, he might resent Evan."

"Oh my goodness, *yes*. You are quite right, Paula. He might regard her as some sort of threat." His eyes narrowed. "Jonathan has been a great disappointment to me. I know he has no love for me, and he doesn't care a jot about my health. I've hardly seen him since his mother died, nor did he come much when she was alive, and Valerie was the best mother in the world. You'd think he'd pop by occasionally; I am eighty, you know. But he never does, not even when he goes to see his fancy woman in Thirsk."

Taking a deep breath, Paula plunged in. "I think Jonathan is dangerous, Uncle Robin. I want to warn you about him."

He listened as she recounted everything Sarah had told her.

"I'm not at all surprised," he said quietly when she had finished. "I have begun to think that he's a sociopath. He has no morals, and he believes he's above the law. Certainly he never thinks he is doing anything wrong. He is indeed dangerous, Paula. He will not hear about Evan Hughes from me."

The next two days were hectic for Paula, between settling Tessa in, calming her, and listening to her stories of life with Mark. She backed her daughter, as far as a divorce was concerned, but purposely did not mention Sarah's visit. She had to protect her cousin against Jonathan Ainsley's wrath. And they had plenty of grounds for divorce without involving Sarah.

Then there were the plans for the weekend to finish, menus from Friday through Monday morning, plus seating plans for the lunches and dinners. But as usual Paula pushed ahead determinedly, and Tessa helped her by writing the place cards and doing other small tasks.

By the time Linnet, India, and Evan arrived on Friday afternoon, Paula was just about finished and ready to relax with them over tea in the upstairs parlor. They had lots to recount to her: the success of the retrospective, the number of people visiting the exhibition, the press coverage, the accolades, and a surge in business on the fashion floors.

"It's a triumph for you all," Paula said, smiling. "I have a feeling the retrospective is going to be a fixture in the store for quite a long time. Well done, all of you. Now I want you to forget work and enjoy the weekend."

Linnet stood up and headed toward the door. "I want to go and unpack."

"I should do the same," Evan said.

"Oh, please don't go, Evan. I'd like a word with you," Paula murmured, touching her arm.

Evan looked at her questioningly and sat down.

"I have to iron a dress," India said,

jumping up. "It's chiffon, so I can't use a steamer on it."

Linnet pretended to shudder. "Never. Come on then, India, let's go."

Once they were alone, Paula said, "I have something to tell you, Evan, regarding your grandmother. But I think for the moment what I'm going to say must remain confidential. I don't want it spreading through the family just yet."

"You found something in the diaries after all?" Evan asked, leaning forward anxiously.

"No, I didn't. But I did find some old letters from your grandmother to my grandmother here at Pennistone Royal the other day, and quite by accident. In several of the letters Glynnis refers to Owen's father . . . his biological father." Paula paused, smiled gently at Evan, and continued. "Richard Hughes married Glynnis when she was pregnant by another man during the war. He did not care because he loved her so much, and he loved the child she bore, brought him up as his own. He was a good man, and a very good father to Owen."

Evan sat staring at Paula in stunned silence. After a moment she swallowed hard and said in a low voice, "You're telling me my father is *illegitimate?*"

"Technically, yes."

"Who was Dad's father? Who is he really? Who am I?"

"Your father is the son of Robin Ainsley, my uncle and Emma's favorite son. He's a Harte. And so are you, Evan. Emma Harte was your great-grandmother."

"Oh my God!" Evan had turned very pale, and she sat back against the cushions on the sofa. Suddenly she burst into tears and brought her hands to her face.

Paula went to her desk, brought a box of tissues to Evan, sat down next to her on the sofa. "I know it's a shock, suddenly finding out that things are different than one thought. But please don't cry, Evan. All of this happened fifty years ago, you know."

Blowing her nose, wiping her eyes, Evan nodded. "Yes, I realize that. I looked up to Gran. I believed she was the most wonderful woman . . ." Evan paused, stared at Paula, the tears welling again.

"You mustn't let this make a difference in the way you think about Glynnis. She must remain the same wonderful woman in your memory . . . because she was exactly that, Evan. I am going to give you her letters to Emma, and when you read them you will understand so much more." Paula sighed and took hold of Evan's hand. "We must always take into account human frailties and remember that *none* of us is perfect."

For a moment Evan was silent, her mind awash, and suddenly she exclaimed, "I'm related to Gideon! *We're cousins.*"

"Several times removed," Paula pointed out.

"Does *he* know about me . . . my real grandfather?"

"Yes. I told him on Wednesday, the day I found the letters."

"What did he say? Does he want to meet me?"

"Yes, he does. Do you?"

"I don't know. . . . Well, yes, I guess I do," she murmured, sounding hesitant.

"There's a slight problem we have to overcome," Paula said. "Robin Ainsley has one son, Jonathan Ainsley. Amongst other things, he is my enemy, and that's why Gideon was upset the other night when he came over to speak to you. But not to digress. Jonathan was married and divorced, but he never produced any grandchildren for his father. So more than likely he will see you as a sort of threat, since you are Robin's granddaughter. Because of his inheritance —"

"I don't want anything!" Evan interrupted. "I don't want Robin Ainsley's money."

"I know. But things have to be dealt with properly. First, Jonathan Ainsley has to be informed by his father of your existence, and he must be told that you do not affect his inheritance in any way. Once Jonathan knows this, we can tell the family . . . about the new development, about who you actually are. Do you understand?"

"Yes, I do." After blowing her nose again, Evan asked quietly, "Can I tell Gideon?"

Paula had foreseen this question, too. She said quickly, "Tomorrow evening before dinner, Shane and I are going to have Gideon and his parents for a quick drink here in the upstairs parlor. You are invited, too. But no one else."

"What about Linnet?"

Paula shook her head. "I want to keep this very quiet. Linnet will know next week, once Uncle Robin has spoken to Jonathan. Do you understand?"

"I understand."

Paula went over to her desk, took out the bundle of letters tied with blue ribbon. "These are for you, Evan dear," she said, returning to the sofa. "Your grandmother's letters."

Evan took them from her and walked across the room. She paused at the door and said, "Thank you for these. And I'd like to meet my grandfather this weekend. Do you think that's possible?"

Paula frowned, then exclaimed, "I don't see why not. I'll phone him."

Forty-five

Evan sat waiting for Paula in the Stone Hall. She felt a little anxious about the meeting with Robin Ainsley, which was due to take place in less than an hour. She glanced at the tall grandfather clock in one corner, saw that it was almost ten. She knew that Paula would arrive at any moment to drive her to Lackland Priory.

Last night, just before dinner, Paula had drawn her aside and told her in a low voice that Uncle Robin had agreed to meet her in the morning. She had worried about it all night, mostly about their reaction to each other but also about what to wear, wanting to make the right impression.

This morning she had dressed in a beige pantsuit with a cream silk shirt, deciding it was casual enough for the country but a bit smarter than a skirt and sweater. A pair of gold shrimp earrings and her watch were her only pieces of jewelry, but she had tied a beige, red, and blue Hermès silk scarf around her neck.

After reading many of her grandmother's

letters to Emma Harte, she had understood so much. At first, when Paula had told her about Glynnis and Robin, she had been upset. But during the night she had come to love her grandmother more than ever. For as she read the letters she had begun to realize what a good person Glynnis had been, a truly kind and generous woman who had not wanted to hurt anybody in any way.

It seemed that when Robin had rejected her, she had stepped away from him with dignity. And she had been honest with Richard Hughes, had told him the truth. The letters had been poignant, happy, sad, positive, optimistic. Her grandmother had run the gamut of emotions over the years. But one thing was certain, she had lived her life to the fullest and without regret. And she had remained devoted to Emma Harte until her death.

There had been a moment during the night when Evan had almost picked up the phone to call her father, but then she had decided against it. She wanted to meet *his* father first, give Robin the once-over before telling Owen about these developments. Another thing had shone through the letters most forcefully, and that was Glynnis's devotion to Richard Hughes. Theirs had been a successful and happy marriage, and Evan was glad of that. But she had known this anyway, hadn't she? Certainly they had never been anything but serene with each other in front of her, and Glynnis had told her so many times how important compatibility is in a marriage, as well as love.

In one of the letters her grandmother had discussed money with Emma, and now Evan knew where that large legacy had come from. Emma Harte had sent money to Glynnis for many years, and Glynnis had saved most of it, spending only when it was really necessary. Apparently Richard had insisted on supporting Owen, whom he considered his son.

There were still a number of letters to read, and she planned to look at them this afternoon. In the meantime, she would soon meet her biological grandfather. She took a deep breath and stood up as Paula came down the stairs, greeting her with "Good morning, Evan."

"Good morning, Mrs. O'Neill."

Paula laughed as she came to a standstill next to Evan and took hold of her arm, kissed her cheek. "I think it might be a good idea for you to call me Paula, since it turns out we're related. I've been trying to figure it all out, and you're my first cousin once removed, I think." She laughed again.

"I was trying to do the same, Mrs. O'Neill, I mean Paula, but it's been quite a lot for me to absorb since yesterday afternoon."

"I know it has, Evan. Come on, we can talk as we drive over to Uncle Robin's."

They walked out together to the garages. Evan waited in the cobbled yard while Paula pulled the car out, then she got in, saying, "I read a lot of Grandmother's letters last night; in fact, I was up half the night poring over them."

"I thought you might be. I didn't actually read many of them, Evan, only enough to find out who Glynnis's wartime lover had been. I just want you to know that."

"Thanks for telling me, but you could have read them. They're yours really, since they were sent to your grandmother." A sudden thought struck her, and Evan exclaimed, "I wonder why Emma kept the letters, I mean, to what purpose?"

"Evan, I've no idea. I thought of that myself, when I found them, and I wondered why she had left the key in the back of the frame holding Robin's picture. And the photograph of Glynnis, Owen, and herself. And I could come to only one conclusion."

"What's that?" Evan asked, an eager expression on her face.

"I believe Emma Harte wanted the key found, and she bargained that I would be the one to find it. Since I'd pestered her about that casket from childhood, she knew I'd know at once that the silver-scrolled key was for that special box."

"Why not just keep the letters in a safe, or tell you about them?"

"I wish I could answer you, but I can't. Perhaps she hid them the way she did because she didn't want them found while she was alive. And then possibly she forgot about them. She died rather unexpectedly, you know. Shane has another theory; he thinks she kept them because they gave her a sort of hold over Robin. But I'm not certain he's right. However, their discovery and the advent of Evan Hughes is certainly going to upset Robin's son, Jonathan."

"Yes, you explained that last night. Why is he your enemy?"

"Basically, he believes he should have inherited much more than he did from Emma, most certainly the department stores. He's been very disgruntled about everything to do with her legacy. And at one point he did Harte Enterprises great harm financially, through the real estate division he ran, and he tried to grab the stores by buying up a lot of stock, and also getting voting control of more shares through a friend. But he didn't succeed. Anyway, Evan, he's bad news, take my word for it."

"Gideon sort of indicated that after the retrospective. He was upset that I'd been talking to Jonathan Ainsley. But I had no idea who he was."

"I realize that." Paula glanced out of the window and said, "We're going to a lovely little village called Masham. Uncle Robin has

637

lived at Lackland Priory for many, many years. It's a beautiful old place; you'll be struck by its simplicity, yet it's an architectural gem."

"I can't wait, but I am a bit nervous about meeting Robin . . . my grandfather." Evan made a face. "That sounds funny, saying *grandfather* when I think of my grandfather as Richard Hughes and he's dead."

"You don't have to be nervous, Evan. I think Uncle Robin is rather pleased to know you exist. Jonathan has become a genuine disappointment to him."

"What do you think of him, Paula?"

"Naturally I detest him, because he's damaged us. I think he's a rather sinister presence in the family . . . and a bit dangerous. Ah, look, Evan, just ahead. Those are the gates of the hall. We'll be there in a few minutes."

Once they had driven through the gates, Evan gazed at the beautifully kept lawns, the copse of trees to the right of the house, and the house itself. Solitary. Simple. And yet so beautiful, as Paula had said. Evan loved the gray stone which was used so much in Yorkshire; Gideon had told her it was taken from the nearby quarries.

Paula pulled up at the front door and glanced at her, a brow lifting eloquently. "Are you ready, Evan?"

"Yes." Evan got out of the car and followed Paula to the front door, swallowing hard and straightening her jacket.

Within seconds the door was opened. "Good morning, Miss Paula," Bolton said. "He's waiting for you in the library."

"Thank you, Bolton. And this is Miss Hughes."

The butler inclined his head; Evan smiled faintly, and the two women followed him across the entrance hall to the library.

Robin Ainsley was sitting in the wing chair by the window; there was a book on the Queen Anne tea table, but it was closed, and it occurred to Evan that he might have been dozing.

The butler cleared his throat. "Miss Paula has arrived, sir. With Miss Hughes."

"Ah yes, thank you, Bolton." Robin immediately rose and turned to them, his eyes focused on Evan as the two women walked toward him.

Likewise, Evan's eyes were riveted on him. She saw a tall, slender, white-haired man, rather elegant and refined. He wore an old tweed jacket with leather patches on the elbows, gray slacks, a pale blue shirt, and a brown knitted tie. In a peculiar way, he reminded her of Richard Hughes, and she smiled inwardly, thinking that perhaps Glynnis had been drawn to the same type of man.

Paula kissed his cheek and introduced her. "This is Evan, Uncle Robin."

He stretched out his hand, gazing at her. "I'm very pleased to meet you, Evan."

"As I am, Mr. Ainsley."

A faint smile touched his mouth. "Why don't you call me Robin, my dear? Much friendlier."

"If you'd like that."

"I would. Now, can I offer you something? Tea, coffee, sherry perhaps?"

Paula said, "I'd love a glass of fizzy water please, Uncle Robin."

"So would I, thank you," Evan murmured.

Robin looked across at Bolton, hovering in the doorway, and said, "Two glasses of fizzy water, and sherry for me. Thank you."

The butler departed, closing the door behind him, and Robin said, "Why don't we sit over there near the fireplace? I know it's June, but I do like a fire even now. I feel the cold in my bones rather a lot these days. Getting old, living on borrowed time."

Paula smiled at him, slipped her arm through his, and walked with him to the fireplace, indicating with her eyes that Evan should follow.

Once they were seated, Paula said, "Evan asked to meet you today, Uncle Robin, because she's going back to London tomorrow, and she won't be here again for two weeks. For Linnet's engagement dinner, the night before the big birthday party."

"I'm glad she suggested it." He turned his gaze on Evan. "To be frank, I wanted to meet you at once, but I thought perhaps I should leave the decision to you."

Evan cleared her throat, still feeling somewhat nervous, and said softly, "It seemed rather silly to wait. I really didn't have to think it over much. I wanted to meet *you*, too."

"Have you informed your father of this . . . development?" Robin asked, eyeing her thoughtfully.

"No, I haven't. I did think about it last night, about calling him, but I changed my mind."

"Oh, why is that?"

"I wanted to look you over first," she blurted out, and immediately felt herself blushing.

Before she could say anything else, Robin laughed. It was a deep-throated laugh; he was obviously highly amused. Glancing at Paula, he said, "Evan sounds like Emma." Addressing Evan, he continued, "My mother was always rather blunt, spoke her mind, much to my consternation at times."

"I'm so sorry, I did sound rude, didn't I? But I just felt we ought to meet before I told my father anything. Besides, it's a bit difficult to discuss on the phone. I think I'd prefer to tell him face-to-face. He's supposed to come over in a couple of months. On vacation."

"Is he now?" Robin pondered this for a moment and was about to say something when Bolton came in with glasses on a silver tray. After the beverages were passed around and they were left alone again, Robin said, "What do you think his reaction will be?"

She shook her head. "I don't know, honestly I don't."

"It will be a shock, I suppose," Paula said. "After all, he grew up knowing another man as his father."

Robin was silent; he took a sip of dry sherry.

Evan shifted slightly on the sofa and said quietly, "I think he might suspect something . . ."

Robin turned his eyes to her swiftly. *"Oh."*

"What makes you say that?" Paula asked.

"His attitude really. He wanted me to come to London originally. And then he seemed to change his mind, especially after I started to work at Harte's. I think he might have found something after my grandmother died last November. Some papers." Looking at Paula, Evan added, "The way you found the letters from Glynnis to Emma."

Paula was thoughtful, her brows drawing together.

Robin said, "I understand from Paula that on her deathbed your grandmother told you to come and find Emma Harte, that she had the key to your future. But they were close friends. Surely she knew Emma was dead."

"I'm sure she did, Robin," Evan replied, saying his name for the first time. "I think she wanted to put me in your orbit, by that I mean in the orbit of the Hartes. Perhaps she knew people would think I looked like Paula, and something would happen. . . . I'm just not sure."

"And we'll never know, will we? On the other hand, I think you're probably right." Settling back, Robin studied Evan once more. Then he said, "You don't look like Paula. You have a strong resemblance to my sister Elizabeth." Glancing at Paula, he continued. "You mentioned that the other day."

"I know I don't look like Glynnis," Evan announced.

Robin inclined his head. "No, you don't. I think perhaps they threw away the mold. Glynnis was quite the most extraordinary-looking woman I've ever known . . ." His sentence trailed off.

Paula said, "Uncle Robin, do you mind if I pop out into the garden for a moment? I want to be sure those plants I sent you the other day are in the beds correctly."

He was about to tell her his gardener knew what he was doing when he realized she was being discreet, leaving them alone together for a while. He nodded. "Of course, do go out to the garden, Paula, my dear."

He smiled at Evan a few seconds later. "She's a bit too obvious at times."

Evan smiled back at him. "But she's thoughtful."

"Oh yes." He seemed to be having a tussle with himself, and then he said, "And do you hate me, Evan, for not marrying Glynnis Jenkins?"

"No. It's so long ago."

"Yes, indeed. It wasn't that I didn't love her. I just loved her far too much. And she loved me in the same way . . . too much. We would —"

"Oh my God!"

Robin stared at Evan. "What is it? What's wrong?"

"My grandmother said something . . . *I loved him too much,* that's what she whispered on her deathbed. I thought she was referring to Owen, her son, my father. But perhaps she was referring to you . . . do you think?"

"Maybe she was. That was our problem. Too much passion and too much possessiveness. Our love would have burnt out, or we would have killed each other. Do you understand what I'm saying?"

"Yes, of course." Evan gave him a hard stare. "Were you happy in your marriage?"

"In many ways I was. However, to be truthful, I missed *her* always, missed the passion, the sensuality, the charm of her, and her beauty. Glynnis Jenkins was the most enchanting woman I ever knew. Yes, I missed her . . ."

"Glynnis was happy, you know," Evan told him. "Very happy with Richard Hughes, and they had a good marriage. But she was always drilling something into me . . . the importance of compatibility as well as love. You two weren't very compatible, were you?"

"No. But that didn't stop me loving her."

There was such a strange note in his voice, a gruff undertone, that Evan glanced at him and saw there were tears in his eyes. Without thinking, she jumped up, went to him, put her hand on his shoulder. "Oh, Robin," she murmured. "I do understand . . . and I don't blame you."

He gazed into her face, and for a split second he saw not Evan, or his sister Elizabeth, but Glynnis. And without thinking he pulled Evan into his arms and held her very close. Within a few seconds he released her and said in that same gruff voice, "Forgive a very old man."

"There's nothing to forgive," she said and returned to the sofa.

Pulling himself together, Robin reached for the glass of sherry and tossed it back. Sitting up straighter, he asked, "So, my dear, do you think you and I can be friends?"

"Oh yes, I hope so."

"And your father?"

"That I don't know."

"Mmmm. I understand. Do you plan to stay in England?"

"I want to, yes."

"So I'm likely to see you again?" Robin raised an eyebrow.

"Absolutely."

There was a little silence.

Evan broke it. "Robin, why do you think Emma kept Glynnis's letters yet hid them in that strange way?"

He let out a deep sigh. "I just don't know. It's a mystery to me." A smile broke through, and he exclaimed, "But I'm damned glad she did."

"Who did what to whom?" Paula asked, coming back into the library.

"Emma. She kept the letters, and you found them, and I've found my only grandchild. You are the *only* one, aren't you?" He shot a glance at Evan.

She smiled. "I am. I do have two sisters, but they're adopted."

Paula said, "You two are looking very pleased with each other, Uncle Robin, Evan. But I want to caution you both . . . there's Jonathan to contend with."

"Ah yes." Robin sat back in the chair, steepled his fingers, brought them to his mouth. "I shall talk to him next week. As long as he knows that I am not going to change my will, everything will be all right."

"I don't want anything!" Evan exclaimed,

then blushed when he gave her a stern look.

Paula said, "You know that, Uncle, and I know it, but will Jonathan believe you? Will he accept your word?"

"I shall make him believe me." Robin rose, went and sat next to Evan on the sofa, and took her hand in his. "You and I don't actually know each other, we've only just met, but you are my grandchild, and I am going to create a trust for you. Immediately. I shall attend to it on Monday. But remember, this is between the three of us."

Evan nodded, not daring to say a word.

"What a good idea, Uncle Robin. And you don't have to worry about me. I'm not going to tell anyone, not even Shane," Paula promised.

Later that day Evan read more of her grandmother's letters to Emma. Glynnis had written in great detail, giving colorful descriptions of her life in New York with her son and her husband. And Evan found the letters fascinating. She also understood that the two women had grown closer over the years.

Putting the letter she had just read back in the bundle and tying the blue ribbon carefully, Evan placed the letters under her sweaters in a drawer, knowing she wanted to peruse them again, perhaps tonight after dinner.

As she showered and washed her hair, Evan thought of Glynnis. Her admiration of her gran had grown and grown in the last twenty-four hours, because of her dignity, and the way she had led her life. She had even brought Owen to London several times when he was a little boy, and Emma had met him. Didn't her father remember these occasions? Perhaps he did but had preferred not to tell her. Or maybe he had simply not understood who Emma was, or forgotten or blocked the visits out.

Stepping out of the shower, Evan dried herself, put on a terry-cloth robe, and stood in front of the mirror drying her hair with a blower, thinking now about Robin. She had liked him almost instantly, had found him warm, kind, and courteous, and she was quite certain he liked her. Of course, they had to get to know each other properly — that would take time — but instinctively she felt they would have a worthwhile relationship.

Naturally Robin had been concerned about her father, and she was, too. She had made up her mind not to telephone him in Connecticut, at least if she did she would not tell him about the news. She believed his reaction would be very mixed. He had been devoted to Richard Hughes, whom he regarded as his father. Well, of course Richard had been his father. Her grandmother had once said to her that any man could get a woman pregnant but it was what a man did with a child later that made him a true father. She had often thought about her gran's words, and now they made perfect sense. Glynnis had been thinking about Richard when she had uttered them.

After brushing her hair and putting on a little makeup, Evan moved into the bedroom, where she quickly dressed, choosing a silk dress of pale aquamarine. She fastened Glynnis's string of small pearls around her neck and put on the matching earrings, then slipped her feet into low-heeled silk shoes that matched the dress.

She was the first to arrive in the upstairs parlor, and she went and stood at the leaded window, looking toward the hillside opposite, then she turned back into the room. She saw the photograph at once, recognized him immediately, Robin as a much younger man, perhaps in his thirties. Picking it up, she saw that the broken glass Paula had referred to had been replaced. She held it for a moment, staring at the face, seeing her father and herself reflected there. Odd, though, that Robin Ainsley had a look of Richard Hughes. She smiled to herself as she put the photo back in its place amongst the other framed photographs of Emma Harte's family.

Even though it was early June, these old country houses were cool, she had noticed, and she made for the other side of the room, where a fire blazed on the hearth.

A moment later Gideon came in, his eyes lighting up the moment he saw her. Hurrying over, he took her into his arms, kissed her cheek, and then stood away from her, exclaiming, "You should always wear that color. You look wonderful in it!"

"Thank you, kind sir," she said, smiling up at him.

"My parents will be here in a moment, but what's going on? My mother said Paula wanted to talk to the three of us privately, with just you and Shane also present. Why not Linnet and Julian?"

"We must wait for Paula, Gid, she will explain everything."

He frowned. And because he was quick and bright, he said in a low voice, "Don't tell me the mystery of your ancestry has been finally solved."

Evan threw him a cool, inscrutable look but made no comment.

When Emily and Winston came in, Emily hurried over to her, kissed her on the cheek, and said, "It's lovely to see you, Evan. And I must congratulate you again, the retrospective was so well mounted."

"Thank you."

Winston joined them, also kissed her on the cheek. "It goes without saying that I agree with Emily. My wife is always right.

Now what's all this about, Evan, do you know?"

"I'm about to tell you," Paula announced from the doorway, gliding in, followed by Shane. "Let's sit down," she said and lowered herself onto one of the sofas near the fire. When they were all seated she proceeded to explain how she had knocked Robin's photograph off the library table, taken it apart to remove the broken glass, found the key for the silver-scrolled casket, and the photograph of Glynnis and Owen with Emma.

"The casket was full of letters from Glynnis Hughes to Emma, and it became instantly clear to me that Robin Ainsley was the father of Glynnis's son, Owen, who is Evan's father."

"Oh my God!" Emily cried. "Then you *are* one of us, Evan! Oh, *of course*. Now I know who it is you look like! My mother when she was about your age. Goodness me, you're a *Harte*."

Winston said, "Well, my dear, welcome to the family. You're going to make a wonderful addition."

Gideon simply sat there, his face quite unreadable.

Shane said, "Paula went to see Robin the other day, told him everything, and he confirmed that he had been involved with Glynnis during the war. That is a story for later, however. Paula also informed Evan when she arrived yesterday, and this morning she drove Evan over to the Priory to meet Robin. Seemingly it went very well."

Emily asked, "Did you like him, Evan? And how did he react to you?"

"I liked him, yes," Evan answered. "He was so very nice, and I'm sure he reciprocated my feelings." She looked across at Paula questioningly.

Paula nodded and told them, "I do believe Robin is truly thrilled. He didn't say that exactly, but he was very keen to know Evan better and to meet her father eventually. And we all know what Jonathan is. . . . Yes, I think Robin is over the moon that he suddenly has a grandchild."

Gideon, recovering from his initial surprise, gave Evan a long, loving look, and said, "I second my father, Evan. Welcome to the family, yes, welcome, welcome!"

There was a little amused laughter, and Paula continued, "For the moment, this must remain between the six of us only. No one else in the family can know. Not until Uncle Robin has told Jonathan, and reassured him that Evan's advent in his life is not going to affect Jonathan's inheritance."

"I hope he believes it!" Emily exclaimed.

Shane said, "I know what you mean."

Winston pondered for a moment, then he nodded. "Uncle Robin is not Emma Harte's son for nothing. He's as shrewd as she ever was. And let's not forget he's a barrister, well schooled in the law, and that he was a Member of Parliament and a member of the government for years. He's not going to fumble this one, rest assured. He's going to use the right words, come up with all the right answers when he sees Jonathan."

"And when is that going to be, do you know, Paula?" Emily asked.

"Uncle Robin said he was going up to London on Monday. To see his solicitor. Perhaps he wants his advice about handling Jonathan."

"Possibly," Winston said. "But it's more than likely he wants to draw up some sort of legal papers that give Jonathan the guarantees he'll probably want."

"I agree with you, Winston," Shane said, standing up, pulling Paula to her feet. "Now, let's go downstairs and have a drink. The others are going to wonder what's going on up here."

Paula said, "Remember, not a word to anyone, not even Linnet. We know what Jonathan is; we don't want him going wild before Uncle Robin has placated him. And it's funny how gossip spreads in this family."

Winston and Emily nodded, and followed Shane and Paula out of the room.

Gideon said, "We'll be down in a few minutes."

When the others had left, he went and sat

next to Evan on the sofa. Taking her hand in his, he looked into her large, soulful eyes and said softly, "So how does it feel to know that we're related?"

Evan sighed, her face serious. "It startled me at first, of course, but when I got used to the idea it didn't bother me. Does it bother you, Gid?"

"No, why should it? I was taken aback, I must admit that, because there had been talk about you being a long-lost McGill. As it happens, you're a long-lost Harte." He laughed, then leaned into her and kissed her on the mouth. Her arms went around him, and they kissed for a long moment, intimately and with passion.

Finally Evan pulled away. "I think we'd best go downstairs, don't you?"

Leering at her a little theatrically, Gideon shook his head. "I'd much prefer to stay up here with you, doing this. But I suppose we have to display a little decorum. After dinner I'll take you for a drive so that we can be alone. All right?"

"Very all right," she answered, happiness flooding her face.

It seemed to Evan that the following ten days passed in a flash. She was very busy at Harte's. The retrospective had been such a huge success that they were inundated with requests for interviews from newspapers and magazines, and there was quite a lot of interest from foreign publications. This aside, they were doing record business on the fashion floors.

Evan sat in her office on Wednesday afternoon, going over her appointments for the rest of the week. Fortunately things had eased off a little for her personally, and she had only two photographic sessions to supervise. One was set for tomorrow afternoon, the other on Friday morning. Leaning back in the chair, she thought about the weekend. It was going to be very special. On Friday evening Paula and Shane were giving an engagement dinner for Linnet and Julian; only the three families, the Hartes, the O'Neills, and the Kallinskis, were invited. And then on Saturday night the sixtieth birthday party for Shane and Winston would take place in the gardens of Pennistone Royal.

She was driving up to Yorkshire on Friday afternoon with Linnet and India. They had toyed with the idea of taking the train to Harrogate but in the end had settled on the car as more convenient.

As thoughts of the weekend ran through her head, Evan glanced at the dresses on the rack at the far end of her office. She went over to look at them. For the engagement dinner she had bought a pale gray silk slip dress with spaghetti straps, very simple and elegant, but she was uncertain about what to wear for the birthday party. She knew Gideon loved her in light blues and aquas, and her first choice was a floating chiffon dress in a mix of those colors, with long, full sleeves and an ankle-length skirt. Now, as she looked at it again, compared it with the rose-colored silk India had picked out for her, she knew the blue chiffon was right. It was soft, feminine, and romantic.

The shrill of the phone made her jump, and she hurried back to the desk, picked it up. "Hello? Evan Hughes here."

"Hello, darling. It's Gid."

"Yes, I know."

"I'll pick you up at six-forty-five tonight. Is that all right?"

"Yes, of course. I'll see you then," she answered, then made a kissing sound against the receiver.

"Many kisses in return, my Evan," he said and hung up.

As she began to move back toward the rack, the phone rang again. She snatched it up. "Evan Hughes," she said.

"Hello, Evan. It's your father."

"Hi, Dad, thanks for calling back. How're you, how's my mother?"

"Doing much better, Evan. We're going out more often, and she even came into New York with me this past weekend."

"Oh, Dad, that's so wonderful. I'm really thrilled."

"I got your message that you wanted to talk to me urgently. Is everything all right?"

"No problems, no problems at all, I just wondered if you'd made any plans to come to London. Remember you said you were thinking of taking a vacation here this summer."

There was a small silence, a hesitation at the other end of the line; then Owen cleared his throat and said, "I couldn't make it before August. Yes, I *was* thinking of August. It'll be lovely to see you, Evan, I've missed you."

She heard the sudden wistfulness in his voice, and for a moment she almost told him about Robin but caught herself. And so she said, "I can't wait to see you, and I've missed you, too. Will Mom be coming with you?"

"I'm not sure. Certainly I'll bring her if she's well enough." Owen chuckled. "That's where we met, honey."

"I know. How's business, Dad?"

"Can't complain. And I know you're just thriving, I can hear it in your voice."

"I am. I love London, and I love working at the store."

"Still being nice to you, are they?"

"Very much so, and as I told you last week, the retrospective was a huge success."

"Congratulations again, honey. I'll call you soon. Or call me when you've got a moment.

At home. Your mother loves your calls, Evan."

"I will, Dad. Love to Mom and the girls. Love you."

"I love you, too, Evan."

They hung up, and she stood looking at the receiver for a moment, her mind full of Robin and everything that had happened in the last ten days. How her life had changed.

It was six-fifteen when Evan left Harte's through the staff entrance, and she knew at once that she was going to have trouble finding a taxi. She glanced up and down the street, then decided to walk. It was a nice evening, quite warm, and although it was a good twenty minutes from Knightsbridge back to the hotel, she knew it was wiser not to dawdle looking for a cab. Anyway, she might easily pick one up on the way.

She hurried past the back of the store, so intent on getting to the hotel she did not notice two men and a woman loitering just beyond the parking lot. It was only when one of the men grabbed hold of her arm that she saw them. The woman lurched at her, punching her in the stomach; Evan gasped and doubled over, dropping her briefcase.

She felt a hard blow in the middle of her back, and her legs gave way. She fell onto the pavement, gasping even harder, her breath strangled in her throat. The woman grabbed her handbag, and one of the men leaned down over her, showing a knife. She recoiled, terrified, certain he was going to stab her. "Please don't hurt me," she whispered.

"Gimme the earrings," the thug bending over her hissed. "C'mon, gimme the pearls." He kicked her thigh with a booted foot, and bending closer, he pressed the knifepoint at her throat.

Shaking now, Evan pulled off the earrings, fortunately clip-ons, and dropped them on the ground. The other young thug pounced on them, and the one with the knife at her throat said, "The watch. Gimme the Rolex or I'll cut yer."

With trembling hands Evan took off her watch and threw it down, bracing for another kick from the booted foot. But nothing happened. She lay there curled in a fetal position, hardly daring to breathe. Suddenly she felt the boot smash against her side, and the thug kept on kicking her while his partner bent even closer to her body, pressing the knifepoint on her neck, breaking the skin. "I'm gonna cut yer . . ."

"Hey, what's going on!" a woman's voice shouted, echoing down the street.

Evan heard running feet, and she opened her eyes, saw her three attackers fleeing; a moment later a young woman was bending over her, asking if she was all right.

"I think so," she whispered hoarsely,

touching her neck, then looking at her fingers. "He cut my neck," she said, sounding surprised. "He drew blood."

"So I can see." The young woman hunkered down, stared into her face. "Do you think anything's broken?"

"No. One of them kicked me in the thigh and the side, the others hit me on my back and stomach. But I guess I'm okay." Evan swallowed, tried to sit up but found it difficult.

"Here, let me help you." The young woman put an arm around her and levered her to her feet.

Evan leaned against her for a moment, trying to gather her swimming senses. She began to cough; her throat felt dry, and she coughed again, holding her hand to her face. Finally, she straightened and looked at the young woman. "Thank you. I think you saved me from being badly hurt."

"I'm glad I was around to help. Can you stand? Do you think you're really all right?"

Evan nodded. "Sure. My legs are a bit wobbly, but I'm fine, honestly. Please, tell me your name, I'd like to —"

"No, no, that's not necessary," the young woman answered, giving her a quick smile. "I'm just glad you're all right." She hurried off, obviously wanting to go about her own business.

For a moment or two Evan leaned against

the wall, then she looked down at her beige trousers, brushed the dirt off, started to walk. She was shaken up, could hardly walk steadily, but she had no choice if she wanted to get home.

Spotting a taxi at last, she flagged it down and got in, slumping against the seat. Tentatively, she touched her neck, saw blood on her fingers again, and groping around in her pocket, she found a tissue. She pressed it to her neck, endeavoring to steady herself.

When the taxi pulled up in front of the small hotel, Evan saw Gideon on the steps, looking up and down the street, obviously wondering where she was.

She got out, moving slowly toward him, explaining, "I've been mugged. Could you please pay the cabdriver, Gid?"

He held her against him, took a five-pound note out of his pocket, and gave it to the cabdriver. Then he led her inside, concerned, solicitous, and seething.

"I have to sit down a minute," she said, indicating the sitting room. "Let's go in there."

The room was empty, and Evan sank onto a sofa, stared at Gideon, who was hovering over her anxiously. "What happened? Are you up to telling me?"

"Yes, I am. But could you get me a glass of water first? My throat feels so dry."

He nodded and disappeared, returning a moment later with a glass of fizzy water.

"Would you like a brandy? Would that help?"

"No, thanks, this is fine." She took a long swallow, looked at Gideon, and burst into tears.

"Oh, darling," he said, sitting down next to her. "I'm so sorry this happened to you. London's become such a dangerous city. Muggings happening in broad daylight." He gave her his handkerchief, and she dried her eyes, then pressed it against her neck.

"He cut me," she muttered, taking the handkerchief away. "Is it a bad wound?"

Gideon leaned closer, examined her neck. "Thankfully, it's just a nick. Are you sure you don't want to go to the emergency room?"

"No, no, I'm okay! I am, Gid, honestly. They kicked me, punched me, took my briefcase and my bag. And one of them made me give him my pearl earrings, and my Rolex." Tears sprang into her eyes again. "The earrings were my grandmother's."

He put his arms around her, and soothed her, and when she was calm she told him what had happened. "The thug with the knife really frightened me," she finished. "I thought he was going to kill me. I was fortunate that the young woman came down the street when she did. She scared them off."

"You're lucky she stopped to help, some people wouldn't have," Gideon told her.

"I guess you're right." Leaning back against the sofa, Evan went on. "Fortunately there wasn't much in my handbag, makeup, a little money. My passport and credit card are in my room here. Linnet warned me ages ago not to carry too much unless I was sure I needed it."

"I'm glad she did." Gideon brought her close. "I couldn't bear it if anything happened to you, Evan. You're the most precious thing to me." He stroked her head and went on. "Perhaps we ought to go up to your room, look at your knees. You said they were hurting you."

"Yes, let's go upstairs. Do you mind canceling the reservation at the Ivy? I don't think I'm up to going out. And we could eat here. You said you liked the dining room."

"That's a good idea. Come on." Gideon stood up, helped her off the sofa, and led her to the elevator.

Once they were in her room, Evan took off her jacket and trousers, and sat down. Gideon examined her knees. "They're grazed, that's all," he murmured. "Nothing serious. Stand up, let me look at your back."

She did as he asked and flinched slightly when he touched it. "That hurts. He hit me in the middle of my back. But the more I think about it, the luckier I feel, Gid. I got away with a few scratches and bruises. I could have been seriously hurt."

"That's true. But don't stand here talking, go and have a hot bath, it will ease the pain a bit." He kissed her on the forehead. "Go on, scoot."

She did as he asked, disappeared into the bathroom and closed the door. Gideon sat down in the big easy chair, picked up the phone and dialed the restaurant, and after canceling his reservation, switched on the television set. But he found he could not concentrate. His mind was awash with thoughts of the mugging, her lucky escape. It struck him as odd that the mugging took place so close to the store, but then there was no saying where they would happen these days. They were so prevalent they were becoming a nightmare.

He thought then of Jonathan Ainsley and sat up straighter, his eyes narrowing. Paula had called him dangerous, and Gideon believed she was correct. Jonathan already knew about Evan. According to his mother, Robin was drawing up documents with his solicitors to satisfy several demands Jonathan had made. His inheritance was in no way jeopardized, and he was totally aware of that. On the other hand, might he not bear malice? Might he not want to hurt Evan in some way? Out of spite? A mugging could be arranged, couldn't it?

Gideon pushed these thoughts away, not wishing to think that Evan had been a target. Better to believe this incident had been random.

But the following morning thoughts of Jonathan Ainsley intruded again as Gideon sat at his desk at the newspaper offices. He made up his mind to watch over Evan at all times. He had the feeling that he must protect her from Jonathan Ainsley.

Forty-six

They were all assembled in the great Stone Hall of Pennistone Royal. The Hartes, the O'Neills, and the Kallinskis — the three clans.

The men looked splendid in their tuxedos, the women elegant in their evening gowns and jewels. And there was a feeling of festivity in the air as they mingled and sipped champagne.

Paula, wearing a gown of pale green chiffon and all of Emma's emeralds, slowly moved around the hall, speaking to everyone. Her brother, Philip, had arrived back from Paris the night before and had been amazed when she had told him the story of Uncle Robin, Glynnis, and the hidden letters. He stood with his daughter Fiona, here from Oxford, and Uncle Robin, chatting amiably with Evan and Gideon. Those two seem joined at the hip, she thought, going over to speak to them all for a moment, then moving on.

Uncle Ronnie spotted her and waved, and she glided across the floor, came to a standstill next to him. He was with his son Michael, Julian's father, and they both planted kisses on her cheek and told her she looked wonderful.

"What an occasion this is," Sir Ronnie said, beaming. "Finally they are to become engaged."

Paula laughed. "It's fantastic."

Sir Ronald Kallinski drew her closer and whispered against her ear, "I heard from my bankers in the City that Jonathan Ainsley has put his new company on the market. Apparently he's about to return to Hong Kong. Permanently. That should please you, Paula."

"It does," she murmured, and as she walked on she felt as though a burden had been lifted, and so unexpectedly.

Everyone who had been invited had come; most important to her, Aunt Edwina was there. She was Emma's firstborn child, over ninety now, and the Dowager Countess of Dunvale. And what a countess she makes, Paula thought admiringly. Edwina was resplendent in purple silk and a necklace of diamonds; she looked every inch the aristocrat. "She's something else," Paula murmured to Shane as he drew up next to her.

"Who is?" he asked, putting his hand under her elbow.

"Aunt Edwina. Doesn't she look perfectly . . . wonderful."

"Yes, but then all of the ladies do. Come on, darling, let's not stand here. We've something to do now."

"Yes, I know." She looked up at him. "I wish Grandy and Blackie were here."

"Maybe they are," he answered. "Watching over us."

Together Paula and Shane walked into the middle of the Stone Hall and were joined by Linnet, radiant in pale yellow silk, her red hair a burnished halo. She held Julian's hand tightly, and he looked so proud of her. Within seconds the group was silent, waiting for Shane to speak.

"In 1905, ninety-six years ago now, three ambitious young people living in Leeds became friends," Shane said. "Emma Harte, Blackie O'Neill, and David Kallinski. They remained friends all of their lives, and it was always their hope, their dream that the three clans would be united in marriage. Tonight their wish is finally fulfilled. Let us toast their descendants, their great-grandchildren Linnet and Julian, who will soon be joined in holy matrimony."

Acknowledgments

First, a word about this book. It is the fourth in the series which began with *A Woman of Substance*, followed by *Hold the Dream* and *To Be the Best*. Those chronicled the rise to power of three families, beginning at the turn of the nineteenth century in England. This novel picks up the story in 2001 with the current families, the descendants of Emma Harte, Blackie O'Neill, and David Kallinski.

By popular demand I have brought back my most beloved character, Emma Harte, the protagonist of *A Woman of Substance* and *Hold the Dream*. To do so I had to return to the 1940s and the tumultuous war years in Great Britain for part of this story. In order to give a sense of time, place, mood, and historical events of that period, I have used as a leitmotif segments of the great rhetorical speeches of Sir Winston Churchill. Aside from being my own personal hero, I believe that it is to him we owe the survival of Western civilization. Without his extraordinary leadership during the Second World War, when he fought appeasement of Germany, Nazi terror, and the evil of Hitler, the world would be a very different place today. Certainly we would not have freedom, justice, and the decencies of life we have come to cherish. We all owe him so much.

In the writing of a long and complex novel, many people give assistance in different ways. I would like to acknowledge the debt of gratitude I owe to my friends Edwina Sandys and her sister, Celia Sandys, the granddaughters of Sir Winston Churchill. Edwina generously gave me twelve never-released discs of the great Churchillian speeches, which were invaluable. Celia arranged a private tour of the Cabinet War Rooms in Whitehall, which was most edifying. I must thank Phil Reed, Curator of the Cabinet War Rooms, for being a most articulate guide.

My friend Jane Ogden is owed my thanks for being a patient listener and for sharing her memories of growing up during the war years. Susan Zito of Bradford Enterprises gave me enormous help with research and proofreading, and she knows how much I appreciate her involvement in all my novels. I owe a really big thank-you to Liz Ferris of Liz Ferris Word Processing, who coped with a long and complex manuscript with great diligence, at top speed, and presented a meticulous manuscript.

I wish to thank my literary agents, Morton Janklow and Anne Sibbald of Janklow and

Nesbit, who have represented me since 1981, and have always been there for me. Thanks also to my longtime British editor, Patricia Parkin, of HarperCollins, U.K., who has worked with me since *A Woman of Substance*, and thanks to my editor in the United States, Jennifer Enderlin of St. Martin's Press, New York.

Finally, but by no means least, I must thank my husband, Robert Bradford, not only the greatest sounding board and intelligent critic but my most enduring and loving supporter.

About the Author

Barbara Taylor Bradford was born in Leeds, England, and by the age of twenty was an editor and a columnist on Fleet Street. Her first novel, *A Woman of Substance*, became an enduring bestseller and was followed by eighteen others, including *Emma's Secret*. Her books have sold more than 70 million copies worldwide in more than ninety countries and forty languages. She lives in New York City with her husband, producer Robert Bradford.

Visit www.barbarataylorbradford.com.